Night's Children

My Dearest Emelia:

I trust this letter finds you in good health; and, by now, Basarab has found it in his heart—if he has one—to forgive you...

Santan grows daily. I am worried because he still cannot tolerate the sun. I thought by now he would have adjusted, even just a bit. He sleeps most of the day and wants to play in the night. An unfortunate incident happened the other day. The young man, Randy, who drives me around, thought to take a peek at Santan, and he pulled across the special cover I had made for the baby's car seat. The sun seared Santan's cheeks. I had tried to stress to Randy that Santan had a serious sensitivity to the sun. Well, he believes me now...

Now for the most urgent news I have to burden you with. I am with child again—his child. I guess, in some ways, I should be thankful, for it means Santan will have a brother or sister. However, I cannot help worrying. Will this child be the same as its brother, or will it be more like me? Either way, I could be in trouble. Do you have any advice for me? If Santan eventually partakes in his father's 'habits,' how will I be able to protect this new child? How safe will I be?...

I'll wait (eagerly) to hear from you.

Love, Virginia

Night's Children

To Mary,

Embrace night's children

Mary M. Cushnie-Mansour

Also by Mary M. Cushnie-Mansour

Poetry

Life's Roller Coaster
Devastations of Mankind
Shattered
Memories

Short Stories

From the Heart

Biographies

A 20th Century Portia

Novels

Night's Vampire Trilogy:
Night's Gift
Night's Children
Night's Return

Night's Children

Mary M. Cushnie-Mansour

Cavern of Dreams Publishing

Brantford, ON, Canada

NIGHT'S CHILDREN

Publisher's Note: This is a work of fiction. Names, characters, places, and incidents are a product of the author's imagination. Locales and public names are sometimes used for atmospheric purposes. Any resemblance to actual people, living or dead, or to businesses, companies, events, institutions, or locales are entirely coincidental.

Ordering Information:
Books may be ordered directly through the author's website: www.marymcushniemansour.ca or through booksellers. Contact:
Cavern of Dreams Publishing
43 Kerr-Shaver Terrace
Brantford, ON N3T 6H8
1-519-770-7515
Discounts are available for volume orders.

Library and Archives Canada Cataloguing in Publication

Cushnie-Mansour, Mary M., 1953-
[Novels. Selections]
    Night's vampire / Mary M. Cushnie-Mansour.

(Night's vampire trilogy)
Contents: bk. 1. Night's gift -- bk. 2. Night's children -- bk.
    3. Night's return.
Issued in print, electronic and audio formats.
ISBN 978-0-9868169-1-8 (bk. 1 : pbk.).--ISBN 978-0-9868169-2-5
(bk. 1 : bound).--ISBN 978-0-9868169-5-6 (bk. 2 : pbk.).--
ISBN 978-0-9868169-6-3 (bk. 2 : bound).--ISBN 978-0-9868169-9-4
(bk. 3 : pbk.).--ISBN 978-1-927899-00-7 (bk. 3 : bound).--
ISBN 978-0-9868169-3-2 (bk. 1 : epub).--ISBN 978-0-9868169-7-0
(bk. 2 : epub).--ISBN 978-1-927899-02-1 (bk. 3 : epub).--
ISBN 978-0-9868169-4-9 (bk. 1 : audiobook).--ISBN 978-0-9868169-8-7
(bk. 2 : audiobook).--ISBN 978-1-927899-03-8 (bk. 3 : audiobook)

    I. Cushnie-Mansour, Mary M., 1953- . Night's gift. II. Cushnie-
Mansour, Mary M., 1953- . Night's children. III. Cushnie-Mansour,
Mary M., 1953- . Night's return IV. Title.

PS8605.U83N53 2013   C813'.6   C2013-905509-6
                                         C2013-905510-X
                                         C2013-905505-3

The future belongs
to those who believe in the reality of their
dreams.
To live without a dream
would be like living in a world without
windows.

To my husband, Ed
Without his unconditional support,
my dreams would not have come to fruition.

Acknowledgements

Thanks to Bethany Jamieson and Ella Pankatz for all the hours they spent helping me with the editing of "Night's Children." The hours were long, and the pay was minimal, but I know you enjoyed the homemade lunches, pots of tea and coffee, and the odd goodie that graced the table at break time—well, what breaks this taskmaster allowed you! I appreciated your patience as we battled together against the legions of commas, semi-colons, word usage, and content. Your staying power when dealing with the ever-changing mind of the writer who you were working with is heartfelt. You both are amazing!

Cover design by Terry Davis at Ball Media, Brantford, ON Canada—Terry you did an amazing job creating this little vampire child!

Cover photography of child by Heather Cardle, Photographer—www.heathercardle.com Maesin will forever be *our little vampire!*

Special thanks to Charlie Mansour and Jesse Whalen for allowing me to use a picture of their son, Maesin Mansour, for the second print of *Night's Children*. Maesin, some time in the future, you will point to this picture and say to your friends: "See, that's me! My grandma did that to me when I was little!"

Thanks to Judi Klinck, Mariette Havens, Jerusa Hunter, George Hatton, and Brenda Ann Wright for taking the time to read *Night's Children* and for giving me such wonderful testimonials.

Once again, I would like to thank the Talos family for allowing me the continued use of photos of their property, Wynarden, for my book cover. Wynarden was built in 1864 by the Yates family, and over the years it has often been referred to as Yates Castle. It is a prominent, historical landsite in Brantford, Ontario.

Virginia

Chapter One

I t was hard to believe I had finally escaped. The graveyard was still. It was a good place to collect my thoughts. I stared at my son, still overwhelmed that he was with me, and then placed him in the basket provided to me by Aunt Emelia. It was time to start my journey. I had no idea what life had in store for me now, but I was hoping whatever it threw at me, there would be less turbulence than the past year of my life had immersed me in.

I needed to find a secluded place to live. I secured the ten thousand dollars Emelia had given me under Santan's blanket. It would buy me time until I wrote to her. She had said in her letter that she would provide for me and the child—I was banking on that. A high-rise apartment was not logical, especially with a small child ... not to mention the fact there would be too many people around, something I was not willing to take a chance on. I followed the sidewalk down West Street and then stopped at Henry Street. I decided that might be a good street to check out, so I turned and headed down it. I noticed a small apartment building in the distance and thought that maybe if I rented a ground floor apartment, it might not be too bad.

As I approached the Red-D-Mix plant, I noticed an *Apartment for Rent* sign at the end of a long, narrow driveway that ran alongside the railway track just beyond the factory. I gazed up the lane, saw a large grove of trees, and walked toward them. When I reached the house, I knocked on the front door. A young man opened the door, just as I was about to leave. From the look on his face, he must have thought I was one weird lady, dressed in a black cape, carrying a baby in a basket.

"Hi," I whispered huskily. "The sign at the road says you have an apartment for rent; I'd like to see it."

"Sure," he replied, running a hand through his thick, auburn curls. He smiled sheepishly as his eyes gave me a once-and-twice-over. I hesitated, noting his unkempt appearance, but I was desperate for a place to live.

"Well?" I prompted. His gaze was making me feel uncomfortable. "Is it still for rent?"

"Yeah, yeah ... just a sec, I'll grab the key." He disappeared for a moment. "It's on the ground floor at the back," he informed on his return. "Has two bedrooms, kitchen, living room, and a four-piece bath. There is a small fenced yard off the kitchen. I use the front yard. Fridge and stove come with the place, and there is laundry equipment in the basement, if you want to use it. You can come through my place, if you like, using the door between our apartments. It locks from both sides. Or, you can use the outside side door that leads to the basement. I'll give you a key." He paused. "Name's Randy, in case you were wonderin'. And you are?"

"Virginia," I responded, just giving him my first name. "The apartment sounds like a nice place; when is it available?"

"Right away. The previous tenant moved out last week. You can move in immediately if you need to."

I noticed again how his eyes scanned me.

We walked around to the backyard. There was an abundance of vintage maple trees holding up a half-rotten wooden fence. The gate wobbled as Randy pushed it open. "Guess I'll need to fix this," he mentioned.

That's highly unlikely.

"Watch your steps here; the ground is a bit rough," he added.

Randy opened the back door and we stepped inside the kitchen.

What a mess.

"I haven't had time to clean," Randy was quick to say—he must have noticed the disgusted look on my face.

I got the impression that Randy had had no intention of cleaning the apartment. "Don't worry about cleaning," I said. "I don't mind a little hard work." I placed Santan's basket on the floor and took a quick look-through. The rooms were of an ample size. The ceilings were ten feet high, which dated the house back several years. Old, peeling wallpaper was on some of the walls, flaking paint on the rest. "Could I do some decorating?" I asked, running my hand along the wall.

"Sure, whatever you like," Randy replied amiably.

I expected that would be his answer. *Anything to save you work.* "How much is the rent?" I asked.

"Six hundred a month ... everything included." He looked hopeful.

"I'll take it."

Randy smiled. I noticed he also breathed a sigh of relief. I was making his job easy. I wondered what his connection to the owner was; and, if he was paid to look after the place.

"When do you want to move in?" Randy enquired.

"Right now, if that's okay."

Randy tilted his head to one side. I could tell he was curious about me—about my outfit—about the baby in my basket. He cleared his throat, as though he wanted to say something more.

"That is okay if I take the place now, isn't it?" I asked before he could be too inquisitive about my condition.

"Yes ... yes ... that will be fine; but ... but..."

"But what?" I asked, probably a little too sharply. I could feel the heaviness of milk in my breasts. Santan would be waking for his meal soon.

"I need the first and last month's rent," Randy said, blushing as he shoved his hands into his pockets.

"No problem," I answered. "Just give me a few minutes. I'll come to your apartment with the money. Would it be possible to use your phone so I can arrange to get my own phone installed?"

"Sure." Randy looked relieved as he turned and shuffled off. "I'll leave the key on the counter for you," he mentioned before closing the door.

I walked back to the kitchen and looked down at Santan. His eyes were twitching, and his arms and legs were wiggling under the blanket. "Want to see your new home?" I whispered as I picked him up.

Santan's head bobbed around on my shoulder. His dark eyes shone brightly as they looked around. He whimpered. I sat down on the floor in a corner of the living room and began to nurse him. He fussed until I covered him with a blanket. I glanced at the large windows. I would definitely have to invest in some heavily lined curtains.

I peeked under the blanket. Santan was sucking contentedly. My milk was still a reddish colour. I hoped the blood would soon be gone, leaving nothing but pure mother's milk. After Santan had finished his meal, I counted out twelve hundred dollars from the envelope. I laid my son in the basket and draped the blanket over the handle to protect him from the sun. I looked around the apartment again, picked up the key, and then headed to the front of the house and knocked on Randy's door.

"Hi again," he greeted me with a pleased look. "The phone is on the end table by the couch." Randy pointed at the doorway, which revealed a cluttered living room. I was surprised he had remembered that I had wanted to use his phone. I handed him the money. He looked shocked.

I made my way in the direction he had pointed, stepping gingerly around the various items strewn on the living room floor. *How can people live in such clutter?* "You wouldn't happen to have a phone book handy?" I asked.

"Sure ... sure ... let me see here," Randy mumbled as he dug through a pile of newspapers. "Here it is," he proclaimed, holding up a dirty, torn phone book.

I grimaced at the condition of it, and prayed bugs wouldn't crawl out of the first page I looked at. "I will need a receipt for the rent money, Randy. You can provide one, can't you?"

He nodded.

"Good. My full name is Virginia Casewell." I had decided not to use my real last name. I had no idea, yet, how I would procure new identification, since all of mine was gone. I guessed I would cross that bridge when I got to it.

Randy nodded and ambled off to the kitchen. I flipped through the phonebook until I found the local phone company's number, and then dialled it.

At first the operator was pleasant enough, but when I said I hadn't had phone service in my name before, her tone changed.

"We will need some information, then. Full name?"

"Virginia Casewell."

"Employer?"

I had to think quickly on that question. *Who was I employed by? The Count Basarab Musat? To give birth to his child, and then be laid off—without notice!*

"Employer please, miss," a curt reminder came over the phone line.

"I ... I ... I'm self-employed," I managed to spit out.

"Well, what is it that you are self-employed at, miss?" The voice sounded snippy now.

How the hell do I know what I am self-employed at? What difference does it make anyway, as long as I pay their damn bills? "I'm a freelance writer," I finally informed her, not being able to think of anything else.

"Oh." I pictured a sarcastic look on her face. "Address please."

I gave her the rest of the details she needed, and then she put me on hold. The seconds ticked off on the rusty alarm clock that Randy had propped up on a collection of well-looked-at *girly* magazines. I wondered if he was a pervert. Probably not—most likely he was just a normal young man dreaming the impossible dream of having a *Bunny Girl* for a night or two. From the looks of the messy apartment, I was almost certain he did not entertain much, which suited me just fine—the less people around, the better for me and Santan.

The operator returned to the phone line and gave me my installation time. She also mentioned that I would need to put down a $200.00 security deposit. *You are hoping I will say I don't have the money, aren't you, so you can cancel the order.* "No problem, will your technician accept cash?"

I heard her clear her throat. *Good, I was well under her skin.* "Of course," was her terse reply.

"He will give me a receipt, I hope?" I asked matter-of-factly.

"Of course."

The operator went over the booking with me, and then hung up without even thanking me for the business. I thought of reporting her rudeness, however that would only draw unneeded attention to me—something I didn't want. The more private I kept my life, the less chance there would be for *him* to find me.

Randy was standing in the doorway of the living room. He was wearing his sheepish smile. "Gave you a hard time, eh?"

"A hard time is what I would like to give her," I answered, still irritated. "Do you know the number for a local cab company? I need to go out and pick up some groceries and a few items for me and the baby."

"No need to call a cab; I'll drive you around," Randy offered. "Now the apartment is rented, I am free to do what I want. Besides, I need to pick up a *two-four* of beer, and some groceries."

"That is extremely kind of you, but I need several things besides groceries. I don't want to take up too much of your time." I had noticed how he had mentioned the beer before the groceries—hopefully not an indication that he was going to be a party guy, which would mean I might have to be more vigilant than I had first thought.

"Time is what I have plenty of," Randy countered with a bow. "Randy's limo is at your service, miss, for the entire day, if that should be your desire." He straightened up and took a closer look at me. "You have any clothes besides what you are wearing?"

I glanced at my outfit. "No."

"How say I lend you a pair of jeans and a shirt?" He suggested, without questioning me about why I had no other clothes.

I breathed a sigh of relief. I wondered how clean the clothes would be, but then again, I knew I couldn't go to stores in what I was wearing. "Thanks, I'd appreciate that."

Randy headed to his bedroom. He returned a few minutes later with a pair of jeans and a red cotton shirt—a perfect colour. "You can change in my bathroom," he suggested.

"Thanks, but I think I'll just go to my apartment and change. I can meet you out front in 15 minutes, if that is convenient for you?" I took the clothes from Randy and picked up Santan's basket.

"Do you want me to watch the little fella for you?" he asked.

"Ah ... no ... it's okay; I'd rather have him with me."

"Weird lady," I heard Randy mutter as I headed out the door.

The jeans fit perfectly around my waist, but I had to roll up the pant legs. I was pleased the shirt was roomy, camouflaging the fact that I was not wearing a brassiere.

"Wow!" Randy whistled as I walked up to the car. "They fit you better than they ever fit me!"

I hoped Randy didn't have an ulterior motive on his mind where I was concerned. After all, he didn't know me from a hole in the wall, and he was lending me clothes and taking me shopping.

"Let's boogie!" Randy cut into my thoughts. He opened the car door. "It isn't much, but it gets me around," he mentioned as I was putting Santan in the backseat.

Randy and I spent the next couple of hours shopping for baby items and other necessities I needed for the apartment. I moved along quickly, trying to finish before Santan's next feeding. After the grocery store, Randy made a quick stop at the Beer Store on Grey Street. I mentioned that I had no furniture, so he drove to a used furniture store on Murray Street. I noticed a few baby items displayed in the parking lot. I bought a crib and mattress, dresser, change table, and a buggy for Santan; plus a bedroom suite, a small kitchen table and chair set, and a living room couch and chair for me. The man said he would have everything delivered later in the afternoon.

Randy still hadn't questioned my bizarre circumstances, and for that, I was relieved. Most people would have plied me for answers. How often does a stranger, dressed in a long black cape, and carrying a child in a basket, show up at the front door? And, on top of that, the stranger had enough money to pay cash for everything they purchased, even though her appearance implied poverty.

Randy helped me to unload my parcels when we arrived at the house. I thanked him and tried to give him twenty dollars for his gas and his time. He refused. I made a mental note to buy him a case of *Blue* the next time we were out, and to put gas in his car.

"You have a licence?" Randy asked as he was leaving my apartment.

"I drive," I answered, "but I don't have a current license."

"Well, if you ever get it, you can borrow the *Bug* anytime I'm not using it."

"Thanks." I shut the door and turned to face my new life.

~

In the late afternoon, my furniture was delivered by a burly man with a pungent odour. He insisted that he put everything into its exact location. All he expected from me was directions, and to hold the door open for him.

Earlier, while Santan was sleeping, I had scrubbed the kitchen, bedrooms, and bath. I intended to ask Randy if the carpets could be replaced, or better yet, removed altogether. I preferred wooden floors; the warmth of them was comforting.

"Well, miss," the delivery guy looked around when he had finished bringing the furniture in, "lot of potential in this little apartment if the right person gets hold of it and fixes it up Private too." He hitched up his pants and stared at me. I didn't like the expression in his eyes. "Been in Brantford long?" he asked.

"No," I replied, offering him nothing further, hoping he would get the message that I was not in the mood for a lengthy conversation. I handed him a ten dollar bill. "Thank you very much for delivering my furniture here so quickly. May I give you something for your trouble?"

"Oh no, miss, we aren't allowed to accept tips. Little fellow sounds hungry," he added, as Santan's whimpers began to get louder. "His pa around?" I noticed a greedy look in his eyes.

"Not here—at the moment," I informed, flatly. "Once again, thank you; and, as you can hear, I must see to my son now."

He still took his time leaving. Just before I shut the door, he turned and looked back. I noticed a startled expression on his face. He hesitated a moment, shook his head, and then got into his truck and left. I looked down at my shirt and saw the moist circle around my breasts—thank God the shirt was red!

~

The first week passed quickly. I cleaned. I tended to Santan. I tried to sit with him in the backyard, but even in the shade, the sun bothered him. I was forced to keep him under cover all the time. I prayed time would change that. Randy was gracious enough to take me out a few more times so I could pick up some other necessities for my apartment.

~

By the end of the second week, my milk was a pale pink. I credited the decrease in the blood to the fact that I was no longer drinking Max's *special drink*. Santan hadn't seemed to notice the difference in his meals, and I felt this was another victory for me over the Count Basarab Musat. It would also be one more step toward keeping Santan human and wholly mine.

Chapter Two

The reality of what the rest of my life would be like, waiting for the count's return, devoured my mind day and night. I constantly read Aunt Emelia's letter. I was still overwhelmed by the immense sacrifice she had made to aid me during my flight for freedom.

I decided it was time to write to her…

Dear Aunt Emelia:

I cannot believe two weeks have already passed. I can't thank you enough for what you have done for me. I was fortunate to find a secluded apartment in the back of an old house. It is set way back in from the road and is surrounded by trees, which keeps most of the sun out. I have purchased some heavily lined curtains for the windows because Santan is still highly sensitive to the sun. I am hoping this condition will go away, so he might have some normalcy in his life.

I cannot open a bank account because I have no identification. I have also decided to change my last name. Is there any other way you can forward my funds, until I figure out what to do with this situation? I have been as frugal as possible; however, the first and last month's rent, furniture for the apartment, and my food and other necessities have drained a good portion of the money you gave me. Even if I managed to establish a bank account, I would feel more at ease if I could keep most of my dollars close. If the count were to discover my whereabouts, I would be forced to leave here at a moment's notice. I hate to ask, but--well, I guess I don't have to tell you the predicament I am in.

Anyway, dear aunt, I hope this letter finds you well and that you have not yet been found out. My address is 53 Henry Street, Brantford, Ontario, N3R 5K2. I also have an unlisted phone number, if you should ever be able to call me--1-519-753-6666.

Until next time--love, Virginia.

~

Santan was growing—thriving, in fact. He was only irritable when I tried to expose him to the sun. I decided that my best solution was to take him out for late evening walks. If I were going to succeed in introducing Santan to the sun, I realized it would have to be done slowly and with extreme caution.

Randy was an immense help. I don't think I could have managed as well if he had not been around. I finally met his uncle, who owned the property. He loved what I was doing to the apartment, and told Randy to deduct all of my expenses off the rent, as long as I handed over the receipts.

~

Santan was already a month old. "I think we should invite Randy over to celebrate—what do you think, Santan?" Santan smiled.

Randy accepted my invitation. I cooked a casserole, made a little cake, and bought a bottle of *Baby Duck* wine and a six-pack of beer. Surprisingly, Randy refused to drink anything more than a glass of milk.

"I've been drinking too much," he told me. "I need to focus on getting my life in order. My uncle keeps telling me the early bird gets the worm."

"He must be referring to job hunting," I smiled.

"Yeah … I guess I won't be able to stay here forever, living off him." Randy smirked. "He doesn't owe that much to my parents."

"What do you mean by, *owe that much to your parents*?" I asked.

"Uncle George is my guardian. He promised my parents he would take care of me if anything ever happened to them. They were killed in a car accident two years ago. The trust fund they had set up for me was meant for my education, so it is locked in until I go to college or university." Randy wiped away a tear. "I didn't even have a chance to say goodbye."

"I am sorry," I managed to say before Randy continued.

"As a result, Uncle George had to put his money where his mouth was and look after me. But, what swingin' bachelor wants an eighteen year old kid hangin' around them all the time? So, he came up with the idea to let me live here, entrusting me with the responsibility of looking after the property. He puts a monthly allowance in my bank account for me. He never bothered to think about the possibility that I may have wanted to continue my education," Randy said with a touch of bitterness in his voice.

"Had you planned to continue?" I posed the question to see how serious he was, or might still be.

Randy feigned a hurt look. "I was going to be a journalist. I had been accepted into the three year Journalism program at Mohawk College, and was supposed to have started classes in September … Mom and Dad died at the end of August. There was no way I was emotionally stable enough to attend college that first semester, and I just never got back around to reapplying—which is something I can't blame on my uncle, I guess."

"But it isn't too late," I prompted.

"Maybe not." Randy hesitated. "Say, I overheard you tell that phone operator you were a freelance writer. Perhaps you could help me get started on my career; I wouldn't even have to go to college. I can bring over some of my stuff for you to read— just for an opinion, mind you."

Freelance writer? Was I? *If only he knew.* Better he didn't know what I was writing. Who would even be allowed to read such a story, if the count found out I was writing it? And if it ever were published, I would have to declare it to be a work of fiction—who would believe such a thing could happen!

"Well?" Randy broke into my musings.

"Sure, I'd love to read some of your stuff." I considered it a smart idea to play the charade. It didn't surprise me, either, that he might look for an easy way out of having to go to college. I didn't hold out for the quality of his writing.

Randy's face lit up. He looked very much like a schoolboy who had just asked a girl out for a first date and she had said yes. What a strange world I had landed in again—but, I hoped not as sinister as the one I had just left.

~

Another week passed, but it had been an uneasy one for me. The blood had finally stopped flowing in the breast milk, however I felt overly fatigued. Santan was testy and I wondered if it was because he was not getting any blood. There were moments when I cursed having him with me, but those moments passed quickly.

I still had not heard from Aunt Emelia and my funds were dwindling. I worried what my tomorrows would bring. I ate; I was sick ... I worked; I tired quickly ... I slept; it was never enough. I remembered my mother's words—*life goes on, no matter what happens to us*—I had no choice but to push forward.

For Santan's sake, if for nothing else.

~

In mid-October, I received a package by special courier. The return address on the package was Miss Adelaide Georgian, 10 West Boulevard, Kenora, Transylvania, so I knew that it was from Aunt Emelia. The letter inside was uninformative, where the family was concerned, but it did confirm that she was still my benefactress and that I would have no financial worries as long as I continued to care for the count's son.

My Dear Virginia:

I am pleased you have found a suitable place to live; and I understand your difficulty in opening a bank account with no identification; therefore, I have taken the chance and sent you another allotment of cash. Hopefully, this problem will not last long; a bank account will make it much easier for Adelaide to wire five thousand dollars to your account at the first of every month.

How is the child? I assume, by now, the blood in your milk has disappeared. I hope that this has not caused complications for Santan or trouble for you.

I will only bore you briefly with news about me. The count was furious at your escape, especially with his son! He demanded to know who had aided you. No one spoke up; as well they would not, since it was I who aided you. Basarab turned his wrath on Max, presuming Max to be the most likely candidate to have helped you.

At that point, I interfered. I could not allow Max to be punished for something I had done; however, I was careful not to disclose my own part in your escape. I knew that I would have to confess eventually; however, that particular moment was not the right time to do so. I stopped the assault on Max, but Basarab was still filled with rage. He began to pressure me as to who had done it. After all, if I knew Max had not, then possibly, I knew who had. He took hold of my shoulders and stared into my eyes, searching for the truth. I have to admit, I feared I would not be able to block him from reading my mind.

It was Atilla who finally came to my rescue, saving me from further interrogation. He grabbed Basarab's arm, staying him in his fury, and ordered his son to let it go; there were more urgent matters to attend to at the moment. Basarab was fuming, but Atilla prevailed. Within a few hours, we had closed up the house and were on our way.

Once we were in Transylvania, I confessed. I told Vacaresti, who in turn informed my nephew. Basarab still will not speak to me; I guess I deserve that, though. After all, I did take from him what he had most desired for a long time--his son. Time will heal, I hope, and time is what I have an eternity of.

Continue to write me at the address I gave you, to let me know how things are going with you and the child. If there is anything else you need, or if the funds are not enough, do not hesitate to speak up.
Love, Aunt Emelia

~

I laid the letter on my lap and gazed over at my sleeping son. It was daylight, the hours when he slept the most. At night he was wide-eyed and roaring to go. This played havoc on my sleep; but try as I might to change his schedule, it was mine that had to change.

I was glad to learn Aunt Emelia had been saved from Basarab's wrath. I would have hated myself had something horrible happened to her because of me. I knew the count would not have been quite so irate if Emelia had only helped *me* to escape; I didn't mean much to him—in fact, I was pretty sure I meant nothing at all!

I chuckled at Emelia's assumption that five thousand dollars might not be enough to sustain my monthly expenses. I was relieved I would not have to get a job to support myself and Santan, especially under my circumstances. Of course, I could always put him in a little coffin through the day and only let him out at night … just a joke, but one I was beginning to believe might come to fruition one day. I wondered if the coffins were still in the basement of *The House*, or if they had been shipped to Transylvania. I guessed that might depend on whether *they* would be returning to Brantford. Plus, if *The House* was put up for sale, wouldn't dirt filled coffins in the basement be questioned?

Randy offered, several times, to watch Santan for me so that I could do my shopping unhampered. I didn't have a valid driver's licence, I reminded him. Sometimes, instead of him driving me around, I would just give him my grocery list and the money to pick up what I needed. I had no desire to go out any more than necessary. Who knew what friends the count might have left last minute instructions with, to see if they could locate the whereabouts of his son?

Randy approached me one day and asked me to go out to a bar with him that night. He said he wanted to celebrate something with a friend. I thought it was strange he felt that I was such a person, due to the short span of time we had known each other.

"Come on, Virginia," he began, "Lets you and me split this place for a couple hours. I have something important to share with you." He had smiled his sheepish smile, the one I had come to love.

"You know I can't do that Randy," I replied.

"Look, everyone hires a sitter for their kids once in a while. You have to let go a little, Virginia. You must know *someone*. Santan will survive without you for a couple of hours." Randy reached out and grabbed my hand.

His action startled me. I pulled away sharply: "Don't touch me," I hissed. "And no, I don't know anyone that I would trust enough to leave with my son," I added.

Randy had stepped back, raising his hands in the air. "Wow! Sorry! I didn't mean anything, Virginia." His face was beet red.

I realized I had made a terrible mistake: "I'm so sorry, Randy. It has nothing to do with you, really. I appreciate your offer; it sounds wonderful, but maybe another time, okay?" I extended my hand to him. "Friends?" I begged.

Randy didn't hesitate. He took my hand in his. I noticed how large and warm it was. He smiled. "Friends, for sure."

As Randy was leaving, he turned and left me with a few words for thought: "I don't know who has hurt you in the past, Virginia, but not everyone is bad. I don't want anything more from you than friendship, please be assured of that. I don't know where you came from, or where you may be going, but I do know one thing. You are the strangest woman I have ever come across, and you are also the most fascinatingly beautiful woman I have ever met."

I stood there, speechless, my mouth hanging open. Those were strong words for such a young man.

"What?" Randy smirked.

I shrugged my shoulders. "Nothing." I shut the door.

Randy went out without me. He must have had fun because he was banging around his apartment in the wee hours of the morning, singing away at the top of his lungs! I was sure, whenever he woke up, he would be nursing a colossal hangover.

~

As the days passed, I couldn't believe how queasy my stomach was—there was no letup to it. In fact, after I ate my breakfast, all I felt like doing was throwing up. I was *late*, too, and that worried me. I feared the last night the count had had his way with me had left me with more than a discarded heart. I thought it was time to call a doctor, but who could I trust with my possible condition? What about Santan? As soon as I walked into a doctor's office, would they not start asking questions about why

I wasn't bringing my son in for regular appointments? What if they asked about his birth records? What would I tell them?

I picked up my phone and dialled Randy's number. It rang ten times before a sleepy voice answered. "Hello?"

"Hi Randy ... sorry, if I woke you ... I need a favour."

"Sure ... what do you need?"

"I have to go to the pharmacy and pick up a couple of things."

"No problemo," Randy said. "Give me an hour and I will be at your door with my little red limo."

"Thanks." I smiled through the phone line. "See you in an hour."

God, I felt sick. I wondered if I should be going out at all. I spent the next half hour throwing up in the washroom. By the time I felt well enough to leave my sanctuary, Santan was waking up, and from the sound of his cry he was hungry. I needed a moment to me, though. I poured a glass of water and threw some ice in it, and then went outside for a breath of fresh air. I looked around, taking in the beauty of my little piece of the country in the middle of the city. I was lucky to have found such a place— quiet, secluded, and out of the way of the hustle and bustle of people. Even Randy was a salvation, for he seemed to be a recluse. In fact, I had yet to see anyone pay him a visit, and I couldn't help but wonder if he had any friends.

The maple trees whispered to me as a light breeze rustled through their branches. They seemed friendly, not like the ones at *The House*. These were younger and straighter, standing tall all around the yard. Perhaps they too were soldiers, but instead of hindering my escape, they would protect me by keeping *him* away!

Santan's whimpers turned into full-blown hunger howls. I didn't want Randy to think I was one of those mothers who let their baby cry and cry. It was time to return to reality.

~

"Hey," Randy said as we were on our way to the pharmacy, "how say, after you get what you need, we split Brantford this afternoon and head out to Port Dover?" Randy smiled his sheepish grin.

"I can't," I answered.

"Come on, Virginia, you never go anywhere! You keep that kid cooped up all day in the house, not to mention yourself! I think we will go to Dover whether you like it or not." Randy turned around and looked at Santan who was sitting in a hooded car seat. I had made a special cover for his seat, so the sun couldn't scorch his skin. "How about it, little guy, want to go watch the girls on the beach?"

Randy gazed over to me: "See, he nodded his head."

"I'm sorry Randy, taking Santan to the beach is out of the question."

"Give me one good reason," Randy insisted.

I decided I had no choice but to tell him. "In case you haven't noticed, Santan has a serious sensitivity to the sun. That is why I keep him inside in the daytime, and if I have to take him outside, he is fully covered." I didn't want to provide further information, but Randy kept pushing.

"Have you taken him to a doctor about this condition?"

"No."

"Why not? Do you know what causes it?"

"No," I lied.

"Is it something hereditary?"

"No!" I lied again, wishing Randy would just drop the subject. "Possibly," I added, as an afterthought.

"Do you have a doctor in Brantford? If not, I could put you in touch with mine."

"No, I don't have a doctor here." *How can I get him to stop questioning me about this issue?* An idea struck me: "But, I have found an out-of-town doctor who specializes in skin conditions. I have an appointment to see her in a couple of weeks.

Don't bother yourself about this, really," I stressed. "Thanks, anyway, for your concern," I added.

I could tell by the wrinkles on Randy's forehead that he was not sure whether to believe me, or not. Finally, he sighed, shrugged his shoulders, and let the subject drop.

"There's the pharmacy," I pointed out.

Randy stopped in front of the door. "You want me to go in and get your stuff?"

"No, it's okay." I got out of the car and reached in the back for Santan.

"Come on Virginia; he'll be okay with me for five minutes!" Randy's voice had a hint of sarcasm in it.

I hesitated a moment, then relented. Aunt Emelia had said to guard Santan well, not be his shadow. What could happen in five minutes?

I learned pretty quickly what could happen in five short minutes. On exiting the store, I saw the look of horror on Randy's face, and I heard my son crying. His cry sounded weird, too— like a howl. *No, not possible ... a baby wolf?*

"What is going on here?" I demanded.

"I ... I ... I ..." Randy's face was flushed.

"Spill it!" I shouted, panic skipping through my heart's normal pattern. "You what?"

"I just lifted the shade a tiny bit; I didn't realize how hot the sun was, I guess. I promise never to do that again. Santan is more sensitive than I imagined. Now I know why you don't expose him to the sun; his skin sizzled!" Randy's face was etched with disbelief, as he recounted what had happened.

I got in the car, slammed the door, and ordered Randy to take me home. I knew I shouldn't have spoken to him so sharply; he had no idea who Santan was—that he was the son of a vampire! I made a decision to get my driver's license and a car, so I would not have to depend on Randy to drive me around. Until then, I would take cabs.

When we arrived at the house, I took my package, unhooked Santan's chair from the backseat, murmured a thank you, and headed for my apartment. I was still shaking. I unlocked the door, entered my private domain, and shut out the outside world.

I drew the blanket away from Santan and observed the burn marks on his cheeks. I noticed that he was already beginning to heal—clearly a genetic disposition! There would be no need for drugstore creams.

Even though Santan was healing fast, he was irritable and didn't want to feed. I laid him in the playpen and wound up the music box that hung on the side. After a few minutes, he settled and fell asleep.

I retrieved my package, opened it, and read the instructions. I couldn't do the test until morning. I walked to the window and stared out into the early evening, watching the sunset, as I used to do at *The House*. However, then, *they* would come for me. Now, when the sun settled in the west, I could walk unfettered down the street, or sit out in the yard, wherever I chose, for I was free—for now. My eyes felt heavy; it had been a long day.

I was startled awake by an insistent knocking on my door. "Just a minute," I hollered. I walked quickly to the bathroom, slipped my package into the medicine cabinet, and then went to answer the door.

Randy was standing on the walkway. He was holding a bouquet of red roses in his arms. "I wonder if you will accept these as a peace offering, Virginia. I had no right to do what I did today; you have no idea how sorry I am. I'll understand if you never want to see me again." He handed me the roses.

I couldn't help but to forgive him. I would just have to be more cautious in the future.

"How is the little guy?" Randy enquired.

"He'll be okay. I put some ointment on his skin," I lied. "He's sleeping in the playpen."

"May I see him?"

"I'd rather you didn't right now. He was quite upset— wouldn't even nurse. I don't want to wake him." There was also no way I wanted Randy to see how quickly Santan had healed. I paused. "If you would like to come in for a drink, I'll just put these flowers in a vase."

"Coffee would be good, if it's no bother." Randy stepped in and took a seat at the kitchen table.

I found an empty glass jar on the top shelf of the cupboard, filled it with water, and placed the roses in it. I got my coffeemaker out and made enough coffee for four cups. I glanced at Randy and smiled, as I reached for two mugs.

"Cream and sugar?" I asked, walking to the fridge.

"Both," Randy replied. "I still haven't told you my good news yet." His face lit up with excitement.

I had forgotten that he had asked me to go out the previous night, to celebrate something. "Well?" I prompted.

"I got a job. Not much of one, mind you, but it is in the field I want—writing! Uncle George spoke to one of his friends at Brant News, and he said I could do some freelance work for them, covering evening sports events." Randy took a breath. "Since that seems to be the only time you go out of the house, maybe you and Santan could go with me sometimes."

I smiled. "That would be nice, maybe sometimes." I was not ready to get into another why or why not session with Randy. "When do you start?"

"Monday night."

I decided to treat Randy to supper, to celebrate his new job. We ordered a pizza and then watched a suspense movie. I guessed who the killer was; Randy said it was because I was a writer. I giggled and told him, as a writer, I would not have ended the story that way.

"You have an inside edge on me," Randy said as he was leaving. He paused and leaned against the doorjamb.

"Not really, Randy; it is just common sense that Jake did it. I mean, look at all the clues." I adamantly defended my reasoning.

"Don't rub it in," Randy snorted, looking embarrassed. He paused. "Would you mind letting me read some of your stuff?"

"Maybe … I don't usually let anyone read my material before it goes to my editor." I was getting proficient at pumping out the lies. I prayed that I could keep track of them all!

"Who is your editor?" Randy asked. "Do you already have a publisher?" He sounded excited.

"You wouldn't know them," I answered quickly. "They are in Europe."

"Oh ... well, whenever; I look forward to reading your work."

"Maybe," I repeated as I shut the door.

~

My greatest fear was realized the next morning. I was pregnant! I had no idea how I was going to explain this, much less be able to handle another pregnancy so soon after the birth of Santan. Then again, who was around to explain anything to? Randy? I had never mentioned to him that I had a husband. I assumed that he would take it for granted that I did because I had a child. At the least, he would think I had had someone in my life. I would write to Aunt Emelia for advice. Without the *special drink*, I knew I wouldn't produce the same *formula* for this child; but it would still be *his* child, and I wondered what affects that would have on its future.

I thought, momentarily, of ending its life; but it was a fleeting thought. Life would be lonely for Santan, and I knew all too well the loneliness of being an only child. Maybe this baby, growing in my womb, had been sent by God—a little brother or sister for my son so that he wouldn't have to grow up alone.

However, I was also aware that it was not God who had planted this child's seed!

Yes, I would write to Emelia; she would know what to do.

Chapter Three

It took me a few days to recover from the shock of being pregnant again. My mind was whirling over my precarious circumstances. Having to raise two children on my own would not be an easy task. I was exhausted. Nevertheless, I knew the letter to Emelia must be written; I could procrastinate no longer. I picked up my pen.

My Dearest Emelia:

I trust this letter finds you in good health, and that by now, Basarab has found it in his heart--if he has one--to forgive you. I hope you have not been humiliated in any way that you are afraid to tell me about. If I found out you suffered because of me, I couldn't forgive myself.

Santan grows daily. I am worried because he still cannot tolerate the sun. I thought by now he would have adjusted, even just a bit. He sleeps most of the day and wants to play in the night. An unfortunate incident happened the other day. The young man, Randy, who drives me around, thought to take a peek at Santan, and he pulled across the special cover I had made for the baby's car seat. The sun seared Santan's cheeks. I had tried to stress to Randy that Santan had a serious sensitivity to the sun. Well, he believes me now; but this occurrence has driven me even deeper behind the walls of my secret world. I made sure, though, that he did not see how quickly Santan's burns healed. Do you know of anything I can use to help him live a normal life in my world? I want him to experience life-

-to be able to play on a beach, go to a baseball game or a soccer game, play in the yard--just be a typical kid. Is there a chance for that? Or am I fooling myself?

Thank you so much for your generous support. After the episode mentioned above, I believe I will need to buy my own car. They have them with shaded windows, which will probably be the best kind for me to get. I will have to figure out how to obtain a driver's licence, since I still have no identification. Any ideas?

Now for the most urgent news I have to burden you with. I am with child again--his child. I guess, in some ways, I should be thankful, for it means Santan will have a brother or a sister. However, I cannot help worrying. Will this child be the same as its brother, or will it be more like me? Either way, I could be in trouble. Do you have any advice for me? If Santan eventually partakes in his father's 'habits,' how will I be able to protect this new child? How safe will I be?

I'm also afraid I might have to leave this place; Randy is getting too curious about my situation. I guess this is my plight now, to always have to look over my shoulder. I cry myself to sleep, whenever I can sleep. I cry, inside, all the time, when I am awake. Dear Aunt Emelia--I trust I am still not taking liberties by calling you that--you are the only one I have in this whole world right now, the only person to whom I can confide my secrets to.

I'll wait (eagerly) to hear from you.
Love, Virginia

Later, as the sun was setting, I packed Santan in his buggy, covered him well, and walked down the lane to the postbox on Henry Street. I watched a train chug along the track, and counted the cars, wondering where they were headed. I pictured that it was going somewhere pleasant; and, maybe, one day I would be able to take my children there. I felt a flutter and rubbed my belly. I turned and headed home—to my seclusion—to the life I never dreamed I would end up in.

~

Seven days after mailing my letter, I received a response from Emelia, and some extra cash…

Dear Virginia…

I am most distressed at your news--another child! This must be an enormous burden to you. It is also something we must keep from the count. I will reflect on what to do, how I might be able to help you. I am unable to travel at the moment because I am being closely monitored. I will have to send someone in my stead, possibly Adelaide, to whom you send my letters. I shall speak to her, to see if she is willing to take the trip. She is a friend that I have kept as my little secret, since I met her and then took her into my confidence. Not even Vacaresti knows of her.

Basarab still does not speak to me. My heart is extremely heavy because of this, but in reality, I deserve his wrath. I often wonder why he spared my life. Maybe it was because of the bond we once had; and, of course, he has more pressing matters to tend to at the moment. He knows he will have no problem finding you once affairs here are taken care of. Vacaresti has been apathetic to me, as well, but I am sure he will come around, probably sooner than Basarab.

We have settled into our caves, temporarily, until the hotel in Brasov is ready for us. It is safe here, and fairly comfortable, despite the lack of modern conveniences.

It is proving difficult for Basarab to adapt over here, because he has been away for quite some time. When I observe him from afar, I get the sense that his mind is elsewhere. I can guess where it lies--probably you can, as well. I fear that in doing what I thought was right as a mother, I have done my nephew an enormous injustice, especially at such a tumultuous time when he should have all his wits about him. But having said that, I do not want you to fear anything; I will not betray the trust you have put in me.

I have enclosed some extra cash. I think you are right; it will be a good idea for you to get your own vehicle as soon as possible. I am also going to look into getting you some new identification so that you will be able to open a bank account. I know people who can arrange such matters because we have had to use their services on several occasions. In fact, Adelaide's brother will most likely be the one I will turn to for your papers. He is known in the vampire circles, but he is loyal to me, above all others, and would never betray me. Please send your picture to Adelaide, so Alfred can start the process. I am thinking of having Adelaide bring you the next package, personally. I also think it would be wise to have her brother accompany her, so he can tend to the rest of the paperwork, ensuring everything is in perfect order for you. I trust you will be able to put them up for a few days--have no fears, they are not vampires--just very dear friends to me. I saved Adelaide's life once, and she and her brother also saved mine several years ago. But that is another story, and there is no time to write it now.

I will send you a telegram in a few days, confirming exactly how we are going to proceed.

Remain well ... give my great-nephew a big kiss and a hug.
Until next time, Emelia

~

I didn't know whether to cry or not. I was grateful for everything Emelia was doing for me; but, I worried that it would become too much for her to bear and that eventually she would break down and tell the count where I lived. I feared for myself, for Santan, and for the child in my womb.

Would the horror in my life never stop?

Basarab

Chapter Four

I left my heart in Brantford…

It took everything in my power to keep me from destroying all around me when I discovered that Virginia had fled *The House* with my son. I could have overlooked her escape because she had served her purpose. I knew she would not go to the authorities, as long as I was with the child … but now … I am not too sure what she will do. However, knowing Virginia, as I do, I do not think she will be that dim-witted to betray me; she has seen how powerful I am. She knows I will return for my son.

Because of the pressing family matters in Transylvania, I could not stay and track Virginia and my child down. My father convinced me that no harm would come to my son as long as he was with Virginia…

"It is for the best," he said. "It is not safe in Brasov. You know, as well as I, that if the wrong people were to get hold of the information that you have a son, it would be better if the child were not with us!"

His words have proven to be accurate, and I have thanked him for having convinced me to leave Santan in Canada. However, his wisdom does not alleviate the pain I feel at the separation from my son.

Something else saddened my heart—my beloved Aunt Emelia's betrayal of handing my son over to Virginia. I still cannot bring myself to speak to my aunt, nor can I look at her if she is in the same room as I. She is heartbroken by my alienation of her; because, in the past, she and I had a special bond. My mother died when I was an infant and Emelia had filled that void in those early years of my life. She taught me the gentler side of life, not that I ever showed that side of me to anyone other than her—so it is difficult.

~

It has been a great curse and burden to me, this role of being the leader of the most powerful vampire clan in the world. We were the first. The Gypsy hag, Tanyasin, who had sought revenge on my uncle, Vlad Dracula, who had murdered her husband and son, laid the curse on my uncle and all his blood. There are many vampire cells, but none has ever become as powerful as the Dracul bloodline. If it were not that my father had insisted I return, that I was badly needed to help deal with the problems in Transylvania, I would not be in Brasov now.

I cannot imagine the pain my lovely wife, Teresa, must be feeling at the moment, either. I promised her a child and I had that child delivered into her arms, and then it was snatched away from her. She does not speak of it to me. At times, I think I detect sadness in her eyes, but at other times, I cannot read what is truly behind those pools of darkness that so bind me to her.

Teresa has been deserving of the position of being my queen. She has proven her faithfulness to me, time after time, even to the extent of saving my life during one of the renowned European scourges. Vampire hunters had tracked me down, and caught me alone and unprotected. If it had not been for Teresa, who happened on the scene as they were about to sever my head, I may have disappeared forever. Teresa made short work of the lot of them, pulled the stake from my heart, and then nurtured me until I regained my strength.

The one thing, other than Teresa, that I wanted, was a son. Teresa was unable to bear me a child during the first few years of our marriage. We tried time after time. Several times, she found herself to be pregnant, only to lose the baby before the end of the first trimester. It took everything in my power not to cross her over, but I wanted a son, and I knew she wanted to give me one, so I had to keep her human until we had our family.

Ten years into our marriage, we still had not succeeded in having a child. I distinctly remember the night that Teresa came to me, tears running down her beautiful face as she begged me to cross her over...

"Basarab, love of all that exists for me, it is of no use. It must be obvious to you by now that I cannot bear children. Doctor Balenti does not know what is wrong with me, but he thinks there must have been some irreversible damage when I took that tumble off the horse when I was thirteen." She had paused, and drew in a deep, shuddering breath before continuing. "I need to be one with you, my love ... however ... if you still desire a son ... well ... I am willing to turn my eyes elsewhere while you do what you must do to accomplish that end."

"What are you saying, Teresa?" I had not slept with another woman since I had wed Teresa, and now she was giving me leave to do so, to get the child I so desperately wanted.

"Exactly what you heard me say. It is vital for the king to have a son. I know that, and I want this for you ... and for me. I guess the right thing to do would be to let you go ... maybe your cousin, Ildiko, would have been a better choice..."

"But she is a vampire, my dear; she could not have borne me a son either." I could see the pain in my wife's eyes.

"But she could have given you a child before she took the step to be fully initiated into the vampire world. It would have been possible."

I took hold of her hands and drew her to me, holding her slender, fragile body close to mine. It was not a surprise that she could not carry a baby in her womb. There was nothing to Teresa; there would be no room for the child to grow in her belly. I felt that if she had managed to bring a child to term, it would probably have killed her during the delivery. I did not wish that; I did not want to lose Teresa. I have watched for too many years the pain in my father's heart because of the death of my mother.

"There are other reasons that I did not wed Ildiko," I said, before leaning over and covering Teresa's lips with mine. When we surfaced, finally, gasping for air, I swooped her into my arms and carried her to our bedchamber, and there we stayed for the next two days. I had decided that I would speak to my father later about setting up the ceremony for Teresa's crossover.

However, our two days of lovemaking had spawned another child. For two months, I waited on Teresa, and when I could not tend her needs, I made sure someone else did. My Aunt Emelia even came to the house and stayed with Teresa when I was on a two week business trip. Nevertheless, despite all of our attention, she lost the baby. This time, she could not be comforted. She stayed in her bed for hours, only leaving it long enough to go to the washroom, or to take a few sips of water. Food, she would not touch.

My father told me that I had to do something before she died of starvation…

"If you want to save her, son, we must cross her over, now! Would you like me to set it up?"

"Is she strong enough, Father?"

"While she still has some strength, we must do this. If she gets any weaker, even the potency of our blood will not save her!" My father had been going to walk away, but at the last minute he turned back to me. I noticed the pain in his eyes when he spoke. "Don't let this opportunity go, son; I don't want you to be alone for the rest of your existence, as I am. When your mother died, the biggest portion of my heart went with her."

I finally agreed. Even though it was a month before Teresa was up and about again, the blood that we fed her began to do its job. Once again, she blossomed into the beautiful woman I had married.

For the next few hundred years, Teresa and I lived in harmony. On nights that I would go out, in search of a suitable young woman to bear me a child, Teresa would turn her head the other way. I was discreet, never flaunting any of them to her, or anyone else, in our home or in public. If I thought I had a reasonable prospect, and she became too possessive over me or my time, I would quickly end the relationship. Teresa never displayed jealousy when I crawled into her bed in the daytime, after an evening away. In fact, on such occasions, she was more passionate than ever before.

Until Virginia.

I think we both felt differently about Virginia, for several reasons. First, Teresa met her—she was in our home. Second, my seed grew within her. This was something that had never happened before. I was ecstatic; however, Teresa became sullen, as though it was okay for me to bed women, but the fact that none had ever become pregnant meant that they were no threat to her standing in my household. And, not only did Virginia carry my son in her womb, she was a fascinating woman. I took to spending more and more time with her, assessing and bantering about age-old issues that were near and dear to both our hearts.

I thoroughly enjoyed the sparing. Virginia was a formidable debater, never missing a point, driving her opinion home without fear of repercussion. With each night that passed, I grew fonder of her. And her physical passion for me drew me in on the same level as did Teresa's. Never had two women been more equal when it came to satisfying my *appetite*. I did not think twice about pleasuring them both, and being pleased in return. I used my power over them to get what I wanted—total control.

As the months passed, Teresa became more and more hostile toward Virginia, and toward me. We began to fight like we had never fought before. She displayed unseemly behaviour, and even though there was a time I did not bed Virginia, because of her condition, I also stayed away from my wife, not being able to stomach her intolerable behaviour.

I knew Virginia was playing a game with me, the game of survival. I would have done the same, had I been in her shoes. The trouble was she loved me. Despite the game that she thought she was playing, she would have been willing to stay and give me another child. She had said as much. I used to sit and watch her, after we had made love, and as she dreamed. Her red hair spread freely across the pillow, her features serene in the moment. Her breathing was soft and rhythmic, and her body radiated the warmth that I would never feel.

Teresa continued to burn with jealousy. I would try to convince her that she was my wife and that Virginia was nothing more than the vessel to bear my child, but she told me otherwise...

"Do not lie to me, Basarab," she had stormed one night, as she threw a priceless vase at my head. "I am not a fool; I know the difference between dallying and love. I see the way you look at her, the way you talk with her, and laugh with her. You are falling for her."

I had laughed in her face, and then allowed the snarling beast within me to emerge. I thrust her across the room, and she smashed against the wall. But that only stunned her for a moment. Within seconds, she was on her feet, lunging for my throat with her fangs, even though she knew she was no match for me, strength wise. I sidestepped, and then pushed her into the pile of broken vase glass that she had shattered against the door. Her blood splattered across the floor, exciting me. I took charge, grabbed her by the hair, drew her head back, and found her lips.

She did not resist.

However, Teresa did not let up on her quest to be rid of Virginia.

Nor did Virginia let up on her quest to escape, despite her professed love for me.

~

Upon arriving in Transylvania, we went straight to the caves and waited there until our accommodations were ready for us. We are now settled into one of the hotels I own in Brasov, commandeering the top five floors. I set up a conference room down the hall from my quarters, where I could assemble with some of the family members who had been called upon. One evening, following a meeting, my father came to my room. Teresa was visiting with my aunts, Evdochia and Emelia, so I was alone. I could tell by the look on my father's face that he had something of profound importance to discuss.

"May I offer you some refreshment, Father?"

"No thank you, I have just supped." He took a seat, folded his hands in his lap. There was a concerned look in his eyes. "Where are you, Basarab?"

At first, I was startled by his question, but then it dawned on me what he was getting at. I had not been focused during the meeting, and information had to be repeated several times. I had never been so distracted before, and I realized I needed to pull myself together.

"I am sorry, Father." I walked over to the window and peered out into the night. "I cannot stop thinking about my son."

My father joined me at the window. He laid his hand on my shoulder. "I understand how you feel, Basarab. I was devastated when your mother died; I live everyday with that loss, but I had no choice but to move forward. And neither do you. Your consolation is that your son is alive. Think about that. Virginia is an admirable woman, and a devoted mother; she will look after Santan. You need to focus, and the sooner you do, the sooner you can look for your son. I have heard whisperings among the family; many are wondering what is wrong with you."

"You say I can look for my son, Father, but I do not know where he is. Virginia has probably hidden him well."

"I am sure Emelia knows their whereabouts."

I snorted in disdain. "Yes, my beloved aunt ... I would like to rip her throat out for what she did."

"As we have discussed, despite how you feel, what she did has probably saved your son's life. News travels too fast in the vampire world. You know your son would not have been safe here. You would have had to spend as much of your energy protecting him as you would have to spend trying to solve the issues we are faced with. Do not blame your aunt. Embrace what she has done and get on with what you must do. I am sure, when the time comes, Emelia will tell you where the child is. Until then, it is better that we do not know."

"I know you are right, Father ... it is just..."

"Stop feeling sorry for yourself, Basarab!" My father's voice was harsh. "Put aside your feelings, and be the leader you always have been! If you do not do this quickly, all will be lost—and not just for the vampire race. How do you think humans will handle a full onslaught of vampire rogues rampaging through their cities? What is happening here is just the inklings of an Armageddon like this world has never seen. You do not want that on your shoulders, especially when you could have stopped it."

I turned to my father, his words burning in my ears. "Perhaps I should step aside and let someone else take the throne ... you perhaps?"

My father's face showed his anger, and his frustration. "Do not be so foolish. You are the leader, so decreed by Tanyasin's curse. There is nothing you can do to thwart that. Live with it, or we all die—including your son!" With those words, my father turned and left the room.

I continued to stare out the window for another few minutes. I knew what I had to do, and I knew that I must do so immediately. I went to the closet and retrieved my coat, then headed out into the night. This was one night that I would revert to old ways. To draw blood directly from a body still breathing might stimulate the beast within me—I hoped.

I left the hotel and headed to the bar district. I was sure I would be able to find willing enough victims to leave the bar with me, especially the women. They were always, in the past, too willing to go with a handsome, respectable businessman, such as I portrayed. I hoped that had not changed; it had been a while since I had gone in search of such prey. I had no intention of killing anyone, just of taking their blood.

I walked up to a bar that had a long line of young people standing outside, waiting to be allowed in. Good, it would be crowded, which meant easy pickings. I approached the bouncer standing at the door.

"Back of the line, buddy," he ordered.

I leaned into him. "I do not think so," I whispered in his ear, and then stepped back.

He did not hesitate for a moment, then. He drew the rope across. "It would be our pleasure to have you with us this evening, sir. Enjoy your time." I stepped past him. He refastened the rope.

I glanced back, before going through the door, and noticed the young man slip the money I had pressed into his hand in his pocket. I smiled and nodded. Then I went hunting.

Chapter Five

The sun was just beginning to rise when I arrived back to the hotel. As I headed to my suite, I passed my father. We each paused, looking into the other's eyes.

"Welcome back, son," he said, and then continued to his room.

Teresa was already sleeping in our darkened bedroom. I went to the bathroom and stared into the mirror. My reflection indicated to me why my father had said *welcome back*. My eyes were aflame!

I turned on the shower and stepped in. I needed to wash the women's fragrances off my body. Their blood had been sweet, but that is all that had been sweet about them. As I lathered the soap on my body, I thought about how easy they had been, and I became aroused again. The first woman had sidled up to me, before I was barely seated at the bar. She had whispered in my ear that there were *special* rooms upstairs, and had invited me to join her in one of them. She was pleasant enough looking; however, it was not her I wanted, it was her blood. I had given her what she desired, and then taken what I needed. I left her, sound asleep, on the bed and returned to the bar, my thirst not fully quenched. She would just be a bit tired when she awoke; other than that, she would remember nothing of what I had done to her.

It had not taken long for another woman to find me attractive enough to want to take me upstairs, but I had suggested we take a walk instead. After all, it was a lovely evening. I left her sleeping on a bench in a secluded area of a park in the centre of the city. She had been an adventurous vixen, to say the least, with an almost insatiable appetite. She had commented on how it had been a good idea to come to the park—an adventurous place to *get it on*. I had to put my hand over her mouth to silence her laughter; I could not take the chance on having a passerby become curious and witness what I was about to do. The woman's blood had been sweeter than her predecessor's, and when she awoke, I was sure that she would be more tired than my first victim. I had taken a bit more than I needed to.

As the door to the shower stall opened, I was licking my lips at the memory of what I had just done. Teresa stepped inside, joining me, taking my arousal in her hands. "What is this, husband? For me?" She laughed.

I pulled her to me, and then thrust her up against the shower wall. She moaned in delight, matching my beast with her own.

~

I awoke in the late afternoon. The bed was empty. I wondered where Teresa had gone so early. I walked through our suite; it too was empty. I went to the refrigerator and drew out a bottle of blood. It did not taste as potent as what I'd had the previous night, but it was satisfying all the same. When I was finished, I dressed and then headed out to find my father. I needed to speak with him.

My route took me past my servant Max's room. I paused outside the door when I heard my wife's voice from within...

"I don't care, Father!" Teresa was yelling. "Don't you get it? I never wanted a child. Basarab was all I ever needed in my life!" She sounded at the point of hysteria.

Then Max spoke. "But, Teresa, Basarab did it for you, too; you always led him to believe you wanted a child."

"Those are the key words, Father—*led him to believe*."

"But..."

"No buts, Father. I hope Virginia hides so well that we never find her—or the bastard child!"

"What are you going to tell Basarab? Has he not asked you to return to Brantford to try to find the child?" I could sense the tension in Max's voice.

"I am going to tell him the same as Atilla has told him—that it would not be wise to do so. I will play the loving mother, begging him not to send me on such an errand. I will emphasize, with tears running down my cheeks, that if I were to find the child and return here with him, and if something horrible were to happen ... let's just say that my grief will be too much to bear. Of course, my dear husband will not want to see me so distraught. I know that beneath that tough, ruthless exterior is a man whose heart has holes in it. Some of those holes I have put there, in order to manipulate him! And lately, he has been so besot with the loss of his son that I can hardly bear to be around him! The other day, to top it all off, he was calling out in his sleep ... do you want to know who he was calling for, Father? It was not me ... it was her!"

I could not believe what I had heard. I was aware that Teresa was jealous. But to this extent? And, why would I call out Virginia's name in my sleep? I did not desire to hear any more, but I could not move away from the door...

"My dear daughter, what have you become?" I heard the stress in Max's voice.

"Just what you bargained for, Father—just what you bargained for! Can you fault me for becoming a heartless creature? You did not think about that, did you, when you bargained my hand in marriage in exchange for the release of my mother, Lilly—did you, Father?"

"Teresa ... I had no choice ... I..."

"Don't say it, Father, don't you dare! You had a choice. *You* could have killed her, ended her misery. But you would not do that, would you? Despite your words of love for me, that is all they are, just words. You do not love me—it has always been your precious Lilly. Look at what that love has earned you—pain and servitude!"

"Teresa…"

I heard footsteps approaching the door of the room, and knew at any moment Teresa would come storming into the hallway. Quickly, I stepped back into a hidden corner. As Teresa stomped toward the elevator, Max stood in the doorway of his room, watching his daughter leave, a forlorn, lost look on his face. I waited until Teresa was on the elevator, and Max had closed his door, before I stepped from the shadows and proceeded to my father's room.

This new revelation astounded me. I had not known that Teresa was jealous of the child, as well. Virginia, yes ... but that was understandable. It was hard to believe Teresa was not heartbroken at having lost the child and that she had never wanted him in the first place—that she had only played along to appease me. But I had heard her with my own ears, and now I would have to deal with her accordingly. If she thought for one second that she could manipulate me, I would show her who the master of manipulation was. Teresa was no match for me!

~

My father was not in his suite, so I continued to the meeting room, hoping to find him there. When I entered, he was standing by the window. He turned at the sound of my footsteps.

"I trust all went well when you ventured out last night?" he said. I noticed a slight grin on his lips.

"Very well, Father."

"I assume the young ladies will remember nothing?"

I smiled.

"And you are ready to return to the helm?"

"Very ready."

"Good. I expected as much, so I took the liberty of calling a meeting. Everyone should be here shortly. Have you supped?"

"Yes."

"I mean since last night?"

"Yes."

My father's intense eyes did not leave my face. "Good. Ah, the first to arrive ... welcome, Gara."

Gara entered the room. My cousins, Gara and Ildiko were twins, but Ildiko had the build of a seasoned male warrior, whereas Gara was built with a more slender frame, to the point of appearing effeminately fragile. However, what he lacked in brawn, he made up for in brains, and he was invaluable to me.

I thought back to our early years of the curse, to the day it was time for my cousins to be fully initiated into the family. All the children conceived by our kind, before and after the curse, had to be initiated. Humans who marry into our family, like my Aunt Emelia, must be crossed over. They are *amestecat-singe— mixed-bloods*; vampires, but not with the full powers of a blood family member.

Gara was unsure if he wanted to take this step, even though he knew that if he did not complete the initiation, there was no telling what would become of him. I remember Ildiko mocking him, telling him that he was a coward. And then she would coddle up to him and soften her teasing by saying she could not live without him. They were twins, she had reminded him, which meant that they should be together forever.

Gara had finally relented. It was difficult for him, though, much more so than it was for Ildiko. Her insatiable fires burned uncontrollably. We were forced to lock her up for several months, to keep her from human throats. Gara, we could barely keep alive. It seemed, even though he had decided to join us, he felt that he had made the wrong decision. He began to refuse the nourishment that he needed, as though he just wanted to die. My father had suggested I go to Gara, and convince him how much I needed him...

"I need you, Gara."

"You need no one, dear cousin." His voice had the rattle of death in it.

"That is not true. I must have someone I can trust; who better than one of my blood, who was conceived before the curse, born into it, and then transformed by it, as was I."

"You have Ildiko." Gara had sounded bitter. I wondered why—was he jealous of his sister? He had never displayed such an emotion before. I do not think that I had ever given her or anyone else any indication that she was anything more to me than a cousin.

"She is a girl, and too headstrong to be of any great benefit to me. I would not be able to trust her moods. I need your calmness. Most of all, I need your brilliant mind."

"Ildiko will not be happy about this, Basarab. She expected to be the one by your side. She loves you."

"I know. She has never made any pretence about her feelings for me."

"She still has her sights set on being your bride, too."

"I know that, as well. But I cannot take her as such."

"Because of the bargain?"

"Yes ... and..."

"Ah, yes, I know ... Teresa is beautiful."

"Indeed."

"When will you cross her over?"

"She must still be human to produce a child, so after she gives me a son—maybe two." I had paused. "So, you see, Gara, I need you by my side, for the wise counsel you give me. I insist you cease this foolishness and accept what we are—what you are! We do no harm to anyone that does not deserve it. We do the best we can with the hand that has been dealt us."

I walked away then, knowing that Gara would come around. He loved me as more than a cousin—as a brother. Gara recovered slowly, finally accepting his fate. When it came time for me to marry Teresa, I asked him to be my best man.

Ildiko, on the other hand, was furious when I finalized my plans to marry Teresa. She had been openly flirtatious with me during the years I had waited for Teresa to mature; however, during the immediate weeks before the wedding, she increased her endeavours. I knew she hoped that I would change my mind and marry her instead of Teresa. During the wedding ceremony, when my Uncle Stephen asked if there were any objections to the union, Ildiko had spit on the floor and left the room. We did not see her for the remainder of the celebration.

~

"Welcome, Gara." I walked over and embraced him. "I am so pleased that you have come."

"I would have it no other way, cousin. It is time we put this evil to rest." Gara's voice was soft, but firm. "We have been putting up with small cells of rogues causing problems for the family for far too long. What is happening now, though, is getting out of control."

"My father feels that Elizabeth Bathory is escalating her plans," I began, but Gara interrupted me.

"It is not just her, Basarab. There is someone more powerful than she, whom I think she answers to. I am sorry to say, but I believe it to be our uncle, Radu." Gara paused, drawing in a deep breath before continuing. "He is the only one of our family who has never stood with us over the centuries, the only one never harmed by the rogues when they rampaged. We must consider this, and not let the fact that he is our uncle cloud our judgments."

I considered Gara's words; however, I did not have time to answer because the rest of the family members began to arrive. "Speak of your thoughts at the meeting, so we all might consider this possibility," I said, and then turned to greet the new arrivals.

"My dear Uncle Stephen; It is an honour to be in your company again. I cannot thank you enough for all the years of selfless service you have given to me."

My uncle smiled. He had always been serious about his role as one of my chief advisors. "Likewise, Basarab … it has been far too long since you have graced our borders with your company." He paused. "Dracula sends his regrets; he will present himself to you as soon as possible. He had some pressing business to look after, informing me that it could not wait."

My father joined the conversation. "Well, we all know how much Dracula hates meetings; he usually finds an excuse to be absent from such events." He chuckled.

"Well said, Atilla," Stephen affirmed the joke. "One can always count on you to tell the truth so straightforwardly." He motioned to the table where the others had all taken their places. "Shall we join our kin?"

I took my place at the head of the table and gazed around at my family and friends. These were but a handful of my most trusted people; however, they were ones of prime importance. I turned to Gara, who sat to my right. "Could you elaborate, please, on our earlier discussion?"

Gara nodded and stood. "I have spent a considerable amount of time delving into a particular individual's business affairs, and I have reached a conclusion. Even though we are beset by a scourge like we have not experienced since the last great cleansing, the individual that we have assumed it to be, in my opinion, is not the actual power behind these events. Elizabeth Bathory is only acting on orders that she receives directly from one of our own." Gara hesitated, gazing around the table, as though to make sure he had everyone's full attention.

"Who is it that you speak of?" Lardom, a cousin of Stephen, and who was the head of our legal team, spoke up.

"Radu." Gara looked down at the table.

"You have proof?" Stephen asked.

"Enough to make me believe my suspicions are not far off." Gara paused. "First, we must consider the fact that Radu has never made any pretence about his displeasure of Basarab being our leader. He has even cursed the one who cursed us, yet he has been seen in the company of the Gypsy hag, Tanyasin, on many occasions. More than that, it appears that Radu has gained considerable support within the community. His influence reaches deep into the government offices and media corridors. The TV news stations and newspaper headlines are rife with such words as *sadistic slayings, vampiric bloodbath, callous slaughter*; I am sure that most of you are already aware of this blitz. I have also discovered that Radu owns the TV stations and newspapers that are the most vocal against our family.

"Radu's strategy, to start this battle in the country where the vampire lore began, is a genius move on his part. The people are already overly superstitious, and will gullibly believe most of what is fed to them through the media channels, and through the gossip that Radu is exceptionally good at spreading around."

"So what you are saying is that Elizabeth Bathory, and her friend Jack, are just decoys to throw us off Radu's plans?" Stephen spoke up again.

"Yes. Once again—I emphasise this is just my opinion— Elizabeth and Jack are nothing more than puppets in his organization. Radu would not want us to know of his intentions. How would he be able to come and go, or engage in any of our decision making, if Basarab got wind of how evil his uncle truly is?"

I stood. "Thank you, Gara. You have been most diligent in your research. I would appreciate it if you could spend some time with Lardom, filling him in on specific details about Radu's influence within the legal system."

Gara nodded. "I also want to caution you, Basarab … Radu will continue to play a game with you, but do not let your guard down for a minute, or you might find that you will be being taken away in handcuffs by the authorities. We have already seen what he has been able to have accomplished with the number of our people who are *guests* in the jails and prisons. Our Uncle

Uros has his hands full, burning the night hours, sorting through the correspondence that comes across his desk, before he sends it out with his couriers for daytime deliveries. He has been invaluable to the family, accumulating much of the information I am making known here today. It was a wise decision to set Uros up in the courier business, but I also suspect that his company post as official government courier may be in jeopardy if Radu discovers the extent of what is going on."

"Has Radu not asked for an audience with you?" my father enquired of me.

"Yes. I sent a message back that I would be pleased to meet with him," I answered. "The date is yet to be set."

"Do not be alone with him," Stephen cautioned. I could tell by the look on his face that he worried I might be walking into a trap. "And make sure the meeting is on your ground, not his."

Lardom stood. "Might I speak?"

I nodded.

"I believe there is something else we need to consider. My law team, while speaking with our incarcerated family, have reported to me that they have found them all to be incoherent, as though they have been drugged. I had managed, when I first arrived here, to sneak some *nourishment* through; however, over the past three weeks we have been unable to do so. Everyone, including lawyers, is searched extensively before they are allowed in the meeting rooms."

Ponqor, an *amestecat-singe*, who had married Dracula's bastard daughter Zigana, raised his hand. "Might I speak, Basarab?"

"Of course."

"While practicing at the hospital in Hungary, I also tended, occasionally, to some of the *amestecat-singe* in the area. I recall being called out one night to the home of one who was an exceptionally dear friend of mine. He had been out to a nightclub, but not one in an area where he usually went, one that was more frequented by rogues. He was with a new friend, a rogue, who had suggested this particular place. After having drunk a couple of glasses of blood-wine, he began to feel woozy. He excused himself, headed home, and called me. It took two days for him to feel normal again. I had drawn some blood from him, for analysis purposes, and found some strange properties in the blood; however, I could not discern what they were."

"Did you find out anything more about the bar itself?" Stephen asked.

"I did. I discovered that the bar is owned by a corporation, which one of my friends in the financial district traced to a holding owned by Radu. I also discovered that Radu is the owner of two of the largest wineries in Hungary; therefore, we should assume he supplies all the bars that he owns … and, there is something else. My friend mentioned that when he first entered the bar he had thought that many of the patrons were acting strange, almost zombie-like. If Radu is drugging the blood-wines he supplies to his bars, I am thinking that this might be his way of keeping the rogues under his control." Ponqor leaned back in his chair, signalling he had nothing further to say.

Gara's face had taken on a contemplative look. "If this is the case, we should take exceptional care about where we obtain our blood supplies from. We need to make sure our supplies are not being tainted with the same drug as the blood-wine rogues drink. After all, our blood is delivered to us in wine bottles. Are we sure we can fully trust *our* suppliers?"

My father spoke up. "Yes. The blood we purchase is from a source we have been dealing with for years. The family who supplies us has been with us for a long time. Each generation of that family has been raised up in service to us. I would trust them with my life." He drew in a deep breath before continuing. "You might have a point, though, Gara. Our blood might be safe, but that may not be the case of the supply of all family members. We cannot be too careful in these times. We should send out a discreet warning telling them that at the first signs of any illness we must be notified."

"I will look after that," Gara affirmed.

I gazed around the table. The atmosphere was gloomy. I was tired. The affects of the blood I had partaken of on the previous night had worn off. "I think we have discussed enough for one night," I said. "We will meet back here at the end of the week. If anyone discovers anything of any great importance before then, do not hesitate to come to me immediately."

No one moved. They started to talk among themselves, catching up on personal news. My father walked over to the refrigerator and took out some bottles of blood. Stephen got up and assisted him, fetching several wineglasses to the table. I excused myself from the meeting. "Enjoy yourselves, gentlemen," I told them as I left. "I need to get some sleep."

When I arrived at my suite, it was empty. I assumed Teresa was still with the women. I sat down on the couch and put my feet up on the coffee table. The curtain was drawn back, so I stared out into the night, going over in my mind some of the issues that had been discussed at the meeting. The more I thought about them, the more my concern centred on Radu.

Chapter Six

I had memorized, over the years, the part in my father's diary where he had recorded the curse cast on us by Tanyasin...

Vlad Dracula, better known to all those less fortunate than you as 'The Impaler,' I curse you to an everlasting hell! Your days shall be spent under closed lids, your nights in horrid shadows. You shall run in the night with the swiftness of the wolf; your eyes shall burn red, like the cave bats; and you will coerce your victims into submission. You shall be as cunning and charming as the red fox while you lure your victims to your den of darkness. But at the same time that you are exerting such power, no rest shall ever refresh your soul, and no peace will ever ease your mind. No man shall open his door to you or give you refuge at his table. You, that pup at your side, and all your descendants shall be burdened with this curse from now and into eternity! Those who stand here with me are my witnesses to this blight I cast upon you and yours!

True to Tanyasin's words, the entire blood family of Dracula was stricken with the curse. Most came about over the years and realized that living peacefully, in anonymity, among the humans would be the best approach to take. For centuries, the greatest adversaries we faced were the vampire hunters, men and women affiliated with the Christian churches. Strangers were one entity to deal with, but to be betrayed by our own kind—my uncle!

My Uncle Radu had not been around much while I was growing up. My father told me the stories of how Radu and Dracula had grown up in the Turkish Court. A certain evening, when both uncles had been present, came to my mind...

Radu had always made it quite clear, in the past, his hatred for Dracula. It rang through in the words he spit forth while we sat around the table. "You were never there for me; you left me to the pleasures of the Sultan's son."

Dracula had just grinned—at first. Then he had stood up and leaned across the table toward his brother, and the words that spit from his mouth were tainted with anger and revulsion. "What do you think, brother? That I was having a picnic while you were warming the bed of the Turk? That I had free reign in the Court to do as I pleased? You have no idea what foolishness comes out of your mouth!"

Radu's eyes filled with malice. "You never even tried. I searched for you every day before the sun fell, for months, but you were nowhere to be found. You…"

"I what? I had my own problems to deal with, and trust me, Radu, they were bigger than what you were dealing with. But I used my brains. I learned their ways—their methods of torture––so that one day when I got out of there I would be able to turn those methods on them! You say I was not there for you, yet when our release was finally negotiated, you were too comfortable in the Turk's bed, and you did not wish to leave."

"I was no…"

"Do not tell untruths in front of the family!" Dracula had cut his brother off. "You betrayed all of us when you sided with the Turks. You constantly harped on the fact that our father favoured me; but, it was not me he favoured. It was the true prince of the land he'd had faith in, one who would not betray his own blood!"

Radu seemed to have gathered some strength from somewhere, for he snapped back at his brother, and his words were filled with venomous hatred. "Look where our father's favour landed us, brother—cursed by a Gypsy hag! Does it bother you, that her curse did not give you the power; that she gave it to the pup of our little cousin, Atilla?"

Dracula had laughed in Radu's face, but then he had stormed out of the room. "Pathetic!" he had hissed at his brother on the way out.

I had been aware of Radu's resentfulness that Tanyasin had not cursed him to be our leader. Even though he tried hard to hide his true feelings when he was around me, I had noticed, as time passed, the malice in his eyes as he stared at me, when he thought I was not looking. His presence at our family gatherings decreased, and eventually, he had gone his own way—until recently, when he had contacted me for a meeting.

I turned my mind to what Ponqor had brought up at the meeting, wondering if all the chaos that had broken out had something to do with tainted blood-wine served in nightclubs owned by Radu. Was this how he was controlling the rogues to do his bidding? Elizabeth and Jack could not be responsible for all that was happening.

I feared if we did not get a handle on the situation, it could become the beginning of our eventual demise—like a Christian Armageddon—our moment of reckoning. At times, I thought that might not be such a terrible idea. How I would love to run back to Brantford and find my son … Virginia, too … possibly. Thinking of Virginia stirred sizzling memories in my loins. I closed my eyes, turning my thoughts back to Santan, as he was on the night of his naming ceremony, dressed in his little tuxedo, adorned with a black cape that was lined with red velvet. First, he panicked because of the commotion. Then, trust had radiated from his eyes when I chanted softly to him in the ancient language of my homeland. He was calm when I had cut his finger, and then held the bowl of vampire blood to his lips…

Why was she was there … in the shadows … pushing into my memories … her face filled with horror? *Nooooo!* Virginia's scream shrilled in my ears. Suddenly, she was heading toward me, a vicious expression on her face. I realized she was coming for my son, and I turned swiftly, giving her my back. She attacked me with everything she had; I felt her fists pounding through my heavy cape. I laughed. Did she honestly think she could overpower a roomful of vampires? *What are you doing to him?* Her voice resonated with rage.

What is necessary, my dear Virginia. I nodded to Dracula's sons, Vlad and Mihail. They stepped forward and took hold of Virginia's arms, dragging her off me. I looked over at Teresa. She sneered as she watched the scene unfold. I turned my gaze back to Virginia, and saw on her face what must be on the face of every mother who thinks her child might be in danger—terror. I hesitated for just a moment. She was strikingly beautiful!

I handed my son to my father and approached Virginia. I could tell that she was still straining against the hold my cousins had on her. I reached out and lifted her chin with my hand. *Why do you continue to challenge me, my dear? Have you not learned that you are no match for me? This child you have given me will be what he was meant to be—a vampire. I am his father. It is in his blood, and there is nothing you can do about it.* Despite the words I had just spoken, Virginia held my gaze.

But, there is something you must remember, as well, my dear count. He is our son, which means he is half human, and that is something you may not be able to do anything to about!

I let go of her chin, and laughed. The room filled with chuckles, the walls echoing with mirth. I noticed how limp Virginia's body had become; my cousins released her arms. She crumbled to the dirt floor, reaching for the hem of my cape, as she did, begging me with her eyes. Her lips opened, but no words came out. I shook my cape, releasing her fingers, and then walked out of the room. As I looped my arm through Teresa's, I turned for one last look at Virginia. She was watching me leave; however, this time I saw something different in her eyes, and it was not defeat. Her lips curled slowly upward, smiling at me. I hesitated, unsettled by the look on Virginia's face. I loved a woman with spirit. If there was one thing that Virginia had displayed during the months of her confinement, it was spirit. Teresa could not hold a candle to Virginia in that department.

Still, I walked away with my wife.

~

I awoke with a start. The dream had left me with a feeling of unease, especially because of my current knowledge of Teresa's true feelings about Santan. I went to the refrigerator and pulled out a bottle of blood, uncorked it and downed half of it without taking a breath. I banged the bottle on the counter, a little too hard, shattering the glass and its contents. I walked over to the window and stared out into the night. My thoughts turned to Virginia, and once again I felt the stirring in my loins.

After a few minutes, I turned, retrieved my coat from the closet, and headed out into the night.

Virginia

Chapter Seven

My days were filled with morning nausea, and afternoon fatigue. From experience, I knew this condition would only last the first trimester—at least I hoped that would be the case this time, as it had been during my pregnancy with Santan.

I looked forward to meeting Emelia's friend, Adelaide, however I was also apprehensive. The more people that were connected with Emelia meant there could be a greater chance of the count finding me. And, Emelia had mentioned that Adelaide's brother, Alfred, was known in the family circle. I wondered if Emelia knew for sure that he could be trusted with the knowledge of my whereabouts. What if he were playing both sides?

~

The morning sickness was wearing me down. Two days after receiving Emelia's letter, I had my first dream of *him*. I had thought I would be able to erase the count from my dreams, at least, which up to this point had been nothing more than vague wisps of memory when I awoke. But this dream had been so real...

Virginia, my love, what is this good news that I have heard? Another child? My, my ... aren't you fruitful? The count was standing in the middle of the library at *The House*.

I was sitting in the large winged chair, the same one I had sat in so many times when he and I had conversed during my evenings of confinement. My hands were resting on my swollen belly and I felt the baby kicking. *Come ... the baby is moving.* I reached my hand out to the count, beckoning him over to me.

The count walked to me and knelt at my feet. He laid his head upon my belly; his hands enclosed around each side of it. The room was quiet, except for our breathing, which seemed rhythmically tuned to each other. I laid my hands on his shoulders, gently massaging them. I heard him moan. He looked up at me and smiled. My heart fluttered. How could I have even thought to hate this man, who clearly, by his current actions, cherished me? Love was written all over his face, embedded in his eyes.

She is going to be a strong child, in more ways than you can imagine. The count stood up and walked over to the window. *Where is Santan? I would like to take him out with me tonight.*

I felt apprehension closing around me. I didn't think it was a good idea for the count to take Santan out into the night, on one of his *outings.* I had no idea what he did when he ventured on these excursions, but I think I could have made a reasonable guess. *He is sleeping; Max is watching over him.*

The count was silent as he peered out the window into the starless night. And then, as though he had read my mind ... *It's okay, Virginia, I won't hurt our son. But, I must show him how his life will be, for he is what he is, and you must understand there is nothing you will ever be able to do to change that.* The count smiled, revealing his fangs. He walked over to the doorway and called out for Max.

Within a few minutes, Max appeared. I had the feeling that he had been lurking nearby, as he usually was. *Yes, Count?*

Could you please dress Santan appropriately; he will be going out with me tonight.

I stood up and made my way to the two men. I put my hand on the count's arm. *Basarab, it is time for his next feeding.*

The count looked down at me. His words slipped out through his grin. *He will have no need of you tonight, my dear. I shall make sure he is well nourished.*

My blood froze in my veins as the impact of his words hit home. He was going to feed my son blood! This couldn't be happening. I had no idea where I drew the strength from, or how I even thought that I could get away with doing what I was about to do; but before I could stop myself, I was pounding on the count's chest and telling him that he had no right to do that to my son. The count's laughter echoed through the halls of *The House.* He grabbed hold of my wrists and held my barrage of anger at bay. *Do not distress yourself so, my dear. It is not good for the child that grows within you.* And he laughed again. I felt the evil swallowing me as he released my wrists. I crumbled to the ground at his feet.

And then *she* was there—Teresa! She was standing in the library, glaring at me, taking in the scene. She was laughing mockingly at me. There was a vicious look on her face, or was that a victorious look? *Why Virginia ... what a spectacle! You just don't listen, do you? How many times do we have to remind you that Santan is not really yours? He belongs to Basarab, and to me. We are his parents, as we will be the parents of this child that is in your womb now. There is simply nothing you can do to change that. No matter where you run to, you will never be able to hide from us.* She paused as she walked over to where I sat on the floor. She put her arm through the count's arm. *You would not mind if I were to join you tonight, would you, my love?*

Of course not, my dear Teresa. That is a splendid idea—a family stroll in the moonlight.

I watched the count and Teresa walk away. I watched as Max handed my son to the count. I watched the three of them head toward the front door, the same door that had almost allowed me to escape before I gave birth to Santan. I shook my head ... but I had escaped, hadn't I? What was I doing back in *The House*? Why had I returned to him? Max was walking toward me. There was a strange look on his face. He knelt down and helped me to my feet.

Let me show you to your room, miss ... let me show you to your room ... let me show...

~

I bolted up from the couch, where I had fallen asleep. I looked around the room, nervously, and breathed a sigh of relief. I was not in *The House*. I was in my apartment. I was safe—for now.

Chapter Eight

True to Emelia's word, a telegram arrived a few days after the letter, stating that I should expect Adelaide and Alfred to arrive November 10[th,] and they would be staying with me for a few days. I decided to fix both of the bedrooms for them, since they might not feel comfortable sleeping in the same room. I would sleep on the couch in the living room and put Santan in the playpen.

As ill as I was, especially in the mornings, I needed to prepare for the guests. I gave Randy a list of items to pick up, and asked him to stop at the used furniture store on Murray Street to check if they had any single beds.

"You having guests?" Randy asked.

"Yes."

"Relatives?"

"No."

When I didn't offer further information, Randy pushed for an answer. "Well then, who is it?"

I realized there was no reason to be so secretive about my guests; after all, it wasn't as if *they* were vampires and I would have to keep them hidden. "They are friends of my aunt, from the old country," I finally responded.

"Neat! Where are they from?"

I hesitated. "I believe my aunt mentioned that they live in Transylvania."

"Wow! Transylvania! I wonder if they have ever been to Dracula's Castle. I would love to go there—wouldn't you, Virginia?"

"Not really. I'm not into vampires, or stuff like that," I added, thinking it might be a good idea to distance myself from a conversation that would lead in such a direction.

"Lots of people are into the vampire craze nowadays. I sometimes wonder what it would be like to live forever, but then I think it would be too difficult to give up healthy eating. Not sure if I could handle having to exist on a blood diet!" Randy chuckled.

"By healthy eating, do you mean pizza?" I snickered, my attempt at keeping the conversation light and steering it away from the darkness of the vampire world.

It worked. We both laughed.

~

Randy found a single bed at the used furniture store, and arranged for it to be delivered in the late afternoon.

"Hello again," the burly man greeted me. He looked around my apartment. "Doing a nice job here, miss," he added. "Where would you like the bed?"

"In here." I led the way into Santan's room.

"The boy is still a bit small for a single bed, isn't he?" the man asked. There was an odd inflection in his tone.

"I am expecting guests. I thought they might enjoy their own rooms." I did not like this man. He asked too many questions, and there was something disturbing about him.

"Well, that will be good for the kid to see some relatives. Who are they?—aunt and uncle?—grandparents?" The man grinned. His teeth were caked with yellow plaque. I shuddered.

"They are not relatives, just friends," I stated. I had no idea why I had even told him that much; there was no need for this pushy man to know anything about my business.

"I see. Well, it's nice to have company, whoever it might be." The man set the bed's head and footboard against the wall in the bedroom, and then headed out to his truck to get the railings, mattress, and box spring. "I'll just set this up for you, miss," he said as he went about getting started.

"No need to bother." I didn't want him staying too long, remembering what had happened the last time he delivered furniture to me.

"Won't take a minute," he insisted. "You do look a tad pale; are you not feeling well, miss?"

"I'm fine." I walked out of the room, not wanting to be dragged into any further conversation. His attempt at niceness probably had an ulterior motive, and I wanted him out of my apartment as quickly as possible. *I guess I can tolerate you long enough to put the bed together, though.*

"There you go," he said as he exited Santan's room. "I'll be on my way now. Take care," he added. He paused at the door, as though he wanted to say something more.

Self-consciously, I gazed quickly down at my shirt—*safe.* "Everything okay?" I asked.

He hesitated, eyed me, and then turned and left.

I clicked the lock into place as I watched the man walk to his truck, get in, and leave. I hated this sort of contact. He was way too nosey. Could he be one of the count's people? I shook my head, trying to erase the paranoid thought. Regardless, I would get my furniture elsewhere from now on, if I needed anything more. Maybe, when I purchased a vehicle, I would get a van so that I could transport my own stuff.

I heard Santan waking up. He would be hungry, he was always hungry. He smiled when I entered his room. It was such an innocent smile, making me forget what he was—or at least what he might grow up to be.

~

November 10th arrived too soon for me. I was nervous, not knowing what to expect. All I knew about Adelaide and Alfred was that they were Emelia's trusted friends, and that they were not vampires. Santan went to sleep after his morning meal. I was nervously pacing in the kitchen. The clock on the wall ticked away the minutes too slowly. Finally, there was a knock on the door. I moved the curtain aside for a peek, to make sure it was Adelaide and her brother—not that I knew what they looked like. An elderly couple stood outside, so I assumed it was them. I opened the door.

"Adelaide?"

The woman affirmed with a smile. "Virginia, I presume," she returned warmly. Her English was quite good, despite a slight accent.

"Yes." I opened the door wider.

Adelaide stepped through first, followed by the gentleman. Once inside, she introduced him. "This is my brother, Alfred."

Alfred set the two suitcases he was carrying on the floor. He extended his hand. "Pleased to meet you." His accent was much thicker than Adelaide's.

I smiled and shook his hand. "Let me show you to your rooms," I said, leading the way through to the living room. "Santan is sleeping in the playpen. If you like, after you settle in, I can make you a drink; you must be thirsty after such a long journey."

"Tea would be lovely, for me, thank you," Adelaide replied. "Alfred prefers coffee."

"No problem, I have both. Would you like something to eat, as well?"

"Not for me," Adelaide answered. "But I am sure Alfred will appreciate some biscuits, if you have any. He has a sweet-tooth."

As I plugged the kettle in to boil water for the tea, I wondered why Adelaide answered for Alfred. Perhaps he just didn't speak much English. I poured the water into the coffeemaker and then checked my cupboard for biscuits. I was not in the habit of buying cookies, so all I had was soda crackers.

I set them out with some cheese and a jar of jam, hoping that would satisfy Alfred's craving for sweets.

When Adelaide and Alfred came into the kitchen, the refreshments were ready. Adelaide smiled as she set an envelope on the table. "Emelia thought you might need a little advance, and since we were coming here, she figured we could deliver it." Adelaide sat down and reached for the teapot.

"Would either of you like cream or sugar?" I enquired.

"No thank you." Alfred reached for the cheese and crackers.

"Black is fine for me, as well," Adelaide responded.

"Sorry, this is all I have," I pointed out. "If there is something in particular that you like to eat, please let me know; I can get my friend to pick it up for you," I added.

"Alfred is not fussy," Adelaide spoke for him again. "These will be just fine." She took a sip of tea. This is nice; what kind is it?"

"Spiced Chai." I poured myself a cup of tea and reached for a cracker, which was one of the few foods I seemed able to keep down. I wondered when the small talk would be finished, and they would get to the issues for which they had come. I didn't have to wait much longer.

Adelaide set her cup aside and folded her hands on the table. "Emelia tells me that you are in need of some identification so that you can set up a bank account and get a driver's licence. Alfred is quite adept at fixing things like that, aren't you Alfred?" She reached over and patted Alfred's hand. His face remained stoic.

Adelaide continued. "Alfred has already created a driver's licence for you, based on the picture you sent me. You were born in London, England. We picked London because we thought it would be easier for you to simulate an English accent. Alfred has also made you a passport, with a stamp in it of the date that you entered Canada. When you arrived here most likely won't be questioned, but if it is, we have that base covered." She paused. "How long have you been living here?"

"Four months."

"Good, the dates are in order then. I suggest you put on a slight accent when you apply for things—it will be expected. Alfred put several other stamps on your passport, as evidence for how well-travelled you are. You met your husband in Germany a couple of years ago, while on a writing assignment. He was on business there, as well. We took the liberty of saying you were a freelance writer because it blended nicely with the travelling you have done. You were married in England, where the head office of your husband's company is located. Of course, we had to have a reason for you being in Canada, so we have set it up that your husband is a Canadian, and Brantford is his hometown. Once your child was born, you wanted a quiet place to raise your son while your husband was abroad on business. Unfortunately, he passed away while on his last business trip to Germany." Adelaide paused again. "I guess we should have checked with you first before we made you a widow. Have you told anyone about a father for your child?"

I hesitated, trying to recollect if I had told Randy something—I couldn't recall anything in particular. "Yes, but only the young man who lives in the front of the house. I believe I might have mentioned that my husband travelled on business a lot."

"Now you will have to tell him that we have brought you the bad news of your husband's passing," Adelaide stated. She looked over at her brother who was drinking his coffee, now that he had polished off all the cheese and crackers. She spoke to him in German.

Alfred nodded and left the kitchen, returning a few minutes later with a large envelope, which he handed to Adelaide. She dumped its contents on the table. There was a birth certificate, a licence, a passport, a British marriage certificate, and a bankbook from an English bank. I opened it and noticed there was a large sum of money in the account. I looked questioningly at Adelaide.

"We thought it would be better if you already had a bank account in the country where you were last living. That way, you could open an account here and simply have the funds transferred," Adelaide explained.

I was impressed at how many little details had been thought out for me. I picked up the passport and flipped through it, noting the numerous places I was supposed to have visited before my marriage. *It would have been nice.* I set it back on the table. "Thank you." I looked up at the woman sitting across from me, wondering how she had come to know Emelia.

"What's on your mind?" Adelaide asked, as though she knew I wanted to ask her something.

I took a deep breath. *I guess it won't hurt to ask.* "I was just wondering how you met Emelia?"

Alfred stood. He leaned over and whispered something in Adelaide's ear. Adelaide nodded.

"Alfred is going to lie down; he tires easily lately. I am worried about him. I was not even sure he should take this trip, but he insisted. He knows how much Emelia means to me." There was a lull in the conversation while Alfred left the room, and then…

"I met Emelia outside a nightclub, forty years ago. I was young and foolish, and that was the first time I had entered a bar on my own. Usually, Alfred accompanied me. But I had given him the slip that night; I was 20, and tired of having my big brother chaperone me. I made my way to a side of town I knew he did not frequent, and walked into a nightclub." She shook her head.

"It was dark in there, darker than it had been in any club that I had been in with my brother. The waitresses were all dressed in short, formfitting black dresses, leaving nothing to the imagination. The bartenders were all males, also dressed in black, and they were extremely good-looking in an out-of-the-ordinary way. Being young, and perhaps a bit frisky, I could only imagine what their bodies looked like beneath their skintight shirts! I noticed many of the patrons were drinking wine; at least wine is what I thought it was, at the time. I remember thinking how strange that was because wine is not the typical drink for frequenters of bars. Only a few people were drinking beer, or hard-liquor. I walked up to the bar, ordered a beer, and then found a quiet corner table where I could watch the goings-on.

"I was sitting there, minding my own business, when two young men swaggered up to my table. They pulled out a couple of chairs and sat down. I mentioned to them that I had not invited them to sit with me, and pointed out there were plenty of other empty tables. They grinned. They told me that such a pretty girl shouldn't be sitting alone; there were too many *seedy* characters around that might take advantage of her. I told them that I could look after myself. When they made no move to leave, I stood up. The taller of the two pushed me back into my seat and told me if I needed anything his friend would fetch it for me.

"I was scared. I wanted to shout out for help, but I realized no one would hear me over the loud music. I tried to excuse myself on the guise of using the ladies' room; but once again, I was shoved back into my chair. There was so much festivity in the bar that no one was paying any attention to what was going on in the shadowy corner. Panic crawled through me, like a viper ready to squeeze the life from its prey. Finally, they stood up. I thought they were going to leave, but I was wrong. They each grabbed one of my arms. Their grips were firm, causing me excruciating pain. As they walked me through the club, the taller one leaned over and whispered in my ear that I should not make a scene; it would not go well for me if I did. I couldn't feel my body. I was only moving because I was being carried by those men. I probably would not have been able to find my voice either, I was so distraught.

"They guided me out of the bar and walked me down the sidewalk, stopping about a block away. There was a dark alley to the right. I thought I heard footsteps behind us, but I could not turn around to see who it might be. I prayed it was not another like them, that it might be someone to rescue me. I was shoved into the alley. The tall one, who always did the talking, pushed me up against the brick wall and began to grope me. I could not believe what was happening! I struggled, but he was stronger than anyone I had ever encountered. I felt the buttons on my blouse give way, and the next thing I knew, he was ripping it off me. The other guy just stood there, laughing. I remember tears streaming down my face, but I still could not utter a word. The tall one continued his assault on me. He pushed my bra off my breasts, and then leaned over and put his filthy mouth on me. His tongue flicked in and out of his mouth as he licked my breast and then moved upward to my neck. 'So nice,' I heard him moan. I felt a stinging sensation on my neck.

"And then, I heard her voice. It echoed with authority. 'Let her go!' I dared to move my eyes in the direction it came from and that was when I saw Emelia standing at the end of the alley. She was dressed all in black, but not like the waitresses in the club. She was wearing a cape, and I remember thinking how strange that was. The man who was accosting me turned at the sound of her voice. 'Leave us be!' he snarled. 'I think not, Adrian—you know the rules,' she answered as she walked toward us.

"I noticed the other perpetrator had backed off, as though he was afraid of this woman. Even the one holding me started to loosen his grip, the closer she approached. Then, I heard the shorter fellow mutter: 'Countess, forgive us; we had no idea that this girl was a friend of yours. We were hungry and in need of a little entertainment. She was just sitting there, ripe for the picking!' He pulled at his co-conspirator's arm, telling him that they should leave. The man who was holding me finally let go and I crumbled to the ground. I heard feet scurrying away, out of the alley. I was alone with the woman who had been referred to as a countess.

"She was kneeling beside me, and she had my blouse in her hands. 'They made a real mess of this, didn't they?' she said as she tried to put it around my shoulders. Then she helped me to my feet and told me that I shouldn't be frequenting nightclubs alone. She asked me where my common sense was. I was still too traumatized to speak. I heard her say something about not worrying about talking now; she was going to take me back to her home and get me cleaned up—then I could tell her my story."

Adelaide poured another cup of tea. I couldn't believe what I had just heard. It sounded to me as though those two young men were vampires, and that they certainly knew who Emelia was. Adelaide continued...

"Emelia took me to her place and poured me a bath. She placed a clean set of clothing on the counter, and then left me alone. When I came out of the bathroom, she was waiting for me, with a freshly brewed pot of tea. I noticed that she did not drink any. She was sipping on what I thought, at the time, to be a glass of wine. She reached over and gently laid her hand on my cheek, and then turned my head to the side. She had muttered that it was good that the puncture wounds were not deep and that no blood had been extracted. I was still too confused to understand what she was talking about.

"I studied her closely. I could see how beautiful she was, even though she appeared elderly. But it was her eyes that actually drew me in. They were so green and filled with energy. She asked me to explain how I had ended in that particular club. I told her that I had been trying to escape from my chaperone. She had laughed pleasantly and told me that sometimes friends were good to have around.

"We talked far into the night. She told me that she had only been living in Germany for a few years. I asked if she had ever married; she had smiled and told me that she was married to a wonderful man. He was in real estate. They owned properties all over Europe. I was fascinated. I asked her if she had children, or grandchildren; she told me that she had a son, but he had never married. He travelled a lot, so she didn't see much of him.

"I told her about my family, about my strict upbringing, and about my brother, Alfred, whom I considered to be a genius. I told her that he was a unique artist, even though he had studied to be an architect. Alfred paid his own way through university. It was not until he had finished that I learned how he had done so—by using his artistic talents to forge documents for people, as he has done here for you. There is decent money in that line of work, you know. People pay well to be able to disappear and start a new life. When I told Emelia this about my brother, she appeared quite interested and mentioned that perhaps she could send some *special* projects Alfred's way, on top of his legitimate job with the architectural firm he was working at. She mentioned his job would be the perfect cover, and that her clients paid well for their anonymity.

"Then she asked me what I was doing with my life. I told her that I was still considering my options, debating whether to become a teacher or go to a business college. She suggested I should pursue teaching. In her opinion, it would be a more fulfilling career.

"Eventually, I could barely keep my eyes open, and when I looked out the window, I noticed the sun was just beginning to creep into the neighbourhood. Emelia noticed, as well. She yawned and said she would like to retire for a nap. She asked if I would like to have a rest before heading home. 'Or would you like me to call you a cab now?' she had asked. I still don't know what possessed me to stay. I told Emelia, if she didn't mind, I would just lie on the couch and have a short nap; I would call a cab later.

"I guess I must have been extremely tired, because when I awoke it was already late in the afternoon. Emelia was still sleeping. I worried that all the excitement from the night before had been too much for her. But then I remembered that even though she appeared elderly, there was something about her that depicted a sprightly spirit. Funny, isn't it, when she is older than she looks—much older!" Adelaide chuckled softly.

"I waited for Emelia to awaken. She was surprised to see I was still there, and she suggested we sup together. She would have her chauffeur drive me home afterward. Wow! The woman had a chauffeur! You can imagine how amazed I was. I stayed. She sent her chauffeur to the grocery store, and when he returned she prepared me a lovely meal of fish and rice, with a side salad. I did not even think about the fact that Emelia did not eat any of the meal she had made for me. She just had a glass of *wine*. After supper we talked; and, before I realized it, the clock was chiming in the midnight hour.

"Emelia had stood up then and said she had to go out, but it would be her pleasure to see me home first. Before I exited the car, I asked her if she would mind terribly much if we could be friends—I felt drawn to her. She said that was a lovely thought, and smiled. We made a date for her driver to pick me up on the following Friday night. Emelia mentioned that she would take me to a more acceptable club. I couldn't wait for Friday to arrive.

Of course, when I walked into my house, my mother was frantic with worry. I apologized numerous times for not having called. I told her that I had met a fascinating lady, and had just gotten carried away with the time. I left out the part about almost being raped. My mother didn't even notice that I was wearing different clothes than I'd left in the night before.

"Emelia and I met regularly on Friday nights for the next two months. Finally, she confided in me, saying that what she was about to tell me had to be kept in strict confidence; it was a matter of life and death for her. She told me that her *kind* had friends, like me, who helped with the everyday dealings within a society that lived by day."

"Weren't you afraid of her after she told you that she was a vampire?" I intervened. "I mean that is not something one hears every day ... hi, oh, just wanted to let you know—I'm a vampire!"

Adelaide chuckled. I noticed the warmth in her crystal-blue eyes. I noticed the crinkles around those eyes, crinkles that traveled upward—smile crinkles. She looked elegant and I could tell that she had been exceedingly beautiful when she was younger—still was. Her slender hands were folded neatly on the table, well manicured and free of age spots. I noticed her neck, trim and lacking the extra skin that often accompanied the elderly. There was a gold locket encircling it. I wondered what secret pictures it held.

"Of course, I was not afraid of her," Adelaide answered my question. She reached out and placed her hand on my arm. "Why would I be afraid of the woman who had saved my life, and then befriended me? She had never harmed me." I felt the warmth of Adelaide's fingers on my skin, confirming to me that she was not one of *them*! She continued. "Emelia explained what she needed from me, and told me that, in return, she would make sure I would never want for anything for the rest of my life."

"Did she never suggest that you become one of *them*?" I enquired.

"No. I asked if I could, though. Emelia was quite insistent that I should not even think along those lines. Then she asked if my brother was trustworthy. I told her that he was. I said he was quiet and unassuming and kept mostly to himself when he wasn't working at the architectural firm. She reminded me of one of our earlier conversations, about his sideline work, and asked if she could meet him. I said I would arrange a meeting, and then asked if I should tell him anything about her. Emelia said that would be unwise. She had to be sure Alfred was the type of person that she was looking for before any information about *what* she was, was divulged to him."

"Had you not met any of her family or acquaintances yet?" I was curious to know just how quickly Adelaide had been allowed into the fold, even if it had been as an outsider.

"No. I had asked once if that were a possibility, but Emelia said she would like to keep me as her little secret. She explained that she didn't know when she might need my services for a confidential matter, so she preferred that I not be known in her circle. And, if she made any deals with Alfred, she would need his assurance that he would not divulge his relationship with me—another safeguard. That is the way it has been for forty years. I have never even met her husband, Vacaresti, although I saw him from a distance one night as Emelia and I were about to enter a nightclub. He was walking toward the same club. We slipped into a nearby variety store; but I got a clear glimpse of him beforehand."

"Was he with anyone?" I was curious to know if Adelaide had ever seen Basarab.

"Actually, he was—an older gentleman, and a younger one."

"Did Emelia tell you who they were?"

"Yes. The older one was her husband's half brother, Atilla, and the younger one was Atilla's son, Basarab. Emelia seemed worried at the time. She said she had no idea why they would be in that part of town; it was not one of their usual haunts. She explained that *things* for their kind had been *heating up*, and that Basarab was in danger. I asked her, why him. She explained that Basarab was their king, and it was his head that most of the vampire hunters desired, more than anyone else's. They figured if they captured the king, the family would come for him; then, they would be able to destroy all the vampires."

"Was that during the time of the great cleansing that I heard mention of when I was living in *The House*? The one Teresa spoke of, when Basarab was almost killed?"

"I believe so." Adelaide drank the rest of her tea and set her cup down. I noticed her hands shaking, and wondered if she was tired. She confirmed my thoughts. "I think I would like to lie down, dear. It has been a long trip and telling this story has made me weary." She rose.

I stood, as well. "Thank you for your story, Adelaide. It has been enlightening. And, thank you for coming here to help me. I have no idea how I will ever be able to repay you and Alfred, and Emelia."

"Think nothing of it, child; I would do anything for Emelia. And, I know that whatever she does for someone she cares about, she never expects anything in return." As Adelaide shuffled out of the kitchen, I heard Santan begin to whimper from his playpen. At the sound of his cry, my milk let down.

I spent the next half hour feeding my son. I mulled over all that Adelaide had told me, and wondered how much more she could fill me in on. Of course, she had only been around in the lives of the *family*—Emelia, specifically—for the past 40 years, so how much could she know? *More than I.* When Santan fell back to sleep, I returned him to his playpen. I checked my watch––2:00 p.m. I decided to put a chicken in the oven for supper, and then lie down for a catnap.

I awoke to the savoury aroma of roasting chicken. I noticed Alfred sitting in the armchair in the corner of the living room; he was reading a book. I sat up. "I'm sorry, Alfred; I slept longer than I expected. Can I get you anything?"

He looked up. "No thank you, I am fine." He returned his attention to his book. I studied him for a moment—his demure posture, his tailored grey suit, his shortly cropped grey hair, wire-thin spectacles hanging precariously on the end of a small, pointed nose, and his lips that never seemed to smile. His thin hands didn't look strong enough to hold the heavy book he was reading. There was a slight hump in his back. He was the picture of a man who would never be noticed in a crowd.

I checked on Santan. He was still sleeping, so I went to the kitchen to prepare the rest of the supper. While I was peeling potatoes, Adelaide joined me. She had Santan in her arms.

"I noticed he was awake as I passed by. I hope you don't mind," she said, with a broad smile on her face. "It isn't often I get to hold such a little one," she added. "Although, I have to say, your milk must be good because he is quite sturdy."

I smiled and pulled a kitchen chair out for her. "Not a problem. May I get you a drink?"

"No thank you. I shall just sit here and enjoy Santan."

"Did you ever marry and have children of your own?" I enquired.

Adelaide's response was short; I sensed a hint of sadness in it. "No."

I don't know why I pushed for more; it wasn't very polite of me. I guess I was curious to know if her reason for not marrying had anything to do with her connection with Emelia. "Was it your choice?"

"Yes and no. I was almost engaged, once. I knew the man was going to ask me. My girlfriend saw him buying a ring. I called him the same night I had received that information and broke off our relationship. I thought it better. How would I explain Emelia to him? He knew of her, but not *about* her. In truth, Emelia was far more important to me than he was."

"How did your family take that? I am sure your mother would have liked to have seen you married."

Adelaide laughed. It was a gentle laugh, harmonizing with the smile on her face. "Yes, mother was not pleased. I was 26. She had almost given up hope of me ever marrying, until Lothar came along. He was handsome and well educated, and he had a fabulous job with the government. I could quit my teaching position and stay home and look after my husband, and the children I would now be able to have. Mother thought I had finally *arrived*! But there had been a few too many times that Lothar had gotten pushy about my association with Emelia—to the point of jealousy—I could not take the chance of having her exposed."

"What about Alfred, did he ever marry?"

"Yes, but sadly his wife died while giving birth to their first child. The child died, as well. Since that tragedy, he sort of withdrew from the world, never even attempting to fill that void in his life. In fact, he has kept Gabriele's and the baby's rooms like shrines, just as Gabriele had left them before going into the hospital. He moved his belongings into the spare room, which he had previously used as a study. I tried, once, to get him to give away Gabriele's possessions, and the furniture, toys, and clothing she had bought for the baby, but he had gotten so angry! I never broached the subject again." Adelaide sighed.

I placed the pot of potatoes on the stove and took a seat at the table. Santan saw me and started kicking his feet. "He knows his mama," Adelaide grinned.

"Yes, he does," I laughed, just as someone knocked on the door. There was only one person it could be—Randy. I stood. Adelaide grasped my wrist.

"Don't forget, you should look devastated; we have just brought you the news that your husband has died." Adelaide handed me Santan. "Better yet, why don't you allow me to answer the door; I can explain your circumstances to the young man and then send him on his way."

I took Santan from Adelaide's arms and headed to the living room. I heard the door open. And Adelaide's voice: "You must be Randy?"

"Yeah, is Virginia home?"

"She is resting right now, Randy." A moment of silence, then: "I think it best if you do not come around for a few days;

my brother and I have just brought Virginia some very unfortunate news about her husband. Unexpectedly, he has passed away."

I heard Randy's voice next. "Oh my God! That is terrible. How did it happen?"

"He caught a cold, and it developed into pneumonia."

"Well, will you tell her if she needs a friend, she knows where I am? How long are you folks staying?"

"A few days, until we are sure she is okay."

"Will they be bringing his body back here for burial, or will Virginia have to go to where he is?"

I was curious how Adelaide would answer that question.

"I am afraid neither is possible. Her husband has already been cremated. Virginia cannot travel now, especially with the baby, and another one on the way. Her aunt will most likely bring the ashes here, eventually." There was another lull in the conversation, and then I heard Adelaide thank Randy for coming, followed by the closing of the door.

Randy's shadow passed my window. I wondered how many other lies I would have to tell in my lifetime, so I could conceal the facts of what had transpired in my life. I hoped Randy would not question me too much about why I had not thought to tell him that I was still in contact with my husband, which was something he might assume because of Adelaide's communication to him. I also wondered how many untruths Adelaide had told over the years, to keep things running smoothly for Emelia.

~

Adelaide thought it would be better that we lay low for a couple of days, so as not to cause any suspicion about why I was not mourning my husband's death. Alfred was not thrilled about the delay, but Adelaide was the one calling the shots. I heard him mention, when they were discussing the issue in his room, that he wanted to go home as soon as possible.

On the third morning, Adelaide gave Alfred and me leave to go about the business that needed to be tended to. She would watch Santan. I called Randy to ask if I could borrow his car, so Alfred could take me out to run a few errands.

"You okay?" he asked. I detected concern in his voice.

I had to remember that my *husband* had just died and that I needed to play the role of a grieving widow. "I'll be fine," I managed to return. "Alfred is being a dear; and, this is a good opportunity for me to get my licence, and look into buying my own vehicle."

"Sounds like a busy morning … want me to watch Santan?" Randy offered.

"No thanks. Adelaide will watch him. She is thoroughly enjoying him, not having any grandchildren of her own."

"She knows not to take him outside in the sun?"

I smiled at his concern, thankful that Randy couldn't see my face. "Yes," I answered. "She is aware."

"Good. Well, tell her if she needs anything while you are gone, just to call me."

"Will do. Thanks, Randy. I'll be by shortly for the keys. Alfred and I will try not to be too long."

"Take your time. I'm not going anywhere today, just cleaning my apartment. Talk to you later, Virginia."

"Bye."

~

The rest of the time with Adelaide and Alfred passed quickly, too quickly. I thoroughly enjoyed Adelaide's company, especially our long talks about Emelia and the family. Alfred kept pretty much to himself; his nose was always buried in a book. He had been helpful in assisting with the opening of my bank account, and he had also helped me to choose a suitable, economical vehicle—a small minivan. There were tears in Adelaide's eyes, and mine, as we embraced goodbye. I noticed a couple brimming in Alfred's, as well, especially when he leaned over and kissed Santan on the forehead.

Chapter Nine

Santan was thriving, and my belly was expanding. It was two weeks before Christmas, four weeks since Adelaide and Alfred had left. I spent hours thinking about the information I had learned during my conversations with Adelaide. It had given me a new respect for Aunt Emelia and the vampire family. Adelaide had mentioned that after Basarab had fled to Canada, she had hosted Emelia for a few months. The vampires, especially those from the Dracul family, had scattered throughout Europe, taking refuge in the homes of the trusted humans they had befriended over the years. Emelia had been separated from Vacaresti and had found her way to Adelaide's door. Eventually, the appalling conditions died down, and life for the family returned to normal. They could come out of hiding and resume their former lives.

Adelaide had gone on to say that one day a woman had appeared at her door, asking for Emelia. 'I was cautious about this woman, knowing the story of Tanyasin,' Adelaide had said. 'But the woman had a kindliness about her that made me think she could not possibly be the evil creature that had cast the curse.' The woman had identified herself as Angelique and had told Adelaide that she had come to escort Emelia back to the caves. Vacaresti was waiting for her, beside himself with grief. She enlightened Emelia about Basarab, informing her that he was safe and living somewhere in Canada.

I was informed of how many people the family depended on, outside *their* world. Adelaide had gone on to tell me how many of the vampires, even those who had clung to the old ways, realized that they had to get with the technology of the 20th Century. 'That is where people like me come into play,' Adelaide had pointed out. 'Alfred was quite an asset during this period, as well.' I had laughed and told Adelaide the family was going to have to persevere if they were going to convince Basarab to get with the times. I told her how he had detested modern conveniences at *The House,* stating that such things were an inconvenience to him! Adelaide said, even though he missed a lot of the tutoring, he would have no other choice. The family could no longer depend on pigeons and hawks to communicate with one another.

I had asked Adelaide why she had been kept secret from the family, yet Alfred openly worked for them. 'Does he know Basarab?' I had asked. 'No,' was her answer, 'my brother has never met him. But, I assure you, Virginia, Alfred's loyalty to Emelia is solid—*they* will never know our secret.'

This worried me, nonetheless. Even though Adelaide had assumed they didn't know about her, I was sure the family would have checked out, thoroughly, anybody who was working for them. That meant there was a strong possibility the count knew Alfred had a sister. Now that Alfred and Adelaide had travelled to see me, I felt it would be easier for Basarab to figure out the link. I made a mental note to ask Emelia about this in my next letter.

~

Santan had mastered the art of crawling much earlier than a normal human baby would have. Randy constantly played with him and hovered over me. I had the feeling that now he knew I was a widow, he hoped for something more than friendship. He also persistently badgered me about seeing a doctor. I assured him that I had everything under control; he need not worry so much about me.

"So, what are your plans for Christmas?" Randy asked one day.

"Nothing in particular."

"Not going to visit relatives?"

"No."

"None are coming here to be with you? I thought some might, under the circumstances, and all."

"No." I paused. "I told my aunt not to make the trip, that I was coping well enough," I added so that Randy wouldn't get too suspicious. I put on as sad a face as I possibly could. I needed to show some remorse to legitimize the issue of becoming a widow. I guess I was lucky Randy had no idea about the many things in my life that I did have to grieve about, especially in the past year and a half.

"Well, I haven't heard anything from my uncle; he usually invites me for Christmas dinner. He's probably shacked up somewhere warm with a *hot* woman. So, how say you, Santan, and I have Christmas together?" There was a hopeful look on Randy's face. I couldn't let him down, so I caved, telling him that I thought it was a wonderful idea. In reality, I didn't want to be alone, as I had been on the previous Christmas.

~

Christmas came and went, and January hit with a sharp cold. I didn't mind the winter months. It was easier to get out with Santan because of the fewer daylight hours. The baby inside me was beginning to kick up a storm, too. I calculated an approximate date for its delivery—May 1st. I made a mental note to ask Emelia if she knew of a doctor in the area, one whom I would be able trust. Before she left, Adelaide gave me her email address, suggesting that it might make communication easier. I decided to send her an email and ask her to pass it on to Emelia.

Dear Emelia:

Time is passing so quickly. Santan is already crawling. He is even pulling himself up on the furniture and trying to walk--I think he is going to be an early walker! The baby is kicking the living daylights out of my insides, but at least the morning sickness has subsided now, and I can keep my food down.

Mentioning the baby, I wonder if there is a doctor nearby who could examine me and help with the delivery. You stated, once, that you had 'people' everywhere. I cannot birth this child without help, and I would prefer not to have Randy deliver it!

I purchased a computer. Hopefully this will improve our ability to communicate in a timelier manner. I had the most advanced privacy settings possible put on the computer. Adelaide said she would make sure you received these correspondences, mentioning that you have access to computers, as well.

There is one subject that is seriously bothering me, though--Adelaide's brother, Alfred. Adelaide mentioned that he was completely loyal to you; however, she also said that he does work for the family. I am worried Basarab may be able to trace me here, now that Alfred has been to my apartment. I know this seems silly ... but I worry ... you understand...

It is much easier now that I have a bank account, and my own vehicle to get around. Randy is a wonderful young man, and an enormous help to me, but I do appreciate having some independence from him. He is terrific with Santan, too. But don't worry, if you might be thinking along this line--I am not romantically interested in Randy. I guess I am still in love with Basarab, as foolish as that might sound. I have even begun to dream of him--the intimate moments, and the times we bantered about life, and law, and everything in between. The strangest thing happens, though, when I think of Basarab--that is when the baby in my belly moves the most.

I still cannot thank you enough for everything you have done for me. You are an incredible woman. Despite what life has done to you, you have never forgotten how to be human.

Well, I shall save some news for another email. Trusting this message finds you well. Please let me know about a doctor as soon as possible, as I am in my fifth month. I have calculated the baby's due date to be around May 1st.
Love, Virginia

I received an email back from Adelaide, not Emelia. This worried me, especially after I read what Adelaide had sent.

Dearest Virginia:

Forgive me for reading your letter, which I know was meant for Emelia, but I thought it best, as Emelia is not available to answer you herself. She has left specific instructions for me to make sure you are provided with whatever you might need.

There is a female doctor in Hamilton, not far from Brantford, who will be able to tend to your needs. She is in the employ of the family and is quite trustworthy. I have sent her an email, telling her of your situation, and she will be contacting you directly. She is proficient at doing home deliveries. However, I do not want you to fear her loyalty, because, even though the family uses her services, she is faithful to Emelia, and to me, above all others.

I am happy to hear your morning sickness is over, and that Santan is starting to move around. I think he will be a wonderful big brother. I noticed gentleness in his eyes--hopefully he will have your personality. However, having said that, you will have to work hard to keep him as yours. Emelia has voiced her concerns to me, on more than one occasion. She knows, once issues are dealt with in Transylvania, Basarab will return for his son. I do not believe you will have much time, but then again, I might be wrong.

I am thinking to come and stay with you when it is time for the baby to be born; I am sure you will need help.

Well, I shall close for now. I will let you know how things are here as soon as I hear from Emelia. I know she will get word to me when she can. Until then, I have my instructions.
Adelaide

I set the letter on the table. I was troubled about Emelia. I wondered if it was because of what she had done for me that she was unavailable, or if there was something worse. The baby in my womb gave me a hard kick. I stroked my hand across my belly. "It's okay, little one. I will protect you. You will not be exposed to *him*." But even as I said the words, I knew they were not true. How could I make such a promise to my unborn child, especially with the knowledge I carried inside my head?

~

Within the week, I received a phone call from the doctor Adelaide had written about. The conversation was short.

"Is this Virginia?" The voice was crisply professional.

"Yes."

"I am Doctor Carla Gibson. Adelaide sent me a message that you were in need of my services. Because of your unique situation, it is better that I come to you. I just need your address."

Wow, she is a cold one! I cleared my throat. "I live at 53 Henry Street, apartment two, at the back of the house. There is a cement factory by the road..."

"I am sure I will be able to find it," Carla's interrupted sharply. "I will be there at seven, Friday evening. I trust that will be okay with you?"

I assumed it would not matter if it were okay with me, or not. If I wanted her services, I would have to accommodate her time. "Friday will be fine," I answered.

"Good." Carla paused. "I also understand you already have a child that has yet to be seen by a physician; I will check him out for you, as well. It won't be necessary to give him any immunizations; his *kind* is not in need of such precautions. See you Friday." The phone line went dead.

I heard Santan babbling. He was standing in his crib when I walked into his room. "Hey there, buddy," I smiled. He stretched his arms out to me and began to bounce. *How innocent.* He was going to be okay. He was going to be normal. The child inside my stomach was going to be normal. I hoped I would wake up one day and discover that this entire bizarre affair had just been a dream. But it was a dream that I wished would stop; I knew that I could not sleep forever! I would be so happy if I could just have a typical life, no matter how boring it might end up being!

~

Friday arrived. I saw the headlights of a car advancing up the laneway, and assumed it was the doctor. At seven o'clock sharp, there was a knock on my door. "Come in," I greeted the young woman. "Carla, I presume."

"Yes." She stepped inside and set her briefcase down. She rubbed her hands together. "Bloody cold tonight."

I got the impression that she might be friendlier in person than she had been on the phone. Perhaps she had been brusque because she was busy. "Would you like tea or coffee?"

"Coffee, if you have it," she replied. "Drink too much of the stuff, but it keeps me going." She smiled, businesslike, but it was still a smile.

"Do you make many house calls?" I asked as I poured water into the coffeemaker.

"Only for the family."

I was curious. "How did you come to work for them?" I walked over to the table, sat down, and motioned for her to take a seat. I didn't ask the question that was on the tip of my tongue— how many of *them* was Carla talking about?

"Long story ... not now though ... possibly if there is time after I examine you and the child."

The coffee machine gurgled its last drops of water into the pot. I poured Carla's coffee. "Milk? Sugar?" I asked, holding the cup up.

"Black."

I should have guessed. I went to the refrigerator and poured a glass of milk for me, and then returned to the table. "Who would you like to examine first?"

"Is the baby awake?"

"He will be any time now."

Carla reached into her briefcase and pulled out some papers and a pen. "I need to get some information from you before I examine him."

For the next twenty minutes, I answered Carla's questions. Her eyebrows arched in disbelief when I mentioned the blood that had been in my milk during those early weeks. I explained that it had something to do with the *special drink* Max had been giving me throughout my pregnancy. She asked me when the blood had stopped; I told her a couple of months ago.

I heard Santan babbling from his room, and excused myself. "Help yourself to another coffee," I mentioned as I left. A few minutes later I returned with my son. He was demandingly pulling at my top, trying to get to his meal.

"Determined," Carla grinned. "You better hurry up and whip out that human bottle before he rips your top off!" She actually moved beyond a smile and laughed.

While Santan was feeding, Carla jotted a few more notes on her pad and then sat back and watched me. Her attention to me made me feel uncomfortable. I was lonely for female companionship, but I was not sure if Carla would be someone I might be able to consider as a friend in the future. Time would tell.

"Could you strip him down for his examination when he is finished eating?" she asked. "Bathroom?"

"Around the corner," I pointed to the living room. "I'll take him into his room; you can use the change table to check him out," I added.

Carla spent about twenty minutes examining Santan. I was surprised that he didn't mind that she touched him; I was also surprised at how gentle she was with him. I studied her as she worked. She was built like a string bean, as my mother would have said about someone of her stature. I wondered—was it because she was built that way, did she starve herself, or was she overworked and didn't have time to cook proper food? Her hair was cropped short, like a boy's crew-cut, and it was dyed black. I noticed a tinge of blue when the lamplight hit it from a certain angle. Carla's facial features were petite and pointed. Her eyes were deep-set and appeared hauntingly large for the rest of her facial features. They were the deepest indigo I had ever seen— almost black—like a raven's feathers when the sun glints off them. Her lips were thin, turned down at the corners toward a chin that jutted out slightly. Carla's neck was long and slender, tapering down to a bony collarbone. Bluish veins dominated her pale skin. From there down, she could have passed for a young boy; I doubt she even wore a bra. I would not say she was particularly pretty, but she was cute, in an elfin way.

When Carla was finished examining Santan, she picked him up and gave him a hug. He smiled at her. *Charming, like his father.* Carla handed him to me; I set him in his playpen.

"When do you think I should start introducing solid foods?" This was something I had been wondering about for a few weeks now, especially since Santan was cutting several teeth.

"I think he is doing fine on your milk, for now," Carla said. "I don't believe it would be a good idea, considering who his father is, to introduce food too early. The longer he is on your milk, the less chance there might be problems when we do start to make the transition." She hesitated. "It is my understanding," she continued, "the first ceremony was performed to initiate him into *his* world."

"You mean there is *another* ceremony?"

Carla ignored my question. "The more time we can put between that and an actual human diet, the better. I don't believe we will have the same issues with your new baby, especially since you have not had that *drink*. We still need to keep in mind, though, that *he* is also the father of *this* child. Time will tell I guess."

As Carla prepared for my examination, I wondered how extensive her knowledge of the family was. I also wondered if she had ever met Basarab. I decided not to ask; I didn't know her well enough, yet.

Carla concluded that I was pretty much on with my guesstimated due date of May 1st. She also mentioned the baby was already a decent size. "Do you get out for walks?" she asked.

"As much as I am able, under the circumstances, because Santan's sensitivity to the sun restricts my times for getting out."

"Well, it is crucial for you to keep fit. I'd prefer not to put you in the hospital for the birth—less complicated," Carla said. "I think it is best we do a home birth. I will be here for the birthing, so you need not worry. I carry a pager with me; I'll give you the number before I leave."

"Why is it less complicated?"

Carla scowled. "I would think you would know the answer to that." She offered nothing further—the second time she hadn't answered one of my questions.

"Is there anything I need to buy for the home birth?"

"A kid's pool, preferably one of the blow-up kinds, the sides are softer. Three-foot depth would be ideal."

"I am going to give birth in a pool?"

"Yes. I will explain everything on my next visit. I'll see you in four weeks. Until then, if you have any questions, call my office. After your next appointment, I will see you every two weeks." Carla began to pack her belongings. "Oh, I almost forgot—here are some vitamins." She handed me a bottle that had a *Prenatal Vitamins* sticker on it. "I have plenty at the office; if you run out, call. Salespeople leave samples all the time."

She hadn't been gone ten minutes, and there was a knock on my door. I pulled the curtain across—Randy. I opened the door. "What's up?"

"Just thought to check in on you; not often you have company. In fact, this is a first, other than me and those relatives from Europe."

"That was my doctor," I informed him.

"Your doctor makes house calls?" He sounded surprised.

"Easier for me." I paused, wondering if I should warn Randy that I would be delivering this baby at home. A gust of wind swept in the door. "Why don't you step in for a minute," I suggested.

Randy slipped quickly through the door. "Thought you were never going to ask," he grinned.

"I wasn't." I really hadn't wanted company. I noticed the look of devastation on Randy's face. "I just didn't want to up the heating bill by standing there with the door open," I added with a chuckle. He joined me.

"Is that coffee?" he asked, sniffing the air.

"Not very fresh, but help yourself."

Randy poured a cup of coffee and walked into the living room. Santan was playing in his playpen. "How ya doin' buddy?"

Santan pulled himself up in the playpen and started bouncing excitedly at the sound of Randy's voice. I watched the two of them; Randy was so good with my son. Randy turned to me: "Can I take him out of there?"

"Sure."

"Did the doctor examine him, too?"

"Yes."

"Did you ask about his skin condition?"

"As I thought—a hereditary condition—the doctor confirmed it. There is not much that can be done about it," I answered him, annoyed that he kept harping on Santan's skin sensitivity.

"This doctor must know the family history, then?"

"Of course." I figured it was better for Randy to think along that line; there would be fewer questions in the long run, I hoped.

"Oh well, guess we'll just have to become vampires then, eh, little fella." Randy set Santan on the floor and then joined him, crawling along beside him, as he moved quickly around the room. "Hey, Buddy; you really got this down pat, don't you?" Randy called out to me: "Look at him go, Virginia! He's a natural! Be walking in no time."

I attempted a smile. My mind was still dwelling on Randy's statement about becoming vampires—I think my heart missed a few beats. I was also thinking I might have to move soon, to get away from Randy. He was becoming too comfortable in my life and I knew that was not good. Randy headed for the couch. Santan followed.

"So, how are you doing?" Randy directed to me as he lifted Santan up beside him. "This new baby coming along okay?"

"Yes." I paused. "I guess I should tell you … I will be delivering the baby here, in the apartment."

"Here?"

I nodded.

"Awesome!" he shouted, surprising me. "Can I be there for the birth? I wouldn't mind, you know, and with your husband being gone, maybe I could be your coach."

I was touched that Randy wanted to play the father figure, but thought it would be better if I did this alone, just with the doctor. I assumed if Carla felt she needed someone to hold my hand, other than her, she would know of someone that we could trust, in case anything unusual happened. I decided the best way to keep Randy occupied, when the time came, would be to let him look after Santan for a few hours. "Tell you what, Randy— I'll say no to you being my coach; however, if Adelaide doesn't make it in time for the baby's birth, you can watch Santan for me. How does that sound?"

Randy grinned from ear to ear. He gulped down the rest of his coffee, and then got down on the floor again, taking Santan with him. I watched the two of them, wishing Santan had a real father who would play with him like this. I wondered how a vampire father would be with his child. Then I thought of Basarab's father, Atilla; he was the kind of man who would have spent every possible moment with his son. I had seen the bond that was between him and Basarab. Of course, they'd had hundreds of years to build on their relationship.

"Earth to Virginia," Randy's voice cut into my musings. "I think Santan needs to be changed." Randy plugged his nose.

"And you want to be here for the birth?" I laughed as I scooped up my son. "I'm not sure you would be able to handle Santan for a few hours if you can't even change his diaper!"

Randy reached for Santan. "I can do this, Virginia; I can change a baby's bum."

"Okay, hot-shot, do it then." I handed Santan to Randy.

Fifteen minutes later, after major supervision, Santan was clean and ready for his next feeding. Randy was quite pleased with himself. "Not bad for a first diaper change, eh?" he smirked.

I agreed with him, and then told him that it was time for him to leave. I wanted to feed my son and turn in for the night. Randy didn't need to know that Santan rarely settled at night, even after all this time, even after all my attempts to keep him awake longer in the daytime. Santan was still very much his *father's* son in that area.

When Santan finished his supper, I pulled one of his books from the bookshelf and began reading to him. Soon he was sleeping peacefully. I kissed him on his forehead and lay him in his crib, admiring how handsome he was—just like Basarab. I shivered as I exited my son's room.

Chapter Ten

It had been a few days since I had left my apartment. I looked out my window and saw the last rays of the sun disappearing in the west, so I decided to take a walk with Santan. For some unfathomable reason, I chose to go down West Street, toward the downtown—past the street where *The House* was. When I reached Buffalo Street, I turned, automatically. Even though my damn curiosity had gotten me into trouble over the years, for some reason I wanted to see if someone had moved into the count's house yet. I guess I thought I would be safe, for a longer time, if there were new owners—at least I told myself that. It might mean the count did not intend to return to Brantford—right?

Something strange happened, the nearer I got to *The House*. Santan became extremely excited, kicking his legs and waving his arms, as though he wanted to fly from the stroller. I quickened my pace, foolishly pushing toward my destination. *Just a glimpse—that is all I need.* The iron gates stood open; several cars were in the parking lot—a possible sign that someone new was living there? Outside lights illuminated the yard, and a man and woman came into view. They were carrying folders and appeared to be chatting earnestly. I slowed down. The man walked over to one of the cars and took some signs from its trunk. I sped up again, happy to see the place was going up for sale.

By this time, Santan was straining at the straps that confined him in the stroller. He was babbling excitedly. He threw one of his toys into the snow at the edge of the sidewalk. As I handed it back to him, I noticed his eyes. They had never been so black! And where his pupils should have been, a glowing red light flared. He was staring intensely through the skeletal trees, at the house where he had been born.

Quickly, I turned around and headed back to West Street. How irrational I was; what could I have been thinking? What if the count had sent Max back to the house to settle matters? What if Max had seen me—and the child—and my present condition? Would he come after me? Or, would he call someone to follow me? Fear drove my feet faster, until I was running. Santan, as we left *The House* behind, had begun to cry—not the "I am hurting" cry—the "I am angry and upset" cry! Santan did not settle easily, once we were home, and when he finally slept, I was utterly exhausted. I lay down on the couch and closed my eyes…

Virginia! Why have you left me, my love? A man's voice was calling out to me. It was familiar, sending shivers up and down my spine. *Why did you take our son away from me? We could have been such a happy family. Together.* I was in a room with antique furniture scattered around; but, unlike the room I had been in at *The House*, this one was thick with dust. The tapestry hanging around the canopy bed, which sat in the centre of the room, was ragged and torn in several places. The blankets looked soiled and overused. *Virginia—my love—come to me.* The voice was emanating from the direction of the bed. I walked slowly toward it.

That's right, my love, my little bird—come to me. Let me hold you. Let me touch your belly. Let me feel our child kicking within you. Let me taste of your womanly delights. It has been too long, Virginia—much too long. Do you miss me, as much as I miss you?

From under the covers a body arose. It was facing away from me, but I already knew who it was, and my blood boiled in expectancy. As the figure turned, I paused—and waited. Words could not escape my throat. He was as magnificent now as he had been on our last night together. And he was calling me "his love." He wanted to hold me, to feel our baby within me, to make love to me. I moved forward, tentatively.

That's right, Virginia, come to me. Just a few more steps and you will be in my arms again. The count stood on the bed. His arms were outstretched—beckoning—encouraging me forward. His majesty was more alluring than I could remember it ever having been; the fire in his eyes drew me into him. *How is our son? I trust you have been giving him the best of care; you did tell me that you would be a wonderful mother. But, there is something I do not understand; why did you have to take him from me, Virginia? I was not serious when I said that you were being left behind. I would never have left you! How could you think such of me, after what had just transpired in this bed? I was going to bring you and Santan with me.* He smiled, the warmth of it luring me even closer.

I stood at the edge of the bed, shaking with anticipation. He had returned for me, the mother of his children. He had left Teresa behind. I crawled onto the bed, grasped his feet, slithered up his legs, wrapped my arms around his waist, pressed his desire against mine, and breathed in the scent of him. I closed my eyes as I raised my face to him. My lips parted; I longed for him to meet my passion with his own. I waited—suspended in the moment.

Suddenly, an evil howl resounded throughout the room. I toppled into nothingness, onto the grimy covers, as the count ripped my hands from his body. He stepped back, and off the bed. The howling increased, and then it faded away, until the only sound left was the sobs pouring from my heart. At length, I looked up from the soiled covers, toward the window, which beckoned me. I leapt from the bed and ran to the window. Maybe I could go after him before he got too far, and tell him how much I loved him. I reached out to push the window open, but bars appeared over the glass, blocking my way. In the moonlight, I saw Basarab walking across the lawn. Teresa was with him. They were laughing. And then, I noticed a small figure between them—my son! I raced frantically around the room, from wall to wall, searching for the door—the heavy wooden door—but there wasn't one. I leaned against the wall and collapsed. The floor beneath me opened ... I was falling ... down ... down ... down ... into darkness ... losing him ... losing my son ... losing me ... losing everything!

~

I jolted up from the couch. My body was wringing wet from sweat and from the tears I had shed. Santan was standing in his crib, screaming; his face was crimson. He must have been crying for some time. Someone was knocking at the door. I staggered off the couch, disoriented, not knowing if I should get my child first, or answer the door. Santan saw me, and his cry intensified. Suddenly, he threw back his head, directing his face to the ceiling. What I heard come from his mouth was not natural for a child! I went to my son and gathered him into my arms, then returned to the couch. I sat rocking him until he settled, and his breathing reduced to tiny gasps. Whoever had been at my door must have given up and left—probably Randy. I was sure he would return at some point.

I spent the rest of the evening reading to Santan. He became agitated every time I tried to set him down. I wondered if the count ever entered my son's dreams. Did babies dream? Finally, around ten o'clock, he fell asleep and I was able to lay him in his crib. I wandered into my room and stared at my bed. Did I want to crawl under my covers and sleep? Yes. Did I want to dream? No. I feared the dream would revisit me; I feared being cast aside—again. But sleep has a way of prevailing. My eyes closed ... I reentered my dream world...

I was in a meadow, walking through a field of wild flowers. The sun was shining brightly. Santan was running ahead of me. There was another child with him, trying to keep up. I noticed the tight red curls bouncing on its head. Santan turned to me, laughing. *Look, Mama. Look at all these flowers! Are they not beautiful, Mama?* Santan picked some daisies and raced back to me. The other child followed; I saw that it was a little girl. *Mama ... f'owers ... bootiful.* Her voice was filled with authority. She picked some daisies, too, and handed them to me. *Me f'st!* She pushed Santan aside. He giggled and fell down in the grass.

I laughed, too, and scooped the little girl up into my arms. I swung her around in the air. We toppled to the ground beside Santan, and the three of us rolled around in the meadow. A cloud crowded its way across the sun; well, I thought it was a cloud, until I turned over onto my back, and stared up at the sky—into *his* eyes.

Virginia, my darling—what a beautiful sight I feast upon! He knelt down in the grass and reached for the little girl. She giggled and ran toward him. *Papa! Papa!* I jumped to my feet and tried to grab her, but I wasn't fast enough. She was already in his arms. Santan clambered to his feet. He was staring at the count, his eyes wide with awe. *Hello, Papa; it is good to see you.* The count extended his hand to Santan. *Likewise, my son.* Santan walked to Basarab—into his embrace.

I looked down at the three of them. There was no evil in the air—no darkness—just a happy family romping in a summer meadow. What was I afraid of, then? Wasn't this what I had always wanted, a happy little family?

The count stood and began to walk away with the children. I tried to follow, to be part of the family, but my feet were stuck. I could feel the earth crawling over my skin. I heard the children laughing with their father. Someone was approaching, from behind me. I turned my head. Max.

I told you that he would come for his son. Is the other one his, as well? There was a malicious smile on Max's face. *Did I not tell you that Santan would never be yours, no matter what you did?* I didn't know what to do. I couldn't budge. The earth and grass had reached my knees, anchoring me to the ground. The count was moving farther and farther away.

Help me; Max ... please ... help me!

Max just stood there, laughing. *Why would I want to help you, Miss Virginia, after all the trouble you caused for me and my Teresa?* Max started to fade away.

From across the meadow, the conquering howl of a wolf floated back to me. It was joined by two youthful howls. The earth around my legs released me. I crumbled to the ground and watered the grass with my tears.

Chapter Eleven

At the end of February, I received an email from Emelia. It was vague and not overly informative…

Dearest Virginia:

I apologize for being out of touch. We have finally moved out of the caves, and into a family owned hotel in Brasov. It is about 20 kilometres from Bran, where Dracula's castle is. The top five floors were vacated for our use, as many of our closest relatives have arrived. It is good to see so many of us gathered together; however, it is also dangerous for all of us to be in one place. I have noticed how nervous Basarab is. I fear for his mental health. I am unsure if it was such a wise thing that I did, to take his son from him. He seems unable to concentrate fully on the task at hand. Oh well, what is done, is done. He still does not speak to me, and my heart is heavy.

Teresa is moody much of the time. Max is melancholy. There have been several moments when I have caught him staring toward the mountains. One day, I asked him what was on his mind, and he told me that he was thinking of his Lilly. I could see the pain in his eyes. Another time, while we were walking together in the caves, Max confided to me that he did not resent what I had done for you; he wished he had had the same courage.

Ildiko, Basarab's cousin, still has an eye for him. She is a fierce young woman, one that could have given Teresa a run for her money, had she dug her teeth into

Basarab before he struck the bargain with Max. I was watching her one evening during supper; she did not take her eyes from Basarab. Ildiko also shadows Basarab whenever she can--much to Teresa's abhorrence! I know Ildiko is a strong, determined young woman, but she should take care. I fear that Teresa's patience will wear thin before long.

I will end this letter now. Take care of yourself. I am grateful for Adelaide's help, because I think Basarab is watching my communications.
Love, Emelia

~

Carla was happy with my progress. She was pleased, too, that Santan recognized her and that he reached out his arms to her, even though it had been a month since he last saw her. It was during this visit that Carla opened up to me, telling me how she had become involved with the family.

"I met Emelia through Adelaide," Carla began. "Adelaide used to visit the orphanage where I lived. One day she came into the common room where the children gathered for playtime. I was sitting in a corner, facing the wall. My face was red from the strain of trying not to shed a tear. I had done nothing wrong; but, as usual, the nuns assumed I was the culprit. I knew Adelaide was in the room before I even saw her—she always smelled so divine—like musk in a forest of evergreens. I turned my head slightly, and noticed she was talking to a nun. Adelaide was pointing to me, and she did not look pleased. The nun was shaking her head; she appeared to be trying to explain something, but Adelaide cut her off by walking away from her—to me.

"Adelaide took me by the hand and softly said, 'you are coming with me, child.' I did not hesitate. What was there to be uncertain about? Even at the young age of seven, I knew that any place would be better than where I was. Adelaide forwarded a substantial amount of money to the orphanage, so there were no questions asked when she applied to adopt me. In fact, the paperwork was filled out in record time. I never saw the inside of that place again—neither did Adelaide, once I was securely hers.

"I remember the first time I met Emelia. What a lovely lady … gentle ... concerned for my welfare. I had overheard Adelaide telling Emelia about the numerous bruises that she had found on my skin, when she had first brought me home. Emelia had asked Adelaide if there was anything that she could do to prevent such atrocities from happening to another child at that orphanage. Adelaide told Emelia that she had looked after it. The wheels were already in motion, and it would not be long before the orphanage's administration would be changed.

"I always felt comfortable around Emelia. Every time she visited, she would bring me the most delightful presents. On my tenth birthday, she asked me what I would like to be when I grew up. I answered without hesitation, a doctor. She had smiled and said that was a very honourable profession; she would see what she could do to help me achieve my goal. I was academically advanced for my age, so Emelia started to bring me medical books. I devoured them, passionate for knowledge. When I entered medical school, I was so far ahead of the other students that I accelerated into the second year program. I completed my courses in four years, as opposed to the normal seven." Carla paused a moment and took a sip of her coffee.

"When did you discover *what* Emelia was?" I queried.

Carla smiled. "I had asked Adelaide, several times, why Aunt Emelia never ate with us. In fact, I had begun to wonder if she had an eating disorder because the only nourishment she ever consumed when she visited was red wine, so I thought. Adelaide told me Emelia had a sensitive stomach and was on a special diet. I was unsatisfied with that answer, so I asked Adelaide why she couldn't just cook the special food for Emelia. Adelaide said she would tell me the details when I was older and better able to understand.

"Finally, that day arrived—my sixteenth birthday. I was so excited. Adelaide said I would be allowed a glass of wine with my supper that night. She cooked a delicious meal for me—roast chicken, with a bread and walnut stuffing; garlic mashed potatoes; baby carrots, smothered in butter and maple syrup; gravy; and a tossed salad. Even Alfred joined us. One day I had asked Adelaide why Emelia and Alfred didn't get together because I thought they would make a lovely couple. Adelaide told me Emelia had a husband. When I asked why she never brought him around, Adelaide said that things were complicated––she would explain one day—something else about Emelia that I was supposed to wait to know about.

"Emelia arrived partway through our meal. As usual, she did not put any food on her plate. Adelaide left the room and returned a few minutes later with a glass of *wine* for Emelia. I wondered why she just hadn't poured her a glass from the bottle that was on the table. When Adelaide went to get Emelia a second glass of wine, I excused myself from the table with the pretence of going to the washroom. Instead, I followed Adelaide, keeping a discreet distance between us. To my surprise, she went into her room and opened her closet. She pushed some clothes aside and exposed a wall safe. She opened it, took out a bottle, and poured some liquid into Emelia's glass. Then she returned the bottle to the safe, closed and locked it.

"Before Adelaide could catch me lurking in the hallway, I slipped into the room across from hers. Once she was safely out of sight, I ran to the bathroom and flushed the toilet. Later, after Emelia left, I asked Adelaide, again, why Emelia did not eat food, what her illness was, and why she had to have a different wine from the rest of us. I noticed a heartbreaking look enter Adelaide's eyes. She directed me to the couch. She sat down and patted the seat next to her. Alfred was sitting in a chair, reading a book. He looked up, briefly, as Adelaide began to explain to me about Emelia.

"You can imagine my shock at learning that such creatures existed. I told her that she must be joshing me, but she shook her head, and told me to ask Alfred. I did. He nodded. 'Adelaide speaks the truth.' Adelaide told me that I was never to tell a living soul about the conversation that had passed between us that night. She told me that as much as she was my benefactress, Emelia was hers, and Emelia would be in considerable danger if word of what she was ever fell upon the wrong ears.

"Eventually, I became a doctor. My tuition was fully paid for by funds Emelia forwarded to Adelaide. When Emelia asked me, a couple of years ago, if I would fulfill the family's medical needs in southern Ontario, I did not hesitate. Everything was arranged for me. I upgraded my medical license to Canadian equivalency at the McMaster University Medical Centre. Emelia found a Hamilton doctor who was retiring, and he accepted her generous offer for his practice. I moved in and took right over."

"So you haven't been in Canada long?"

"Not really." Carla looked at her watch. "My goodness, ten o'clock; I better get going." She headed to the door. "I'll see you in two weeks," she stated as she slipped her coat on.

"Thanks." I opened the door.

She paused a moment. "For what?"

"For sharing."

"No problem."

I watched her leave. She opened her car door, turned and smiled, and then waved to me. I shut my door, thinking my world was getting stranger and more complicated by the minute. Just how powerful were these creatures? How far did their influence extend? To whom did it extend? How many of *them* lived *next door* to me?

I heard Santan whimpering. It was time for his next feeding.

~

Through a couple of emails, over the next two weeks, I learned even more about the family. Emelia filled me in, briefly, that Dracula's brother, Radu, was the one behind the unrelenting heinous crimes Elizabeth Bathory and Jack the Ripper were committing and framing many family members with in Brasov and throughout other family strongholds in Transylvania, Moldova, and Turkey, to mention a few. Emelia had written that Radu's quest for power seemed to have no borders.

Ildiko continued her flirtation with Basarab, and Teresa had caused a couple of scenes at the supper gatherings, similar, I assumed, to the type she had exhibited toward me. Emelia wrote that Basarab had confined Teresa to her room due to her latest outburst, something that had thrown her into an even worse fit of temper. Emelia noted that Max was not pleased with that turn of events. She had overheard him talking to another servant about how unjust it was for the count to treat Teresa with such disrespect. Ildiko seemed pleased, though, Emelia wrote, pointing out that Ildiko still felt that she should be Basarab's queen.

Emelia wrote that she hoped all was well with me, and she anticipated Adelaide would be able to make it over in time for the birth. If not, she was sure I would be in capable hands with Carla.

Despite how I had constantly wanted to escape from Basarab when I had been a captive in *The House*, after reading Emelia's letters, something stirred in my heart. At first I couldn't figure out what it was, but as I pondered on it, I realized I was worried for Basarab, and the others I had met—especially Atilla and Emelia. I felt the blood as it rose to my cheeks.

Foolish woman! Don't you know that you are better off without him?

I looked around to see who had said that. I was the only one in the room. *But, I love him.*

How could you, after what he has done to you?

I don't know ... maybe because I have never met anyone like him before ... he is the father of my son...
No reason to love him. He is a beast! He has no heart.
You are wrong ... I've seen glimpses of his heart.
No ... you only saw what Basarab wanted you to see.
You are wrong!
Time will tell ... time will tell ... time...
I awakened with a start.

~

Time was passing quickly. Santan was walking without aid, and his speech was clearer than that of any child of his age. We spent countless hours reading. Now that the weather was getting warmer, once the sun had set, we went for walks. Santan loved to walk. One day he shocked me by saying: "Big house; Santan want to see big house."

"There is no big house around here," I told him.

"Yes, big house; I want to see it again." Santan's eyes glowed red in the darkening evening.

I was shocked. I knew there was only one house that Santan could be asking about; but I had no idea, having seen it only once, how such a young child could remember it! I tried to distract him, but every time we went for a walk, he asked about the big house. I was beginning to get the feeling that no matter what I tried to do to make Santan mine, I would fail.

I prayed for the child in my womb.

Chapter Twelve

One warm day in mid April, as the sun was settling down in the west, I packed Santan in the van, and we headed for a new trail that I had scoped out. I pulled into the parking lot at D'Aubigny Creek and sat there for a few minutes, taking in the beauty of the old trees that lined the top of the hill. There were still a few cars in the parking lot, but I assumed they belonged to some stragglers from the evening soccer events played on the fields below.

"Well, Santan, shall we?" I turned in my seat and looked at him. He smiled. I secured him in his buggy, and we headed down the steep hill, to the path that meandered along the river. I noticed the soccer fields were empty, except, as I had presumed, for a few coaches taking down nets.

I pushed the buggy along quickly, until I passed the fields and entered the forested area. I stopped for a moment, and breathed in the scents of early spring. Santan looked back at me, a questioning look on his face.

"Santan walk now," he demanded. He tried to undo the buggy straps.

I gazed around, up and down the trail. It looked safe. Not many people would be walking or biking on the trails this time of night. "Okay," I said, undoing the straps. "Up you come." I lifted Santan from the buggy and placed him on the paved trail. "You stay with me, though, no running off," I ordered with a grin.

He looked up at me, his eyes warm and filled with love. "Santan not run away from you ... Santan want to see river and big birds." He toddled off down a narrow path that led to the water. I left the buggy at the edge of the trail and quickly followed my son. He was already standing at the river's edge when I reached him. We crouched down on the shore and watched a flock of geese that was swimming lazily on the river.

"Nice birds," he said.

"Yes they are beautiful, aren't they?" A strange voice permeated our space.

I scrambled to my feet and spun around. Not ten feet from me and Santan stood a young woman. She began to approach. I picked up Santan and held him close to me. He seemed to be getting excited, as he watched the woman come closer.

"Hi!" he shouted out boldly.

"Hush, Santan," I whispered in his ear.

"It's okay, Mama ... this a nice lady." Santan cradled my cheeks in his little hands. He looked directly into my eyes. I looked away, and focused on the woman.

"We were just leaving," I stuttered, and began to walk toward the pathway.

The woman extended her hand to me. "Please, don't leave on my account. We can all enjoy the river's beauty. There is plenty of room here." She paused. "My name is Angel."

When I didn't give my name, or Santan's, she continued. "I am new in the area. I just rented a small house near here and haven't made any friends yet. I travel a lot with my job, so I am not home enough to get to know the neighbours. Do you live around here, as well?" She smiled—a friendly smile.

"No." I wasn't about to tell her where I lived, either. I tried to step past her. She laid her hand on my arm.

"Please, I am so lonely ... have you ever felt lonely? We don't have to become friends or anything; but, just for a bit, couldn't you stay and chat? I've had a rough week."

Loneliness was something I understood, and I doubted this woman had any idea what true loneliness was, compared with what I was living. My heart began to soften, though. It had been a long time since I had spoken to someone outside my world, other than Randy, Carla, Adelaide, and Alfred. I smiled, tentatively, and set Santan down. "I guess we can stay a bit longer."

"Might I ask your name, since I have told you mine?" Angel asked.

"Virginia."

"And the child?"

I hesitated. I would probably never see her again, and I could make sure of that by not coming to this trail again. "Santan," I finally answered.

"That is a strange name for a child born in this country," Angel commented. "Did you pick it?"

I shook my head. "No ... his father did."

"It is a strong name, though ... means 'A tree.' Your son will grow up to be kind and nurturing, and he will always be reliable. He will love taking care of others, especially his family, and he will do what it takes to create a harmonious atmosphere for those he loves. You must take care, though, to ensure he is not taken advantage of."

"You seem to know a lot about names ... well, my son's name, anyway." This worried me. Who was this woman, really?

Angel chuckled softly. "I have studied names and languages for years. I am a linguist and I travel all over the world, speaking to groups on the importance of global understanding. Some names just stick in my head—Santan is one of them."

"I see." I relaxed a bit.

"What do you do, besides looking after your son?"

"Well, that is pretty much it," I replied. "Looking after him and this one," I pointed to my belly, "will keep me pretty busy. I was a freelance writer before I had the children," I added.

"I see ... and what of your husband?"

I paused. "Deceased." I could hear the flatness in my voice.

"I am sorry." Angel reached out her hand and set it on my shoulder.

I shrugged her hand off. "I am adjusting," I whispered, taking a step back from her. I noticed that Santan was getting restless. "I truly must get going. It was nice to meet you." I walked over to Santan and picked him up. This time, as I approached Angel, she stepped aside, allowing me to pass.

"Do you mind if I join you on your walk?" she asked, following me to the main trail.

I desperately wanted to say that I did mind, but held my tongue. I pushed the buggy along the trail. Santan walked beside me. Angel caught up, and walked along with us, not saying a word. When we reached the little steel bridge that traversed the creek that flowed into the Grand River, I paused and lifted Santan up so that he could look down at the water bubbling over the rock bed.

Angel rested her arms on the railing. "If you listen closely, you can hear the old stories of where the waters have been, being whispered." She looked directly at my son.

"What are they saying?" Santan asked eagerly.

"Let me see now..." she cocked her head to the side. I noticed the concentrated look on her face as she closed her eyes. "They are telling me that they originally came from a great ocean in the sky, and that they were swept up from the waves by a passing cloud. At first they were scared, but soon they began to make friends with all the other droplets of water the cloud had gathered. The cloud became crowded, though, and all the tiny droplets cried out in despair that there was too little room. They couldn't move. No one seemed to answer their cries for help. But, suddenly, a mighty wind began to drive the clouds across the sky. Faster and faster they went. Bits and pieces of the large cloud broke off, forming their own clouds, and then they each set out on their own journey. However, no matter which cloud they were in, the droplets all felt a tremor within the belly of their cloud and a thundering voice would crackle, telling them that it was time to begin the next stage of their journey. The voice was always followed by a thunderous rumble, and then the cloud would burst open and release the droplets into their new world."

Santan was watching Angel, and his eyes were wide with wonder. I, too, was observing her—the gentleness in her eyes and her voice. Maybe it wouldn't be so bad having a friend, one that wouldn't be around all the time, though. Santan, probably realizing that Angel was finished telling her story, clapped his hands.

"Where did you hear such a story?" I asked.

"Oh ... it is just an old Gy...—an old story that my father used to spin around the campfires when we went camping as children."

I was surprised at how hesitantly the words had come out of Angel's mouth when she related to me the origin of the story. I also wondered why she had been about to say that it was a Gypsy story, and then changed her mind. *Oh well, it is not of any significant importance where the story came from.* I turned to Angel. "Would you like to go back down to the river's edge? There is a spot in this area where people launch their boats into the river, and there are numerous islands where wildlife abounds this time of night. Maybe Santan will get to see a deer or two if we watch closely."

"That would be lovely," Angel replied.

We walked across the bridge and down to the river. It was a quiet evening, not a boat or another human in sight. I was happy for that. We stood there, side by side for several minutes, neither of us speaking. Santan picked up some small pebbles and threw them into the water, giggling each time they splashed.

"I hope me not hurting droplets," he burst out, a serious look on his face.

Angel chuckled. "Oh no, the droplets are quite strong; the rocks cannot hurt them. The rocks are their friends, you see, that is why they live in the river together. When they play, you can always tell how happy they are by their laughter, which is the bubbling water you hear. Humans like to refer to it as a babbling brook."

Her answer seemed to satisfy Santan. He resumed his stone throwing. I noticed some enormous rocks beside the shoreline and motioned to Angel. "Why don't we sit for a few minutes before heading back?

"Good idea," Angel smiled warmly.

~

Later that night, as I observed my son playing with his toys on the floor of the living room, I thought about my newfound friend. Angel had given me her phone number; I had not given her mine, feeling that I still needed to know more about her before entrusting her with something like that. After all, there was a possibility that she could be one of the count's spies, wasn't there? I had let her leave the parking lot first, making sure she was well on her way before I pulled out and headed home. I had also been cautious of any vehicles that came around me, making sure that Angel hadn't doubled back to follow me.

Santan had been fascinated by her and had chattered all the way home, retelling some of the story she had told him about the droplets. There could be no harm from such a warm and open person, could there be? I watched Santan as he built a wall with his wooden blocks. I sighed deeply; my son had no idea, thus far, what walls were all about. He was still an innocent child, not yet exposed to the evil of the world he had been born into—his, or mine!

Basarab

Chapter Thirteen

I continued to leave the hotel, in the middle of the night, to seek nourishment in the nightclubs around the city. I made sure not to frequent the same bar twice in a row; I knew I could not be too careful. One night, I bumped into an old friend.

"Basarab?" I felt a gentle hand on my shoulder and heard a familiar voice.

I turned and looked into Angelique's eyes. "Angelique! What a pleasant surprise."

"It has been a long time."

"It has. What brings you to Brasov?"

"Is there somewhere private that we can go to talk; perhaps a walk in the park? I do not trust the ears in these places."

I nodded, and together we left the club. Angelique did not say anything until we reached the park. The silence gave me time to think and to observe the beauty of the woman who walked beside me. She had not aged since the day I had met her. Her hair was longer, but still fell in soft blond curls, an unusual colour for a Gypsy maiden. Her eyes were an icy blue, yet when she smiled they exuded warmth. Her skin was soft and unblemished, untouched by time and weather. She caught me looking at her.

"What is it, Basarab?"

"You have not changed."

"Just the clothes." She laughed. The sound was music to my ears, soothing. "I discarded my usual clothes for this." She motioned from her neck to her feet—to the baggy t-shirt, jeans, and running shoes.

I smiled. Angelique had been invaluable to the family over the centuries, always appearing at the moments we needed her most. I wondered what brought her to me now.

She pointed to a bench that was sitting next to the fountain in the middle of the park. "Shall we sit a moment?"

Once seated, Angelique turned to me. "I have news of your son, Basarab."

I felt my heart constrict in my chest. I could not think of a response.

"He is well, and healthy," she continued with a smile.

"What of his mother?" I raised my eyebrows; even though, as I asked, I regretted my impulsiveness. I wanted no one to think I bore any feelings for Virginia.

"She too is well."

"Where is she?"

"This I will not tell you. I only wanted to let you know that your son is safe. Your job, at the moment, is to rid the family of this blight before it gets totally out of control. I felt the knowledge of knowing Santan was okay would ease the painful turmoil that I know you must be dealing with."

"How do you know?" I asked curiously.

"I keep watch over all the family members that I care about, especially during these times." Angelique sighed and stood up. "I am afraid I must leave you now. I have other matters to attend to."

"Will you keep me informed about my son?" I stood, as well, and we headed out of the park.

When we reached the sidewalk, she turned to me. "As best I can."

I watched her walk away, and then headed back to my hotel. A dark foreboding enveloped me. If Angelique had seen my son, I could not help wondering who else might have. What if

Radu had rogues across the ocean? We still had not been able to
determine how far his borders extended. Since I had not taken
any nourishment yet, I felt the thirst rising up in me, like a savage
beast. I happened on a lone young woman, a nurse, making her
way home from work. I detained her for only a few moments; she
would remember nothing in the morning.

~

Teresa continued to be outraged by Ildiko's actions, and I
cannot say that I blame her. Ildiko had been hounding me with an
unrelenting, wanton flirting. Teresa brought the subject up to me
several times when we were alone, only she did not speak with
the respect due to me. Instead, she shrieked like a banshee. I was
so tired of her behaviour, especially when it flowed over into
family dinners, as it had on several occasions. One evening, after
one of her displays, I lost my temper on her. I told her how tiring
her atrocious conduct was—that she had made a spectacle of
herself in Brantford, in front of my family, and now she was
doing the same in Brasov. I had stomped from the room, leaving
her in a crying heap on the floor.

As I stormed out of the hotel, my thoughts had turned to
Virginia. She was making a habit of invading my waking
thoughts, as well as my dreams. I smiled as I walked down the
sidewalk, remembering the dream I had just had the previous
night...

*Basarab, my darling, why do you shun me? Have I not
been a perfect lover and a devoted mother to our son?*

You have been both.

Then why?

Her eyes were aquiline pools that drew me into their
depths; her long red curls fell over her body, covering her
womanly fruits. I tried to draw her into my arms, but she pushed
me away.

I will no longer play second fiddle to your wife, Basarab. You must make your choice—her, or me. I hope you make the right one.

She took her hand and pushed her curls behind her ears, allowing me a clear view of her lovely breasts, still filled with mother's milk. I reached for her, again. She smacked my hand, teasingly. And then she walked around me, slowly, running her hands up and down my arms, my shoulders, my back, my chest … pausing but a moment before she took hold of my desire. How I burned for her…

Come, Basarab … tell me that this is what you truly want … and it shall all be yours…

~

I could feel my excitement, and quickened my pace. I almost lost control with the young woman whom I had fed on that night; but luckily, I checked myself in time. I hoped that no one would find her in such a comatose position … that she would just awaken and get herself home, with nothing more than a headache.

~

I was sitting with Gara one evening, when Evdochia's nephews, Kerecsen and Laborc, and Kardos, the son of Dracula's cousin Bajnok, entered the sitting room where we were. All three looked serious. They said they had something important to relay to us. Kardos spoke first.

"Kerecsen and Laborc were late for our meeting tonight; we were supposed to meet at a club at 11:30. I was annoyed. A stranger approached me and tried to pick a fight. I told the man to leave through the same door he had entered, or I would physically put him through it. He jeered at me and told me to try it, so I picked him up by the throat and put him up against the wall. You should have seen the look on his face. My fingers tightened around his neck, and his legs began to twitch. I heard someone shout my name, breaking the trance I was in. I dropped him and stormed out of the bar, but not before I threatened that if I ever saw him again, I would finish what I had started."

Laborc continued the story from where Kardos had left off. "As Kerecsen and I approached the club entrance, we noticed Jack dragging a man into an alley. We stepped back into the shadows and waited a few moments before following him. We were too late; Jack had already ripped into his throat. He was setting a walking stick by the body—Kardos'. Jack must have sensed our presence, because suddenly he stood up and turned around, and sneered at us. I do not think that he realized, at first, who we were when he bared his fangs. I suppose he was thinking it was his lucky night—that he might have a little extra dinner."

"We snarled at him, exposing our fangs," Kerecsen continued, "and then we began to walk slowly toward Jack. There was no other way out of the alley, not for Jack. Laborc grabbed Jack by the throat and held him up against the chain-link fence, while I whispered in Jack's ear. I scraped my fangs along his neck, cutting his skin just enough to draw blood. Laborc asked him why he had been placing Kardos' walking stick beside a dead body."

Kerecsen nodded to Laborc, who relayed the rest of the story. "When Jack refused to answer, I advised him that it would be wiser to confess than to succumb to the fate he would encounter if I were to step back and let my brother take over! Kerecsen flexed his hands, and his talons emerged. There is a legitimate reason that my brother is often called *The Hawk*, as you well know, Basarab. My brother's talons are lethal when it comes to extracting information. Jack looked from me to Kerecsen, and back. He still hesitated, until Kerecsen scraped lightly along Jack's cheek. Then, he shrunk like a coward and spilled his guts.

"He told us that Elizabeth had him set up family members, so it looked as though they had committed the heinous murders that were inundating the cities and countryside of

Transylvania and its border countries. We asked who the mastermind behind Elizabeth was, and his lips sealed again. Kerecsen had but to scrape his talons, a little deeper this time, down the side of Jack's neck, crossing over the spot where his fangs had broken the skin earlier. Jack was swift to report, then, that Radu was the real architect behind everything, something I realize that you have suspected for quite some time.

"We finally let Jack go, sure that he would not rush to Elizabeth and tell her anything. Kerecsen told Jack that if he so much as breathed a word of what had transpired in the alley— well, let us just say, whatever Elizabeth or Radu might have done to him, would be nothing compared with the damage we would wreak on him. Jack is no fool; he will keep his mouth shut."

I thanked my cousins for their information, and then they left.

"It is as I suspected, then," Gara stated.

"It appears so."

"You are still going to meet with Radu?" Gara's eyebrows rose questioningly.

"Of course. What better way to know your enemy than to face him?" I returned.

Gara smiled. "I believe I will retire to my room. I have a few things I need to look into. Goodnight, my dear cousin."

"Goodnight, Gara."

Later, in my quarters, I thought about that night's incident, knowing that if Kerecsen and Laborc had not happened along when they did, Kardos would have been arrested and put in jail.

~

The meeting with Radu followed closely on the heels of Kerecsen and Laborc's revelation. It had not lasted long, and it had not gone well. As had been agreed, I did not meet Radu alone; my father, Stephen, Dracula, and Gara were with me.

Radu opened with the statement that he had heard rumours that I suspected he was trying to usurp the throne. "How could you think such of me, my dear nephew?" Radu's voice had a slithering silkiness to it.

I was shocked when Gara spoke up before I could answer. He was not usually so bold. "We know more of your doings than you might think," he said, looking Radu directly in the eyes.

Radu turned on his brother. "Is this your doing? To put me down, as usual?"

Dracula guffawed sarcastically. "Do not flatter yourself … you are quite capable of being obvious all by yourself."

"I came here to tell you that I know who is behind all these killings … now, I think I shall not." Radu's face had twisted into a pout.

I stood, walked to where he was sitting, and leaned over until our noses were almost touching. "I suppose that you are going to try to tell me Elizabeth Bathory is the responsible party … is that what you would like us to believe? So you can continue with your own plans? I am not a fool! Tanyasin did not place me on the throne because she thought I was going to be manipulated by creatures such as you."

"Tanyasin's putting you on the throne was guided by her hatred for my brother; she thought she was going to be able to control you…"

"And how would you know this?" I sneered.

"He knows because he is in constant contact with Tanyasin," Gara intervened, again. He turned to Radu. "Is that not correct, uncle?"

Radu stood. His lips pursed with anger; his eyes blazed with fury. "I do not need to listen to this any longer. I came here in good faith, to warn you, and you have treated me like a common rogue on the street." He stomped across the room and hesitated in the doorway. "Do not ask for my backing when her hell rains down on you; I shall not give it." The echo of the door slamming shut resounded throughout the room.

~

I excused myself and headed out of the hotel. I needed some fresh air. I needed to think. Gara had told me a couple of days ago that Tanyasin had been seen fraternizing on several occasions with Elizabeth Bathory. What game was she playing?– –meeting with Radu, and now Elizabeth. Was Tanyasin playing them both? We had not seen her for years, and now she was resurfacing just when we were being faced with all our problems. Although we believed Radu to be the real power, and Elizabeth was not to be underestimated, just where did Tanyasin fit in this puzzle? Jack, I know we did not have to worry about; he did Elizabeth's bidding at the snap of her fingers.

Elizabeth has become quite cunning over the years, though, even moving in some respectable social circles. However, an unfortunate incident happened to her a couple of weeks ago. Three young women were found murdered, and Elizabeth had been the last person seen with them, at a party in her home. The police had picked her up for questioning, but she was not interrogated for long. Lardom happened to be at the police station that night, checking on one of our friends who had been arrested. He saw Elizabeth leaving with a lawyer, one whom he had seen in the company of Radu on several occasions. Lardom relayed to me that he was also pretty sure the lawyer was a rogue.

As I approached a nightclub, still lost in thought, a young woman sidled up to me. She had a cigarette hanging out of her mouth. "Got a light, mister?"

I looked down at her, disgusted. Then, I noticed the veins pulsing in her neck. *Why not?* I ran the back of my hand along her cheek. "Smoking will ruin your beautiful skin," I commented.

She giggled.

I took hold of her elbow and escorted her through the crowd, up to the front of the line. As I did so, I leaned over and whispered in her ear, telling her that I would give her much more than a light.

She giggled again.

~

When I arrived back to my room, the young woman's blood still pulsing through my body, Teresa was sitting on the edge of our bed waiting for me. She rose as I entered, folding her hands in front of her. Her gaze went to the window. "The sun is just about to rise," she stated.

"Yes." I had no idea where she was going with this. She looked different, almost serene, compared to what she had been lately.

"You have had a good night?" She was smiling, but I could not tell how deep her smile went.

"Very, thank you." I paused. "What is this all about, Teresa?"

"I have been thinking."

"Yes?"

"I want to apologize to you for my recent ill behaviour."

"Okay ... continue."

"I am sorry I embarrassed you in front of your family. I do not understand what has come over me; I never thought I possessed such jealousy, to the extent I have displayed. I would like to make it up to you, to prove how much I love and care for you and all that is dear to you, in particular, your family."

"And my son?" I had never mentioned to Teresa anything about the conversation I had overheard, but I wanted to see her reaction to my question.

She swallowed hard. I noticed her hands begin to shake slightly. She stared directly into my eyes. "Yes, our son, too." She emphasized the word *our*.

I held my remarks back, wanting to hear what else she had to say.

"I have an idea that I would like to run by you. What would you say if I were to try to approach Elizabeth, with the pretence to join her?"

"Stop right there!" I ordered. "You will do no such thing." Even though I was angry with my wife, I would not allow her to put herself into danger of that kind. Elizabeth was not a woman to be tampered with.

"But it could work. I could play on the fact that you are being unfaithful to me, that we fight constantly, and that I can no longer stand to be in the same room with you. I will go out to one of her haunts one night, and introduce myself to her. I know she will remember me. Anyone who is anyone in the vampire world knows that I am your wife. I will make sure there are tears in my eyes, and I will have news of a fresh fight to relay to her, to get the door open. From the rumours that I have heard, Elizabeth does not have much use for men. If I play my part well enough, I am sure I can convince her that I need saving. I can also provide her with fragments of information about the family—not truths, of course, but enough that will wet her appetite.

"Once I have established a rapport with her, you and I will inform a select few individuals of our plan, and then we will stage a fight, for all the others to hear, and I will run to Elizabeth. Of course, you will have to beat me so that I will have scars when I show up at her door, making the unpleasant incident look legitimate."

I reached out and drew Teresa into my arms. This was the woman I had married, the one who would do anything to ensure my safety. I stroked her long black hair, and then, without agreeing, or disagreeing to her plan, I picked her up and carried her to our bed.

After Teresa fell asleep, I remained awake for a long time, pondering her plan. I watched her rhythmic breathing and drank in her beauty. I did not want to sleep because my slumber was constantly interrupted with dreams of my son—and of Virginia.

I went over in my mind what I had heard Teresa tell her father, and was not sure if I could trust this change of heart she seemed to be having. I had actually been contemplating leaving her. Never, in the history of our family, had a vampire of such a high station ever set aside his wife; and I had wondered if I would be setting precedence. The more Teresa had displayed her unseemly behaviour, the more I had dreamed of Virginia taking her place by my side. However, after the night's revelation, I was unsure which woman I would choose, if I were ever forced to decide.

I closed my eyes. I needed to sleep…

Papa … why are you with that lady? She is not my mama. I looked into the eyes of my son as he stood beside the bed I shared with Teresa. He was older than I had expected him to be, an intense young boy. Had I been away longer than I thought?

She is not a nice lady; she hurt me the other day. Santan's eyes were dark and serious. His lips shut firmly, arched down in a frown.

I hoisted myself up on my elbow. *This lady is my wife, son; therefore, she is your mother.*

Being your wife does not make her my mama. Santan pointed to a corner in the room. *She is my mama … tell him, Mama … tell him!*

I looked in the direction my son was pointing. Slowly, from the shadowy corner, Virginia stepped forward. She walked leisurely toward Santan, giving me time to take in every movement of her body. My breath caught in my throat at her exquisiteness. She was dressed in a white silk gown that clung to her splendidly curved body. The neckline of the gown plunged in a V, disclosing the firmness of her full breasts. She kept her focus on Santan, so I could not read what was in her eyes. She knelt down and gathered him into her arms.

Yes, Santan, you are right; I am your mama. This woman who is in bed with your papa is his wife, though, and your papa wants her to be your mama ... but, you and I know that should not happen, don't we?

Yes, Mama.

We know how she really feels about you, don't we?

Yes, Mama.

We know that she would rather you were not born, don't we?

Yes, Mama.

I could not believe what I had just heard. How could Virginia and Santan be privy to such knowledge? And, how could my infant son have such an understanding of the situation? *How have you bewitched my son?* I glared at Virginia, despite the nagging memory of what I had overheard Teresa tell her father.

Teresa began to stir. She stretched, and pushed herself into a sitting position, propping her back against the pillows. Her eyes opened wide when she realized that we were not alone in the room. *What is going on here? Virginia! What are you doing in my bedchamber; is it not enough that my husband visits yours? Do you have to invade my privacy with your sorcery?*

It is you who has invaded my life, Teresa. It is you who has deceived your husband, leading him to think you wanted a child as badly as he did. But you and I know better, don't we?

You know nothing!

Oh, but I do. The walls have ears, dear Teresa. And your body language, when you are around my son, exudes the truth!

My eyes flitted back and forth between the two women. Then Santan did something unexpected. He took hold of

Virginia's hand and led her around to my side of the bed. He reached for my hand, and then he placed our hands together.

This is as it should be. His voice was firm. He stared at me with authority—my son, no longer an infant.

I looked at Virginia. She had a peculiar smile on her face. I turned to glance at Teresa, but she was fading away. In the dying moments of her image, I heard her scream, like the banshee she had been over the past few months.

You will all be sorry for what has passed here tonight … you will all be sorry!

~

I awakened, disturbed by the dream. I gazed upon my sleeping wife, the woman who had stood by my side for centuries, who had even saved my life, who had just proposed to me an exceedingly dangerous liaison to gather information for the family. But the words from my dream kept resonating in my head—Teresa's words, *you will be sorry*—and then, Santan's words, *this is as it should be.* I saw Virginia's face, clearly, and I was not dreaming. I saw her smile, warm and genuine, filled with love for me, and for my son. I heard her laughter tingling in the room, and somewhere her voice saying to me, *I can give you more, Basarab, my love; oh so much more can I give you...*

I thrust the covers aside, slipped from the bed and strode from the bedchamber. The sun was beginning to set in the west—it was time to appease the beast within me.

Chapter Fourteen

We discovered that Radu protected much of his worldly wealth within holding companies. Stephen suggested we try to obtain more details by infiltrating some of the holdings we were positive that he had interests in. During one of our meetings, I pointed out that it was beginning to look as though Radu was more powerful than we had realized. We were going to have to exercise extreme caution, as the loyalty to Radu, from both humans and rogues, was appearing substantial and unshakeable.

My father suggested that one possible way to gain access to Radu's order was to find someone he had done an injustice to, someone who would want to seek revenge. Gara said he would investigate that avenue.

Dracula probed into the many strongholds held by Radu. There was one in particular that had captured his attention— Hunedoara Castle, also known as Cornvinesti Castle. Dracula signed up for one of the castle's guided tours. He disguised himself as an old blind man, layering on his clothing, walking with a white cane. Ildiko dressed in a burqua and accompanied him as his guide.

"I wanted to see what was going on behind the walls of the castle; I had suspicions that particular location might be where Radu had set up his headquarters," Dracula relayed to our gathering. "Once Ildiko and I were inside, we slipped away from the group of tourists. As you all know, I had been incarcerated in that castle in 1462, so I know it well. We made our way down to the prison area, and my assumptions were confirmed. The cells were full of rogues lying drugged and listless on their beds. We were able to pass along, unnoticed, and we ventured further, to where I knew there were meeting rooms, deep in the bowels of the castle. Nothing was happening in that area, though, so we turned around, intent on heading back to the tour group. That was when we heard footsteps approaching. Ildiko noticed an open doorway, and quickly we slipped through it, into an empty room.

"I recognized my brother's voice. He was telling his companion that she needed to be patient a while longer; he would allow her to exact her revenge when the time was right. Then, I heard her voice, grating and as ugly as ever. I felt Ildiko's fingernails dig into my arm at the sound of it. 'Do not go back on our bargain, Radu ... it will not go well for you.' 'You shock me with your accusation that I might do such a thing, Tanyasin. Our main goal has always been one, has it not? To rid this world of my brother, the man who savagely murdered your family?' Tanyasin's cackle had rung through the stone hallways. 'I am afraid you are twisting the facts here, Radu. I want to exact my revenge on Dracula; for you, his elimination would just be a bonus. You want to dethrone Basarab.' Radu's laughter filled the empty caverns. We waited until it faded away to nothing. When we were convinced that it would be safe, we cautiously made our way back to our group."

"So you believe that Cornvinesti Castle is Radu's headquarters?" Stephen asked.

"Yes. His other castles do not have the same buzz of activity. Cornvinesti, as we know, is in a most tactical location, in the Cerna Valley at the south-western part of Transylvania. It is also surrounded by The Poiana Ruscai Mountains. The castle is a fortress, located on a rocky cliff. Its three massive towers are strategically located; anyone approaching can be seen from miles away. The castles only entrance is a suspended bridge, strung high above the Zlasti River."

"And you are sure it was Tanyasin's voice?" I questioned.

Dracula scowled at me. "Were you not paying attention, Basarab? He called her by name."

"Of course ... I apologize, uncle ... my mind must have drifted for a moment."

"As it does, lately," he returned.

I ignored his disrespectful comeback. "Thank you for the information; it will serve us well." I turned to Gara. "I think it is time we sent some of our people into Hunedoara."

"Consider it done."

"What holdings do we have in that area?" I asked.

"None that I know of," Stephen replied. "But I am sure it will not take much to acquire some," he added with a smile.

"I will look after that as well," Gara stated. He shuffled through the papers that were sitting in front of him, and then slipped them into his briefcase. Gara was judicious when it came to recordkeeping, the same as my father was.

"Take Kerecsen, Laborc, and Kardos with you. None of us should go out alone anymore," I said. "Also, we need to carry our cell phones with us at all times. Laborc's wife has set them all to the highest security available. There should be no critical information discussed over the hotel phones from this point onward."

Everyone nodded. It had been a blessing to have Kerecsen's and Laborc's wives join us. They were computer experts and my cousins had met them when they signed up for a computer class. Since they joined the family, the women had been invaluable in setting up a high security computer network.

I stood. "I think this meeting is adjourned then, unless there is any other pertinent information to bring forward." I looked around the table. Everyone shook their head. "Good, we will meet back here at the end of the week. Be safe." I nodded to the gathering, turned and left the room.

I did not wish to return to my suite because I had been trying to avoid Teresa since she had presented her proposal to me, and since I'd had *that* dream. I headed out the front door of the hotel, into the night, to walk the streets of Brasov alone.

~

It became impossible to avoid Teresa, despite how hard I tried. She dogged my path, constantly bringing up her proposal to me, asking me if I had made my decision yet. Finally, against my better judgement, I gave in. I cautioned her to be extremely careful, and to fill me in on every detail. I also told her that we would wait to see how the plan unfolded before we told the others.

Ildiko took advantage of Teresa's frequent absences, seeking me out whenever possible. One night, she followed me when I left the hotel. When Ildiko approached me outside the nightclub I was about to enter, I hissed at her, and then ordered her back to the hotel.

"I know what you are doing," she had laughed. "Do you mind if I join you? I could use a little…" she ran her tongue along her lips … "fun."

"You have no idea what I am doing! You only think you do." I did not want to draw any attention our way, so I kept my voice low.

"Oh, Basarab; I do know, and I don't mind. I think it is quite exciting that you are going down that road."

"You will tell no one," I ordered angrily.

She had sidled up to me. "What can I get in exchange for my silence?" she purred.

"Your life." I gripped her shoulders, turned her around, and gave her a shove. "Now go home, Ildiko. I will see you when I return."

She left, but not before throwing me a defiant glare. Maybe she thought she might have something on me now. I turned my back on her and entered the club.

~

We suffered another massive blow. Uros, who had been getting us classified information for many of the court cases our family members were embroiled in, was arrested. He faced several charges—theft of government documents being the primary one. Lardom had been unable to obtain bail for Uros; the judge indicated Uros was too high a flight risk. Lardom pointed out to me that the District Attorney handling the case was the same one who was in charge of all the family's cases. He was also a man whom had been seen in Radu's company on several occasions.

I was aware of the net closing over us, and there were moments that I felt powerless to quell the tide of invasion that was ravaging through our family. Those were the moments when I was consumed with thoughts of my son, and of Virginia, and they usually occurred after one of my dreams. However, the amount of time I dwelled on the dreams, I kept secret from everyone, including my father. To admit to such feelings would be a sign of weakness, which was one thing I could not afford. I knew the time would come when I would be able to embrace my son in my arms, and deal with my choice between the woman I was married to, and the woman who had borne my son!

Virginia
Chapter Fifteen

I had decided to keep my meeting with Angel a secret, even from Randy. I figured it was nobody's business if I had a friend outside the cocoon I was living in. In fact, there might come a time when I would be in need of such a person, if she turned out to be a true friend.

Carla was pleased with my progress. She said the walks I was taking were keeping my body in good condition and she didn't anticipate any problems with the birth. I bought a three-foot deep pool for the birthing. Randy laughed at me; he thought it was ridiculous to give birth to a baby in a pool of water. I explained to him that babies existed in amniotic fluid for the first nine months of their lives, so they were used to breathing in liquid.

I was not sleeping well; the dreams had started again. I mentioned my lack of sleep to Carla, but not the dreams. She said it was normal to be restless, especially during the last couple of months. She had laughed and said if I thought sleep was difficult now, just wait until I had two children to look after. At least with one, I could rest when he napped.

I was beginning to think there was something strange about Carla, though. After her visits, the baby was abnormally restless, and my dreams were more disturbing than usual. The most disturbing one happened two weeks before my estimated delivery date; I had just returned home from a walk along the river trails. Santan was napping. I decided to lie down, as well...

I was walking the trail that ran along the Grand River's shoreline near Wilkes Dam. Santan was beside me, his hand clutched tightly in mine. I was pointing out the wildlife that graced the river in the twilight hours—the geese, a blue heron, and a mother deer and her fawn. He was thrilled when we spotted the deer on one of the little islands. I picked up some small flat stones and tried to show Santan how to skip rocks on the water. I was not particularly skilled at it. Santan, as he had done before, just threw the stones into the water and laughed.

Virginia ... Virginia ... it is almost time, my love. Why do you keep such a distance between us? How many times do I have to prove to you that you are my true love—the mother of my children? I gazed around, trying to locate the all-too-familiar voice. I feared it, yet anticipated its arrival in my dreams. The fear occurred when *he* left with my children; the anticipation was my longing for him to hold me in his arms again, for him to take me on his wings to the hell only he could fly me to. I tightened my grip on Santan's hand.

Santan looked up at the sound of the voice. *Papa! Papa! I am so glad you have come. Mama needs you!* Santan shouted excitedly. *Stop hiding, Papa, come out and play with me!*

Basarab stepped out from behind a large, fallen tree trunk, just ahead of where Santan and I were standing. He smiled, and then crouched down and opened his arms to his son. Santan broke free of me and raced to his father, faster than a child his age should be able to move. He leapt into his father's arms. Basarab lifted him up and dangled him over his head. Santan squealed in delight. Basarab was laughing, too, with joy. I watched the sight before me, not being able to help the grin that spread over my face.

A sharp pain ripped through my abdomen. I doubled over and fell to my knees on the stony shore. I tried to stand, but couldn't. Suddenly, Carla materialized, standing in the river, reaching out her hand to me. *Come, Virginia, it is time. The child will be born on this night. There is no time to return to your apartment; we will have to do the birthing here, in the river waters.*

The pain riddling my body was keeping me in a crouched position on the riverbank. I tried to locate Basarab and my son, but they were nowhere to be seen. I could still hear Santan's laughter, and the sound of Basarab's voice; although, I could not catch what he was saying. Carla continued calling to me. *Virginia, why do you hesitate? You must enter the water now. I have everything here that we will need.*

Slowly, I forced myself to a standing position, trying to breathe through the jolts of pain that were assaulting my body. I stepped into the water. I shivered. Spring's sun had not yet warmed the water to a tolerable temperature. Carla called to me, again, with words and open arms. I continued walking toward her. I glanced back at the shore, fearfully, because I couldn't hear Santan's laughter anymore. Where was Basarab taking my son? But then I saw him. He was still there, smiling and waving to me from his father's arms—arms that once surrounded me with love and passion. Arms that would soon hold another one of his children—one I presented him with— something his wife, Teresa, could not give him. Despite my pain, I smirked, relishing my victory over her.

I reached out and grasped Carla's hands, just as another excruciating pain shot through me. She led me deeper into the water. I felt the currents pushing against my legs, trying to sweep me off my feet. Carla held me steady. She drew me closer and wrapped her arm around my shoulder. *We must do this quickly. There is not much time before Basarab has to leave.* I wanted to ask what she meant by 'not much time before

Basarab has to leave,' but another pain invaded my already weary body. I needed to focus.

I pushed ... again ... and again ... and again! I screamed ... again ... and again... and again! I did not stop to think about why the water was not rushing into my mouth. Suddenly, I felt a sense of release as the child entered the world. Carla was holding my baby. She took a knife from her pocket and cut the umbilical cord. *It's a girl.* She smiled.

As I tried to manoeuvre to a standing position, Carla's foot pushed me back down to the riverbed. This time, as the rocks dug into my back, pain seared through my body. I couldn't move. I watched Carla walk out of the river, toward Basarab and my son. I could not follow. I opened my mouth to scream, but the water rushed in this time, almost choking me. I sputtered. I tried to hold my breath as the water began to flow into my nostrils. What was she doing? Where was she going with my baby? Why had she left me alone?

I watched as she handed my baby to Basarab. He was waiting for her, with a pink blanket in his hands, as though he knew I would be giving birth to a girl this time. He wrapped the baby in the blanket and then crouched down so that Santan could see his new sister. I saw the smile on their faces. Santan pointed to the water, in my direction. I saw Basarab shake his head. He took hold of Santan's hand, and together they turned and began to walk away. I struggled, but still couldn't move. My head was spinning from lack of oxygen. I watched as Basarab climbed the hill to the main trail, disappearing with my son, with my daughter.

Carla was still standing on the shore. She was staring in my direction, her face contorted with evil. She waved her arms in the air, and the water started to bubble. I broke free from the river's hold on me and floated in the choppy water. Then, I noticed the blood—crimson—flowing from me, mixing with the river's foam—turning it pink. The last image I saw, before the current swept me away, was Carla's open mouth—and fangs. She was laughing. Or was that a howl?

The water cast me into a swirling tunnel of black and red. As darkness closed around me, I heard the sound of my son's voice, faintly on the river breeze. *It's okay, Mama, don't worry. Papa will look after me and my baby sister!*

~

I awoke dripping wet, as though I had just crawled out of the river, for real. Santan was crying. I staggered off the couch and into the bathroom and splashed my face with water. I glanced at my reflection in the mirror. Dark circles held my eyes captive. My face appeared drawn, older than my years. I leaned on the sink for a moment, before going to my son.

Another week flew by. Each night was tormented by the same dream, however there were slight variations. Sometimes Teresa was there with Basarab, and she and Carla mocked me as they had their little tête-à-têtes. And then, they would go off with Santan and the baby girl, only my children were no longer babies; they were toddlers, podgy and hearty looking, romping on the river's shore. The dreams always came to me in the evenings, when the stars twinkled in the sky and the moon shone down on his domain.

Basarab, domineering and as omnipotent as always, was the only constant in my dreams. One night the dream began with *him*, walking with me—alone…

I was leaning against him. He had his arm around my shoulders and he was carefully manoeuvring me around obstacles on the pathway. We were talking, just as we had done at *The House*. He laughed when I got too serious, and then he would hug me closer to him—to the beat of his heart? Basarab leaned over and whispered something in my ear. I smiled and nodded. He led me deeper into the woods, to a small clearing layered with pine needles. He removed his cape, spread it on the ground, and then turned to me.

It has been too long, Virginia darling, much too long. How I have missed you! I heard the excitement and expectation in his voice. My blood heated up. I could feel the flush of it in my cheeks. I slipped my sandals off and stepped onto his cape, sinking my toes into the silkiness of the material. My fingers were shaking as I began to unbutton my blouse. I could feel the baby moving within me, dancing. Basarab reached out to me, taking my hands in his. He kissed my fingers, lingeringly. *Let me.* He continued to undo the buttons, from where I had left off, and then slipped the blouse off my shoulders, letting it fall to the ground. *Beautiful!* His voice choked with emotion. He unclasped the hooks on my bra. It joined my blouse.

Basarab stepped back and stared at me. I noticed his rising passion. He stripped his shirt off and threw it to the ground. I could feel the anticipation burning in my veins. It had been so long since I had been in his arms, since we had been one. Memories rushed back to me, pleasurable memories. I had forgotten about the way he had left me on the floor that long ago night. Basarab slid my skirt down, over my hips, dropping it to the cape. Then he fell to his knees and rested his head on my belly. I felt the baby kick in the spot where its father was resting. I saw the smile on Basarab's face. I felt his hands caressing me, gently, before they guided me down onto the cape—onto the forest floor.

He removed his trousers and then nestled in close to me. *I will not hurt you, will I, Virginia darling? I know it is almost time for the birthing. I can wait, if I must.* At that point, my body was screaming for him to consume it. I drew the count to me—into me. Time left us alone, temporarily, as though it knew it had been too long, and we needed to rediscover our passion for each other. There were no other sounds in the forest; quiet had taken over, leaving us to our lovemaking. How I burned for him! How I wanted this moment to be my never-ending story.

The sun was just beginning to rise when he finally released me from his arms. If I were a cat, I would have been purring. Actually, I think I was. *It is time, Virginia.*

Time for what?

Time for the birthing. Come, let me take you to Carla; she will look after you now. Basarab helped me to my feet. He drew my skirt back onto me, and then handed me my blouse. As I fasten the buttons, he donned his clothing, then picked up his cape and shook the pine needles from it. Once again, Basarab placed his arm around me, and then led me out of the clearing. As we walked, I felt the birth pains working their way through my stomach and my back. I lost my balance several times, but his arms were there, always, keeping me from falling to the ground.

Basarab guided me down to the river's edge. Carla was waiting, a smile on her face as she reached for my hand. Santan was playing on the shore. Teresa was with him, but she was watching me, her face void of expression. Carla led me into the water. The blood in my veins froze. What a difference a few moments could make!

The labour pains became intense. I stumbled. He was not there to catch me this time. I plunged into the water. Carla's hands were there, though, but something was terribly wrong. I realized that she was not helping me. She was pushing me down ... down ... into the murky depths, until I could no longer open my mouth to protest. She reached inside me and pulled the baby from my womb. There was no umbilical cord tying the child to me! Then she stood and walked away with my child. She was laughing—I think—it was hard to tell, because the laughter was drowned out by the echoes of howling wolves—a large male—and a pup. I saw no more. As usual, the river water swept me away.

~

I awoke to the telephone ringing. "Hello?" My voice was hoarse, as though I had been crying. I wiped my hand across my cheek—it was damp.

"Virginia? Is that you? Did I catch you sleeping?" Adelaide's voice came over the line.

I sat up. "Yes, but it's okay; I need to get up, anyway. Santan will be up soon, wanting his supper."

"I have some good news for you." Adelaide sounded excited. "I am taking the next plane to Toronto. Alfred and I discussed the situation, and he feels I should be with you for the birth of the child."

"Alfred said that?" I was surprised.

"He is not as crusty as he would have people believe," Adelaide laughed. "In fact, he is quite taken with you." She paused. "I have another surprise for you, but for that, you will have to wait until I get there."

"That isn't fair, Adelaide. I need to hear something good right now."

"What is the matter, child?"

"Dreams, Adelaide—constant dreams. They always end the same, no matter how beautiful they begin, they become nightmares! Without fail, Basarab walks away with my children. And Carla is in league with him, too. In one dream she even had fangs!" I paused. "Is there something about her that I should know?" I tried to say my last sentence with a hint of humour, but I don't think it came across that way to Adelaide because there was a moment of silence on the line.

Finally, Adelaide answered. "No, there is nothing you need to know about Carla that you don't already know. I hope you don't think for a moment that she would ever hurt you!" I detected the shocked tone in Adelaide's voice.

"Of course not; these are just bad dreams I am having." I was quick to try to put right what I might have insinuated about Carla. "Carla has been nothing but good to me over the past few months," I added. I realized Adelaide's first loyalty would lay with the girl that she considered her daughter, not with me, the newcomer.

"Good. Well, I need to finish packing; I shall see you tomorrow. Alfred and I will take a shuttle from the airport." Adelaide hung up the phone.

I leaned back on the couch and watched the baby dance in my stomach. Boy or girl, it was a strong baby. Sometimes I thought it was going to kick right through my skin! I stroked my belly, wondering what it would be like if Basarab were here to hold me, as he had done when I was pregnant with Santan. He had always caressed my belly, and he had talked to his son, and then he would take me in his arms and make love to me. I drew in a deep breath. The shudder that I gave off startled me, as did the tears that ran down my cheeks.

A knock interrupted my thoughts. I wiped the tears away, grabbed hold of the arm of the couch, and struggled to pull myself up. As I lumbered to the door, I was thinking that I just couldn't wait until this pregnancy was over—until I held my child in my arms. It would be my child, mine alone. I still hoped, despite my dreams. I even prayed for it. Sometimes, I prayed that the count would return, so that he could look after us all.

Randy was just about to knock again, when I opened the door. He was standing there with a smile on his face and a crock-pot in his hands. "Supper?"

I am famished. "Come on in." I moved aside.

Randy stepped in and set the crock-pot on the counter. He plugged it in and then reached for some plates from the cupboard. "Will Santan be joining us for some real food?"

"Not yet," I answered. "And if he did join us, it probably wouldn't be for something you cooked up," I added with a chuckle.

"Well, you are going to have to get him eating something soon. You are having another baby, Virginia—any day now. I don't think it's wise, or convenient, to be breast-feeding two babies; you'll never get any sleep!"

"Carla suggested that I feed him as long as possible before I introduced solid foods. Besides, women who have multiple births feed more than one child at a time," I stated matter-of-factly.

"Well, I am no expert on kids, but I still think the time for adding solids is well past," Randy pushed on, "and babies from multiple births are usually the same age."

I was annoyed. Why did he have to question everything? Who did he think he was, anyway? Why couldn't he just leave well enough alone? "Actually, Randy, I really don't think this is any of your business!" It shocked me when I heard the sharpness in my voice, but I plunged on. "You don't have children, so you have no right to criticize me, or give advice! I will listen to my doctor, thank you very much! She is the professional here!" My words hadn't come out exactly as my thoughts had been, but just the same I was sure they stung with the same hostility that I felt. The look on Randy's face confirmed my assumption.

He stepped back, looking confused. "Sorry, Virginia; I didn't mean anything. I was only thinking of you." His voice sounded strained

A little voice, calling out from his room, broke the tension. "Randy! Randy!"

I watched as Randy headed to get Santan. *How I wish my life could be different.* When Randy returned to the kitchen with my son was in his arms. Just looking at the two of them, I knew Randy would be a terrific father one day, maybe even a good husband. He certainly had matured. When I had first met him, he had been dressed in faded ripped jeans and a heavy metal band t-shirt. His hair had been long and scraggly, and his beard had looked as though it hadn't seen a razor or a comb in weeks. Now, he was wearing a pair of kaki pants, a matching shirt; his hair was trim, and the beard was nonexistent. But deeper in my thoughts, even though Randy would be the one who would be able to give me a normal family life, I was thinking that he would never measure up to the father of my children!

After supper Randy and I retired to the living room to watch a movie. I told him that I had just found out that Adelaide would be arriving the next day. He was happy to hear I would have someone besides Carla with me during the birth. After Randy left, I fed Santan and put him to bed. I didn't want to sleep. I didn't want to dream. I stretched out on the couch and turned on the television.

But I did sleep.

And I dreamed.

And the pain just wouldn't go away!

Chapter Sixteen

I awakened with a severe headache. I stumbled to the bathroom and turned on the water, hoping that a hot shower might help me feel better. As I walked into my room, to get some fresh clothes, I heard Santan playing in his crib—*so much for my shower*. I returned to the bathroom and shut the water off.

After breakfast I changed the bedding on my bed, getting it ready for Adelaide's visit. I was relieved she was coming, but was curious about what her surprise was. Santan was being cooperative, playing in his playpen. I turned the television on for him; the early morning children's programs seemed to keep him occupied. I slipped into the bathroom for my shower, leaving the door open so that I could still keep an eye on my son.

Carla called before lunch to enquire how I was feeling. She mentioned that one week wasn't long; the baby could arrive any time. I told her I was feeling OK, and then mentioned that Adelaide was coming.

"I know." Carla sounded excited. "It will be good to see her again. I didn't get to see her when she was here with you last time; I was away at a seminar."

"You must miss her."

"Very much. She saved my life ... then gave me a new one." Carla paused briefly. "You wouldn't mind if I dropped in this evening, would you? I would love to see Adelaide, and I think I should make sure everything is set up and ready for the baby's arrival."

"No problem. Would you like to come for supper? I can order out."

"That would be nice, thank you, but I will probably eat before I come over. I'll see you around seven." Carla hung up.

I wondered why Carla didn't want to have supper at my place. In fact, I mused, she had never actually *ever* eaten any food when she had stopped in to check on me and Santan she drank lots of coffee, but never ate any food. I envisaged my dreams of Carla standing on the shore, laughing at me, fangs protruding from her mouth. I had never witnessed the count or Teresa drinking coffee, but maybe Carla had been *turned* recently and could still tolerate such beverages.

There was something else that had begun to bother me, too, especially since Carla had entered my dreams in such an *unnatural* manner. I wondered if the vitamins that she had so conveniently provided me with were a mixture that would produce blood in my milk. Was Carla working against me?—with Basarab and Teresa? I rationalized that Emelia wouldn't know about this possible liaison. However, if Carla was in league with the count, then wouldn't he know of my whereabouts by now? If he did know where I was, maybe he was just biding his time, looking after affairs in Transylvania, knowing that I wouldn't be going anywhere that he could not find me when he was ready to. My mind churned with questions—questions, but no answers. I felt as trapped now as I had felt when I was a prisoner in *his* house.

A knock on the door startled me. I looked at my watch, noting that it was almost noon. To my surprise, there were three people standing on the sidewalk. One of them was wearing a burqua, and a large pair of sunglasses. My heart skipped a beat … *it can't be*!

"Emelia!" I cried out, and then fell into her arms as she opened them to me.

When I finally looked at my other guests, I saw the grins on their faces. Adelaide motioned to the door: "Are you going to invite us in?"

We stepped into my apartment. I noticed they only had one suitcase with them. "Are you not all staying here?"

"Alfred and I have taken a room at a hotel," Adelaide informed. "We know that you do not have much room here, and we did not want you sleeping on the couch in your condition. Besides, we thought you might like to have some alone time with Emelia. I am sure she has a great deal to fill you in on."

Emelia took her head covering off. "You keep it quite dark in here," she noticed.

"Yes, Santan still cannot tolerate the sun," I pointed out.

Emelia turned to Alfred. "Alfred, could you be a dear, I left my other bag on the backseat of the car. It has my *supplies* in it."

Alfred nodded and left to get Emelia's bag.

I looked at Adelaide. "I am glad Alfred came with you ... it is nice to see him again."

"He wanted to see Santan," Adelaide beamed. "It is as though that child has breathed some life back into my brother," she added.

Emelia approached me. "You look well. I can see that Carla has been taking good care of you." She paused. "Now, where is my little nephew?"

As though on cue, Santan started to holler from his playpen. "Mama! Mama!"

Emelia clapped her hands and laughed. "He sounds just like his father, when he was little, only Basarab used to say, Auntie! Auntie!" Emelia headed into the living room. I followed close behind and was amazed when I saw my son reach his arms up to her. She rewarded his gesture by picking him up. I was even more surprised when he put his arms around her neck and kissed her on the cheek.

Adelaide and Alfred entered the room. Alfred was grinning from ear to ear. "The little fellow has grown." He turned to Emelia. "I put your case in the refrigerator."

"Thank you, Alfred."

"Would you like some lunch … tea or coffee?" I asked my guests.

"Lunch would be nice," Adelaide replied. "But please don't bother too much; Alfred and I are not fussy, as you already know."

From the kitchen, I could hear Emelia and Adelaide talking, but I couldn't make out what they were saying. I glanced into the living room, and was shocked to see Alfred sitting on the floor playing with Santan. There seemed to be something different about Alfred this visit, an informality that hadn't been present in his first visit. I wondered if maybe he had met someone special and fallen in love. This change couldn't just be all about Santan.

Carla phoned after lunch. "Hey there, Virginia, I'm just checking in to see if Adelaide has arrived safely."

"Yes, we just finished lunch; would you like to speak to her?"

"Please."

I handed the phone to Adelaide. She took it into the living room. When she returned she told us that she and Alfred would be having supper with Carla later, and that Carla would be stopping by to check on me beforehand. Adelaide said that she would return in the morning.

Carla arrived mid afternoon and examined me. "Won't be long," she commented as she folded her stethoscope and placed it in her bag. "The baby has already dropped into position. I think I might hang around in Brantford for the next few days, just in case." She turned and addressed Adelaide: "That will give us more time together. I'll give my secretary a call and have her reschedule my appointments; I don't believe any of them are urgent."

"That would be nice. I do miss having you around." Adelaide looked pleased at the prospect of spending time with Carla.

As Carla was preparing to leave, I remembered my concern about Santan's eating. "I am wondering when I should start giving Santan real food. With my condition, I would have thought I should already have weaned him. It might prove difficult, shuffling an infant and a toddler for meals."

Carla looked at me, a quizzical expression on her face. "I am so sorry, Virginia; I thought we had already put Santan on solid foods. By all means, get him started. From the looks of all those teeth, he won't have any problems chewing." With that statement, she headed out the door.

Well, thank you very much! Just land that on me and then walk out—no great physician's words of advice for the inexperienced mother! I observed Carla walk to her car. When she reached it, she swivelled around, looked back, and smiled. *Were those elongated teeth caressing her bottom lip?* I shook my head and tried to refocus. *Must have been mistaken*; her teeth appeared normal now. I watched as Carla drove away, and then I returned to the living room where my other guests were congregated.

After a couple of hours, Adelaide announced that it was time for her and Alfred to be on their way to the hotel. Emelia mentioned that she was tired and would like to lie down. She went to the refrigerator, took a bottle from her container, and then retired to the room I had prepared for her.

With everyone gone their separate ways, and with Santan sleeping in his playpen, I decided to lie down. I was eager to hear news of happenings in Transylvania, especially news about Basarab, but it would have to wait until Emelia had rested. I closed my eyes...

I was in a big house. It was dishevelled. I walked through the rooms, stepping gingerly around the broken furniture. There was a familiarity to the rooms, but in my dream, it was vague. I noticed a long, winding staircase looming in the centre of the foyer, beckoning me toward it. I cautiously tested the first few steps, making sure they were safe. Other than a few squeaks as I ascended, they held. I gazed around when I reached the top, searching for something, but I was not sure what.

Virginia darling, is that you? I thought you would never come back to me. I have been waiting so long for your return into my arms. The voice was soft—musical. I spun around and walked down the hallway, toward the room from where the voice was coming. The door was shut, but not latched. I pushed it open. Dust particles danced in the air, disturbed by the movement. I stepped inside.

Hello? Are you in here? I called out.

I heard a scuffling noise coming from one of the corners. I turned toward the sound and noticed a large shadow crouching there. Slowly, the shadow rose. At its full height, it rotated and faced me. *Ah, Virginia darling, how you have made me suffer. Why did you leave me? Why did you take my son from me? You were both my life—what I lived for. Teresa could not hold a candle to you, my love. It was only a matter of time before I would have cast her to where she should be. You were the one who was meant to be my true partner in this world. It was you who gave me a son, and are about to present me with another child! How could you think that I would have abandoned you?*

The count was walking toward me, his arms open, welcoming. I faltered, but for only a moment, before going to him, into his arms. I placed my head on his chest, where his heart beat for *me*? His arms closed around me. He lowered his head and buried his face in my hair. I could hear him breathing in my scent. His fingers massaged my tired back muscles. I moaned and leaned in closer to him, raising my face to gaze into his eyes.

Reality! His eyes were like flames from the fires of hell. There was a smirk on his lips, which had not been there minutes before. He was mocking me. His hold tightened, but now it was not so gentle. Two more shadows appeared from another corner. Why hadn't I noticed them when I had entered the room?

Max ... Teresa ... look, I have recovered our little bird that you so carelessly let fly from your keeping. I don't know what I am going to do about you two—you have both been careless, so many times. Teresa darling, your position in my household is in jeopardy; do you realize that? I don't understand your lack of watchfulness. And Max, have I not been a good master to you; how could you let me down like this? Is Carla the only person I am able to trust—able to depend on? Fetch her for me, Max; it is time for Virginia to present me with my daughter. Teresa, go to Santan's room and sit with him. Do not let him out of your sight. If you lose him, all that you have now, shall be lost to you.

I struggled to free myself from the count's arms. Why was I so foolish, time after time? Had I learned nothing from all my experiences—from all my crushed dreams? The more I strained against the count, the firmer he held me. *You should know by now, dear Virginia, you cannot escape me. You will always desire to seek me out. And, I will always find you—you are mine—to do with as I please!* He threw back his head and an evil howl filled the room.

Carla walked through the door and bowed her head to Basarab. *Is it time, my love?*

I screamed.

~

"Virginia ... wake up, dear!" Emelia was shaking my shoulder. She gathered me into her arms. "Oh my, you poor dear." She held me, comforting me until my tears subsided.

I stayed on the couch while Emelia went into the kitchen, returning a few minutes later with a pot of tea and a teacup. "I thought you might like a hot drink." She sat down beside me. "Now, tell me what is going on with you."

The words gushed from my mouth. I told Emelia about my dreams and my fears. I was hesitant to speak of my feelings about Carla, but when I talked about the dreams with her in them, I just kept going. Emelia didn't interrupt. When was I finished venting, I leaned back and shivered, even though I was not cold.

Emelia reached over and patted my knee. "You have been through so much, my dear, and this pregnancy is just adding to your turmoil, isn't it? I wish I could do more to ease your pain."

"Oh, Emelia, you have already done more than enough! I doubt I would even be alive today, had it not been for your intervention. Santan would be lost to me, too. And despite how difficult it might be to be having a second child, I consider this child a blessing, for I can hope that it will be truly mine, as Santan most likely never will be. As wonderful as he is, I have already noticed some disturbing traits to his personality."

I detected a sorrowful look pass over Emelia's face, as I mentioned the new child being *truly mine*. However, she spoke before I could continue. "Yes, from what you have told me about his connection to *The House*, it is disturbing; although not unrealistic, considering he is his father's son." Emelia walked over to a window. She peeked through the curtain. "I would like to bring you up to speed on what is happening in Transylvania— maybe after supper, if you are up for it."

"I would like that." I almost asked Emelia what she would like to eat, but stopped short as I remembered how she sustained herself. Instead, I said: "Maybe you would like to help me feed Santan; Carla said I could introduce real food to him now. I guess this should have been done sooner, but we both forgot after she told me to keep him on my milk for as long as possible—due to what he is. She felt the transition, once started, would go much smoother."

"I hope it does ... even now." Emelia walked into the kitchen. I followed. Emelia's statement unsettled me.

I prepared puréed oatmeal for Santan, adding some of my breast milk, which I had stored in the refrigerator. When he cried out from his room, Emelia went to get him. "I can feed him if you like, unless you want to be the one to give him his first solid food," she proposed.

I observed Emelia holding my son. My heart surged. How I wished she could stay with me forever. Watching her reminded me how much I missed my own mother, and how she would have been enthralled to have a grandchild to spoil. "No, I think you should be the one; he looks comfortable on your lap. And he might give you less trouble than he would give me," I added. I handed her the bowl of oatmeal and a baby spoon, and then sat down and watched as Santan ate his first meal of solid food. To my surprise, he loved it; he even grabbed the spoon from Emelia and tried to feed himself.

"He is going to be very independent," Emelia commented, "like his father." I thought I detected a wistful note in her voice.

"I am sorry that you are in the position you are in with Basarab, because of me. I cannot imagine how it must hurt."

Emelia didn't look at me as she spoke. "It does not hurt, most of the time. There is so much going on that I barely see my nephew." Emelia finished feeding Santan, while I fixed myself something to eat. I couldn't help thinking that she was lying to me—I knew it hurt—a lot.

~

Later that evening, after Santan settled, Emelia and I retired to the living room, and she brought me up to speed on what was occurring in Brasov. I began to wonder if the family had any regard for human lives. I felt that I should start being more careful of everything I said and did, even around Emelia. I also thought it might be a good idea for me to stash away some of the money Emelia was sending, in case there came a time when I needed to get away quickly.

Emelia laid her hand on my knee. "Are you okay, dear?"

Her question returned me to the present moment. "Yes ... yes," I nodded, and then stood. "I think I should check on my son."

Santan was still asleep. I gazed into his crib, taking in the sweetness of his expression. I ran my fingers, ever so lightly, through his mass of curly hair. I breathed in his scent—his sweet scent—no hint of death. My son was very much alive! He stirred. I watched him for a few more seconds and then left the room.

"Santan must have enjoyed his supper," I said as I reentered the living room. "He's still sleeping."

Emelia was standing by the window, again, gazing out into the night. She turned and smiled. I caught a glimpse of her fangs. "Yes, I was amazed at how well he took to food. I hope that will continue." She returned to the couch and sat down.

That was the second time that Emelia had been hesitant about Santan taking to solid foods. It bothered me enough to ask: "Is there a chance it might not?"

"Time will tell." Emelia cleared her throat. I noticed her fidgeting with the lace on the sleeves of her dress. She appeared agitated.

"Is there something bothering you, Aunt Emelia?"

"No ... I guess I am just tired. All this talking about the family troubles has unsettled me. Sometimes I think there will be no end to it; and, if the end does come, it will not be good for those of us who have tried to live unobtrusively in your world. Basarab is feeling the strain of it all, the loss of his son and the turmoil we are embroiled in; I can tell when I observe him. He has taken to leaving the hotel at night, seeking solace on the streets. On a couple of occasions, I bumped into him upon his return. There was a smouldering fire in his eyes. I fear that he will get caught doing something he should not be doing, something he has not done for many years. I notice more and more how he leans upon the strength of his father. Atilla has always been so strong and wise. Many times I have wished Tanyasin had cursed my brother-in-law with the throne, instead of my nephew."

"We don't have to talk any more tonight, then. Besides, I am feeling tired, too, and a bit queasy. I think I'll grab a glass of water and a nap. Is there anything I can get for you?"

Emelia shook her head. "No, I am fine; thank you, dear." Emelia retired to my room.

Chapter Seventeen

Despite how poorly I felt, as soon as my head hit the pillow, I drifted off into my land of dreams…

I was in a large room with stark white walls. I was standing beside a bed, also white, with bleach-white bedding. Santan was in the middle of the bed, lying on his stomach. He was wearing a white suit. He was flipping through the pages in a book; however, the book was nothing but blank pages. I turned around, slowly, searching for windows—for a door—for a way out, should I need one. All I saw was frosty-white walls.

Santan raised his head. *Mama, come read to me.* His voice was commanding, like his father's. I smiled, and then sat on the edge of the bed and picked up his book. He clambered onto my lap and snuggled against my chest. I flipped through the pages; as I suspected, they were blank. Santan giggled. *Just tell me a story, Mama.*

As I began to speak, the words I voiced appeared on the empty pages. Santan's eyes grew wide with wonder. *It's a magic book, Mama!* He squealed in delight. I continued telling the story—a story of a young, handsome prince who ruled his kingdom with wisdom and compassion. And the words continued to script across the pages. Pictures also appeared, periodically, at will. The prince resembled Santan, with only a hint of Basarab in the young eyes and the finely chiselled features.

Suddenly, I sensed another presence in the room. I looked up, into the count's eyes. He was smiling. Santan looked up. *Papa! Papa!* He cried joyously, as he leapt into his father's arms. Basarab easily caught his son and hugged him close. Santan smothered his father's face with kisses. *I have missed you so much, Papa! Why do you stay away? Don't you love me?*

Basarab gazed down at me; I noticed the look in his eyes—menacing. But his moment of warning passed quickly. He returned his attention to Santan. *Your papa is a very important man; I have much business to attend to; unfortunately, it keeps me away from you. I am trying to fix things so that you can come and live with me.* Basarab looked directly at me again.

What about my mama … can she come too?

Maybe.

I want her to live with us.

No promises. Basarab sat on the edge of the bed, his leg brushing against mine. My body tingled at his closeness. He reached for the book. *What a handsome little prince—he looks just like you, Santan!* Santan giggled. Basarab continued with the story, from where I had left off. The words and pictures continued to inscribe on the pages. A distinguished king appeared on the page, and he bore a remarkable likeness to Basarab. That picture was followed by other individuals, all of whom looked familiar to me. Why was he destroying my story? Was there nothing in my life that he wouldn't contaminate? I began to back away from the count and my son, allowing them their special moments together.

I reached the edge of the bed and stepped off onto the cold stone floor. My head began to spin, or was it the room that was spinning? Everything became cloudy. Grey clouds, smelling like smoke, choked me. I was drawn into a tunnel of swirling mist. I couldn't catch my breath as I was propelled deeper into a world void of colour. The pain, as I landed on something hard, blasted through me. I cried out, and my body doubled over. I managed to look up, just long enough to see that I was alone in a barren wasteland. I tried to stand, but my body was stuck to the ground.

Let me help you. I recognized the voice—a woman's. Adelaide appeared before me. She was smiling, but it was a peculiar smile, not like her usual one. It was more like the smiles on the faces of the women in the pictures in *The House.*

Adelaide. I choked out her name.

Come, my dear. Adelaide helped me to a standing position. We walked. A bed appeared in the middle of the harsh environment. Standing beside the bed was Carla, in a starch-white nurse's uniform. She was smiling peculiarly, too. In the distance, I detected a small group of people, but I couldn't clearly see their faces. Another pain battered my body. Adelaide prevented me from falling to the ground.

Suddenly, I was lying on the bed, and pillows were being shoved under my shoulders—by whom, I could not tell. Carla's hands were on my stomach. *It is almost time, Virginia; your baby is about to be born.* She disappeared, momentarily, returning with the people that had been gathered in the distance. I gasped for breath! *No! Not again! This baby is different!* They shouldn't be here; I didn't want them here. They had no right to be here this time! I opened my mouth to scream at them—to tell them to leave me alone.

Then, my eyes centred on *him.* He was holding our son, talking to him, pointing to me, smiling. I relaxed, until another pain rocketed through me. Carla was bustling about. She went to the end of the bed and pushed a button; the end dropped down. She caught my legs, just in time, and placed my feet into the waiting stirrups. Someone's hands were holding me upright. The pain that was assaulting my body intensified to an intolerable throbbing. I noticed a circle of bodies forming around the bed, and the chanting began. Carla was busy examining me. I noticed her head shaking, and a look of concern on her face. She motioned to one of the men in the circle. As he stepped forward, I recognized him—Count Balenti, the doctor who had delivered Santan. Carla whispered something to him, and then he examined me, too. He stood back and nodded his head.

I was correct then? Carla.

Yes, you will have to turn the baby, or we will lose it. Have you ever done this before? Balenti.

Only on a dummy when I was in medical school; but, I should be OK. You are here, right, if I need assistance? Carla.

Count Balenti nodded and returned to his place in the circle. I wanted to cry out and ask what was wrong with my baby. Nothing could go wrong with this one ... I couldn't lose it ... this one would be *my child*. Something invaded my body— Carla's hand. Water poured from me, soaking the bedsheets. The hand continued to move inside me. I didn't think I could ever have imagined such pain. Other hands held my shoulders down on the bed. Basarab stood at my side, still holding our son. Santan's eyes were wide open, but I could not tell whether he was afraid or amazed. I felt something turning within me. I closed my eyes, trying to block the pain as I attempted to force the intruder from my body.

Do not push! Carla.

It won't be long, now. Basarab.

I love you, Mama. Santan.

I experienced a sense of release as Carla withdrew her hand. Then, I was lifted off the bed and carried out of the wasteland, and into a beautiful oasis of lush green plants and trees. There was an abundance of flowers blooming all around. I was lowered into a warm, bubbling pool of water ... down ... down ... until only my shoulders and head were protruding. It was so comforting—until the contractions began again, in earnest.

Carla stepped into the pool. Once again, she pushed my legs into a bent position. I lost track of time as the pulsating pain continued, without a moment's relenting. The chanting in the background was no longer an issue for me. I was losing all sense of surrounding, all strength to carry on. I was losing … just losing...

I could hear a baby crying—loud and insistent.

~

"Virginia! Wake up!" Emelia was shaking my shoulder.

Santan was sitting in the doorway of his room, crying. I tried to sit up, but a sharp pain prevented me from moving. I felt as though I was sitting in a pool of water.

"I have called Carla," Emelia informed me. "She should be here any minute now. It is good that she is still visiting with Adelaide and Alfred at the hotel."

My stomach tightened. It was time. But it was too early! I wasn't ready yet.

Emelia picked Santan up and he stopped crying immediately. "I'll give him some breakfast," she said, leaving the room.

I didn't want to be left alone; but, I knew that my son needed to be tended to. I was in no condition to look after him. A few minutes later, I heard the kitchen door open; Carla rushed into the living room. Quickly and efficiently, she examined me. I looked up and saw Adelaide standing in the doorway. Carla nodded to her. Adelaide hurriedly walked away. I heard the kitchen door open and shut again—then again. Carla left the room, telling me that she would be right back. I was to try to relax and breathe through my contractions.

I had no idea how much time had passed. All I knew was that it was filled with pain. Carla and Adelaide aided me up from the couch and steered me toward the pool that had been set up in the middle of the room. Steam was floating over the water. Carla supported me as Adelaide stripped my clothes off. I shivered as they guided me into the pool.

As I sank into the water, its warmth swathed me, soothing my tired muscles. Carla stepped into the pool and dropped down to her knees. She pushed gently on my legs until they were in a bent position. I felt Carla examining me. There was a worried look on her face when she looked up at Adelaide.

"Is something wrong?" I heard Adelaide ask.

"The baby is breech. I don't know how this could have happened. It had already turned a couple of weeks ago. I thought this was going to be an easy birthing for Virginia." Carla was shaking her head.

I panicked. *Had I not just dreamed this*? I looked around for the *others*. They weren't there—only Adelaide, Emelia, and Santan were in the room.

Carla stepped out of the pool and approached Emelia. "I think you should take the child to Randy. I am going to need you and Adelaide to help me with this birth." Emelia nodded. She disappeared into Santan's room, returning a few minutes later with his diaper bag.

I had no idea how long I had been in the pool, trying to give birth to my child, but I knew the pain I experienced was real. I was not dreaming anymore. I had never felt so exhausted, and I kept praying for it to end sooner rather than later. The pain, as Carla worked to turn the baby, was excruciating. I thought I heard Carla express the baby was in position; I think I prayed that I had heard correctly. I heard her tell me to keep breathing through the contractions. I felt someone wiping the sweat from my forehead. Someone poured hot water into the pool. I was breathing—panting—wishing for something to ease my discomfort. Someone in the room was crying; I realized it was me. Someone turned on a radio. Classical music floated through the air. It didn't reduce the pain, but it calmed me—a bit.

"One more big push." Carla tried to keep me focused. "Come on, Virginia; it's almost over."

I pushed again. From where my strength came, I had no idea. I experienced a sense of relief as my body expunged its burden into the water. Carla worked furiously with what I assumed was my baby. Emelia was holding me, under my arms, to keep me from slipping under the water. I felt drained of strength. I noticed Adelaide standing beside Carla, a large white towel spread open in her hands. Carla was lifting something from the water and passing it to Adelaide.

I heard a cry! Not a whimper, but a strong, demanding wail. I attempted a smile.

"It's a girl!" Carla exclaimed.

"Look at those red curls!" Adelaide sighed.

"Like her mama," Emelia smiled.

"Did Virginia have a name picked out yet?" Adelaide enquired.

"Not that she mentioned," answered Emelia.

I closed my eyes, losing all sense of the moment.

~

"Okay sleepyhead, wake up. This child is searching for its first meal." Carla was shaking me gently. I could hear the baby fussing.

My eyes fluttered open, and I looked up. I was in my own bed. Emelia must have moved her belongings to Santan's room. She and Adelaide were standing at the end of my bed; they looked concerned. They both sighed with relief when they saw that I was awake.

"Would you ladies like to help Virginia to sit up," Carla directed.

Once I was in a sitting position, Carla handed me my daughter. She reached over and untied the ribbon on the nightgown that someone had dressed me in. She pushed the material aside, revealing one of my full breasts, and then helped me guide the baby to the nipple. I tensed, as a picture of what had happened the night Santan was born sprang to my mind. *There is no possible way that I will produce a mixture of milk and blood this time, is there?*

"Relax, Virginia. Here, this might help so you don't have to hold the full weight of the child." Carla placed a large pillow under the baby. She smiled. "She is a healthy baby girl, and strong too. She weighs eight pounds, ten ounces. And what a set of lungs she has!"

"Have you chosen a name?" Adelaide asked.

I had thought of a few names, keeping them to myself until I saw whether the baby was a boy or a girl; but, I didn't want to make a final decision until I spent some time with the baby. "Not yet," I finally replied.

"A hint?" Emelia prodded.

I winced as the baby pulled extra hard on my nipple. "No … not yet." I relaxed as she settled into a rhythmic sucking. I noticed the disappointed looks on the faces of the two elderly women. Suddenly, I realized someone was missing. "Is Santan still with Randy? And where is Alfred?"

Emelia was first to respond. "Oh my, we have forgotten all about the child; I do hope Randy is not having any problems!"

"Santan loves Randy," I quickly enlightened, in order to alleviate Emelia's fears. "If he has problems, I am sure he would have been knocking on the door by now. However, if one of you could get Santan, I would like to introduce him to his little sister."

"I'll go," Adelaide offered. "Alfred is with Randy, so I am sure between the two of them, they have been able to handle that sweet child." She paused. "What if Alfred and Randy want to come along, too?" Adelaide asked as she was leaving. "Are you ready for that many visitors?"

I sighed. "That will be fine."

A few minutes later, Santan bounced into the room, with Randy and Alfred right behind him. They all wore big smiles. Alfred hung back in the doorway, but when Randy saw the baby, he stopped short in his tracks and let out a long, low whistle. "If I didn't know better," he exclaimed, "just looking at that baby, one might think she was my daughter! Look at those red curls!"

I laughed. The baby jumped—startled—and began to cry. I settled her down. "Of course, my curly red hair doesn't have anything to do with that?" I looked at Randy and smiled. I noticed the uneasiness on the faces of the three women in the room. I wondered if they might be considering the possibility that this child was not Basarab's! I looked over at Alfred; he was just standing there with a smile still plastered on his face.

"She's beautiful," Randy commented as he reached down and picked Santan up. "Want to see your baby sister, buddy?"

"Baby sis'er; baby sis'er!" Santan kicked his legs excitedly. Randy set him on the bed, and he crawled up and cuddled beside me. He reached out his hand and stroked his sister's hair. "Nice baby sis'er," he said.

The baby paused in her feeding. It appeared as if she turned and looked at her brother. She gurgled contentedly.

"Santan is going to be a wonderful big brother," Alfred remarked.

~

Later that evening, the subject of the baby's name cropped up again. I had not yet fully decided on the name, but there was one on the tip of my tongue when Emelia asked me a second time. It was out of my mouth before I could stop it.

"Samara."

Emelia beamed. "That is beautiful, and it is Hungarian, too. It is a strong name and has the strength of God behind it. Samara—*mountain—ruled and guarded by God.* It also means *seedling,* and that is what she is, isn't she?" There was an added element of excitement in Emelia's voice when she spoke of

Basarab's child, confirming that this child was *his*, no matter the possibility that Randy had previously insinuated.

As Emelia related the meaning of the name I had chosen, foreboding crawled over me. *Seedling—his seedling!* I began to remember the curse that had been written in Atilla's journal—*to you and all your blood is this curse cast upon, from now until eternity!*

I gazed down at my newborn child's head, at her mass of red curls. I gazed over at Randy who was sitting on a nearby chair. Why couldn't he have been Samara's father? What chance did my child have; really, not to join her brother in the family to which they had been born? What hope was there for Samara? Probably no more than there was for Santan! I knew that now.

Defeat was a difficult thing to bear.

A tear slid down my cheek.

No one noticed.

I was alone.

Chapter Eighteen

The next week was a blur to me. Somehow, I had developed a fever. I had vague memories of those hours—of people coming and going from my room—of a baby sucking greedily from my breast—of a little voice calling me mama—of cool cloths being applied to my forehead—of a curly redhead smiling at me—of an elderly woman, two, I think—of an efficient younger woman—all coming and going—going and coming...

~

Seven days after the birth of my daughter, the fever broke. I opened my eyes and saw a shadow sitting in a rocking chair near my bed. It was slouched in an awkward position. One long leg was slung precariously over the arm of the chair, and the other leg was stretched full-length to the floor. The head of the shadow was pillowed on a shoulder. I sat up in my bed; the shadow stirred. Stretched. Readjusted to an upright position. Stood. Walked toward me. Randy.

"What are you doing here?" I couldn't think of anything else to say and I hoped my question hadn't sounded too harsh.

A familiar grin greeted me. "Welcome back, Virginia." He paused briefly. "You are back, aren't you?" His brow creased worriedly.

I managed a smile. "Have I been away?"

"Sort of."

"I thought I heard voices in here." Emelia walked into the room. She was holding a baby in her arms—mine? She smiled when she noticed that I was sitting up in bed. "Ah, Virginia," she uttered as she handed me the baby. "Samara is about ready for another meal. She certainly is a ravenous child."

"If I have been *gone*," I hesitated, not knowing if I should ask—"how did I manage to feed the baby?"

"We brought her to you," Emelia responded. "Of course, you were unaware of most of what was going on, but Carla said we needed to ensure that you fed the child, so your milk would not dry up. Adelaide and I took turns holding Samara while she fed."

My mind began to clear. "How did I eat?" I raised my concern, before noticing the intravenous in my arm, the pole, and the bag of liquid. "Oh ... I see ... Where is Santan?"

"Still sleeping."

"How is he taking to real food?"

"Well, there have been a few *moments*," Emelia looked concerned. Or, was it an apprehensive look, as if she were considering whether to tell me more about the *moments*?

"Like what?" I prodded.

"He has been throwing up some of the food we tried to feed him. It appears that he is more tolerant of foods with a liquidly consistency. But Carla says not to worry too much, yet. She realizes, now, that she should have introduced the solids earlier. We will know better with Samara."

Samara began to tug at my nightgown, searching for the treasure it concealed from her. I undid enough buttons to reveal my breast. Samara didn't hesitate a moment more. She latched on greedily. I felt the milk letting down. She patted my breast with one of her tiny hands. I watched the rhythm of her cheeks, sucking in and out. Were those growls I heard coming from her throat ... like a wolf pup? At least the excess spillage was white ... no trace of blood!

Randy decided to leave the room. "I think I'll check on Santan." On his way out, he avoided looking at me—embarrassed?

Samara cried and pulled angrily on my breast. I switched her to the other side. She settled down as the milk spilled generously into her mouth. "Does she not take a breather?" I looked up at Emelia.

"Not really." Emelia chuckled as she turned to leave. "I think I will give Adelaide and Carla a call and let them know you are awake."

I looked at my child. Why was it that I did not *feel* much emotion for her? I had been waiting so long for this child to be born, but now that she was here all I felt was a vacuum inside me—an ominous sense of loss. *Loss of what?* Samara pulled her mouth off my breast. She stared up at me. I was shocked at what I was staring into. Her eyes were blacker than coal, but the fringes of her pupils blazed a bright red, like jagged flames—the beginning of the fire to come?

I lifted Samara up and placed her on my shoulder, heart to heart. I needed to hear her heart beat against mine. It was there, strong, pounding rhythmically. I patted her back. She burped. At least that was normal. Maybe all was not lost; perhaps I had just imagined the colour of her eyes. I lifted her off my shoulder and took another look. Samara glared at me, eyes wide—no change. I returned her to the burping position and continued patting her back. Once again, disillusionment was casting a steel net around my world.

Emelia returned to the room and informed me that Adelaide and Carla were on their way. I asked if Alfred was still around. She told me that he had returned home; he was sorry he couldn't stay longer. She was to say goodbye to me, for him.

"When will you be leaving, Emelia?"

"Soon."

My heart sank.

"But Adelaide will remain on with you, if you want her to. I must return before Vacaresti becomes too suspicious. He has already contacted me and is wondering what I am doing. It is difficult for me, deceiving my husband the way I have had to." Emelia looked sad.

"Does he know where you are?" I was worried. "And, *how* has he been in contact?" This knowledge worried me—especially if he could trace her here!

"Not exactly," is all Emelia would divulge. She reached out and laid her hand on my shoulder.

I flinched.

"Are you cold, dear? You should not overexert yourself; you have been through so much." Emelia reached for Samara. "Here, let me take the child and change her."

Before I could protest, Emelia took Samara and left the room. I heard Emelia singing in a strange language to my baby. It resembled the chanting I had heard when Santan was born, and when he was *baptized* into the family. I shuddered and pulled the blankets up under my chin. I lowered myself down, turned over, and buried my face into the pillow. The tears came again. From where, I had no idea. I thought all my tears had been shed.

~

Night closed in. After Santan was settled in his bed and Samara was fed and in her cradle, Emelia entered my room and pulled a chair beside my bed. She looked thoughtful.

"I am leaving tomorrow," she spoke with a melancholy tone. "I just received a message from Vacaresti; things are much worse than anticipated. Brasov is overrun with murders and break-ins, and all the fingers are being pointed at *us*. The police have been to the hotel, and they questioned Basarab. Vacaresti mentioned there was more to the story; he would tell me the rest when I returned home." Emelia rose. "I think I will rest now; it is going to be a long trip tomorrow. Carla will drive me to the airport. And, as I mentioned earlier, Adelaide will remain with you for now. After she leaves, Carla will check in regularly." Emelia headed to the door. "You will be well looked after, my dear. I will not desert you. I promise."

Samara began to stir in her cradle. Emelia hesitated in the doorway. "Would you like me to get her for you?"

I nodded.

Emelia placed Samara into my outstretched arms. My daughter looked at me with her fiery eyes. I looked away, still not able to accept that Samara seemed more Basarab's child, than mine. She might have my hair colour, but she obviously had his temperament! She pulled at my nightgown, groping for her meal. Quickly, I undid the buttons on my nightgown and rewarded her.

"You will be okay?" Emelia asked, pausing in the doorway.

"I'll be fine," I affirmed.

After I had finished feeding my daughter, I changed her and laid her in her cradle. I lingered a moment, gazing at her. She stared at me—and smiled? I guessed it was better to think of it as a smile, rather than something sinister. I returned to my bed and crawled under the covers. I noticed the cradle rocking; Samara was fighting sleep. Every so often she whimpered, but soon the room quieted. I closed my eyes...

Ah, Virginia darling, she is beautiful! You have done well. It is good that Santan will have a playmate. And you—you are more radiant than ever! Motherhood suits you. The count was sitting on the edge of my bed, a warm smile on his face. He reached over and stroked my cheek. I leaned into his fingers and breathed in his scent.

Suddenly, Santan was on the bed, jumping excitedly. *Oh, Papa! Have you seen what Mama has given me? A baby sister all of my own!* He jumped into Basarab's arms and threw his little arms around his father's neck. Basarab's laugh filled the room— a joyous sound. Santan was wiggling in his father's arms. Basarab told him to calm down, so as not to wake his baby sister. Santan buried his face in his father's shoulder and giggled. Basarab hugged him closer.

Samara was whimpering. I started to get up. Basarab set Santan on the bed and laid a hand on my shoulder, gently pushing me back onto the pillows. *I will get her.* He walked to the cradle. My eyes drank in the magnificence of his body. What perfection God had created! But, it wasn't really God who had created him, was it?

Basarab gathered Samara into his arms. She crooned to him, reaching a tiny hand to his face. He took hold of her hand and raised it to his lips, brushing it lightly with a kiss. She giggled. I noticed her legs were moving excitedly under the blanket that was wrapped loosely around her. Basarab returned to the bed and placed Samara beside me. She looked at me ... scowled ... returned her gaze to her father ... and smiled. My heart dropped. Basarab laughed.

Santan curled up to his little sister and kissed her cheek. *I love you.* Samara gurgled and grabbed a handful of his hair.

Let your mama feed your sister. Basarab gathered Santan back into his arms. *I will return shortly.*

Bye, Mama. Santan waved to me.

I was alone in the room with Samara. She cried as soon as Basarab and her brother left. Hastily, I picked her up and put her to my breast. Between sobs, she sucked angrily, all the while pounding on my breast with her fist. I could see the fury in her eyes—the fiery ring around the black centre. Teeth chomped down on my flesh. I screamed. Samara laughed. She looked at me and laughed a deep belly laugh. It was then that I noticed the blood. But how could this be?—she was too young to have teeth! Her little tongue flicked out of her mouth and began to lick up the droplets of blood. I had to look away.

I screamed ... a large shadow entered the room ... the bed felt lighter ... voices faded away ... *Bye, Mama!*—two small voices in unison ... one more good-bye ... a voice so velvety—so soothing. *Goodbye, Virginia, my darling ... rest well ... rest well ...*

rest well ... the voice disappeared gradually—leaving me alone in a room, gloomy and cold.

Chapter Nineteen

A delaide stayed with me for the remainder of the month. There had been no word from Emelia since she had left Brantford. This bothered Adelaide and I, because we knew things were not good in Brasov. We also had no way of knowing if Emelia was okay. I often wondered just how Vacaresti had contacted Emelia. If he knew where she was, would he tell Basarab? How deep was his loyalty to his wife? If Basarab discovered just how far Emelia's deception went, would even Atilla be able to stop the wrath that would be unleashed on the beloved aunt?

My apartment felt empty. Randy tried to visit as much as possible, but he had started back to school. Classes and homework took up most of his time. There was still an inseparable bond, though, between him and Santan. Carla mentioned she would stop by periodically to check on me; however, if I needed something right away, I could call the office and leave a message. I couldn't say I was sorry she wouldn't be around too much; in a way, I still had doubts about Carla. My dreams, where she and the count were both laughing at me, played vividly in my mind, even when I was not sleeping.

Santan's speech was becoming amazingly advanced—he never ceased to amaze me. "Where's Randy?" he asked me one day, his little forehead crinkling with worry.

I looked up, startled. "Randy is studying," I answered, not believing my son would understand.

I was even more shocked by Santan's next question. "Why can't he study here?"

"He doesn't live here," I answered warily.

"He should." Santan stomped off to play with his toys. As I watched him leave, I realized that not only were his verbal skills superior, so were his motor skills.

On the other hand, as much as Santan was attached to Randy, Samara wanted absolutely nothing to do with him. Every time Randy tried to pick her up, she screamed. One day, his hand got in the way of Samara's fingernails. She scratched his skin, drawing blood. Randy was too busy shaking out the pain to notice— but I did—I saw the smile on my daughter's face after she licked the speck of blood from her finger!

There were moments, too, when I wondered how Samara felt about me. It seemed as though she only tolerated me long enough to get what she needed—her meals and clean clothes. The rest of the time she was content in her cradle, or to spend time with Santan. When she was fed and clean, but not happy, he was the only one who seemed able to calm her down. Even though her teeth had not yet broken through her gums, she had begun to bite me while feeding. Each time I took her off my breast and told her not to bite, she just looked up at me and smiled— peculiarly—the smile that tormented my dreams.

I was anxious because there was still no word from Emelia. Adelaide emailed me every week, and I could tell from her letters that she was worried, as well. Carla called faithfully, every couple of days, but she never stopped by. Despite my apprehensions about Carla, I missed that female companionship she had periodically provided. I rationalized that she probably figured my health was fine enough now, but I also felt she should be checking on Samara; although, in reality, there couldn't be a healthier child. And, even though I was uneasy about befriending an *outsider*, I often thought of Angel. I wondered what she was up to, what country she might be in, and when she might be back to Brantford. I hoped to have another chance meeting with her.

July arrived. I planned a little celebration for Santan's first birthday. I was still having a difficult time with how highly developed my son's speech and motor skills were. Even if he were a prodigy, he was still way too far advanced. It also appeared that Samara was following in her brother's footsteps—but at an accelerated rate. She was already trying to crawl and pull herself to a standing position. Santan hovered protectively over Samara, encouraging her along the journey of discovery. Randy was constantly amazed when he observed my children's unique abilities.

I continued to walk in the evenings, after the sun set. Much to my frustration, Samara was also showing sensitivity to the sun. One day, while Santan was napping, I decided to take Samara outside. Despite the shade in my backyard, as soon as the sun touched her, she began screaming. I noticed her skin turning a bright pink, and then it bubbled. Quickly, I wrapped the blanket around her and hurried back inside the apartment, my heart beating hard against my chest.

Hope was failing me.

~

Randy was on a school break. He had done well in his courses, and he wanted to celebrate. "Why don't we take a road trip for a few days?" he suggested.

"I don't think that is a good idea."

"Why not?"

"Samara is still too young, so is Santan. Can you see you and me travelling with two babies?"

"Yes." There was a strange look in Randy's eyes. "I can see us doing a lot with two babies—maybe even more than two." He blushed.

Randy's last statement knotted up in the core of my stomach. I deduced I should have expected this subject might crop up again, especially because of the amount of time we spent together. And the door was wide open now, wasn't it, with Randy knowing that I was a widow. What he didn't know was that Basarab, the father of my children, was very much alive and that he would one day be returning to reclaim what was his. Strange as it seemed, I hoped that I would be considered *his*, as well. But my hope was nothing more than a daydream. In the sleep induced dreams, the count always walked away with my children, laughing mockingly. And he always left me behind in a heap of emptiness.

"Earth to Virginia," Randy waved his hand in front of my face.

"Ah ... yes?"

Randy's face took on a look of excitement. "Yes? To the road trip?"

I shook my head fervently, realizing my mistake. "No ... no to the road trip; I just don't think it's a good idea." I spent a couple of moments thinking, before I continued. "What did you mean by *more than two*?"

Randy blushed again. He reached for my hand. His fingers were warm and clammy. His voice shook. "I ... I just thought that maybe ... maybe someday you might consider me more than just the guy who lives at the front of the house."

It was my turn to blush. I felt my body temperature rising. I was hesitant to respond. "I already consider you more than that," I began.

His face brightened, and his fingers tightened on my hand. I pulled away.

"I consider you a friend, Randy. That is all. Just a friend––my best friend."

"We can be more." I noticed the hope in his eyes.

"No. No, we can't." I stood.

Randy stood, too. I hadn't actually taken notice, before, of how tall he was; I barely reached his shoulder. And, he had filled out, too, since I had first met him. He no longer looked like an adolescent. He put his hands on my shoulders and turned me to face him. I could feel anger welling up inside me. *How dare he touch me like this*! I tried to pull away, but he held me fast.

"Would you just stop a minute and listen to me, Virginia." His words had urgency to them. "Your husband is dead! He is not coming back! You need to start thinking about what you are going to do with the rest of your life, about how you are going to raise two kids by yourself. Think about it, Virginia! I am offering to be in your life forever—by your side, helping you to raise Santan and Samara. Santan already loves me; Samara will come around eventually."

I stared into Randy's pressing eyes, tears welling in my own. "You have no idea what you are asking of me."

"I am asking you to be with me, Virginia. Can't you see how much I have changed since we first met? It is because of you and Santan, but especially you. I think I love you!"

"Oh Randy, don't love me, please don't. You don't love *me*—maybe the *idea* of me, but not me. I can't be with you—I can't be with anyone. My life is just too complicated." I realized, too late, what I had said.

"Too complicated?" Randy's eyebrows rose questioningly.

I pried his fingers from my shoulders. He released his grip. I stepped away from him. "I am not ready, Randy. My husband was the love of my life, despite some of the tumultuousness we experienced. Most of that was because of my jealous possessiveness. He was more than I could have dreamed of, and I constantly second-guessed how such a naive girl as I could be his wife, when he could have had anyone. There will never be another man who will be able to fill his shoes." I almost choked on my words, realizing the grain of truth that was in that statement. I still had not been able to erase from my mind the tender moments I had spent with the count. Did that mean he truly was the love of my life? Or, was I just a twisted woman controlled by my lust for the phantom in my dreams? But, he wasn't a phantom, was he? The verification of that had grown inside my belly, and were now a part of my living world!

"I could try," Randy pleaded.

"It wouldn't work." I heaved a heavy sigh. "Believe me, it just wouldn't work."

"I'm not going to give up asking."

"I can't stop you from that, I guess."

"Promise me that you might consider this proposal someday."

"Maybe—someday." I knew I shouldn't give Randy false hope, but I also felt if I didn't give him something he might leave, move away, and I would miss his friendship. Selfishly, I said: "Give it time Randy; my husband has not even been dead a year yet."

Randy nodded. He looked defeated. He glanced at his watch. "I have some errands to run; need anything while I'm out?"

"No thanks."

"Mind if we have supper together tonight? My treat."

Not wanting to let him down any more than I already had, I nodded. "What time?"

"I'll be over at six."

I locked the door after Randy left, and then leaned my back against it and slid down to the floor. The tears started, slowly at first, building their momentum until they poured from the wells of grief within me. Santan came over and put his arms around me. He didn't say a word; he just hugged me. I encircled my arms around him and buried my face in his mass of curls. There was no way that such a loving child could be *his* spawn— no way. I hugged my son closer to me.

An angry cry broke into our special moment, reminding me there was another child in my house. And she was unquestionably developing into what very well was *his* offspring!

~

The evening after Randy's proposal, I decided to take a walk along the D'Aubigny trail again. I was hoping to bump into

Angel. I needed another friend with the way my life was going. I
pulled into a spot at the far end of the parking lot, away from the
few scattered cars that were still there. Santan was excited. I
fastened Samara in her buggy, and with Santan walking by my
side, we headed down the steep hill. When we arrived at the spot
in the path where we had previously met Angel, I paused. Santan
didn't hesitate, though; he plunged down the small foot-beaten
path to the river. I followed him as quickly as possible, arriving at
the river's edge right behind him, despite the difficulty I'd had
manoeuvring the buggy through the weeds that crowded the
passageway.

To my surprise, Angel was sitting on a rock near the
water. She was barefoot, and her feet were dangling in the waves
that lapped on the shore. My breath caught in my throat. How
could I have been so lucky? "Angel?" I approached her.

She smiled. "Why hello, Virginia ... and you too, Santan,"
she added. He ran up to her and hugged her; she tousled his hair.
She stood up and walked toward me. "Who do we have here?"
she asked, leaning over the buggy.

"Samara ... my baby sister!" Santan replied excitedly.

"I see." Angel stood up and faced me. "She is beautiful ...
and just look at all those red curls ... she is going to be a *man
killer*." She laughed softly.

You have no idea ... "I hope not." I joined in her laughter.
I looked around, and then returned my gaze to Angel. "Do you
come here often?"

"Well, since we met here, I come whenever I am home. I
am sorry I missed the birth of your baby; I would love to have
been there for it, but I was lecturing overseas. Did everything go
well for you?—you look fantastic."

I paused. Why not? Why shouldn't I confide in her? I
needed to talk to someone besides Randy. "There were some
difficulties, but the doctor managed. Samara somehow had turned
the wrong way at the last minute, and she had to be manoeuvred

back into the right position. After the delivery, I developed a fever, and I was seriously ill for about a week. I had no idea what was going on. The doctor stopped by to check on me every day; my aunt and her friend persistently stayed at my side. My aunt had to return home, but her friend stayed until the end of May," I rambled on. It felt good to talk about my birth experience.

"You must miss them?" Angel's voice sounded concerned.

"Yes," I breathed. Now that it was mentioned, I realized how much I did miss Emelia and Adelaide, and I had no idea when I would see either one of them again.

Angel laid a hand on my arm. "I understand what it is like to feel alone; I have been alone for a long time." I noticed the faraway look in her eyes. My heart melted. How I wanted to reach out to her.

And then, for some reason I will never know, or understand, I decided to invite Angel to my apartment. My need for female companionship was greater than my need to be shut off from the real world. Angel had been only too happy to visit me, and she followed me home. After the children had fallen asleep, we sat talking until the rays of the sun began to dance through the cracks at the edges of the curtains. When I saw her to the door, I felt so fulfilled—refreshed. She said she would see me again, soon, but she would be out of town for a short time because she had another overseas' lecture.

I watched her car disappear down the lane. And then, I turned to face the reality of my world, hoping that I hadn't relayed anything to Angel that might present a problem for me or my children in the future.

Chapter Twenty

The more time that passed, the more I wondered about how I could protect Santan and Samara against the family. There were fleeting moments, too, when I pondered that maybe it was me who would be in need of protection—unless I became one of them. But that was not a viable option, was it? I kept asking myself, just how far I would be willing to go to remain with my children. I had also reflected on how far I would be *allowed* to go. Once the count returned for his son, what manner of outrage would be inflicted on me when he found out about Samara?

~

I decided to resume my studies, to keep my mind sharp, and prepare for my future. Angel had been instrumental in encouraging me to do so. I revisited our conversation…

"Santan and Samara will grow up and leave the nest, eventually," she had said.

"I know. But that is a long time from now; they are just babies."

"The time will pass quicker than you think."

"You are probably right, but it is difficult for a mother to think along those terms."

Angel had taken hold of my hand. "Still, you should consider it; you will need something to fill your life when it does happen. There are several universities that offer correspondence courses. When the children start school, you could be ready to start looking for work."

At the time, my stomach had curdled with the thoughts of what my children were, and that they would never be able to attend a regular school with normal children. But of course, Angel didn't know anything about that. How could she?

I decided to continue the path I had previously started on when I had been living in Toronto, and I signed up for two courses—Criminal Profiling and Abnormal Psychology.

I had several pages to read before I wrote my next paper, but I was tired, and I knew the children would be waking soon. Well, Samara for sure. She still had an insatiable appetite; whereas, Santan was still trying to adjust to solid foods. Sometimes, I allowed him to take comfort at my breast. It was difficult to watch my child eat, and then throw up what he had just consumed.

I was continually dumbfounded at how mentally advanced my children were for their ages; it was as though centuries of knowledge had seeped into them through their father's seed. Santan loved books, and now he was reading some of the words in the stories, even before I did. I remembered the first time this happened…

"I am going to read the story for Samara today," he said, his words ringing out clearly, his brow wrinkled seriously.

Samara was sitting in a baby chair that I had set beside me on the couch. She started kicking her feet when Santan began to read. Her eyes glowed. Then she opened her mouth and spoke her first word—coherently—"Santan."

"Listen now, Samara!" Santan ordered, and then giggled. The giggle sounded good to my ears, because it was the music of a child of his age. But I wondered, watching him, just how old was Santan, really? How much of the ancientness of his ancestors was in the soul of my baby?

"Me listen," Samara returned and giggled along with her brother.

I had sat there in total shock. Santan should be speaking a few words at his age—but, Samara? No way!

~

I set my books aside, stood up, and stretched. I heard Samara stirring in her bed. My peaceful moments would soon end. I walked into my children's room and was rewarded with two smiles and two sets of arms reaching out to me.

After our supper, we cuddled on the couch, Santan beside me, Samara beside him. That was the way she preferred it. Just as we were about to open a storybook, there was a knock on the door. Santan looked up in expectation. "Randy!"

I headed to the kitchen and opened the door. Randy was standing there with a bouquet of wild flowers in his hand. The flowers looked as though they had been freshly picked from someone's garden; I wondered whose.

"The sun is about ready to go down, m'lady," he began, a sly grin spreading across his face. "How say, m'lady and I and her two beautiful babies take a lovely stroll when the stars come out?"

I had not been making myself or my children so available to Randy since he had opened his heart and confessed his love to me. I felt that his outburst of wanting us to spend the rest of our lives together had been prompted more because of his attachment with Santan, than from his affection for me. I didn't think he was ready for full-time parenthood, let alone becoming a husband. I prayed every day that he would start dating, like a normal young man of his age should be doing. But Randy just kept knocking on my door. I constantly thought about moving; but, I guess I was being a bit selfish—actually, a lot selfish. I was too comfortable and too scared to leave. I felt safe, secluded behind the towering maple trees—away from *his* eyes—for now, anyway.

My heart softened; I opened the door wider. "Come in, Randy. We were just about to read a story to Samara. I think a walk would be lovely, afterward."

Randy followed me into the living room. He turned to me. "Am I to believe what I am seeing here, Virginia?"

I smirked proudly. "Yes, it appears that my son is even more of a genius than we first thought. All the reading I have done with him seems to have been absorbed into his brain, and now he is spewing out words as though he were already in school." I paused, trying to determine how to explain this to Randy so that he wouldn't hammer me with questions.

"Actually," I'd thought of something brilliant—"their father was a genius. I think they both take after him. Samara is also beginning to speak. I almost fell off the couch when I heard her say her brother's name for the first time!" I laughed.

Randy looked shocked. "You're kidding me!"

"Nope, clear as a bell."

Santan stopped reading when he noticed Randy. "Randy! Come and sit with us." Santan patted the sofa cushion.

"No!" Samara screamed. "Samara don't like Randy! Him not Papa!"

Now it was my turn to be shocked. How could she know that? Samara had never met her father! The words I wanted to say froze on my tongue. Randy saved me, by speaking first.

"Wow! It looks and sounds like your kids certainly have drunk from their father's gene pool!"

I stopped short of bursting into laughter when Randy said *drunk from their father's gene pool.* If only he knew.

"What did your husband do for a living?" Randy asked. "I don't believe you ever told me." He paused. "And I don't think you ever told me his name, either." His eyebrows rose enquiringly.

"No … I didn't." I detected the flatness in my statement. What was I supposed to say? I had no idea how Basarab earned his money, and there was no way I was going to tell Randy his name. What if he were to look it up on the Internet and discover that Basarab had been born in the 1400s?

"Well?" Randy didn't seem willing to let the issue go.

I prayed for some divine intervention, so I would not have to answer his questions. I needed time to make up a story, and an untraceable name. I didn't even think, until much later, that I would not have had to give the real name. After all, I was Virginia Casewell, which would most likely mean my husband's last name would have been the same.

Santan came to my rescue. "What is this word, Randy?" Santan shoved the book at Randy, pointing to a word on the page.

Randy looked stunned. He glanced at me. I shrugged my shoulders. He looked down on the page. "Hippopotamus."

Santan giggled. "Hippopotamus," he repeated, annunciating each letter.

"Wow!" Randy gasped in a gulp of air.

I was glad that Randy seemed to have forgotten his questions to me. We listened as Santan finished reading the story. I prepared the children for our walk, putting Samara in her buggy. Santan preferred to walk now, so I put a small children's harness on him.

~

As I lay in bed, later that night, my mind wandered back to Randy's questions. I began thinking of moving again, but to where? I closed my eyes, whispering an appeal to God before sleep overtook me—a plea for just one peaceful night's sleep. My dreams usually never gave me a chance for respite, though. They started out well enough, but the night creatures soon sewed their way into the seams of my mind, knotting themselves off, eliminating all avenues of escape. This night was no exception…

I was standing on an enormous expanse of white sand. The wind was whipping around, disturbing the sand particles from their resting places. Santan and Samara, heavily clothed, were trying to build a sandcastle, but the sand wouldn't bond because it was too dry, and the wind constantly swirled it elsewhere. I looked around, hoping to see water.

Virginia, my love, why have you brought the children to such a desolate place? You should know better—the sun is not good for them! Their skin will simmer.

But I have covered them well. I turned at the sound of his voice and tried to defend myself, even though I knew I should not have brought them to this place.

Yes, I can see that, but look under the sleeves of their shirts, my love.

I walked over to the children and rolled up one of Santan's shirtsleeves. His skin was bubbling with blisters. I gasped.

See? He gathered both of the children into his arms and began walking away from me. *Follow me.* He ordered.

I was dumbfounded that he wanted me to follow him. This was a first. Usually, he just walked away with my children, leaving me alone. I hurried, trying to keep up. We entered a grove of trees, which canopied us from the sun's rays. I glanced down at my feet and noticed that I was still walking on sand, only now it was moist and cool. A small, clear blue body of water, surrounded by a sandy beach, appeared in the woods. Basarab set the children on the ground. He dropped down on his knees and began building a sandcastle. Samara squealed in delight. Santan crouched beside his father, smiling as the castle walls took shape.

Mama didn't mean to be so foolish, Father. She just doesn't know any better. Please don't punish her. I listened as my son begged his father not to hurt me. So far, in my dreams, Basarab had not harmed me, physically, anyway. Was this dream going to be different?

Mama is bad! Samara looked at her father, a serious cast to her face. *Mama doesn't love us, Papa—not like you do. You would never hurt us! You would never take us out in the sun!*

Samara threw a disgusted look my way. My heart stopped beating, momentarily.

Basarab roared with laughter. *Don't worry, my precious little Samara; Papa won't let your foolish mama hurt you ever again. She just does not know better; she is not one of us, is she?* I watched as my children shook their heads no, and my heart beat accelerated. I felt a blazing sensation race through my veins, burning so deeply that I thought I was going to explode. I turned and staggered toward the water, hoping to exterminate the fire that was swelling within me. But even as the water closed around my body, there was no relief. From the shoreline, I heard his voice ... *Now you know, Virginia, how my children suffer when you expose them to the sun! Come children, we will leave your mother to think about how she has treated you. Nagypapa Atilla has a surprise for you and Teresa has also planned something special.*

I stood in the water, unable to move. Only my head could turn. My eyes focused on Basarab and my children as they disappeared. Santan's words reached my ears. *Why can Mama not come with us, Papa? I think she has learned her lesson.* Was there hope strung to those words?—my son was coming to my defence. But the next string of words shattered my expectation. *Leave her there, Papa; she has been bad! She always takes us out in the sun. She is evil. You must punish her!* My daughter's voice rang out clearly, radiating hatred!

~

I awoke from the dream, dripping wet. I sat up in my bed. My limbs shook uncontrollably. Was there no end to the torment? Should I take my chances and accept Randy's proposal? But that would mean we'd have to leave Brantford—leave my nest—the place where Emelia and Adelaide, my benefactresses, knew I was; where my new friend, Angel, knew I was. How would I survive without them, or without the financial support that

Emelia provided? Randy didn't have a real job at the moment, just the odd sport's article for the newspaper; and, those had been few and far between since he had started studying. I could probably get a job in a law office somewhere, but the fact that my children would never be *normal* would force me to impart to Randy my darkest secrets. No ... there was no way out for me. I would just have to make the best of my situation and prepare for *his* return. Although, how I was going to do that, I had no idea. In reality, no manner of preparation was going to prevent the count from reclaiming his son!

~

The end of October arrived too soon. Its coming meant my life had been in turmoil for two years. I didn't want to celebrate anything, but Carla came by the Friday night before Halloween and suggested we take the children trick-or-treating. I told her that they were still too young, but she laughed and said she hadn't gotten to do those kinds of events when she was growing up. She would appreciate it if I'd let her live vicariously through my children—just this once.

"Come on, Virginia ... please."

Randy must have noticed her car in the driveway, because, shortly after Carla's arrival, he was knocking at my door. Carla raced to let him in. I couldn't believe how excited she was about Halloween. "Randy..." and she told him everything she wanted to do. He thought it was an excellent idea. With the two of them ganging up on me, I had no choice but to give in.

"Let me buy their costumes," Carla suggested.

"Whatever," I said as I walked out of the kitchen. Samara was crying for her next feeding, and she was a child no one kept waiting! Carla followed me.

"Maybe we should start Samara on some solid food. I think it will be much safer for her, since she was not born under the same circumstances as Santan."

I was in no mood to argue. "Whatever you say, Carla, you're the doctor." I gathered my daughter into my arms and headed for the easy chair.

Santan had woken up when he heard Randy's voice. Randy hurried through the living room, heading to Santan's room. "I'll get him," he mumbled as he passed by.

Carla came into the living room with a bowl of baby cereal. "When she is done that side, let's try to give her some of this," she proposed.

When Samara finished, I set her in the baby chair. Carla handed me the cereal. Samara was watching with those eyes of hers, not missing one movement. She watched as I took the spoon and dipped it into the bowl. The spoon hovered by her mouth. Suddenly, her little fist struck my hand, sending the spoon to the floor.

"Carla feed me!" she screamed.

I sat back in my chair, shocked! Carla quickly came to my aid and fetched another spoon. Somehow, I had managed to keep hold of the dish of cereal. Carla took it from me, gently prying my fingers from the bowl's edges. I watched in dismay as Samara smiled. Carla fed *my* baby her first meal. I bore in mind some of the dreams I'd had—dreams depicting a deceitful Carla—portraying her as one of *them*. I also remembered my most recent dream—the one where Samara was in her father's arms, and she was telling him that I was bad, and that I always tried to hurt her and Santan. How could this child be mine, when no part of her seemed to have any conscience, at all?

~

I had heard Carla and Randy whispering and laughing like co-conspirators; unfortunately, I hadn't thought to ask Carla what costumes she was going to buy for my children. Naively, I had pictured something cute, to suit their ages: a kitty, or a puppy, or a bunny. Halloween arrived, and so did Carla, followed closely by Randy.

"Did you get them?" His voice was full of excitement.

"Sure did."

Randy rubbed his hands together and chuckled. "I can hardly wait to see them!" He turned to me. "Wait till you see what Carla and I have cooked up!"

Carla plunked a large box on the kitchen table. She pulled out two bags and handed one to Randy, and one to me. She took another bag from the box. "My costume," she said. She pulled out two smaller bags. "You get Santan ready," she ordered, giving him one of the small bags. "I'll dress Samara."

They disappeared from the kitchen, heading to my children's bedroom. "Don't peek inside your bag until we come out," Carla called back to me.

I sat down at the kitchen table. I glanced at the clock. Six-ten. I tapped my fingers nervously on the table. My camera was sitting on the kitchen counter, so I got up and brought it over to the table, getting it ready to take a picture of my children dressed in their costumes. The bedroom door opened at six-thirty. I lifted the camera and focused on the doorway. But, what I saw coming toward me stilled my heart. The camera crashed to the floor. My stomach lurched. How could Carla do this? I assumed this had nothing to do with Randy; but even if it did, he was not aware of *what* my children were—Carla was. She should have known better!

"Look, Mama!" Santan ran up to me. "I'm a vampire!"

"Vampire," Samara repeated, from Carla's arms.

Carla and Randy were dressed as vampires, too. I didn't need to look inside my bag to see what my costume would be. I staggered to the bathroom. Everything in my stomach hurled into the toilet. I remained on the cold floor for several minutes after the heaves died down. I heard a light knock on the door, and Carla speaking to me. She sounded far away. I looked up. The room was spinning. I felt someone lifting me from the floor, leading me out of the bathroom and into my room. I felt someone drawing a blanket over me. I thought I heard someone say that everything was going to be all right ... that they were sorry I was sick ... that they would take the children trick-or-treating ... that they wouldn't be long ... that I was not to worry. Everything went black.

It wasn't until the next morning that I found out what had happened the night before. When I emerged from my bedroom, I saw Randy sleeping on my couch. I walked over and shook his shoulder roughly. "What are you doing here?" I shouted.

"You were sound asleep when Carla and I returned," he explained sleepily. He rubbed his eyes. "And I hadn't wanted to leave you alone with the children, with you not feeling well," he added. Randy paused and pushed himself up into a sitting position. "I need to tell you something, though. Something pretty bizarre happened during the trick-or-treating last night." I noticed the puzzled look on his face.

"We decided to go to another area," he began, "one with more houses. We drove down to Buffalo Street, and Carla parked the car in the parking lot at the beginning of the street." Randy stopped and stared at me. "What's wrong, Virginia?"

At the mention of Buffalo Street, I had begun to shake. I hadn't been near that street since the day I had walked Santan down it. Memories flooded my world ... of how Santan had gotten excited about *The House,* and how he had gotten upset when I steered him away from *The House!* I drew in a deep breath, and choked. "Sorry, Randy," I finally managed to say. "I guess that I am still feeling a bit queasy. Go on ... tell me what happened."

"Well, we were walking along, going from place to place. Everything was fine, but it seemed the further down the street we went ... the kids, especially Santan, began to get overly eager. And then Santan started to talk about the big house and how he wanted to go and see the big house. I asked Carla what he was talking about, and she told me there was a mansion at the end of the street. I had no idea how the little fella would even know such a house existed. Do you walk that way?"

"No." My reply was short.

"Never?"

"Never." I looked away, briefly. "Well, once—a long time ago."

"I guess that is all it took because Santan got majorly pumped the closer we got. Carla said that we just needed to let him see the house. As we walked up the back lane, Samara got excited too, as though her brother's enthusiasm had rubbed off on her. And then ... well, you know how strange Samara's eye colour is, so different from Santan's ... well, as we approached the house, Santan's eyes started to glow, like his sister's. He pointed to the house and said, 'Papa.' I couldn't believe what I had just heard!

"Tell me, truthfully, Virginia, is your husband still alive ... maybe? Did you live in that house with him? You were told that he died, but you never got to see his body. Are you sure he is dead? I have always had a hard time figuring out what you are all about. You are such a mystery. You tell me that your husband was the love of your life and that no man would ever be able to fill his shoes; yet, you do not return to the place where you obviously made a home together. And, you never talk about him. If he meant so much to you, wouldn't that be something you would talk about ... to me ... to your children? You showed up at my door that day with hardly any clothes on your back, yet you also seemed to have a deep source of financial resources. Your child recognized that house, as young as he is, and there is also the fact, one which is difficult for me to understand, that both your children are tremendously advanced for their ages..."

"Stop!" I felt the anger welling up within me, like a volcano ready to explode. How dare he question me like that! How dare Carla take my children down *that* street! I turned to Randy. "My past life is none of your damn business, Randy. My husband is dead. I have no reason to believe he is not, despite not having seen his body. Aunt Emelia has no reason to lie to me. He supported me lavishly before he died; now I live off the money from his estate. It was a vast estate. He loved me, and he loved his son. He never got to see his daughter, but I know he would have loved her, as well.

"As for the condition I was in the day I showed up at your door, that was my fault. We'd had a fight. I was sulking. I decided to punish my husband, the man I loved and adored, by taking his son from him. I knew he was leaving on an urgent business matter, and that he would not be able to come after me because he had to catch an early plane. He would have just assumed that I would come to my senses, and when he returned home I would be there waiting for him, as I always was. This wasn't the first time I'd taken off after a disagreement. But, this time, I had made plans; I had been stashing money away. I was going to teach him a lesson! I can't even remember, now, what it was I was trying to teach him. Unfortunately, life dealt me a cruel blow."

I was on a roll. I had no idea where the words were coming from, but they continued to flow from my mouth. "My husband died! I didn't have a chance to tell him how sorry I was. I didn't have a chance to say good-bye. His son didn't have a chance to say good-bye. His son will never get to know his father, as I knew him. His daughter will never know what it is like to have her father's arms hold her. How dare you even suggest that I am lying—that my life is just a huge fabrication!

"Who do you think you are? You are my landlord—that is it. Actually, you are not even that. Your uncle allows you to stay in your apartment for free, as long as you look after the house. You are nothing but a worthless young man who has wasted most of his life, so far, and you will probably squander the rest of it in your quest for whatever it is that you are searching for. From now on, consider me nothing more than your tenant! I think it will be better that way." I paused to catch my breath, and because I couldn't think of what else to say. I hoped Randy wouldn't push for an answer as to why I hadn't returned to my *matrimonial* home. I had no idea how I would reply to that question!

Randy's face was redder than fresh strawberries. But it was his eyes that captured my attention. They were not alarmed; they were angry. He began to speak, slowly, at first—his voice bearing the tone of a mature man. "Wow! You certainly are something, Virginia. Have you forgotten how much I helped you when you first came here? You had nothing—the clothes on your back, such as they were; a kid; and some money!" Randy ran his hand through his hair. His voice picked up momentum. "I drove you around. I was there for you and Santan. You allowed me into your life. You used me? Is that what you are saying here? You and your husband had a whopping fight, so you were using me to get back at him? If he hadn't died, would you have run back to his arms, eventually, after you taught him his lesson? I don't believe a word of what you are telling me, Virginia! You have some big, dark secret hidden inside that head of yours; I have always felt it. I have to wonder why you didn't return to your home, especially if you love your husband the way you say you do. And, wouldn't his property be part of the estate that you would have inherited? I am not a fool, Virginia! There is something, actually several *somethings*, just not right about you!

"And, these people who visit you from Europe are a strange lot. Your Aunt Emelia—she is the strangest. Does she have the same skin condition as your son? I have never seen her outside in the daytime unless she was wrapped up to the hilt! Adelaide is hovering, and her brother, Alfred, is just weird, never saying a word. The only normal one, in the bunch, is Carla, and there are times that I think she is a bit odd too."

At the mention of Carla's name, I asked the question that had been lingering on the tip of my tongue. I needed to divert attention away from Randy's questions, especially the one about running back to my husband's arms. If I was given the opportunity, would I run back to Basarab and give him my all again? "By the way, Randy, whose idea was it to dress up as vampires?"

"Mine—why?"

"Not Carla's?"

"No, it was mine. I don't tell untruths, Virginia. I have nothing to hide. I have always been fascinated with vampire lore, and I thought it would be cute to dress up like a vampire family."

I turned away and walked over to the kitchen sink. My hands gripped the edges of the counter. I could feel my blood surging through my veins. Randy had no idea what he was talking about. How could he? Vampires, to him, were like what they had been to me at one time— stories created by some overly imaginative writer. Just because I knew better, now, didn't mean everyone else did. I turned and faced Randy. I willed myself to be calm.

"I am sorry, Randy. I guess I am still not feeling well. I have had so much happen to me in the past while that sometimes, I guess, I just don't say the right things. I have never been partial to vampires. I think they are a ridiculous figment of people's imagination, and all the stories that are written about vampire allure are just that—stories. Vampires are the last creatures that I would want my children to be dressed as, let alone be." I choked on my last three words. "I think you better leave now. I need some time alone."

Randy took a few steps toward me, his arms outstretched. "Virginia…"

I raised my hand. "Don't, Randy, not right now. Please go." I walked to the door and opened it. He hesitated. "It's okay. I'll talk to you later. I'll call you," I assured him.

Before Randy passed through the door, he had hesitated and looked down into my eyes. Was he searching for the truth in my head—or for the lies he felt I was telling him? I breathed in deeply, absorbing his closeness. I felt flushed. Then he was gone. I shut the door, turned around and leaned against it. My body inched down to the floor. I wrapped my arms around my knees and squeezed tightly. My fingers interlaced until I felt them tingle, as the blood stopped flowing to their tips. I tried to cry, but the sobs that wrenched out of me were nothing but scorched gulps of air.

~

I needed to talk to Carla. I stood up and walked to my phone, picked up the receiver, and dialled her number. Randy might be innocent about what had occurred in my life, but Carla wasn't. What I needed to know was why she had taken my children to a place where she knew I would never want them to go. Carla answered on the fourth ring.

"Hello." Her voice sounded sleepy.

"Carla … Virginia, here."

"Hi. I hope you're feeling better; you gave us quite a scare last night. What happened to you? You seemed OK one minute, and then the next…"

"You should know why, Carla. Randy tells me that it was his idea for us to be vampires; but, wouldn't you have known how that might have bothered me? Couldn't you have talked him out of such foolishness?"

"Your Randy can be rather persuasive when he wants to be. I mentioned that I didn't think vampire costumes were suitable, especially since the children were so young, but he insisted. So, I finally caved."

"But *you* purchased the costumes."

"Yes … what of it?"

"You could have bought something else and then just told him that you couldn't find little vampire costumes."

"But that would have meant I would have had to lie, wouldn't it? I don't like having to do that, Virginia. What if he had gone out and found them in a store that I had already looked in?" I sensed a hint of sarcasm in Carla's voice.

What?—neither you nor Randy lie? "Another thing, Carla ... you and Randy both have said the vampire costumes were his idea—okay, I'm willing to accept that fact; but, it had to be your suggestion to go down Buffalo Street. Why would you have considered that might be an appropriate place to go?"

There was a pause on the other end of the line. I could hear Carla breathing. When she spoke, her words were hesitant. "I ... wanted ... to see ... *The House.*"

"You could have seen *The House* any time you were in Brantford," I cut in. "Now, you are lying to me! What were you thinking—that I would be happy to have my children anywhere near that place—especially, Santan!"

"You are overreacting, Virginia!" Carla's voice escalated angrily. "How could the child remember anything?"

"Oh, he remembered, all right! He remembered! I didn't tell you about the time I took him for a walk near *The House* and what his reactions were, the closer we got. Those reactions told me that my son remembered something! I swore I would never take him near it again. And now, from what Randy tells me, my daughter is reacting to it, as well!

"There is something I want you to understand, Carla—these are *my* children. For how long, I have no idea. But the farther I can keep them away from the count's world, the better chance my children will have to grow up normal. If I had my way, Santan and Samara would never see their father, ever; but, the voice inside my mind keeps reminding me that is not going to happen. I know Basarab will return for his son one day. I am not sure if he knows about Samara yet, but I am sure, when he does find out, she will go with him, as well. She is actually more his daughter than I could have believed possible. You are never to take them near that place again! Have I made myself clear? In fact, from now on, you will be nothing more to them than their doctor!"

"But the children are so attached to me, especially Samara; how will you explain my lack of visits?" The despair in Carla's voice surprised me.

"My daughter will adjust to you not being around; after all, she is just a baby."

"True. But she is not just *any* baby. She is *his* daughter. And, like you said, from all indications she is more like her father than Santan is. Your children are exceptional, 'prodigies' our world would label them. There is nothing you can do about what they are, Virginia. You need to accept that fact."

Carla wasn't telling me anything that I did not already know. "I will do whatever I have to, to protect my children, even if it means moving from here. I will hide somewhere that he will never find me." I realized, too late, the implication of my words.

"You cannot hide from him. Maybe, for a time, but it will be brief. He will find you. They have their ways." Carla's voice sounded assured.

"Well, we'll see about that. There are ways to disappear."

"For you, perhaps, but not for the children. Eventually, their blood will call out to their father!"

The receiver clicked. Silence. I thought about Carla's closing statement. *Their blood will call out to their father.* I flopped down on the couch and buried my face in a pillow. For two years, I had been fighting for my survival. Every time I thought I might be gaining ground, another obstacle was dropped in my path. If Carla was right, then there was no hope; so, what was the point of even trying? I closed my eyes…

You must not worry; everything will work out. You must continue to be strong and have faith. Angel had her arms around my shoulders, and was trying to comfort me.

I gazed up into her eyes, my own brimming with tears. *I just don't know how much more I can take; I don't even know who I can trust anymore.*

You can trust me. I will never fail you. Angel looked sincere.

I so desperately wanted to believe her, but the agony of my life kept building roadblocks for me. *I'd like to believe you. But I thought I could trust Carla and Randy, and look what they did at Halloween? They dressed my children as vampires!*

Angel sighed deeply. *I understand how you feel. It must have been horrifying when you saw your children dressed like that. But, my dear, you must take it for what it was—just a Halloween costume. That is all! Paranoia over life's little details will be your downfall.*

But you don't know the count... I stopped as I realized the slip I had made. I had not told Angel of the count, only that I had been married to a businessman and that my husband had recently passed away.

Angel did not miss my statement. *Count? Who is this count to you?*

I pulled away from her. *No one ... forget you even heard that ... I don't know why I said that ...* I was fumbling over my words.

Is there someone hurting you, Virginia? You can tell me, if there is. I can help you. Let me help you ... let me help you ... let me...

~

"Mama? Are you okay, Mama?" A tiny hand touched my arm. I looked up from the pillow, into Santan's warm, dark eyes. He was smiling. I sat up and gathered my son into my arms. Maybe there was still hope. Angel had just said she would help me. And, in my last dream of the children, Santan had spoken out protectively for me. He had wanted to save me. I hugged him closer, against my heart.

He leaned into me and wrapped his arms around me. "I love you, Mama."

Yes.

There was still hope.

Chapter Twenty-one

S amara was calling for me. She no longer cried like a normal baby when she wanted something; she demanded now that she could speak words. "Mama! I need you … now!" I gathered my school papers and placed them in the desk drawer, and then went to my daughter.

Santan was standing beside Samara's crib. He had insisted that he was too big for a crib, so I had bought him a junior bed. Samara had pulled herself up and was gripping the crib rails. She was strong for a six-month baby, stronger than Santan had been at that age.

"Look at me. Look at me stand." Samara bounced in her crib. Suddenly, she lost her balance and plopped on her bottom. She scowled and then heaved herself back up. She and Santan were laughing.

It was good to hear laughter in my home. There had been so little of it in my life. I lifted my daughter out of the crib and headed to the kitchen. Santan followed.

"Samara … down!" Samara strained against my arms. "Samara walk … like Santan."

"But you can't walk yet," I said.

Samara continued to struggle, so I set her down on the floor. I tried to hold her hands. She yanked them away from me. "Let go!" she screamed. And then she was on her bum again. Quickly, she moved into crawling position and took off after her brother. Despite how she had screamed at me, I grinned. She certainly had spirit, something I was going to have to keep a harness on, without breaking it.

In the kitchen, I went about preparing our meal. Santan was still having problems with some solid foods, but I had honed in on the ones he was most able to tolerate. Samara was eating mostly baby cereal, although I had started to puree vegetables and fruit for her, as well. There was a knock on the door just as I was about to feed Samara.

"Randy!" Santan shouted excitedly as he headed for the door. "Randy is here!"

It had been a couple of weeks since we had seen Randy—since our *misunderstanding*. I walked over and opened the door. Randy was standing on my doorstep, holding a bouquet of roses. I softened. He was such a romantic. This was the third time, since I had moved into the apartment, he had brought me flowers.

"Peace." He smiled sheepishly—a smile I couldn't resist.

I sighed and then opened the door wider. Santan was ecstatic.

"Where have you been Randy?" Santan grabbed Randy's leg, trying to drag him through the doorway.

Randy glanced at me. "Oh, I've been around, but I have been busy, little man. I had to go away for a few days."

"Come, read a book with me, Randy. Mama is going to feed Samara; I'm not hungry."

Randy looked at me and raised his eyebrows questioningly. "Is that okay, Virginia?"

I shrugged my shoulders and nodded. Randy and Santan disappeared into the living room. Samara kicked her feet on the highchair footrest. "Samara want to go with Santan!"

"Let's finish your supper first," I suggested to her.

"No!" Samara pounded a fist on the highchair tray. "Samara eat supper there!" She pointed to where her brother was.

I decided it was time to start putting my foot down. If I didn't, she would be out of control by the time she was a year old. In fact, sometimes I felt that she already was. "No … Samara will eat her supper here, and then Mama will take her into the living room so that she can listen to Santan read the story." I kept my voice firm.

The dish of food flew across the kitchen, splattering against a cupboard door. I noticed how red my daughter's eyes were. The flames that normally just clung around her coal-black pupils began to flash; they were consuming her whole eye! I stood and backed away from her. Santan, having heard the commotion, ran into the kitchen; Randy was right behind him.

When Randy saw Samara's face, I noticed a look of horror cross over his. "My God!" he exclaimed.

Santan went straight to his sister and climbed onto the chair I had just abandoned. "Samara!" His voice was deep and commanding. When had he acquired such a tone?

Samara looked at her brother. I watched her calm down as he continued to gaze into her eyes. The flames began to wane. I stood rooted to the floor while my year and a half old son calmed his sister. This was not natural—none of it. I glimpsed at Randy, noticing the confused look on his face.

"Your children truly are *special*," Randy murmured.

I nodded, unable to speak.

Santan turned to me. "You can feed Samara supper now––she will be good."

"How do you know this?" I had not heard Santan say anything more than Samara's name.

"I have ordered her to behave, Mama."

"But you only spoke her name?"

"That is all that is necessary," he said as he climbed down from the chair, took Randy by the hand, and returned to the living room.

I shook my head in disbelief as I mixed another dish of cereal for Samara. This time she ate eagerly. When the bowl was empty, she smiled. "I go sit with Santan now."

I lifted her out of the highchair and set her on the floor. She crawled quickly into the living room. Randy reached over to pick her up; I noticed her body tense. She still didn't like him much, but with one look from her brother, she relaxed. Randy snuggled Samara between him and Santan, and then Santan continued reading the story.

"You want to stay for supper?" I called to Randy, even though I knew I shouldn't be encouraging him with such an invitation. But, I was lonely for adult company. I was being selfish again; I realized that, but I didn't care.

He looked up with a startled expression. "Sure."

Later in the evening, after the children were in bed, Randy brought up our last disastrous conversation. He told me how sorry he was that he had doubted me and said so many unpleasant things to hurt me. He told me that he'd had no idea how much I hated the vampire craze that had infected so many people. He asked my forgiveness.

I gave it.

Soon, his arm was around my shoulder…

I fell asleep…

Nestled against his chest.

~

When I awoke the next morning, I was still on the couch. The quilt from my bed had been thrown over me.

"Good morning, sleepyhead," Randy sauntered into the living room. "I just put the coffee on. What would you like for breakfast?" He was beaming.

"You're still here?"

He smiled. "I didn't want to leave. You were so tired. I thought if one of the kids woke up I would look after them and let you sleep." He paused. "I hope that's okay?"

I sat up. "Sure ..." I grinned. "Just don't make a habit of it," I added, trying to look stern.

I heard the patter of little feet behind me. "Randy!" Santan shouted joyfully as he ran to him. He raised his arms, signalling he wanted Randy to pick him up. Randy bent over and grabbed my son up into his arms.

"How's my little man this morning?" Randy gave Santan a generous squeeze.

"Good. And how are you, Randy?"

I burst out laughing. Randy and Santan stared at me, probably thinking I was crazy.

"What's so funny?" Randy asked.

"Santan asking how you are," I managed to say between tiny bursts of mirth. Randy looked puzzled at first, and then he laughed, too. We were soon joined by Santan. A voice, calling to me from the bedroom, jolted me back to reality.

"Mama! Samara is awake ... come now!"

By the time I had breastfed Samara, Randy had a breakfast of eggs and bacon, and toast laid out on the table. He had also made a bowl of oatmeal for Santan, one breakfast my son seemed able to tolerate. A cup of coffee, freshly poured and steaming hot, was sitting by my plate. I surveyed the scene. How I would love this to be my life. But I knew it would never be that simple for me. A shiver passed through my heart. *What am I thinking, giving Randy hope?* I needed to stop this before it went any further. Randy didn't deserve the wrath that would rain down on him should the count find him in my company, or in the company of his son, Santan. Something told me that Randy's life would be expendable.

Maybe it was time for me to pick up and leave— seriously. My procrastination could result in the death of my friend, an innocent person who would be disposed of with no forethought; it would be just because of his association with me. I could not bear that on my conscience. I ate the rest of my meal in silence; the joy of the morning dissipated into the wretchedness of my life's reality.

Randy left after breakfast, saying he was tired and wanted to catch a nap. He must have stayed awake all night watching over me. Santan and Samara were playing in the living room. I watched them for a few minutes before I went to my desk and took out one of my textbooks. I opened it to the next section I needed to read: *Abnormal Psychology of a Serial Killer*. Great.

One of the first names appearing on the page was Vlad Tepes, but I already knew his name would show up. Basarab and I had discussed him enough, back at *The House*. I skimmed over the page. In the 1400s, there was a Gilles de Rais, a Breton nobleman, child-murderer and companion-in-arms to Joan of Arc ... in the 1500s, Elizabeth Bathory (Erzsébet Báthory), the same individual Basarab and I had talked about—the Blood Countess, as she was known then, and probably known now, for I knew she was still very much alive.

I paused with interest at Peter Stumpp, known as the Werewolf of Bedburg of Danvill, also from the 1500's. I made a note to use him as one of my case studies. I had to choose two— one male, one female. I perused down the page and came across a female serial killer from Italy, Giulia Tofana. She had been accused of poisoning over 600 victims in the mid 1600's. I thought she might be intriguing to write about, as well, so I wrote her name down.

I couldn't believe the atrocities that some of these individuals had committed. One woman, Mary Ann Cotton, had killed a number of her husbands and offspring; another woman, Amelia Dyer, was convicted of only one murder, but it was estimated that she had killed over 400 individuals. She had been dubbed the "Baby-farm Murderess." Jack the Ripper was on the list, too. It was noted that he had never been caught for the atrocities he had committed. The man listed after Jack was Gilles Garnier. He had cannibalized young children, claiming their corpses created a magical ointment that enabled him to transform into a werewolf... The list went on—and I hadn't even touched on the 20th Century yet!

I snapped the book shut. How many of those criminals now walked with vampires? Basarab had indicated to me that he knew of several. I couldn't help wondering, after having read those accounts, was Basarab safe from such monsters? I couldn't see him committing such abominable crimes, just for the fun of it.

My children voiced their desire to do something different. I glimpsed out the window. It was late afternoon, and cloudy. Maybe, we would take a walk after an early supper.

~

It was an anxious time for me. I had heard nothing from Emelia and Adelaide, or from Carla. Since I had spoken so sharply to her after the Halloween incident, Carla had been keeping her distance. Randy was a constant in my life, though, which delighted Santan. I feared it, yet continued to do nothing to stop it. Humans were meant to be with someone; Randy was a definite comfort to me.

Angel called me two weeks before Christmas, and conveyed to me that she would not be making it home for the holiday. She told me to expect a parcel in the mail; she had sent a gift for the children. The next day I received a postcard from her. There was a picture of the pyramids of Egypt on the front, and a hastily scribbled note on the back, stating that she couldn't wait to see me and the children. The gift arrived two days later, a lovely collection of children's books—*1001 Arabian Tales*.

With December on us, the weather turned for the worse. Freezing north winds made walking with the children in the evenings almost impossible. I hated being cooped up in the apartment. My nerves were beginning to fray, especially with Samara, who became more challenging by the day—by the minute. Only Santan seemed able to control her.

Randy was filled with anticipation for the upcoming holiday season. I couldn't remember the last time I had been excited about Christmas, and I could not tap into the specialness of the season. After all, what was there that was so good about my life at the moment? I lived with the constant fear the count would walk through my door and take my children from me. If he left me alive, that would be a miracle.

I had been careful to make sure Randy never stayed overnight again, but other than that, he spent most of his waking hours with us. One afternoon, he walked in with a giant Christmas tree, which he set up in the corner of my living room. He left and returned a few hours later with bags of decorations. Santan was excited, especially after Randy explained to him what happened at Christmas.

"Wouldn't it be better to explain the real meaning of Christmas?" I suggested.

"He wouldn't understand." Randy picked out a box of decorations from one of the bags. "Want to help me put these on the tree, little buddy?"

Samara crawled over to Randy. Using his pants, she pulled herself to a standing position against his leg. "Me help too," she squealed.

Randy looked at me and burst into laughter. "I think there is hope yet that she will take a liking to me!" He reached down and tousled her curls. "Of course you can help, Samara. In fact, you can put the first decoration on the tree; I'm sure Santan won't mind, will you, son?" Randy calling Santan *son* startled me, but I decided not to comment on it. There was no point opening a can of worms I had no desire to pick through.

Santan shook his head. He reached into the box Randy had just opened, picked out a bright red ball with silvery snowflake sparkles, and handed it to his sister. She grabbed it eagerly. With the help of Randy and her brother, it was soon fastened to a bottom tree branch.

It never ceased to amaze me how mature my little son was—a young man in a baby's body. I headed to my room, returning a few minutes later with my camera. These were memories I wanted to be able to treasure forever; well, at least as long as my forever was.

Randy motioned to the decorations and the tree. "You aren't going to help us?"

"Nope. I think I'll have more fun taking pictures."

"Mama, look at me!" Samara surprised me with her excitement. I snapped a picture of her smiling, which was something she seldom did. I snapped more pictures, in succession: Santan ... Randy and Santan ... Samara ... Samara and Santan ... Randy and Samara ... all three together. Before long, I had used an entire roll of film.

The tree was almost decorated when someone knocked on the door. "Are you expecting anyone?" Randy enquired.

"No." I went through to the kitchen.

Carla was standing outside my door, shivering. She had an apprehensive look in her eyes. "May I come in?"

I stepped aside. I couldn't hold a grudge forever, and she had helped me through my pregnancy, and brought Samara safely into the world. "Sure. Why don't you join us? Randy and the kids are decorating a Christmas tree in the living room. I'm taking pictures."

I enjoyed the rest of the evening. I put another film in my camera and continued to take pictures. I wished I had bought a video camera because the scene unfolding before me was priceless. Carla helped finish decorating the tree. I made popcorn and hot chocolate for everyone. Even Santan and Samara had a few sips of the hot chocolate after it cooled off. We turned on the TV and watched "Charlie Brown's Christmas," and then "Rudolph."

I had never seen Samara so relaxed; she was interacting with everyone. I fed her, and then she crawled to Carla, who picked her up. Carla took out a storybook to read to the children. Santan made his way to the couch and settled in beside Carla. Randy joined them, and plunked himself beside Santan. I sat in the chair opposite the couch, took more pictures, and listened to the story Carla was reading. It wasn't long before both Samara and Santan closed their eyes. It had been a long day.

After I put the children to bed, Randy said goodnight. Carla lingered.

"Would you like something else to eat or drink?" I asked, after seeing Randy out the door.

"No thanks." Carla reached for her purse. "I have a letter for you from Adelaide."

My pulse quickened. *About time.* "That's wonderful," I commented. "It has been a while since I have heard from her, or Emelia."

"The envelope is quite fat," Carla pointed out as she handed it to me. "There might be something in there from Emelia, as well."

"I wonder why they didn't use the computer this time."

"Adelaide mentioned in her letter to me that it was not going well for the family." Carla glanced at her watch. "I think I will be on my way. It looks like we are in for some snow; I saw a few flakes coming down when you opened the door to let Randy out."

I didn't argue. I wanted to be alone to read whatever news had been sent to me. After Carla left, I curled up in my chair and opened the envelope. As Carla had assumed, there were two letters—one from Adelaide, one from Emelia. I decided to read Adelaide's first.

Dearest Virginia:

I am sorry for not having written to you for a time, but I have been ill; possibly with something I caught from someone on the plane while on my way home from Canada. Since I am not getting any younger, these types of viruses take much longer to recover from. I am better now, though.

Alfred sends his regards. He is quite taken with your Santan. I think Alfred is fascinated with your son's intellect--after all, how many 'babies' can a person have a conversation with? It has been a long time since I have seen his eyes light up as they do at the mention of Santan's name--since Gabriele. He has suggested we come to Canada for Christmas, and he has been out buying presents for Santan. He told me that I was responsible for buying Samara's gifts.

We plan to arrive on the Monday before Christmas. That way, I will be able to spend a few days with Carla, as well, because Alfred and I must return home before the New Year. Unfortunately, Emelia will not be able to come with us this time; she will explain some of the reasons in her letter.

Carla will pick us up from the airport. We will stay in a hotel again, so as not to put you out of your room.
Love, Adelaide

~

I was overjoyed that Adelaide and Alfred were coming for Christmas. After all, they were the closest thing I had to a family right now. I smiled, recalling Adelaide's statement about Alfred being so taken with Santan. I thought about asking Adelaide if Santan could call her brother, "Grandpa Alfred." It would be beneficial for my children to have a grandfatherly figure in their lives—pictures and everything. Maybe, Adelaide could fill in as their grandmother.

I set Adelaide's letter aside and unfolded Emelia's. The writing appeared hurried and frail. My heartbeat accelerated; I feared what I might find written on the pages...

My dearest Virginia:

It is with a heavy heart that I write this letter to you. Things are in a great turmoil here. The police raided our hotel. I was watching from my bedroom window when they stormed in. Officers surrounded the building, blocking off all exits of escape. Basarab went to the lobby to see what the commotion was about, while the rest of us gathered in one of the rooms and pretended we were dining, just in case there was a need for alibis. Basarab was informed that his description had been given by the lone survivor of a mass murder that had taken place that evening. Unfortunately, the witness had slipped into a coma. Basarab brought some of the police up to the room where we were all gathered; but I guess the officer in charge became confused because the descriptions given to him had been so vague that they could have been any one of the men in the dining room. The police left, but we were told not to leave the city.

Basarab is beside himself. I worry for him, but there is no consolation I can give him because he still does not speak to me. Adelaide informed me that she and Alfred are going to spend Christmas with you. I am pleased. How I wish I could be there, too. I have forwarded enough money to Adelaide to cover for the next few months because I do not know when I shall be able to do so again.

I am sorry that I have nothing more to say, even though there is much going on here. I have not the will to write of it at the moment.

Stay well, Virginia. Give Santan and Samara a hug for me. It looks as if it will be some time before I will be able to see them, or you, again.

Love, Aunt Emelia

I laid the letter on my lap and pondered on what its contents could mean for Basarab and the family, especially now that his description had been given to the police as a potential mass murderer. I was sure that would complicate matters even more for him. I wondered how he was going to get out of this mess any time soon. On the other hand, I assumed that the more complicated things were for Basarab, the longer he would have to remain in Transylvania. If that were the case, I might have more time with Santan and Samara before the count returned for his son. I felt a moment of guilt for thinking like that, because I was also aware of how fast my heart had beat while reading of the accusation against him. I folded the letter and returned it to its envelope.

I was sad, too, that Emelia was not going to make it for Christmas. I was hoping that Angel might return early from her trip, but didn't want to get too excited at the possibility. And, at this point, I was still not sure if I wanted to share my new friend with the others. Oh well, at least I would have Adelaide and Alfred … Carla and Randy, too, I assumed. I smiled, thinking of Randy, and of how he had matured in the short time I had been living in the apartment. I had not seen hide or tail of his uncle since our initial meeting; it would be good if he could see his nephew's progress.

Since it was so close to Christmas, the Discount Store was open twenty-four hours, which made my shopping easier. I trusted Randy with Santan, but Samara was another story. I thought that maybe if her brother were around, Samara might behave, but that was a chance I was not willing to take yet. So, I left Santan with Randy while I headed out with Samara to do my Christmas shopping. I had to buy presents for my children, and all my guests who were spending the holiday with me. Randy told me that he was buying the food for the Christmas dinner, and he would do all the cooking.

To my surprise, my shopping experience with Samara turned out to be a pleasant event. She was fascinated with everything in the store. Of course, she put several items that I didn't want into the cart, but it was wonderful to see my daughter relaxed and happy. When we arrived back to the apartment, Randy and Santan were busy reading. I noticed a worried look on Randy's face when I asked him how everything went.

"I am still worried about Santan," Randy began. "He does not eat enough, and he throws up so much of what he does eat. Maybe Carla should arrange an appointment with a specialist to see if there is something seriously wrong with his digestive system."

I needed to be careful how I phrased my words; I didn't want Randy pursuing this any further. He was always so pushy where Santan was concerned. "I have already mentioned that to Carla; she is arranging for Santan to see a specialist." I figured that a little white lie wouldn't hurt.

"Good." A boyish grin spread over Randy's face. "Now, what did you buy me for Christmas?"

I giggled. "Nothing."

"You don't mean that!" A look of disappointment wiped out the grin he had been trying to charm me with.

"I spent all my money on the children and the guests: Adelaide, Alfred, and Carla." I continued my charade.

"Not fair! I'm a guest too!"

"No—I don't consider you to be a guest," I snickered.

"Randy is my friend," Santan entered the conversation. "Why didn't you buy him a present, Mama?"

Randy and I looked at my son. Once again, the depth of this child's understanding shocked me; although, by now, I had no idea why it should have. Randy came to my rescue.

"It's okay, little man; your mama doesn't have to buy me anything. Just to spend Christmas with you, your sister, and your mama is enough of a present for me." Randy wrapped his arms around Santan; my son snuggled closer to him. Randy helped Samara onto the couch; she climbed onto his lap.

It was the portrait of a perfect family, only I knew it wasn't real. I was aware of *what* my children were. I knew this ideal picture was false and could never be. I knew I was going to have to leave, soon, before matters got totally out of my control. But to where? After the holidays, I would think more about where I might move.

Later, after Randy had gone home and the children were tucked into bed, I sat in my chair in the living room and stared out the window. I thought about the events that had led me down this pathway in my life—all the way back to Toronto—to John, with whom I had thought I was going to spend the rest of my life. If he hadn't cheated on me, I would most likely still be working for Mr. Carverson, or maybe, I would even have my degree in Criminal Profiling by now. I wondered what my old boss was doing now, and if he had ever pondered what might have become of me. I wondered if the Brantford firm had told him of my sudden disappearance, or if they had just swept it under the carpet. I wondered if they had even bothered to file a missing person's report—probably not.

I envisaged the night when I had been so foolish to peek into the window of *his* house. I saw him clearly, sitting there, and then standing up and arguing with the woman who had entered the room. I saw me, running away from the scene when *he* opened his mouth…

I was in the room again—in the large bed with the heavy, red velvet curtains drawn all around. I felt warm and safe. I opened my eyes; *he* was there, lying next to me. He must have heard me stir, for his eyes opened. He moved on his side, propping himself up, with his head resting on his hand.

Ah, Virginia, my love, you are awake. I cannot believe your beauty; what a fortunate man I am that you happened on my home. His smile was warm and inviting. I moved closer to him and buried my face against his chest, breathing in his scent. He smelt like the polished wood of antique furniture, like the mist from the ocean waves crashing against rocks, like the fragrant pine trees in the forest. I did not smell death on him.

I felt his fingers under my chin as he lifted my face toward his. *What would you like to do tonight; where would you like to fly?* He leaned over and covered my lips with his. I felt the trembling of my heart as it beat faster—anticipating. I opened to him—taking charge—climbing onto his soaring manhood. His arms encircled me; he smiled knowingly. His fingers played a melody from my shoulders to my thighs, electrifying my skin. I began to dance on him ... for him...

Suddenly, the curtain was drawn back sharply and a shadow lurked over the bed. A female voice called out his name. *Basarab! My husband! What are you doing with this whore?— this bewitcher!*

The count's body tensed. I froze. The warmth I had been enjoying dissipated as my lover flung me off his body. *Teresa!* I heard the sharpness in his voice. I prayed it was from anger— that he was annoyed with her for invading his moments with me. But his next statement stole my dream. *You know why I am here, why I do this—to impregnate her so that we might have another son!*

I covered my nakedness.

~

Tears flowed down my cheeks. The gloomy night stared at me through the windowpane. I walked over to the window and watched the last of a freight train's cars disappear, and then I closed the curtain and headed to my room. I lay down on and stared at the ceiling until the sun's rays crept into my room through the edges of my curtains. I was not willing to succumb to sleep again, at least not on that night.

Chapter Twenty-two

The Monday before Christmas arrived, and so did Adelaide and Alfred. I greeted them with open arms. Carla was with them. Alfred, after giving me a flimsy hug, asked where Santan was. Santan must have heard his voice because he came running into the kitchen, followed closely by Samara. She was crawling as fast as she could as she tried to keep pace with her brother. Alfred sat down on a kitchen chair and opened his arms to my son. Santan folded comfortably into the old man.

It wasn't long before there was another knock on the door, but I knew I would not have to answer it. Randy came over so often now that we had made a deal—if the door wasn't locked, he could just walk in; when the door was locked, he knew that I didn't want to be disturbed.

Adelaide pulled out a kitchen chair and sat down. "So, what are the plans for Christmas?"

"Randy is going to do all the cooking," I informed them. "He says he is whipping us up a big surprise."

"Interesting," Carla commented. Samara crawled over to her. Carla picked her up and set her on her lap. Samara started playing with Carla's red beads. "Careful, honey, don't pull too hard on my necklace," Carla gently pried Samara's fingers from the beads.

"Samara not break. Samara love Carla."

Adelaide laughed. "I see we have another child prodigy here."

"Appears so," I replied. I turned to Randy. "So what are you going to cook for us, Randy?"

He grinned. "Secret."

We decided to take the greetings into the living room where there was space for everyone to sit comfortably. Alfred pulled a small gift box from his pocket and handed it to Santan.

Santan's eyes lit up. "A present for me?"

Alfred nodded.

Santan tore the paper. Alfred helped him to open the box. Inside was a gold pocket watch. "It was my father's," Alfred enlightened us. "I want you to have it; I have no children of my own to pass it on to. Your mama will keep it safe until you are old enough to look after it by yourself."

Samara was watching the scene. "Where my present?" she screamed.

I noticed the discriminating look Adelaide threw Alfred's way. "What did I tell you, Alfred; you cannot give something to one, and not to the other." I saw the twinkle in her eyes as she reached into her purse and drew out a small package wrapped with bright pink paper. Adelaide handed it to Samara. "This is for you, my dear."

Samara grabbed it and ripped off the paper. Inside was a folded piece of white cotton. Carla helped my daughter unfold the cloth. Inside was a gold chain, with a heart locket attached. Samara snatched the necklace before Carla had a chance to pick it up.

"Let's see what is inside, shall we," Carla said, as she carefully took the locket from Samara's little hands, and pried it open. "Look, Samara, it's a picture of you and Santan." Carla turned the locket so that Samara could see inside the heart.

"I should probably put that away for her," I suggested, reaching for the locket—"until she is old enough to wear it."

"No! Samara wear it now!" I watched as my daughter's eyes flamed with anger.

"Just until you are bi…" I tried to say.

"No!" she screamed again.

Carla came to the rescue. She fastened the necklace around Samara's neck. "Okay, rascal, but just until nap time."

Samara's arms flung around Carla's neck, but not before she threw me a look that suggested victory.

~

Christmas Day arrived. Savoury scents wafted through the walls of the old house. Randy must be cooking up a storm. Santan and Samara had gone to bed early on Christmas Eve, and had slept through the night—probably because Randy had told them Santa Claus would not come and leave presents if they were awake. After the children had fallen fast asleep, Randy and I had wrapped their presents and then laid them under the tree.

When I came out of my room, I found Santan and Samara sitting among the presents, their eyes wide with wonder. I was surprised that they hadn't tried to open any of them yet, but Santan divulged the reason.

"Call Randy, Mama." Santan pointed to the phone. "We can't open our presents without him here."

As though Randy had heard Santan's request, the doorknob on my back door started turning. I rushed to unlock it. Randy's face was flushed, and he was holding a large box in his arms.

"Randy, the children have enough," I exclaimed, annoyed that he had bought something else, especially after we had discussed he was not to do that.

He snickered. "It isn't for them; it's for you."

"Oh," I blushed and opened the door wider.

Randy piled the children's gifts in front of them, and then we helped them unwrap their presents. Santan was composed, but I could tell by his body language that he was delighted with his new books, and with the train set that I had purchased for him. Samara squealed in delight at the play dough and the puzzles, but she cast the baby doll away and screamed that she did not want a baby. She was a baby, and that should be enough for me!

I handed Randy the gift I had gotten for him, and he pushed the box he had brought over toward me. I waited as he opened mine. He held up the new shirts and pants—"just what I needed for my next semester." He smiled at me, warm and tender. "Now open your gift."

I picked at the paper; but suddenly, two sets of little hands and a freckled pair of hands were helping me to tear the wrapping off. Underneath was a plain brown box, sealed with clear packing tape. Randy went to the kitchen, returning a moment later with a knife. I sliced down the seam and opened the box. Inside was another box, but this one displayed a picture of a large wooden jewellery chest with legs. It looked to be about three feet tall and was covered with painted wildflowers.

Randy helped me pull the chest out of the box. He set it on the floor beside me, and then pushed the empty carton to the side. "Open the top drawer."

Inside the drawer was a small, blue velvet box. I hoped it was not what I thought it might be. Slowly, I took it out, and opened it. I opened the box. Inside, nestled in the velvet slit, was a silver ring with several small Sapphire stones. I looked at Randy. "You shouldn't have done this." I was trying to keep the harshness out of my words.

"It is just a ring—a friendship ring—nothing more." Randy defended himself. "Put it on ... please."

I wavered for a moment, not wanting to put the ring on. I felt, if I did, it would give Randy a hope that could never be. He reached across the pile of torn wrapping paper and placed his fingers beneath my chin. He lifted my face, forcing me to look directly into his warm brown eyes.

"It is only a friendship ring," he reaffirmed.

Gently, I pushed his fingers away. I slipped the ring on my right hand. It was Christmas. I could always remove it later. Randy smiled and excused himself, saying he had to finish cooking. I was left alone with my children—and my thoughts.

Strange that I was wondering what Basarab was doing at the moment. Stranger still was the fact that, in my mind, I was comparing Randy to Basarab. Not so strange was, there was no comparison—Randy, despite how much he had matured since I first met him, was still just a *boy*.

~

Carla, Adelaide, and Alfred arrived shortly after three o'clock, their arms full of packages for the children, I assumed. Randy phoned and asked if someone could come to his apartment to help him carry over the food—everything was done. Carla went. Soon my kitchen counter was lined with several blanket-wrapped pots.

"Smorgasbord style, ladies and gentlemen," Randy announced as he unwrapped the pots and removed their lids.

Randy had cooked a feast fit for a queen's table—an orange-glazed roast duckling; a turkey with bread and walnut stuffing; potatoes whipped, creamy and smooth; green peas with sautéed onions and mushrooms, sprinkled with caraway seeds; and asparagus, lightly seasoned and oven-baked. He had also made several dips and sauces to go with the poultry and vegetables. Randy kept one course covered, saying that dessert was hidden within, and it would not be unveiled until it was time to eat it.

Alfred rubbed his stomach and licked his lips. "Why do you never cook like this, sister?" he questioned Adelaide, an impish smirk on his face.

"For the same reason you don't!" she returned, just as playfully.

Everyone laughed. The mood around the table was one of joy and family togetherness. I watched as my children delighted in their surroundings—as Santan ate and was not ill—as Samara relaxed, a constant smile on her face—as Carla laughed and joked. Randy was exuberant when he unveiled the dessert, which turned out to be a steaming hot, homemade Christmas pudding with a savoury sauce that smelled of cinnamon, allspice, and nutmeg—and perhaps a hint of rum.

"I made the pudding myself!" Randy informed—"from a recipe that I found in one of my mother's old cookbooks. It was called 'Grandma's Secret Christmas Pudding Recipe.'"

The pudding was so rich that it melted in my mouth. Never had I tasted anything so delicious and I wished I had not eaten so much of the main course. I sensed, by the looks on everyone else's faces, they were wishing the same.

We retired to the living room after the meal. The children opened their new presents. Randy turned on the TV and found a channel that was playing Christmas carols. When the choir sang *The First Noel,* Adelaide and Carla sang along, easily hitting the descant notes. Randy and Alfred had Santan scrunched between them on the couch, and Santan was reading them a story from one of his new books. Samara was sitting on the floor. I watched my daughter—closely.

She was staring at the television screen. Her face took on a shrewd look as she listened to the carols. She looked even more discerning when the singing finished, and when the priest began to tell the story of Jesus' birth. Suddenly, an earsplitting screech filled the room. "Off! Off! Off!" she howled. Samara turned to me, her eyes flaming—no dark centre—just the red dancing blaze. "Off!" She crawled toward the TV and pulled herself to a standing position. She pounded on the screen. "Off!"

Quickly, Randy grabbed the remote and turned the TV off. Samara plopped down on the floor. At first, I thought she was going to cry, but she didn't. She just looked around the room, at each one of us—and then she smiled, strangely, and crawled over to Santan. She used the couch cushion to pull herself to a standing position, and reached out to her brother. She was shaking. Santan grasped hold of her hands and stared into her eyes. Not a word passed between them, but her little body relaxed under his gaze. Finally, she smiled sweetly and nodded her head.

Santan released her hands. With the aid of the coffee table, Samara walked over to Carla, who settled my daughter onto her lap.

The only sound, now, in the room was Santan's voice as he continued to read his storybook, unfazed by the recent event. I looked at my daughter, bewildered. Suddenly, it occurred to me what had set her off—the story of the birth of God's Son. But why had it not affected Santan in the same manner? This appeared to be just another indication of why Samara was truly more Basarab's child than Santan was.

~

The rest of Adelaide and Alfred's visit passed too quickly for me. Before I was ready to say goodbye, they were embracing me and telling me that they would try to return at Easter. They hoped Emelia would be able to accompany them then. Carla drove them to the airport. Randy stood by my side, and together, we waved goodbye to our guests.

"I would like to be alone for a bit," I told Randy. I was tired.

He took the hint and left. "I'll call you later, so we can make plans for New Year's Eve?" His voice sounded hopeful.

"Call me tomorrow." I shut the door.

The children were sleeping. I sat down on the couch and picked up a pillow and hugged it close to my body. I squeezed it so tightly that had it been a living person I probably would have killed them. I glanced at my hands and noticed the ring. I had almost forgotten about it, with all the hustle and bustle of the week. Slowly, I took it off and laid it on the end table beside the couch. I was remembering Carla's and Adelaide's words, when they had noticed the ring on my finger.

"He is a good person, Virginia," Carla had stated. "Maybe it is time you moved on."

"You have no idea what you are suggesting, Carla," I returned.

"Your husband is dead."

"Don't I know that, and don't you know that, as well!—
more dead than any of us will ever be, unless we were to embrace
his world!" Even an untrained ear would have heard the sarcastic
irony in my words. "So how can you even suggest that I bring
Randy into my life, leading him to think there could be anything
more to our relationship, beyond friendship?"

Carla had cleared her throat and looked away. It was
Adelaide who came to my rescue. "Virginia is right, Carla, she
cannot be with Randy, or with any other man. We are all aware
that Basarab will return for his son, and when he finds out he also
has a daughter, only God knows what the count will do then.
Virginia is wise not to get romantically involved."

"But what if something happens over there? What if it
goes so badly in Brasov that Basarab does not return for years—
maybe never? Should she just bury herself in a hole and not live
her life?" Carla posed the question to Adelaide.

"Better she bury herself in a hole, than Basarab bury her–
–and Randy." Adelaide had walked out of the room, leaving
Carla standing there in shock, her mouth open.

~

Once again, I fell to crying. Life continued to treat me
unfairly. However, I knew that it was time to stop feeling sorry
for myself and do something about my situation. My tears
shuddered to a stop. I took a deep breath. Tomorrow would be a
new year. I could no longer procrastinate.

To save my life and the lives of my children, the ultimate
weapon I would be able to wield against the vampire world that I
had been sucked into, was to continue learning how *their* minds
worked. Weren't vampires just like the serial killers in my
textbooks? Well, some of them, at least. As I walked to my
bedroom, I held my head high. It was time to stop being a victim.
Life was what one made of it, and I was ready to live again!

I crawled under my covers and closed my eyes, resolute in what I needed to do. I relaxed, not even fearing the dreams that might invade my night...

I think it is time that you left me alone. Don't you have something better to do, other than tormenting me? I stared up into Basarab's eyes, as he strode toward me.

He laughed, and then did something unexpected. He placed his hands on my waist, picked me up, and twirled me in the air. *It is over! I have come for you and my son.* His voice was filled with joy.

Put me down! My voice was piercing, filled with anger. *How dare you come to me and think you can just take over my life again ... you are too late ... I have found someone else!*

Basarab stopped and set me down. His face furrowed into a deep frown. *Did I hear you correctly? You have found someone else?*

Yes.

He burst into laughter. I felt his evil surround me. *And you think that I will allow you to be in another man's arms ... that I will allow another man to be a father to my son ... how is it that you have become so foolish in the time that we have been apart?*

Do not speak to her like that! Randy stepped into the room. His presence filled the empty spaces and sucked up the fear I had begun to feel. I moved to his side. I looked up into his brown eyes and saw that they were darker than I had ever seen them before. He pushed me behind him.

Basarab laughed again. *She is giving me up for the likes of you? You are nothing ... nothing against me.*

I love her.

Love has nothing to do with this ... boy.

It has everything to do with it. Randy took a step toward the count.

To an average sized man, Randy might have appeared formidable with his height, and his well-muscled body, but beside the count, he was small, at least it seemed that way. I reached out to hold him back, but he brushed my hand away. *I won't let him have you, Virginia ... you are mine ... he has no right to you...*

The room began to swirl. I was falling down a deep well. Randy and Basarab followed, each trying to grab hold of me. We splashed, one after the other, into the water at the bottom of the well. As I surfaced, gasping for air, I was between the two men. They each grabbed one of my arms and pulled. Blood was everywhere, as my body split in half.

~

I awoke screaming, raced to the bathroom, and pitched the contents of my stomach into the toilet. I crumbled to the floor and wept. Why did life keep eluding me?

Basarab

Chapter Twenty-three

I am tired.

How many more centuries must we endure this curse? There are times I think we should spawn our personal apocalypse, thereby ending our miserable existences. However, we, like most of humankind, cling to life. That is the one thing Tanyasin could not take away from us—the human desire to live!

I continued to worry about Santan. Even though my father constantly assured me that my son was safe with Virginia, I still wished I had not had to leave him behind in Brantford. I tried to understand why Emelia helped Virginia, but my anger toward my aunt clouded my judgement. Emelia was family—she should have known better. So, no matter how many nights I walked the city streets, drinking of their fruits, I still wallowed in misery.

I had thought of forcing Emelia to tell me where Virginia and the child were, something that I could easily do. However, if the wrong people ever found out about Santan's whereabouts, and if harm were to come to him because of that, my heart would be crushed. I realized I needed to keep my focus on the situation the family was embroiled in. If I did not, there would be no hope for any of us, including my son!

~

We have had a few victories lately. Lardom's litigation team managed to get some of our accused family members freed. We celebrated with a small dinner party. Unfortunately, there was quite a commotion in the dining room beforehand, which I happened to witness prior to everyone else's arrival. Teresa was still coming apart at the seams. With her constant absences, as she pursued our plan, Ildiko's flirtations continued to escalate. I overheard the women arguing as I approached, so I lingered outside the door, to watch and listen. It had begun when Ildiko slipped into the chair beside where I sit—Teresa's chair.

"I believe you are sitting in my chair," Teresa had said to her, icily.

"I believe that it is first come, first take," Ildiko had returned, just as coldly. "Except for Count Basarab's chair, of course," she had added with a smirk.

"You seem to forget, my dear Ildiko, I am the count's queen, not you; therefore it is I who sits next to him at the table."

Ildiko had pointed to the chair across the table. "Take that one then." I heard the sarcasm in her voice.

"That chair is his father's." From where I stood, I saw Teresa put her hand on Ildiko's shoulder. "I think you should move, now!"

Ildiko brushed Teresa's hand away. "I think you should not touch me, Gypsy!"

I had never seen Teresa so furious, not even when she had fought with Virginia. Teresa attempted to slap Ildiko across the face. "Why you insolent…"

Teresa never had a chance to finish her sentence. Ildiko grabbed my wife's wrist in midair. "Don't think that you will ever be strong enough, or fast enough to lay a finger on me, Teresa! I will say and do what I want. You are nothing more than a dirty Gypsy! The count is stuck with you because your conniving Gypsy father tricked him into making a bargain to save the worthless soul of his own unfaithful wife—your mother! I am of the true blood of the family; I did not have to be *crossed over*!"

It was at that moment that Emelia and Evdochia arrived to the other entrance of the dining room. They tried to defuse the situation, but there was no taming the shrews that spit forth that night. Emelia went immediately to Ildiko and put her hand on the young woman's shoulder. "Ildiko! Let her go. Basarab will not be happy about this. Don't you think he has enough to worry about right now, without having you two at each other's throats?"

Evdochia approached. "Ildiko, you know this is Teresa's place at the table. You cannot change what already is." Evdochia's voice was soft as she spoke, but I noted, from the look in her eyes, she meant business.

Ildiko looked from Emelia to Evdochia, and then to Teresa whose wrist she still held. Finally, she let go. She pushed away from the table and stood up. "You are correct, my dear aunts. I should be thinking of my beloved cousin more than anything right now; he has enough to contend with." Ildiko turned and faced Teresa. "Your time will come, Gypsy. Basarab will tire of you and realize what a mistake he made by taking you as his wife. Then, he will come to me, his blood. I will be waiting for him, and I shall relish the moment when he casts you into the pit of darkness!" Ildiko inclined her head to her aunts. "I shall dine elsewhere tonight," she commented on her way out of the room.

Her brother, Gara, almost bumped into her as she was leaving. "Ildiko, where are you going?" he called to her. She did not answer.

Gara's eyes swept over the circumstances. He looked as though he were about to call after his sister, again, but I stepped out from the shadows, into the room, and put my finger to my lips. "Later," I mouthed. He read my lips and nodded.

Teresa appeared shaken. I cannot say I blame her for her reaction toward Ildiko. She had become a member of the family through no choice of her own. Max should never have made the bargain with me. He had seen enough of *what* we were. But then again, how can I blame him? He loved his Lilly, and was willing to sacrifice anything to release her from the hell I had entombed her in. Had the shoe been on my foot, to what extent would I have gone to have found a way to save the life of someone I loved? To what extent would I go to protect my son, who, besides my father, seemed to be the only person I truly loved? At the moment, I only tolerated my wife, and my feelings for Virginia were no more than fascination—or so I told myself whenever she entered my mind.

As I walked into the room, Teresa stared at me for a few seconds, pain pooling in her eyes; then, without a word to anyone, she turned and left.

~

The friction between the two women, even though they steered clear of each other over the next couple of days, weighed heavily in the air. I needed to speak to my father, to gain his wisdom on how to handle the issues between Teresa and Ildiko. As I approached his study, I heard voices, and noticed that his door was ajar. I hesitated, and then leaned against the wall...

"Uncle, might I have a word with you?" Ildiko's voice was almost a whisper.

"Of course, my dear, how might I help you?"

"I have some information for you to take to my cousin, but I do not know if you will believe me, or just think I am being vindictive, especially after what happened the other night between me and Teresa."

"What is it, Ildiko?

"Do you have any doubt, uncle, that I love your son?"

"No."

I shook my head. There had never been any doubt in my mind that she loved me. When we were younger, I had thought it was just a crush that would eventually wear off. Ildiko had always been a *wild child*, and I had no idea how much she loved me until Gara had confided to me that his sister had always assumed she would one day become my bride. After all, we were blood, and that was how it was supposed to be done.

"The other night, after the scene in the dining room with Teresa, you know we both left, right?" Ildiko's question returned my attention to the conversation beyond the door.

"Yes."

"I was in my room, looking out my window, when I saw Teresa leave the hotel." There was a lull in the dialogue.

"Go on." I heard my father encourage her.

"I decided to follow her."

"And...?"

"She met with Elizabeth Bathory."

I wished I had been in the room at that moment, so I could face my cousin—see into her eyes—see the truth, or the lie. I hoped that my father would seek the same answers I would have, had I been there.

"How long was she with her?" my father questioned.

"Over an hour."

"Did you hear what they were discussing?"

"No. I was too far away and did not want to get closer; I did not wish to be detected. But I can tell you this much, whatever they were talking about, it looked to be serious."

"Did anyone else join them?"

"No."

"You have no reason to bring me a falsehood, do you Ildiko?" I detected an unusual firmness in my father's voice.

"Uncle! How could you even think I would do that? Even though I am repulsed by Teresa, I would never consider lying to you, or to Basarab. She will soon enough bury herself. I have but to wait for my moment."

I heard the elevator bell, and remembered that I had asked Max to tell everyone about the meeting I had called. I had failed to inform him that I would let my father know because I had wanted to speak with him before I met with the others. I stepped into the room that was across the hall from my father's, keeping the door cracked slightly so that I could still hear what transpired. Max knocked on my father's door.

A few seconds later, my father appeared. "Max ... what can I do for you?"

"Basarab sent me to ask you to come to the meeting room. He has gathered the family council for an emergency meeting." Max bowed his head, then turned and quickly walked away. I wondered at his behaviour, thinking about how distant he seemed to have been of late.

Ildiko approached the doorway. "Do you think he heard what I told you about Teresa?"

"I have no idea," my father replied. "We do not know how long he was outside the door; but, if he has overheard us, it will not be long before Teresa knows that you saw her with Elizabeth. Conversely, he will realize if I am privy to such knowledge, it will not be long before my son knows of his wife's deception!"

After Ildiko left, I slipped out of the room. Instead of going to my father, as I had planned, I headed back to my quarters, hoping that Teresa would be there. I knew that my wife was not betraying me, and soon the others would know of our plan, as well. It was time. The fact that Ildiko had told my father of this possible betrayal made it even more necessary for Teresa and me to lay our plan on the table. Teresa was curled up on the bed, resting. I filled her in, briefly, and then asked her to present herself at my meeting in about an hour. That would give me plenty of time to deal with other matters.

~

My father was last to arrive to the meeting. I noticed the pained look on his face as he entered. The room overflowed with a sombre atmosphere. I gazed around the table, at each of its members, and saw the looks of despair, frustration, and anger at this blight, more diabolical than ourselves, which had infiltrated our family and was attempting to destroy it. I noted the fury in Dracula's eyes.

"Ah, Father, you have arrived." I stood up and stepped forward to greet him. "Dracula has been filling us in on some of what he has learned about Radu's traitorous intents. He is clearly in league with Elizabeth Bathory, as we thought, and with others whom we were unaware. It appears Radu has gathered a collection of what this modern-day world would consider 'serial killers.' His most trusted ones, he recruited over a hundred years ago. Somehow, Radu was able to defer their executions and the expulsion of their souls. Humans, who believe these people to be dead, are in for a revelation."

Dracula spoke up. "My sources have told me that Radu worries constantly about the rogue loyalty, and their willingness to comply with his wishes, thus the reason for him keeping most of them drugged. He also thinks he can trust Elizabeth—that she would not betray him because he is the one who turned her, saving her from living out the rest of her life in a stone cell. I am almost positive, despite her brilliant mind, that she is not aware of Radu's full and true objectives. My brother cannot be trusted. She believes that she will sit next to him when he ascends to the throne, but I wonder if she realizes his true feelings toward women. I am surprised he has been able to demonstrate such restraint, considering his lust for men. If truth be told, Radu is partial to Jack, a secret that those two have kept extremely well hidden from Elizabeth. Then again, perhaps Radu should watch *his* back; Elizabeth could know of his deceit. Maybe she has *her* own ambitions!" Dracula had posed several items for us to consider.

Bajnok stood. He was as tall and thin as I remembered him to be; but today, everything about his personal appearance was unkempt. As he began to speak, everyone around the table paid close attention. "There are several large cells of rogues in Moldova. Although we know, from Dracula, that Radu's main headquarters is in Cornvinesti Castle, we have also learned that Radu has rogues hidden in many of the castles he owns in the regions. The massive castle dungeons make the perfect hiding places. I am convinced that legions of rogues are scattered elsewhere, as well. Radu has been a busy man, purchasing numerous fortresses in Hungary, Romania, and the Ukraine—and possibly countries we are not yet aware of."

I nodded my head. "Thank you, Bajnok. We will need to execute a plan to discover which castles are housing the rogues, and then, either destroy the cells or destroy the entire building. It would be a shame to wipe out such architectural history, but I am sure the human tourists, walking the halls by day, have no idea what evil forces lay beneath their feet. It will only be a matter of time before Radu unleashes his horrors on our family and humans." I paused. "I also have some additional information for us…" I turned toward the door and called out: "Teresa, you may come in now; we are ready to hear what you have to tell us."

I noticed the puzzled look on my father's face. I figured that he was pondering the information he had just heard about Teresa meeting Elizabeth; and, he was probably wondering what game his daughter-in-law might be playing, as well. Ildiko's words rang through my mind as I watched Teresa walk across the room, and take her place next to me. She bowed her head respectfully to the council. "My Lord," she addressed me.

I decided to skip formalities and delved right in: "Teresa has been meeting with Elizabeth Bathory, trying to infiltrate her organization."

There were several gasps around the table. Finally, Gara posed a question. "How so, cousin?"

I deferred to Teresa.

"My fellow comrades, keepers of our family and all that is right about it … as you might have noticed, Basarab and I have been at each other's throats since soon after we arrived in Brasov. We do apologize for this, but it was a necessary façade that we needed to present. What is going to be said here in this room must stay with every one of you. It is not to be told to wives, children, friends—no one."

I grimaced when Teresa referred to our fighting as *a necessary façade.* Most times, it had been anything but that!

She continued. "I have gone to Elizabeth, begging her to take me in, telling her that I can no longer remain happy in my husband's arms, since he is so focused on being in someone else's. I even mentioned how he spent time with the woman, Virginia, when we were in Canada; but be assured, I did not tell Elizabeth that Basarab has a son. I told her about Basarab's cousin, Ildiko, who is so enamoured with my husband, and that Basarab is returning to her the same favours that she is offering up to him!" Here, Teresa turned to Gara, and to Farkas, the twins' father: "Forgive me for this, but it was necessary. All will be explained to Ildiko, in due time. It has to be this way so that she will play her part well.

"I am aware that Ildiko followed me the other night, and saw me meeting with Elizabeth. Therefore, I am sure, by now, Ildiko has told at least one of you that I have met with Elizabeth." Teresa looked directly at my father. He nodded affirmatively. "Just as Basarab and I thought, she would go to Atilla first. Actually, I have met with Elizabeth several times, and I think I have finally gained her confidence. She believes I am willing to betray my husband—that I am tired of being treated like a piece of disposable property. We even laughed together, joking about how we were more like the modern women of this world than our men would think, or want us to be!

"However, in order to ensure Elizabeth believes that this deception is genuine, there is something I must do. I am going to have to move out of the hotel. Elizabeth will never believe I am betraying Basarab unless I do so. That is another reason this information must not leave this room. Tonight, at supper, Basarab and I will have an enormous argument, after which I will leave and flee to Elizabeth. It is a dangerous game I will be playing because Elizabeth Bathory is an astute woman, and she has not survived all these years by being anyone's fool." Teresa took a deep breath and turned the floor back over to me.

"We have decided that you, Bajnok, will be our liaison with Teresa. The details of how we are to work this out have not yet been exacted, but before tonight is over we will have our plan in place."

Bajnok nodded. "I am honoured, Basarab; I will do whatever it takes to bring down this evilness that is disseminating through our family."

"Thank you," I returned with a strained smile. I turned to Teresa, again. "Now, my dear, is there anything else you can tell us? What do you know, so far, of my dear Uncle Radu's plans for us?"

"Well..."

Before Teresa could answer, a loud commotion broke out on the street in front of the hotel. Quickly, I went to the window and looked down on the scene. Police cars were everywhere, roaring up to the front entrance.

"Everyone, get to the dining room!" I ordered. "We must make sure that we all have alibis in case the police are here for us. What better alibi could we have, than all of us sharing a meal together? Gather the women and children, as well." I turned to my father. "Make sure that Max and the other servants get some food spread out on our table. As distasteful as the smell of it is, we shall have to set the scene. I will head down to the lobby and see what this commotion is all about. For all we know, it might not even have anything to do with us, but I cannot take that chance, especially with everything else that is going on."

I waited until everyone had left the room, and then turned to Teresa. "You must slip out of the hotel at the first available moment that you are sure you will not be detected. I will instruct

Bajnok to meet you in the restaurant on the south side of The Square tomorrow night. You know which one I mean?'

She nodded. "It will all go well, Basarab; I assure you."

I studied her, my thoughts turning to her erratic behaviour of late, to the conversations I had overheard, and to the moment when she had first come to me with her idea. Could I fully trust her? When did the sweet young woman, whom I had married, change so drastically? There were moments when I could not stand being in the same room with her.

"Basarab?" Teresa laid her hand on my arm.

I smiled to her, assuring her that all would be well. "Yes ... I am sure you will be safe if you stick to the plan." I said the words of assurance, even though I did not believe them. I had a deep foreboding about the whole plan. I ran my finger along her cheek, and down her throat. "I could not bear it if something terrible were to happen to you," I added. I noticed how she winced at my touch, but I said nothing.

"Nor could I bear it if something horrible were to happen to you, my dear husband," she returned, with her eyes downcast to the floor.

I headed out the door, leaving her in the room, and took the elevator down to the lobby. As the elevator door opened, I noticed two police officers talking to the desk clerk. She was checking something on the computer. Then, she glanced up and looked directly at me as I entered the lobby. I read her lips: "That's him." I walked toward the front desk, nonchalantly, as though I had nothing to do with why the police were at the hotel.

The taller of the officers approached me. "Excuse me, are you Basarab Musat?"

"I am. How might I be of assistance?" I kept my voice calm.

The officer cleared his throat. "Is there somewhere private we might talk?"

The clerk must have heard his question. "There is a meeting room just down the hallway," she pointed out. "I believe it is empty at the moment."

The officer who had spoken to me motioned for me to lead the way. As we left the lobby, I noticed the hotel entrance was totally blocked off by police, and there were also several officers scattered throughout the lobby. However, only the two officers who had been at the front desk followed me into the room. One of them stood by the door while the taller one motioned for me to take a seat at the table. He sat down, opposite me. I tried desperately to keep my emotions under check, but inside I was seething. How dare they ... this was my hotel ... my domain!

"I am Officer Skultety. We are sorry to bother you at this late hour, but we are looking into a mass murder."

"That is awful!" I exclaimed, trying to sound shocked. "When did this happen?" I was hoping that it was within the last few hours, to ensure my alibi.

"This evening," Skultety continued, "we have been informed that you and some of your guests here at the hotel may be responsible for this bloodbath." He scowled. "Can you tell me why you were coming down to the lobby?"

His question threw me off guard momentarily, but I recovered quickly. "I was heading out for a walk, something I do most evenings. You can check with the staff; they see me coming and going all the time. I and my guests were just finishing our meal." I patted my stomach. "I think I overate." I ran my tongue over my lips and sighed deeply.

"Where are your guests right now?" Skultety asked.

"When I left the dining room, they were all still there, chatting about how we are going to spend our next few days." I smiled, thinly, not wanting the officer to catch sight of my fangs.

Skultety did not return my warmth. "Could you tell me why so many of you are gathered here in this hotel?" His face was poker-straight.

"Of course. We are having a family reunion, which is something we do every five years. Since I own this hotel, and it has been a while since we have held a reunion in the country of our ancestors, we decided to meet here."

"You have been here for some time, though, I have been informed." Skultety pushed forward.

"You seem to be well-informed," I stated sarcastically. "However, to answer your statement, yes, we have." I offered nothing further, unsure of where Skultety's line of questioning was headed. I thought it better to err on the side of caution.

"Do you always have such *long* reunions?" His eyebrows rose inquisitively.

"Not always," I replied. "This year is special; my father is turning 70."

"I see ... well, I will need to speak with the others when we are finished here." Skultety reached into his jacket pocket and pulled out a pad of paper and a pen. He flipped to an empty page. "Where were you at 8:00 this evening?"

"I told you already; my guests and I were having supper. If you wish to check, I am sure most of them are still sitting around the table—we have a tendency to linger over our meals." I smiled again, still being careful not to reveal anything out of the ordinary.

"What time did you start your meal?"

"We arrived in the dining room shortly after seven, I believe."

"All of you?"

"Yes."

"And that includes?"

"All of us ... although, I assume by now that some of the women and children will have returned to their rooms," I added.

Skultety tapped his pen on his booklet. I could tell from the look on his face that he wanted to ask me another question; however, before he could speak, I continued. "I honestly do not understand who would be pointing fingers at me and members of my family for such a heinous crime as what you have described. We are business people, with companies and properties all over the world; what cause would we have to murder anyone?" I looked directly into the officer's eyes. My tolerance was running thin.

He hesitated a moment more, before he spoke again. "Actually, the people who were murdered are prominent business people, themselves. We were informed they had business dealings with you, and that these dealings had ... gone sour. Our witness told us that the victims had discovered you were being underhanded." Skultety leaned back in his chair and stared at me. His eyes were dark, and deep-set, and were difficult to read—typical for a cop.

I leaned forward in my chair. Inside, I was seething. I did my best to hold my anger in check. "You say these people who have been murdered are here in Brasov?"

Skultety nodded.

"And they were doing a business deal with me?"

Again, he nodded.

"And is this a recent deal ... that you know of?"

"So I have been informed."

"Well," I stood. "I think we are finished here then. I have no current business dealings with anyone here in Brasov. Whoever has informed you of such is sadly mistaken. I have been patient, so far, but the more I hear from you, the more ridiculous this entire affair sounds."

The next question was dropped like a bomb. "Do you know someone by the name of Uros Musat?"

"Yes ... of course, he is my uncle. Why do you ask?" I queried cautiously.

"He is in jail now, isn't he?"

"Yes ... on some trumped-up charges. Our lawyers are working on getting him released."

"Your legal team seems to have quite a job right now, don't they? Are there not several people connected with you and your family in jail at the moment?" Skultety grinned, for the first time in the interview, as though he was the cat who had just lured a giant rat into an open trap, and was getting ready to slam shut the cage door.

I threw my head back and laughed. And then leaned over, placing my hands on the table in front of Skultety. "Yes ... it would seem there is someone out there who is trying to destroy my family name. So, in a way, I am not surprised at your little visit here tonight to my hotel. My legal team has already gotten a few of our people out of jail, proving the charges against them were farcical and unfounded. In fact, I have started my own investigation into the legal system here in Brasov ... I feel there is some corruption that needs to be weeded out.

"If this harassment continues against my family and friends," I continued, "I will have no choice but to remove all of my businesses, which are many, from this city. As I already mentioned, my family has assets everywhere, all around the world, so that will not be a difficult task! And then we will see what happens, won't we? The economic impact on this city will be catastrophic! So, whoever this informant is, I think you should go back and tell them that they are sadly mistaken..."

"I would tell them if I could; however, the guy's in a coma," Skultety cut me off.

"Excuse me?"

"He was the one victim who survived the attack. Before losing consciousness, he actually described you to a T. What do you think of that?" Skultety grinned again.

"I think, for someone who must have been in the throes of near death, he was most informative. I also think it is a total setup, just like all the other allegations toward us have been. Whoever is behind these lies has not been able to oust me through previous charges to my family and friends, so now they are attacking me directly. This entire façade is too ridiculous for me to waste any more of my time on. If all you have is the testimony of someone who is now in a coma, I think we are finished here. If you want to come upstairs, my family will confirm my whereabouts during the questioned time frame, and that of anyone else in the family who might be implicated in this sham!" I turned and headed for the door.

The officer who was guarding it looked questioningly at his superior. I did not hear a word uttered, but he stepped aside and allowed me to exit. As I reached the elevator, I became aware of a small group of men behind me. I turned. Skultety and three officers.

"I think I will take you up on that offer," Skultety said, "just for the sake of checking out a couple of other descriptions we were given."

"Incredible. This person not only detailed the events precisely, he gave you accurate descriptions of the perpetrators!" I retorted as the elevator door opened. I stepped in and pushed the button for the floor where my relatives would be gathered around a dining table. The police officers stepped in after me.

The ride up was quiet. I studied the men who were with me. They had no idea who I was, or what I could do to them. There was a time when I would not have tolerated such an infringement on my life; I would have just eliminated the problem. I noticed the sweat breaking out on the brow of the two younger officers and wondered if they were nervous about something. The door finally opened, and I led the way out.

When I opened the door to the dining room, I breathed a sigh of relief. My family was sitting around a table laden with the end of what looked like had been a sumptuous feast. In the centre of the table sat a half-eaten cake, which could easily pass for a birthday cake. I smiled at the irony of it.

My father rose as we entered. "Is everything okay, son?"

"It seems to be, Father, just a little mistake in identity. These gentlemen want to check where I was, and where some of you were this evening. I told them that we were here celebrating your 70th birthday." I was watching the officers from the corner of my eye, especially Skultety.

"I see." My father approached us. He was smiling. "Would you gentlemen care to have a piece of birthday cake? I am afraid that we have stuffed ourselves so much that none of us has any room left to finish it off. I can have Max bring some clean plates?"

I noticed Skultety studying my father. "You look young for seventy," he commented.

"I am fortunate to have aged well … and having a good plastic surgeon helps, too." My father grinned.

Skultety scowled; apparently he did not see the humour in my father's statement. "You also look a lot like one of the descriptions we were given," he directed to my father. He looked around the room; I noticed his brow furrow.

"Is something wrong?" I enquired.

"Well, there is one thing I can see for sure ... it is obvious that you are all related."

"Are your descriptions beginning to become a bit foggy, now?" I asked.

"Possibly." I could tell that Skultety did not like having to admit to that.

"Then I think that you should return when you are better informed," I stated.

Skultety gazed at me, hard, and then turned to his fellow officers. "Let's go." He paused in the doorway and looked back at me. "Don't any of you leave town until we get this matter settled. I'll be in touch."

"Indeed," I replied. "I look forward to seeing you again, to hear what other untruths might be directed toward me and my family. Enjoy the rest of your evening, Officer."

I turned to Kerecsen and Laborc after the police were gone. "There is someone who was just taken to a nearby hospital; he is in a coma. I need you to follow the police captain because I am sure he will be checking in at the hospital where his witness is. I don't need to tell you two to be discreet. It is imperative that we find out who this witness is because he has incriminated me, and some of you, in a mass murder that took place tonight. Report directly to me when you have found out what we need to know. Take the back way out of here."

~

After everyone else scattered to their rooms, I returned to my own quarters, hoping that Teresa might still be there, so we could discuss what had just happened. I still could not shake the awful feeling I had about what she was going to do. I entered into silence.

I had never had much use for televisions, but decided to flip through the news broadcasts while I waited for a report from my cousins. Scenes of the mass murder were splashed across all the channels. I snorted in disgust, not recognizing any one of the victims. On one of the TV stations, paramedics were loading someone into an ambulance, but I could not see the victim's face. I flicked the TV off, stood up, and began to pace.

There were many times, especially lately, when I wished that my life could just be normal, like that of humans. To be born … to love … to have children … to grow old … to die. Yes … even to die.

~

Kerecsen and Laborc returned sooner than I had expected, and the news they brought with them was disturbing.

"The cop was not difficult to follow," Laborc laughed, "and the hospital is only about five blocks from here. We watched, from the lobby, which floor he got off, and then took the stairs. When we stepped into the hallway, we heard the officer shouting at a nurse. He was demanding to know how she could have allowed someone to come into the ward and move a comatose patient to a different facility. The nurse appeared quite distraught at being yelled at by a police officer. We moved closer, and ducked into a patient's room so that we could better hear what was being said."

"You can imagine our surprise when the nurse mentioned that a woman named Elizabeth had come for her brother, Jack, saying that she would be taking him to a private hospital where he would receive specialized treatment. We had to stop ourselves from bursting into laughter," Kerecsen smirked.

I grimaced, trying to hold back my own mirth at the irony of the situation. "Of course, Jack would be able to describe us, and fill in numerous innuendoes about the family. You have done well. The stew in the pot is thickening, and I fear it is about to bubble over. Get some rest, my friends. Darker days are yet ahead of us."

Chapter Twenty-four

After Kerecsen and Laborc left my room, I sat for a long time, alone, thinking about the plan that Teresa had convinced me to go along with. I had not believed, for a moment, that Teresa had the wit or the fortitude to carry out such a deception; but she had insisted, saying there was no other way to get information as quickly as she would be able to. I still feared for her life.

Teresa, despite what I overheard her say to her father, and all the annoying things she had done lately, was still like a drug to me; although, I would never openly admit that to her, or to anyone else. When Max had first come to me with his proposition, there had been no hesitation in my mind. I saw, even as young as she was, she was going to be a potent beauty. From the moment I had laid eyes on her, the day she was born, I knew that one day she would be mine. The bargain that I made with Max, to release his Lilly, hadn't really been necessary, but I guess I owed that much to Max, for all he had done for me. I would never admit that to him, though. So many secrets I have concealed in my heart...

This curse, which has been inflicted on the family, especially on me, goes beyond my inner psyche. I never asked for the responsibility of leadership. I am more like my father than many would believe, so it has been a difficult role to play—a fine line I have been forced to walk, to keep up the façade. The only one who truly knows me is my father; yet, even he is not aware of all the demons that feast off my soul. I have done some horrible things in my life, to facilitate my family's survival in the human world.

One of those *things* was Virginia—a beauty who happened on a beast who decided to use her for his own needs. I knew I had snatched her from her human life and plunged her into my sinister world. I enjoyed her company—her mind, and her body. And then, I just discarded her. Granted, I was going to leave her alive and just take my son, but she escaped with him. This angered me, almost beyond her redemption. There were moments, when it first happened, that I had wished I had killed her. Then, I would have had my son with me; my family would have been intact.

I was confident that Emelia was financially providing for Virginia and my son. She would not just have helped Virginia escape with Santan and then forget about them. However, I have been too immersed in this turmoil that Radu and Elizabeth are causing to do anything about it right now. It seemed to me that Radu would stop at nothing to seize the throne of power. Unfortunately, I and the family know that Radu will not rule with the same peacefulness that I have over the past few hundred years. He must be stopped. Elizabeth, as well. I was deluged with thoughts that she might be the more dangerous of the two. Her actions, over the centuries, indicated clearly that she was not a woman to be trusted. I feared for my Teresa. However, there was no turning back now.

~

Bajnok informed me that Teresa had not shown at the meeting place, as we had scheduled. He feared something had gone amuck. "I sent Kardos to a local bar that is frequented by rogues, to see if he could glean any information. Kardos befriended a group of rogues who were becoming quite drunk, and he pretended to be drunk, as well. Once he felt the rogues had let their guards down, he questioned them about the impending *movement*."

Kardos appeared in my open doorway and knocked softly on the doorframe.

"Ah, here he is; I will let him fill you in on what else transpired." Bajnok moved forward and embraced his son.

Kardos smiled. "What have you told Basarab so far, Father?"

"Just to the part where you were going to question the rogues."

"Ah…" Kardos turned to me. "It was an entertaining evening. One rogue had a lot to say. He told me that Radu was the new king of the vampires, and he had laughed heartily when he mentioned how your days were numbered. He even caressed his lips with his tongue when he spoke of the beautiful queen that Radu would have sitting by his side, when he ascended to the throne, of course. His eyes had glowed with lust when he mentioned that Radu's queen was not as fine-looking as your queen; but, he also pointed out that she was still a *looker.* However, she had a temperament not to be crossed! The rogue had snickered as he suggested, in many ways, she was more powerful than Radu, who at times seemed too feminine to be in the company of *real* men. The other rogues had nodded in agreement."

"Is that all you found out?" I asked when Kardos stopped talking.

"They clammed up, all of them, when I asked about the rogue armies I had heard rumours of. One of them slipped, though, mentioning that they had heard their master's queen-to-be had left on a trip to somewhere in Canada."

An icy hand, colder even than my own, clutched my heart. Were my worst fears being realized? Was Santan in danger, as well? "Did they say whether she had gone alone?"

"I asked, but they ignored the question; which tells me that they knew, but for some reason that was a line they had decided not to cross. A couple of the rogues, who were less drunk, had begun to show wariness at my questions, so I excused myself and left."

"You have done well, Kardos. Thank you." I gave him leave to go, and turned to Bajnok. "I will be in touch with you soon, in order to determine what our next step will be. I fear the worst."

"As do I," Bajnok returned; then he left, as well.

Now, not only were the burdensome circumstances that I had returned home to resolve still looming, my Teresa was missing. How much more could I be expected to take—my son—now my wife? In truth, it was Teresa I feared more for. Virginia, I was sure, would do whatever it took to ensure that no harm came to Santan. Teresa was with the enemy, and she was no match for the evilness exuding from every pore of Elizabeth Bathory's body. She could do what she wanted to me, but I would not be able to bear it if Elizabeth struck Teresa down. I decided to call another meeting, to see where we stood on all our fronts. I would consult with my father beforehand, though, for he had been my strength over the years—my voice of reason.

~

"It has gone badly, Father," I told Atilla, once he settled into a chair.

"I know."

"Then you have heard about Teresa not showing for her meeting with Bajnok."

"Bajnok enlightened me."

Why was Bajnok telling others of our business, before running it by me first? Before I could express my thoughts, my father continued.

"Bajnok did not want to tell me. When he returned early from the scheduled meeting, I just happened to bump into him in the hallway. I noticed that he appeared troubled, so I pressed him to tell me what was wrong. At first he refused to discuss the matter, stating that only you should hear what he had to say. I told Bajnok you were deployed in other matters…"

"Deployed in what, Father?" I intercepted, feeling that even my father had no right to such assumptions.

"You were resting, son, something you have not done too much of lately. I did not want to interrupt your sleep." I noticed a look of concern in my father's eyes. "Do you not trust your own father, Basarab? You should know that I, of all around you, would do naught to harm you. Since the day you were born, you have been my sole reason for living—especially after your mother died."

I conceded to his query by shaking my head and murmuring that I trusted him above all others. After an uncomfortable pause, I suggested we call everyone together to establish a definite game plan, and that we should send someone out to find Teresa. My father's next statement sent another shock wave through me.

"Emelia has disappeared, too."

"Emelia! … When?"

"About the same time as Teresa, maybe the day before. I am not sure. Max told me that Emelia left him a note, stating that she had to leave, but she did not explain her reasons. The note said that she would contact us when it was safe to do so."

"And the note did not divulge where she was going?"

"No."

"Why did Max not come to me with this information?" I sputtered angrily.

"He said Emelia's note instructed him to speak with me." Atilla stood up, walked over to my refrigerator and withdrew a bottle of blood. He held it up. "Would you like a glass, son?"

"No! I have no appetite. Everyone seems to be going behind my back, assuming they are protecting me. I need to know every move that everyone close to me is making; I should never be kept in the dark about anything! If someone else wants to be the king of the vampires, let them step forward. Our family was cursed, but I more so than any. Remember, Father, I was still in my mother's womb when Tanyasin cursed me with this role. Tell me, was it her way of getting even with you for the support you gave to Dracula, the one for whom the curse was actually meant?"

"I have no idea what the reasoning behind her curse was, other than retaliation for the deaths of her husband and her son. I have no idea as to why she cursed the entire family, other than to say that hatred that festers into revenge is the most vile hatred one can imagine. Angelique has been solidly behind us, trying to lighten the blows inflicted by Tanyasin; yet even with all of her power, I do not think Angelique is a match for such a witch."

"Is it not said that Tanyasin acquired her power from a witch who lived somewhere in our mountains?"

"True. Many have tried to find the sorceress; no one has been successful. Many think she does not really exist, that it was solely Tanyasin's obsession that turned her into what she has become." Atilla poured a glass of blood and took a sip. "However," he continued, "at the moment, we have more urgent matters to see to. I will send a message to everyone to join us here in your chambers at midnight. Is this okay with you?"

I nodded.

Atilla finished his glass, set it on the counter and headed for the door. "Until midnight, then."

I felt ill with all that had transpired. My son—my wife—my aunt—what manner of a leader was I? Despite the power I had originally gained from taking my nourishment directly from a warm body, that strength was waning. My time in Transylvania was draining me, mentally and physically. Or, was it because I was channelling my strengths elsewhere?—that my subconscious was so set on finding my son that it overshadowed all else I needed to focus on. What I needed now was some nourishment; I could not remember when I had last drunk; however, I was not in the mood to head out into the night. I filled a glass from the bottle my father had left on the counter—probably on purpose. I downed the blood in two gulps, and then picked up the bottle and walked over to the couch. I sat down, put my feet up on the coffee table, and raised the bottle to my lips.

As the liquid raced through my veins, an enormous sense of tranquility overwhelmed me. I leaned back and closed my eyes, drained the remainder of the bottle, and then hugged it against my chest. I felt as empty inside, as the bottle of wine now was. I would rest a few moments … there was time … before they came…

What are you doing here?

I came to see you, my count. It has been far too long since you have held me in your arms." The sweetness of her voice overwhelmed me. *"Are you not happy to see me? I brought someone with me. He has been asking for you lately, so I thought it was time for me to make this trip.*

I strode toward her and gathered her into my arms. Her scent was as breathtaking as I remembered it to have been; I buried my nose into her crimson curls. Virginia. I thought you were forever lost to me. I am so thrilled you have come. And you have brought my son—how kindhearted of you.

Oh, my dear count, it has been insensitive of me to have kept your son from you for so long—and to have kept me from you. I know how you love me, not Teresa. It is I who gave you what you most desired—a child.

You must not say such a thing. I do love Teresa.

How could you, after all she has said and done? Do you not know that she does not want your child? That she only tolerated this union between us because it was what you wanted? I would be afraid to leave Santan with her, especially if she were to go into one of her jealous rages!

She would not harm him...

Wouldn't she?

Virginia's arms curled around my neck. I could feel the heat of her body pressed against mine, and then realized that we were both naked. Her face was turned upward, her lips slightly parted, as she waited for me to start the dance we had danced on so many nights. She smiled—radiant! She ran her fingers through my hair, along my face, down my back, over my buttocks. She moulded into my body, a perfect fit, massaging my manhood with musical movements. I immersed myself into her ... there was no turning back...

Papa! What are you doing to my mama?

I stopped and turned at the sound of the voice. My son was standing in the room. He was still a child, but he spoke as an adult. And he was beautiful—like no child I had ever seen. His black hair was full of softly woven curls that cascaded to his shoulders. His eyes were raven-coloured, set deep in their sockets, mysterious, and yet, sparkling with life. The lines of his facial structure were much softer than my own. Actually, he resembled his grandmother, Mara, as I had seen her in the portrait my father had had painted of her before her passing. He also resembled Virginia; they had the same smile.

From somewhere behind him, I heard another voice— female—young, but strong. *Santan! I want to play! Leave Mama and return to me!*

We came here to see our father, and time is short. Mama told us so.

Mama is always dictating to us; I am tired of her. I stared deeper into the shadows behind my son and saw another child, but I could not distinguish its features.

Virginia pulled away from me and walked toward Santan. She knelt in front of him. I was shocked that she would display her nakedness to the child; but when I took a second glance, I saw that she was fully clothed—as was I. *I told you that I would* come and get you as soon as I had had a few moments with your father—did I not say so, Santan?

Yes, Mama. But I was impatient; you were taking so long.

Virginia laughed. I smiled. It was so good to see her, to hear her voice again, to hear her laughter. It appeared, though, that she did not see the other child that I had heard. She took Santan by the hand and led him over to me. I gathered him into my arms and hugged him close. There was a warmth to him that was not in me. I assumed that it was the human side of him. Virginia stepped back, looking pleased.

I am sorry we cannot stay longer. There is much to do at home, and I must return before I am missed.

Before you are missed?

She did not respond to my question. She just continued to smile—beautiful—amazingly more so than I could remember her ever having been.

And then the other child's voice penetrated the peaceful moment, again. *Santan!*

Santan reached to the shadow and drew it up beside him. I still could not make out its features—only, that it was slightly smaller than my son, and it had the voice of a young female child. The shadow curled into me and giggled. Santan was smiling as he watched the creature he had guided up onto my lap. *See, I told you that he was wonderful. Papa is the most powerful man alive … the most powerful man alive … the most powerful man alive …* the voice began to fade, as did Santan and the shadow. Virginia remained for a few moments more, but the serene look on her face had changed.

I am sorry to do this to you, Basarab, but I felt I owed you this much—to let you see your son before I go into hiding. I have learned the basis of your power. I will not hesitate to wield my new knowledge over you, should you try to take my son from me.

Your enemies have been liberal with their information. I am also to tell you that if you wish no harm to come to Santan, you will leave Brasov now. You will go anywhere you have to, even into exile if need be. You should leave the ruling of the vampire race to someone better suited. She started to chuckle. I noticed vindictiveness in her, for the first time, ever. Virginia had never been evil—desperate, yes—never evil.

I reached out to her. *Who are you in league with?* But she just backed away, sneering wickedly. Away from me ... away ... shadows disintegrating into the walls ... banging ... something falling ... more banging...

~

The wine bottle thumped onto the floor. I sat up, startled, and realized that someone was knocking on my door. I checked the time. Midnight. It must be my father and the others. I tried to collect my thoughts as I walked to the door. Why were there two children in my dream? Santan had known the child and had introduced me as her papa. I heard my son's words in my head ... *Papa is the most powerful man alive!* I straightened my shoulders and opened the door, Santan's words returning power to me.

"Welcome gentlemen. I apologize for my tardiness in getting to the door; I must have slept too deeply." I motioned them in. As I was about to close the door, I noticed Ildiko lurking in the hallway. I paused a moment, before shutting the door, dismissing her. As I turned to my guests, I heard a door down the hallway slam shut.

"Would anyone like some refreshment?" I asked.

"No, we have all supped," Gara stated. "We did not want to waste more time than necessary. Shall we begin, dear cousin?"

Everyone gathered around the council table. I took my place at one end, my father at the other, and the meeting began. My father and I filled our brethren in on what we knew and asked them, in return, if they had any new, important information to divulge.

Chapter Twenty-five

Lardom was the first to speak. "I have finally managed to procure bail for Uros, but I am afraid we have lost one of our best sources for obtaining information, now the courier contract has been awarded to someone else. Radu has closed the city up tighter than a doubly waterproofed ship."

"When will Uros return?" I enquired.

"Tomorrow; I am to pick him up."

"How is he mentally coping?"

"Not well. He appeared broken when I last spoke to him. Even getting released on bail did not cheer his spirits. I assume he has been drugged, like the others." Lardom looked thoughtful.

"It is good that we discovered the tainted blood issue early on," Ponqor commented. "When Uros arrives tomorrow, I will draw some of his blood, and continue working on an antidote. I have depleted the samples I have drawn from others. I am close to a solution, though; I can feel it in my bones."

"No one, including our human friends, will be safe from Radu's drug," Stephen brought up. "I would not put it past him to start slipping his drug into the wine supplied to the key people whom he has a desire to control, if he has not already done so. Our cities think this scourge that is tormenting them now is horrific—it is nothing compared to what Radu's rogues will do once he releases them on the entire population."

"It makes sense that he would be building up supplies of the drugged blood-wine and storing it in the same fortresses where he keeps his rogues," Gara pointed out.

"I am just thankful that, so far, only one batch of blood that has come through here has been tainted. Ponqor, you have done a superb job in double-checking our supplies," Atilla said.

"There might be a way…" Ponqor had a thoughtful look on his face, "of discovering where Radu's main storage units are. If we were to snatch some rogues who Radu allows to roam freely in the city, we might be able to obtain that information. Of course, we should target the stable ones, because they would most likely be the ones Radu has overseeing the others."

Kerecsen grinned broadly. He flexed his fingers. "Laborc and I would be honoured to assist you with this, Ponqor."

Laborc appeared to be contemplating something. His brow was creased with worry lines. "This is a fantastic idea, but are we to release these rogues after we get our information? Would they not run to their master and tell him all?"

I nodded to Laborc. "Well mentioned, my friend. You and your brother bring us the rogues; we will extract whatever information possible, and then I will dispose of them."

Gara laid his hand on my arm. "Let that be my pleasure, Basarab; you have more important matters to concentrate on."

"I think Gara is correct, son," Atilla affirmed. "And, if I might add, it may be a good idea if some of us ventured out and toured some of the other cities, inspecting them for ourselves, to locate as many of Radu's sites as possible. One cannot always depend on the word of a rogue, even if he fears his life is at stake. Most of these fellows probably fear Radu's wrath more than they fear their own death." He directed his attention to Gara. "You and your father can oversee goings-on here, while we are gone."

Up to this point, Farkas had been silent. "I understand," he opened, "that you want me to stay and assist my son while you are gone; but I feel a trip back to Turkey might be in good order. A friend of mine, who is also one of my apartment superintendents, mentioned that a crazy woman, who goes by the name Tanyasin, has moved into one of my buildings."

"When did you find this out?" I asked. I tried not to let the anger that I felt creep into my words. It was not like Farkas to keep such information to himself.

"This morning," Farkas replied without hesitation.

"Was it your superintendent who rented the apartment to her?" I probed.

"Well, he told me that he had spoken with a man who wanted an apartment for his mother. He never actually met Tanyasin until yesterday. He told me the moment he laid eyes on her, he felt unsettled. Her appearance was eerie—evil. She was not your ordinary old, wizened Gypsy. Tattoos covered every inch of her neck and arms—tattoos of men impaled on stakes, their faces contorted with agony, blood dripping from their wounds ... a necklace of skulls—some of the skulls looked as though they had been freshly drawn ... snakes slithered around the impaled men and the skulls ... but, there was one tattoo etched on her face that did not follow the same revolting theme. It was of a beautiful, young Gypsy maiden dancing around a flaming fire."

"Tanyasin, for sure," Atilla's voice was barely audible. "The men on the stakes are representative of her husband and her son—both were impaled by Dracula. The Gypsy girl is representative of whom she used to be. I wonder what she is up to."

"That is what I want to find out," Farkas said. "I have my suitcase already packed, Basarab; I just await your approval."

"You have it."

Farkas nodded.

"And, I think you should take someone with you." I turned to Tardos. "How say you accompany him? Remember, none of us should go out alone any more."

Dracula started laughing.

"What is so funny, uncle?" I questioned.

"Have you forgotten about Officer Skultety? Did he not tell us that we were not to leave the city?"

Stephen smiled a ghost of a smile. "We will just have to use other methods of movement, then, won't we?"

At first I did not comprehend what he was saying, but then it dawned on me. We could leave the city on all fours, or on wing; the authorities would never know we were gone. I mirrored my uncle's smile, and then turned to Gara. "It will be your responsibility, when we are out, to make sure to cover for us if the police come knocking, and then contact us straight away on the cell phones so that we can return immediately."

Atilla stood and walked over to the window, drawing the curtain slightly aside. "The moon has begun its descent; we have only a few hours to prepare our exodus."

"We must all be vigilant," I stated. "I feel it in my bones that Radu is not far from unleashing his horror on the world. We must keep in regular contact with one another..."

I was interrupted by Vacaresti. "What of Emelia and your wife? Should we not send someone to seek them out? Possibly, to Brantford where you resided when you were in Canada?"

"My wife should be able to get access into the airport files, to find out where they went," Laborc stated. "At least the destination of the plane they boarded from here. That will give us a starting point."

"Okay, but we cannot waste too much time on them right now," I articulated. "I will need everyone here with me when Radu makes his move."

Atilla spoke up. "But, if it is true that they have gone to Canada, it must also be considered that Elizabeth knows of your son, Basarab. If this is the case, it would be much wiser to get to him before she does. Vacaresti is right; we must try to find the child." Atilla turned to Vacaresti. "You were not in the room with us the night the police visited, so you would not be missed if they were to show up. Would you be willing to go to Canada, to Brantford, to seek out your wife and the child?"

"I would have no other go but me. If my Emelia is in any danger..." he could not finish his statement.

I noticed the lost look in Vacaresti's eyes. It was the same look that I knew had been in my own when I discovered my son was gone. "You may go, uncle ... and why don't you take Ildiko with you? She, too, was absent that night. If you find Virginia and the child, Virginia will be more inclined to open the door to a woman she does not know, rather than open it to you, whom she does."

After a few more moments of small talk, I dismissed the meeting. Everyone dispersed to begin preparations for what was vamping up to be the battle of our lives—our existence—and that of humankind, as well. If Radu got his way, there would not be a human on earth that would be safe. There were moments I wished I could pray to the God my forefathers had once prayed to in the great cathedrals of Walachia, but the very thought of such a deity burnt into the nucleus of my mind.

I needed to prepare for my trip with my father, but first I had to seek out Ildiko in order to explain to her what she must do, and how crucial a role it would be.

~

Ildiko had not taken too well to having to accompany Vacaresti to Canada. She had complained furiously, at first, but finally agreed. I had cajoled her into doing it, by saying that to do so would earn substantial favour with me. I had even pulled her into my arms and held her tight for longer than a normal cousinly hug. When she had reached her lips up to mine, I did not push her away. Finally, she left to prepare for her journey. I could tell that she was not happy; however, I was hoping that she would be spurred on by the fact that if she followed through with my request and returned my son safely to my arms ... well, who knows what she might think her reward would be? At the moment, I honestly did not care what Ildiko thought she might gain, where I was concerned.

My greatest distress, now, was my son, and then Teresa, although I was not going to send anyone to follow after her. I could not afford to; she was on her own. I sat down in an easy chair and closed my eyes, waiting for my father to come and get me...

What? Are you not concerned for my safety, Basarab? Is all your talk of loving me, and wanting to be with me, just that— talk? Virginia circled my chair.

I attempted to stand, but her hands pushed down on my shoulders with a strength I had no idea she possessed.

Do you think for one moment that I will allow anyone, whom you might send, to take Santan from me? Why don't you come yourself? Or are you too much of a coward? Virginia came around to the front of the chair and leaned over, peering straight into my eyes. My loins stirred at her scent, at the closeness of her body.

There was something different about her; I could not put my finger on it. This boldness she displayed was so out of character. Who did she think she was, calling me a coward? I pushed my shock aside and grabbed hold of her wrists, noticing how hard she tried to control her pain as I squeezed tighter. I stood and lowered my face to hers, covering her mouth with my own, pushing the fire that was burning within me into her. She fought me, for only a moment, before we tumbled to the carpet.

We were lying spent, in each other's arms, when the door opened. Teresa entered with an enraged look on her face. *Is this how you repay me, husband, for my loyalty to you? You run to this whore's arms?*

I jumped to my feet, despite my nakedness. *Loyalty to me? Is that what you are, my dear Teresa?*

What do you mean by asking me such a question? Have I not endangered my own life by going to Elizabeth Bathory, to get information to help you?

Is it really to be of assistance to me, Teresa? Or is it to facilitate your own agenda?

The look of shock on her face was glorious to behold. At last, I was going to confront her with what I knew, with her deceit. By this time, Virginia was standing, as well. She had stepped over to where Teresa stood.

The first words out of her mouth sent a shock wave through me. *Are you going to allow him to talk to you like that, Teresa? Has he not controlled and ordered you about long enough? You and your father?* She paused. *I think it is time we women took that power away from him … if we stand by each other, we can win.* Virginia laughed maliciously.

I noticed the hesitation in Teresa's stance; the disbelief on her face. I was too stunned to move. I detected a movement in the doorway and looked up. Santan was standing there, taking in the scene. Slowly, he walked over to us. I smiled to him and reached out my arms. Actually, I did not care about either one of these women—Santan was the only one who really mattered to me.

My son stared at me for a moment. Then he reached out and took hold of, first Virginia's hand, and then Teresa's. He did not take his eyes off of me, until he turned and walked out of the room with his mother, and the woman whom I had asked him to call mother. I was too shocked to follow.

~

I awoke with a start. My father was standing by my chair, staring at me. He looked worried. "Are you okay, son?"

I gave my head a shake, trying to erase the alliance I had just seen in my dream. I stood, resolute in the fact that such a thing would never happen … that it was not possible. "I am fine, Father. Are you ready to leave?"

Virginia

Chapter Twenty-six

Christmas and New Years were over. My guests had returned home. I spent many of my quiet hours on my computer, studying and recording the events of my life. Santan and Samara played well together; Santan was even teaching his sister to read storybooks. Randy visited as much as possible, but he was busy with his studies. I received a postcard from Angel, saying that she would be home sometime in January, and would stop by to see me and the children. She was sorry she hadn't made it back for Christmas; she would have loved to share the holiday time with a friend. I had not heard anything from Emelia since her letter before Christmas. No news is not always good news, especially in this case. Adelaide had not been in touch, either.

It was snowing again. The children had been tucked into bed, settled in for the night, I hoped. I fired up my computer and opened the document of my time at *The House*. It was finished, finally, edited and gone over several times in order to make sure that I had all the details correct, as I remembered them, anyway. Most readers would never believe such a story was true, so when I sent it to a publisher, it would go through as a fantasy, gothic romance, psychological thriller—maybe all three. I chuckled softly at the thought.

I went online to search for publishers that might be interested in the vampire genre. There were several. I perused through them, running off the details of the ones that looked the most promising. When I finished, I had information on ten publishing companies sitting in front of me. I read each one thoroughly, noting the submission guidelines, and then I wrote a rough draft of a query letter.

I selected a couple of sample chapters, which I thought would grab the attention of any reader, to submit with my cover letter for the publishing houses. The long hours were beginning to capture me; I was tired. I glanced at the time on the computer screen—2 a.m.—way past bedtime. I shut down the computer, gathered my papers, and locked them in my desk drawer. That was something I had started to do since the day I had caught Randy glancing over some of my work. I hadn't wanted him to ask questions and get excited about me writing a vampire story, especially since I had given him the distinct impression that I had no use for such legends!

I had been sleeping reasonably well since the New Year. I was still dreaming, but not bad dreams. These new ones, I had no recollection of on awakening. It was a pleasant respite for me. But, as I laid my head on the pillow, trepidation spun a frigid, silvery web around me. A tremor convulsed through my body. I closed my eyes, anyway, because having to look after two extremely active children equalled needing rest once in a while…

Virginia, you are in grave danger. You must take your children and flee from where you are. Find someplace where they will never be able to find you. They are coming for you— more than one! You cannot trust any of them … any of them … any of them…

I heard the voice, but I couldn't see who was speaking. The voice was so muffled that I couldn't even detect whether it was a male's voice, or a female's. I felt cold, though—frightfully cold.

The voice continued. *There is little time, Virginia. Wake up and gather your children together, and flee…*

But where do I flee to? I found my voice. *And, who are you? Where are you?*

I am a friend—that is all you need know. Once you get outside, and into your vehicle, let your intuition be your guide. Trust me—trust your intuition.

What are you suggesting?

Think, Virginia ... use your common sense and you will discover the answer. Only put your trust in those that you know, in your heart, you can trust ... but go ... get out now!

And then I was running in a narrow, winding tunnel, one filled with eerie looking shadows—shadows that resembled diabolical creatures. Bats flew at my face. In the distance, I heard the echoes of howling wolves. I ran faster. Suddenly, Santan and Samara were in my arms. I pushed on. I had no idea why I was not fleeing in my van. My breathing was laboured ... my legs felt like jelly, almost giving way from under me ... I needed to stop.

Don't stop, the voice encouraged.

I thought I detected a light at the end of the tunnel, beckoning me forward. When I reached it, I realised it was just a street lamp, but the street was vaguely familiar. I noticed a row of trees just beyond the light.

Keep going.

I pushed forward, stumbling over the protruding roots as I plunged through the tree, and into a familiar yard. I dared to look up, even though I didn't want to because I knew where I was. *The House* loomed in front of me!

~

I awoke screaming, sweat pouring from every orifice of my body. I sat up and looked down at my hands; they were shaking uncontrollably. So were my legs. What was the meaning of the dream? I got out of bed and staggered into the washroom. I gazed into the mirror, and I was not happy with who stared back at me. Dark circles, swirling like voluminous angry black and deep-purple clouds, surrounded my eyes—eyes that had no life left in them, as though they had already accepted defeat.

I rested my hands on the edge of the sink, leaning heavily on the porcelain. After a few moments, I turned on the cold water and splashed some on my feverish face. I continued splashing, as though possessed, as though I could not get enough water to extinguish the fire within my head. The water spilt down my chest, much of it landing on the floor, forming a puddle around my feet. And I kept splashing … splashing…

"Mama! What's wrong, Mama?" Santan's voice sliced through my agony.

The next thing I felt was his little arms around my legs. I turned the tap off and leaned on the sink again, staring down at my son. Slowly, I knelt down and wrapped my arms around him. We stayed like that for a few minutes, and then I heard the patter of feet approaching. Samara had climbed from her bed and had decided to join us. Then she did something very rare for her—she reached out her arms and hugged me. I folded her into my embrace, along with Santan.

~

I spent a quiet morning with my children. We read books, coloured pictures, and erected some buildings with the big *Lego's* they had received from Carla at Christmas. Before I knew it, it was almost noon. The phone rang. The call display showed Randy's number.

"Hey there," I greeted him.

"Hey ... want some company for lunch? My treat. I've been cooking all morning, and trust me, what I have conjured up, you will not be able to resist."

"You don't have school today?"

"Cancelled … teacher was sick. So … want company?"

"Sure, why not."

Randy was at my door within a few minutes, as though he had known I would say yes. He walked in, carrying a pot of something that smelled delicious. He set it on the table and went to the cupboard for some bowls.

"Where did you get this recipe?" I asked as I polished off my second bowl. "This is the most scrumptious soup I've ever tasted!"

"Another secret," Randy grinned. He leaned back in his chair, a pleased look on his face. "Look, even Santan is eating it. Should we let Samara try some?"

"Might be too spicy for her," I pointed out.

"I doubt that. I don't think there is much that will ever hurt that child—she is tough."

"She might be tough, but that doesn't mean her stomach will be able to tolerate these spices yet."

"Just a couple spoonfuls…" Randy was already hovering a spoonful of soup in front of Samara.

"Soup … Samara want soup … like Santan!" She opened her mouth, and Randy obliged her. At first she screwed up her face, but then she swallowed and opened her mouth for more. I sighed in frustration and let Randy feed her as much as she wanted.

After lunch, Randy suggested we bundle the children up and go for a car ride. I pulled the curtain aside and noticed that it was a dismal day, but I still didn't want to go out. "Possibly, after the sun goes down. We were building a village with the *Lego* blocks before lunch; maybe you would like to help us finish it?" I suggested.

Randy, as usual, was easy to please. "Sure." He pushed his chair back from the table and began to clear the dishes. Within a few minutes, he had them washed, dried, and put back in the cupboard. "I'll just put the rest of the soup in your fridge," he remarked, "and then I'll join you guys in the living room." Watching him in the kitchen, I thought that I could get comfortable having someone like him around. But, how long would it last?

We spent the next couple of hours working on our *Lego* village. Santan was intense, making sure we did everything the right way, which turned out to be *his* way. Samara mimicked her brother so much that she had Randy in stitches several times throughout the afternoon. For the most part, after the first half hour of construction, I sat on the couch, reading one of my textbooks, glancing periodically at the handiwork of my children and my friend. Before long, my eyes closed.

"Mama! Look, Mama! We are finished!" Santan was shaking my shoulder.

I opened my eyes and looked at the completed handiwork. As my eyes moved from building to building, numbness slithered through my bones, like a giant cobra. I felt as though I was being devoured. Sitting in the centre of the village was a huge house towering over all the rest. It was a house surrounded by trees created from the *Lego* accessories, with shaded windows, with a room at the top, and a door that lead out to a widow's walk. The train set that Santan had received for Christmas bordered one side of the house he had built. My hand reached to my throat. I struggled for breath as the cobra squeezed harder, circling in for the kill.

"Do you like my big house, Mama?" Santan sounded excited. "Look, here," he pointed to the room at the top. "Wasn't this your room, Mama?"

I felt the blood draining from my face. I noticed a puzzled look on Randy's face as he watched my reaction to the house my son had built.

"Answer Santan, Mama!" Samara's voice rose to a lofty crescendo as she ordered me.

I was not sure how I managed to speak, but I did. "Yes, Santan, that was my room—yours too—for a short time." Somehow, despite how little strength I felt in my body, I managed to leave the room. In the kitchen, I grabbed my coat from the rack. "Randy, do you mind watching the children for a bit? I need some fresh air." I could barely hear my own voice. Before I heard Randy's answer, I was out the door.

Despite the frigid temperature, and the slipperiness of the ground, and how drained I felt, I took off running, trying to distance myself from my apartment, and from my children. I knew I couldn't be gone for long, and that I would never leave them, but the pain of what had just happened was too much for me to bear. As I ran, the tears began to empty from my wells of grief. Despite their saltiness, they froze on my cheeks, but I took no notice. I reached the end of the laneway and stopped for a breather, and then turned right and headed to West Street, walking quickly and with purpose.

At West Street, I turned left, and then right on to Buffalo Street. As my steps drew me closer to *The House*, I felt my body heating up. *What is wrong with you, Virginia? He is gone. They are all gone!* I stumbled up the laneway, which had led me to my freedom on the day that now seemed so long ago.

The House sat quietly serene. There were no cars in the parking lot, a probable sign that either whoever lived there, now, was at work, or *The House* was still empty. I looked around for the *For Sale* sign that I had seen a real estate agent set up the day I had walked by with Santan. I couldn't see a sign, and was unsure if that were a good indication, or not. I ventured closer, up on to the large white veranda. I crept along until I reached a window, then stopped and peered in. There was no curtain, so it was easy to see inside. I noticed white sheets had been thrown over the furniture, indicating that *The House* was most likely vacant. I wondered why it had not been sold; perhaps it was overpriced.

I continued, looking in each window I passed by. They all confirmed the same story. I walked up to the front door and tried the doorknob. Of course, it was locked. What else could I have expected? And what would I have done had it been unlocked— entered? Entered *The House* that had held me captive for almost a year? What was I doing here, anyway? I swivelled around and headed down the steps and across the lawn. I manoeuvred my way through the trees, back to the street. I needed to prove the trees could no longer hold me prisoner.

The sun was already setting when I arrived back at my apartment. Randy was busy serving up another bowl of soup to my children. I hung up my coat and sat down at the table.

"Feeling better?" Randy enquired.

"A bit," I lied. How could I tell him how I truly felt? How could I tell him the house my young son had built brought back memories of a dreadfully dark period in my life, memories that constantly haunted me?

"Good." Randy placed a bowl of soup in front of me, and as though he knew better than to ask me any more questions, the rest of the meal was conducted in silence.

After supper, we watched a movie with the children. Samara fell asleep, leaning on Randy's arm. Randy gathered her up and took her to her bed. Santan finished the movie with us, and then I tucked him into his bed. When I returned to the living room, Randy had turned off the TV and put on some classical music. He patted the spot beside him on the couch. I hesitated.

"I won't bite you," he grinned. I noticed his brown eyes dancing with mischief.

I sat down beside him, even though I didn't think it was a good idea. We stayed like that, side by side, for a few minutes, silent, listening to the music as it filtered gently through the room. Finally, Randy spoke.

"I was just wondering if you have thought to reconsider what I talked to you about—about us getting together and being a family."

I didn't understand why his question hadn't shocked me. Maybe it was because I expected him to ask me again? And why shouldn't he? We spent so much time together; Santan loved Randy, and even Samara seemed to have come around to him. I enjoyed his company, even craved it sometimes, especially when he hadn't come over for a few days. But then again, why shouldn't I crave it ... who else did I have?

"No," I answered, simply—softly.

"It is time to move on, Virginia. You could do a lot worse than me, but honestly, it is I who needs you. You have given me a purpose in life. Look at me now, compared to the lazy bum who opened the door to you that day and rented you the apartment, happy that I didn't have to clean it up. I want to be with you, and with the children." He slipped his arm around my shoulders and pulled me closer to him. I sensed his lips drawing near to mine.

I didn't push him away, at first. But as his lips brushed against mine, I froze. This was so wrong! I couldn't allow this to happen, as much as I might have wanted it to. My hands came up and I laid them on his chest, pushing him gently away. I noticed that his cheeks had turned red. "It's not you, Randy," I hurriedly assured him. "It's me. I am simply not ready yet."

Randy stood up. I noticed his desire. "I need to go." He hurriedly left the room, heading for the door. After a few minutes, I heard Randy's car start, followed by spinning tires. I knew there were some deep snowdrifts in the laneway. I hoped he would be careful.

I felt empty. My selfishness had just sent out the door the one true friend I had in the world. If only my life were different ... *if only*. I looked at my watch. It was later than I thought, almost midnight. I turned off the music and headed to my room. I didn't bother to put on my nightgown; I just lay down on top of the covers. I stared at the ceiling, thinking of what I should do—knowing what I had to do—but not wanting to. Tomorrow I would put my affairs in order. I had no other choice now; I had to leave. If Basarab returned and found Randy with me...

I closed my eyes ... the dream returned ... the faceless voice...

You are right, Virginia, you must leave; but not just because of Randy, because you and the children are in danger. They are coming for you—more than one. Time is running out! Let your intuition guide you. As the voice faded away, I found myself plummeting through the shadowy tunnel, again—with the bats and the howling wolves! Only this time, it went on forever!

~

I was awakened by a loud knocking on my door. I tried to focus my eyes on my alarm clock. It was three o'clock in the morning; who dared come by at such an hour? The pounding continued. I looked around for something I could use as a weapon. Most likely, it was just Randy returning, drunk—maybe to beg me again; but I couldn't be too careful, especially after the dreams I had just had. The words from my dream were spinning around in my mind. The biggest problem I had was there was no other exit out of my place, unless I used the common door between the two apartments. However, Randy and I had agreed to keep it locked, from both sides.

Cautiously, I made my way into the kitchen, feeling along the walls in the darkness. I pulled the corner of one curtain aside, just a bit, and peered out. I noticed two figures standing in the yard. They looked as though they were in deep discussion. It was difficult to determine if they were male or female because they were both quite tall. I noticed smoke from a car exhaust. It was too dark to see the car clearly so I had no way of knowing if there might be a third person. I turned around and headed to my phone, deciding, despite the hour, to call Randy and get him to open the door. Then, I would get my children up, and we would get out before it was too late. I realized that I had no choice but to listen to the voice from my dream—I needed to leave—*now*.

I stopped in my tracks when I saw Samara. She was standing in the doorway of her room. Her eyes burned brighter than I had ever seen them glow before.

"They are here, Mama! They have come for us! You must open the door and let them in!"

I lost control of my legs and crumpled to the floor. I had not had enough time, and now they were here. I had no idea whom Basarab might have sent after me; or, if he was one of the two standing outside my door. However, if it was him, I would have known; he would have been a towering shadow. That was not the case of either silhouette. Plus, *he* would never have knocked! Before I realized it, Samara moved toward the kitchen, heading for the door.

I tried to go after her, but my legs were unresponsive, not allowing me to regain my feet. "Samara! Don't go near the door, honey!"

Samara stopped. *Good, she's going to listen to me.* Somehow, I managed to stand by using the couch to pull myself up. I staggered my way to Randy's door. I pounded on it as hard as I possibly could, praying all the while that he had returned home. From the corner of my eye, I noticed Santan in the doorway of his bedroom, rubbing the sleep dirt from his eyes.

Suddenly, I heard Samara speaking, but this time it was not in a language I understood. However, it was one that was terribly familiar to me. I had heard it before—chanted—on several occasions. I watched in horror as the doorknob began to turn. I heard the dead bolt click.

Samara's voice continued chanting … the same sentence … over and over … the door began to open…

"Welcome," Samara said. She opened her arms wide; there was a radiant smile on her face.

Arms—strong arms—grabbed hold of me, as I collapsed to the floor.

Chapter Twenty-seven

I awakened in a strange room. My head felt as though I had been drugged. There were no windows, but I thought I heard wind blowing close by. I heard a child laughing from beyond the walls. My eyes searched for a door; I couldn't see one.

I attempted to sit up. I needed to find my children. Pictures of my last recollected moments flipped through my mind, like a slideshow on fast-forward.

The dream ... *They are coming for you...*

The shadows in my yard ... two...

Samara walking to the door...

Samara chanting in the strange language...

Me, pounding on a door ... Randy's?...

A lock clicking ... which lock?...

A door opening ... which door?...

A car speeding down the laneway ... me in it...

Randy's car? ... *Was it?*...

Me pounding on a car window ... trying to get Randy's attention ... but he didn't see me...

There were two children in the car ... one was silent; one was chatting with *them* ... a man who was driving ... a woman beside him...

Darkness ... after the woman touched me...

I felt a presence in the room. I looked around, still not able to locate a door. It was then that I saw him, leaning against the wall.

"Hello, Virginia. Finally, you are awake."

Fear wrapped its arms around me as the figure stepped closer—*Vacaresti*.

I managed to find enough courage to speak, although I could feel the tension in my vocal chords. "Where are my children?"

"They are safe. Ildiko is with them."

"Basarab's cousin?"

Vacaresti's eyebrows rose questioningly. "How would … ah … of course … my wife has been in contact with you." He smiled. "Yes … Ildiko accompanied me to find you and Santan, and Emelia. Imagine my surprise when I saw that you had two children. From the behaviour of the girl, I would say that she is also Basarab's?"

"Yes," I managed. "But, why would you be looking for Emelia?"

"Basarab sent me to recover her. She disappeared a few days ago, and we had a hunch that she might be coming here to find you, with the intent to get you to safety before Elizabeth Bathory and Teresa found you. Elizabeth is after Basarab's son."

"Has Teresa betrayed Basarab?" I was slowly beginning to realize what might be happening.

"No … Basarab believes that she is in danger, but that is not of any importance to you at the moment."

I looked around the room. "Where are we?"

"In Basarab's house." Vacaresti sat on the edge of the bed. "I am going to have to leave for a few days, to look for Emelia. You should be safe here with Ildiko until I return."

I picked up on the words *should be safe,* and shuddered. Suddenly, I became aware of another presence in the room. I looked over to the spot where I had first seen Vacaresti, just in time to detect a door melt away into the wall. A woman was standing there, staring at me. My children were beside her. I wondered how they had entered the room so quietly. Samara appeared jubilant … Santan serious. I felt as though ice was coursing through my veins. I shivered.

There was something about the woman that terrified me. She stood tall, over six feet. Her hair was black, like Teresa's, but unlike Teresa's smooth, silky strands, Ildiko's was crammed with long, untamed curls. Her facial features were sculpted to perfection, and the eyes that glared at me were filled with fire— much like Samara's. Noting her muscular physique, there was no doubt in my mind that she would stand up to any man if she was ever forced into a fight. Emelia had been right when she had told me that Ildiko would give Teresa a run for her money. Where Teresa's exquisiteness was delicate and feminine, there was a crystal-clear, untamed beauty about Basarab's cousin.

Vacaresti stood. "Ah ... Ildiko ... how nice of you to bring the children in to see their mother." He turned to me: "Virginia ... Ildiko; Ildiko ... Virginia."

We stared at each other. I had the feeling that she detected the fear in my eyes, but I could not read her eyes. They were like two uncut black diamonds. Neither of us spoke. Santan left Ildiko's side and ran to me. Samara gripped hold of Ildiko's hand and glared at me. My heart fell as I saw that my daughter had chosen her side, as young as she was.

The silence was awkward. Finally, "I shall be leaving shortly, Ildiko. You have your instructions." Vacaresti said.

Ildiko nodded.

"I can trust that all will be well?"

She nodded again. I assumed that Vacaresti was trying to assure me that I would be safe with this wild woman ... that she would answer to a higher order if anything were to happen to me or the children, especially the children.

"There are enough supplies here to last you for a couple of weeks; however, I do not think it will take me that long to find Emelia."

"I hope not; I am anxious to return home."

"As am I, my dear."

After Vacaresti departed, Ildiko left with the children. I could tell, by the look on his face, Santan hadn't wanted to go with her. On the other hand, Samara gave me the impression that she could not wait to get away from me.

~

It seemed hours had passed since I had seen anyone. The silence within the walls was deafening. I paced, just as I had done when I had been a prisoner in this house before—in my room— on the widow's walk. My mind was spinning, trying to think of a way out of my situation. The first time I was a prisoner, I had been pregnant; and, despite my condition, I had still managed several attempted escapes. This time I had two children to consider. I couldn't leave them behind, but they would also be an encumbrance if I took flight. Samara would be, for sure, because I was almost certain that she would not want to leave with me. Maybe, if I got the chance, I would just try to get out with Santan. I knew that he would come with me willingly.

The door opened, and Ildiko entered with Santan and a tray of food. By the look on her face, the very smell of the food disgusted her. I decided to try a conversation. "Where is my daughter?"

"Sleeping."

"How long are you planning on keeping me locked in here?"

"Until Vacaresti decides what to do with you; or, is instructed by Basarab what to do with you. I am sure of one thing, though; we will be returning the children to their father." She paused. "Basarab is angry with you for taking his son, you know. What a surprise it will be to him when he finds out about Samara!"

I decided to play a different game; however, I wondered if she were going to be as tough an opponent as Basarab and Teresa had been. I thought that eating humble pie might be the best route for me to take, under my present circumstances. "I know—as well he should be." I lowered my eyes to the floor.

I sensed that Ildiko was studying me. I dared to glance up. Once again, I looked into a dark pit of emotional nothingness. Then: "Don't think for a moment that you are going to play games with me, Virginia. I know what you are all about. What Teresa did not tell me about you, Basarab did. Vacaresti also warned me that you were an escape artist; so, if I do allow you out of this room, it will be temporary, and under my ever watchful eyes." She placed my tray on the end of the bed, took Santan by the hand and dragged him from the room. I noticed the tears in his eyes as he looked back at me, just before the door closed. I heard the lock click into place.

I thought it strange that Santan hadn't spoken a word this time, as though he were terrified to talk to me. I picked through the food on the plate, thinking. She hadn't said that she *wasn't* going to let me out…

There was hope.

Let the game begin.

~

I divided the next several hours between sleeping and pacing. I had no idea of exactly how much time had passed, but I assumed, by the rumblings in my stomach, that it was the next evening. Ildiko entered without knocking, but she did not have a tray of food with her this time. Perhaps, I was mistaken about the time, or maybe the order had come down to kill me by starvation. "I thought you might like to join your children for supper," she said.

I noticed a smirk on her lips and wondered at her sudden change of heart. Well, at least it wasn't starvation that was going to end my miserable existence! I was not going to be foolish enough to think that she would not be far away, so I stood up, and bowed my head demurely, as I thanked her for this small favour.

"Don't mention it," she returned. "Besides, I would rather not sit with your children while they eat. The smell of food makes me gag. It is traumatic enough that I have been forced to cook for you what I already have, and to feed them." She laughed. It was not a pleasant sound. "I have decided to allow you to make your own meals. But, be assured, I shall not be far away. Don't try anything funny." It was as though she had read my mind.

Ildiko led me out into a narrow, musty smelling corridor, similar to the one that I had been in the night Max had led me to Santan's naming ceremony. As we rounded a corner, I saw the stairs, confirming that my assumption had been correct. The doorway at the top was ajar, and I pushed it open and stepped into a familiar hallway. Ildiko came up beside me and grasped hold of my arm. I winced, and thought that her grip was firmer than necessary.

"Not that I think you would attempt to run and leave your children behind," she stated, "but I am not willing to take any chances." She led me into the dining room where I had had my meals when I had been Basarab's captive, and then proceeded across the room and opened another door, which led into a small kitchen area. "Everything you need is here," she pointed out.

"Where are the children?" I asked.

"I will get them and bring them to you." She turned to leave, and then hesitated. "But don't be getting any crazy ideas," she reminded me. "They are not far, and I have a keen sense of hearing. If you should try anything foolish ... well, let's just say that it would not bode well for your children ... especially the boy." With those words ringing in my ears, she left.

I clenched my hands into fists and pounded them on the counter. I could feel tears of frustration rising in my throat. *This is no time for tears.* I squelched them back to my heart, to rest with the other ones in my watershed of grief. I opened the refrigerator door and peered in. It was well-stocked with food. I set about preparing something light to eat, for my stomach was in turmoil and I knew I would not be able to consume a heavy meal.

As I prepared the food, I wondered what Ildiko had meant by, *especially the boy*. She wouldn't do anything to harm Santan, of that I was sure. She would not dare risk the wrath that would come down on her, from Basarab, should any harm come to Santan—particularly, if the harm was administered by her own hand. No ... she was bluffing.

Finally, I heard my children's voices. Samara's sounded excited. I heard Santan tell her to calm down. I turned to the cupboards, opening them until I found one that housed dishes. Pulling out what I needed, I headed to the dining room. Santan's face lit up when he saw me. Samara scowled. I set the dishes on the table and went to my son. Samara slunk behind Ildiko. I knelt down. Santan threw his arms around my neck and kissed me on my cheek.

Suddenly, there was a loud crash. It seemed to come from the study across the hall from the dining room. Ildiko raced to the window and pulled the curtain aside.

"Damn!"

"What is it?" I asked, following her.

She turned quickly, letting the curtain fall back into place. "There are two cars in the parking lot, and neither one belongs to Vacaresti." Ildiko grabbed hold of my arm. "Take the children into the small kitchen. There is a door on the far side; it opens into a narrow passageway that leads to the main kitchen. Find a place in there to hide until I come for you." She pushed me toward the children. "Hurry!"

I secured Santan and Samara's hands and headed to the kitchen. I could tell from the look on Ildiko's face that she sensed we were in great danger. Regardless of how much she most likely despised me, I knew that she would protect the count's children. For a brief moment, though, I thought that this might be a good opportunity for me to escape. To where, I had no idea, but it still might be worth a try.

As I was about to open the second door, I heard Ildiko shouting. "What are you doing here, Tanyasin?"

And then, the ugliest voice I had ever heard … "I have come for Basarab's son."

I could not shake the shiver of terror that bolted through me at the mention of the name Tanyasin. And, the sound of her voice was enough to send anyone into cardiac arrest. Why was she was here, in *The House*? My greatest fear, over the past months, had been the return of Basarab; I had not reckoned that my son might fall into the hands of the count's enemies. How I wished that *he* was here, now, for Tanyasin would be no match for him!

I reached for the doorknob. To my surprise the door began to open. A woman, dressed in Gypsy garb, stepped through, a finger to her lips. In the light of the small kitchen, I finally saw her face … Angel? But how … why … what was going on?

"There is no time to explain right now," she whispered. "Follow me," she said, turning back toward the door from where she had just come.

But before I could move, the door leading into the dining room flew open, and a foul smell permeated my nostrils. Samara screamed and clung to my leg. Santan stepped behind me. I looked into the eyes of a crazy woman. I noticed Ildiko behind her, a powerless look on her face, her body motionless, as though someone had cursed it to a frozen wasteland.

"Well, well … what do we have here?" Tanyasin's voice grated into the room. "Two little treasures … how lucky can I get!" She looked past me and snarled. "Angelique!"

"Hello, sister."

My mind became a jumble of confused thoughts. I looked from one to the other, not seeing any resemblance between the two women. How could this be? Angel? Angelique? Tanyasin? I could feel my legs beginning to crumble beneath me, and I fought hard to keep control of the tremors. Thank God, the counter was close by. I leaned against it. The children still clung to me.

More commotion was coming from the hallway. Doors opening and doors closing … hushed voices … footsteps approaching.

Angelique stepped forward, guarding me from Tanyasin.

Samara was still whimpering, so unlike her, and Santan just watched, his body tense.

How much more of this turmoil could God expect me to endure?

Epilogue

Teresa managed to slip out of the hotel while the police were busy questioning the family. Before leaving, she went to her father's room. She needed to tell someone, besides Basarab's closest council members, about the plan. The prospect of his daughter getting close to Elizabeth Bathory did not thrill Max.

"She is a bloodthirsty monster," were his exact words.

"And *we* are not?" Teresa leered. "Well, I guess I should clarify that, right, Father?—I am the one who lives on blood—not you."

"Tread carefully, daughter. I would die if anything happened to you."

"I know, Father." She paused. "We have just told Basarab's main council," Teresa said, "but the police raided the hotel, and we were stopped short of disclosing everything I have learned. I need to leave immediately. My greatest difficulty will be to convince Elizabeth that I am willing to betray my husband because I have not had enough time with her, to convince her to fully trust me."

"If you tell her about Virginia," Max suggested, "that will infuriate her."

"I already have," Teresa interrupted.

"Good. From all the rumours that I have heard, Elizabeth has no *use* for men, other than to use them for her own advancement. Look at poor Jack, how he bows to her every whim." A sinister look entered Max's eyes. "Maybe you should tell her about the child. It will be the most convincing part of your story. For you to disclose that your husband fathered a child with another woman, and that he is considering to replace you with her—what better picture is there for you to paint? The discarded wife! Elizabeth will be furious."

Teresa considered her father's words and thought of a compromise. "I guess that I could tell her there is a child, without giving up its whereabouts. Although I am not pleased about this child's birth, I wish him no harm. Technically, I would not be lying; I do not know where Virginia is. It would be foolish of her if she has stayed in Brantford."

"I also believe that you need to take even greater precaution of Radu. I am sure you will cross his path if you are with Elizabeth. He is to be feared." Max looked worried.

"I agree, Father; but at the moment, I need to focus on Elizabeth. I have a favour to ask of you; however, it is one that I am sure you are not going to be happy about. I was to go to Elizabeth fresh after a fight with Basarab. He was to have scarred me enough to convince Elizabeth that I had good reason to leave him. I have already hinted to her about the succession of beatings the count inflicted on me over the years."

Max looked petrified. "I hope that you are not going to ask me to strike you?"

Teresa nodded. "I am."

"I have never struck you."

"If you won't do it, I will have to find someone else who will, or do it myself."

Max shook his head. "I cannot."

"Very well. I will arrange something else."

Max shook his head. He was not happy about the danger Teresa was putting herself in. Old wounds surfaced. "You are risking everything for this family, Teresa. Are you sure that is wise? Basarab does not deserve you! Think about all the times he has scarred your beautiful face! And, I cannot forget how many times I have heard whispers of *dirty Gypsy* on the tongues of family members when they are speaking of you!"

As much as Teresa agreed with her father, she would never say her thoughts out loud. There was much that she kept hidden. There were moments she despised Basarab, despite how much she loved him. Teresa had known that Virginia had played a game—the game of survival. She played the same. And, Teresa was good at the game, having practised it for a few hundred years.

"It will be okay, Father; I will be in touch." Teresa embraced Max and then left the room.

~

"Your husband is a violent man." Elizabeth walked around Teresa's chair. She stopped and leaned on its back. Teresa felt Elizabeth's breath on her skin. Elizabeth scraped her nails across the veins on Teresa's neck. She traced the fresh scars Basarab had just meted out. She did not know that it was not really *him* who had done the inflicting. "What is it that you did that he would do this to you?" Elizabeth enquired.

Teresa's words came out slowly. "I stood up to him in front of his tramp girlfriend."

"Basarab dares to flaunt his whore in front of you?" Elizabeth's eyebrows rose questioningly. "I know our men are from the old world and think they can do whatever they want, but most of them have the decency not to parade their whores for all to see."

Teresa lowered her eyes. "She is not actually a whore; she is his cousin, Ildiko. She has always been in love with my husband, and she has never been inhibited in her pursuit of him. She feels that she, not the daughter of a filthy Gypsy, as she so often calls me, should have been Basarab's queen. Since our time overseas, it has not been well between Basarab and me. There, right under our roof, he *took* a human woman. He would leave my bed to crawl into hers."

Elizabeth moved quickly to the front of the chair. Her eyes pierced into Teresa's. "What happened to this woman? Did he turn her?"

"No ... but ... she had his child."

"A child?—boy or girl?"

"Boy."

"And where is this child now?"

"We don't know. The woman escaped just before we left. Basarab wanted to stay and pursue her, but Atilla said he was needed here, immediately. He told his son there would be plenty of time to find the child once we had dealt with you."

Elizabeth laughed. "I have caused quite a stir, haven't I?"

Teresa tried to stand. She wanted to look Elizabeth in the eyes; however, before she could move, Elizabeth put her hands on the arms of the chair and leaned over, driving her gaze into Teresa. Teresa was aware of the coldness of Elizabeth's eyes, even though red flames glowed around the dark centres. Her breath smelt of freshly drawn blood. Her face, although beautiful, was heavily made-up—her beauty not natural, as was Teresa's. Her skin was whiter than bleached bed linens, her hair the colour of the flames in her eyes. The mass of curls stood out starkly against her pale skin.

Elizabeth had a voluptuous figure. In the old world, it would have been pleasing to many a male taste; in the modern world she would be considered overweight. Her ample breasts flooded seductively from her dress. However, there was no hint of softness to her. Elizabeth's arms rippled with muscles, as did her neck and shoulders. She smiled and ran her tongue along her lips and then over her incisors. They were the sharpest fangs Teresa had ever seen, as though they were specifically filed that way.

She began to speak, and with each word, Teresa felt her blood turning into icicles. "I must know where this child is. You will find out for me."

Teresa chose her words carefully. She could not endanger the life of Basarab's son. On the other hand, she needed to be convincing enough that Elizabeth would believe her intentions were in *her* best interests, not Basarab's. "Trust me," Teresa's lips curled in a sarcastic grimace, "if there was any way I could have stopped that woman from escaping, I would have. She was a thorn in my side from the moment she stepped foot on our property. However, someone else had a hand in helping her to escape..."

"Who?" Elizabeth interrupted sharply.

"Someone I never thought would cross Basarab." Teresa paused, realizing she might have gone too far. She had not intended on involving Emelia.

"Who?" Elizabeth insisted.

Hesitantly, Teresa whispered: "Emelia."

An evil flicker raced through Elizabeth's eyes. "Emelia! Yes, you are right; I would not have suspected her. She has always adored Basarab!" She commenced pacing. "Unbelievable ... Emelia ... unbelievable!" She stopped and turned to Teresa. "She must know where the woman is, if she helped her to escape." It was a statement of fact, not a question.

At that point, Teresa realized what a horrible mistake she had made. Elizabeth was going to force her to get the information of Virginia's whereabouts from Emelia. Elizabeth would then kidnap the child and use him against Basarab. The child wouldn't stand a chance in the clutches of Elizabeth, or Radu. Basarab would be destroyed! Teresa knew he loved his son, above all else.

"I honestly don't know, for sure," Teresa finally managed to say.

"Then find out, *for sure*," Elizabeth snarled. "Prove that you are with *me*, Teresa. Consider this your first big test! I am sure you will find a way."

"She may not know, though," Teresa tried to defuse the situation before it worsened. "She helped the woman escape, but we left right afterward..."

"Ah, Teresa, please do not toy with my intellect. She would not leave this woman without financial support. Trust me, Emelia knows; you will find out for me—and quickly." She headed toward the door. "I must go now. It is good we are what we are; your physical scars are healing rapidly. Think about what I have just said; when I return I shall expect your answer."

"Where are you going?"

"Out."

Teresa watched through the apartment window as Elizabeth exited the building and disappeared into the night crowds. She began to pace. *Think ... think ... how do I keep Emelia safe?* She knew that Elizabeth would get to Emelia if she didn't come up with the information. Teresa thought hard about whom she could get a message to—fast. And, that person had to be someone Elizabeth would not suspect, if she had Teresa followed.

Max! Elizabeth would just assume that Teresa wanted to see her father. Teresa quickly left the apartment and headed toward the hotel, hoping that whatever the police had been after had been dealt with. She looked around the foyer, searching the shadows. All was quiet. Teresa sensed an icy shiver across the back of her neck. It circled to the front of her throat, squeezing tightly. *Is she here—lurking?* Teresa shook off the feeling and walked over to the check-in counter.

"Could you please ring room 1201?"

The receptionist threw her a puzzled look and then checked her watch. "Rather late, isn't it?"

Stupid girl! Teresa smiled. "That is not your business now, is it? Just ring the room."

The girl picked up the desk phone. "I am sorry to bother you, sir; but there is a woman here who insisted I ring you." There was a pause. "Yes, she is young and beautiful."

Teresa noted the disgust in the woman's words. *She probably thinks I am a prostitute sent to fill the needs of a hotel guest.* The woman replaced the phone into its receiver. "The gentleman will be right down." She turned away and busied herself with paperwork.

Teresa lurked in a corner while she waited for her father. Once again, the icy fingers crept around her neck, accompanied, this time, by a frosty whisper. *What are you up to, Teresa? Be careful now.*

Finally, Max entered the lobby. Teresa stepped out of the shadows and greeted him. She leaned over and whispered in his ear that they needed to find a secluded place to talk. He nodded. The woman behind the check-in counter glared at them. Teresa smirked as they left the hotel, her arm strung through Max's. There was a swagger in her step, too—just for effect.

"I didn't think to see you so soon, Teresa." Max sounded concerned.

"I did not think it would have to be so soon, either, but something has come up. I made a mistake with my wording, and now Emelia might be in danger."

Max was silent, waiting for Teresa to continue. There were times when her father's quiet demeanour bothered her, but this was not one of them. "I foolishly thought I could gain Elizabeth's trust by infuriating her with the fact the count is unfaithful to me and that he flaunts his infidelity openly. I thought she would buy my story much quicker that way—like you and I talked about. So, not only did I play up his obsession with his cousin, Ildiko, I mentioned the woman overseas. Elizabeth's astuteness is unmatched. She asked me if Basarab had *turned* her. I replied, too quickly I guess, that he had not, but that she had had his child."

"Santan will not be safe now," Max mumbled, even though it had been his suggestion, first, to tell Elizabeth about the child.

"No, he will not. Elizabeth demanded I tell her where the child is. I told her that I had no idea; the woman had escaped with the child, and there had not been time to go after them before we left for here. When I slipped and mentioned that she had had help, Elizabeth forced me to tell her who had helped them escape. I had to say that it had been Emelia. Now, Elizabeth is positive that Emelia knows where they are and has demanded I find out, proving that I am being true to her. I do not know what to do."

"Did you name Virginia?"

"No. Her name did not pass my lips."

"We must get Emelia out of the country, immediately. That way, you will be able to tell Elizabeth you could not reach Emelia to get the information." Max laid a hand on Teresa's arm. "Don't worry; I will deal with this."

Teresa noticed a bench. "Shall we sit a moment?" Once seated, she turned to her father. "You must do this tonight. Tell Emelia only what is necessary. I am sure she will listen to you, especially if she knows that Santan is in danger."

Max nodded, and then shook his head.

"What is wrong, Father?"

"It is so bad right now," he replied. "I have not witnessed such evil for many years—maybe never. It is one thing to fight the vampire hunters, another to have to watch our backs with our own kind."

Teresa laid her hand on Max's knee. She felt the bones protruding through the material. "Elizabeth is evil, Father. She was before she turned, and her turning created a bigger monster than Radu could even imagine. He has no idea what she is capable of. Maybe, eventually, they will destroy each other."

Max stood. "I better get back to the hotel and seek out Emelia." He reached over and embraced his daughter. "Be safe,

Teresa. You are the breath that keeps me from walking into the ocean, to drown my worthlessness."

Teresa started to follow him. "I will walk back with you."

"No, it is better I go alone." He hesitated. "Meet me here tomorrow night so that I can fill you in on how it went. You must think of something to tell Elizabeth, to keep her from your throat." With that, he disappeared into the night shadows.

Teresa headed back to Elizabeth's apartment, thinking hard on what she would tell her. When she arrived, the apartment was empty. Teresa grabbed a bottle of blood from the refrigerator and uncorked it. The cool liquid flowed easily down her throat. She felt a trickle on her chin and wiped it away with her hand, and then licked her skin clean.   Despite   getting   some nourishment, Teresa was still tired. She closed her eyes and fell into a deep sleep.

A sensation, more foreboding than anything she had ever experienced, wrapped around her, like a veil of ice. Her eyes opened. Elizabeth was sitting in a chair, a smile on her face—a knowing smile?—Teresa wondered.

"You slept well?" Elizabeth purred.

"Yes, thank you."

"So, how did you make out last night?"

Teresa decided that some truth was better than none. She was remembering the icy clutch on her throat and the voice of warning. "I went to see my father."

"I know. What did you and *your father* discuss?"

Teresa noticed the serene look on Elizabeth's face, as though she were waiting for her to make a mistake. Teresa stood and walked to the back of the couch. She rested her hands on the soft material and prayed that Elizabeth would not see her knees trembling, or her fingers. Yes, Teresa prayed—even though the words scorched her throat.

Finally: "We discussed how my father would get the information you need. Emelia would be too suspect of my intentions because she knows I had no use for the woman, so I thought it best to ask his help. Emelia would never suspect Max of double-crossing her; she knows how much the child means to my father. He is going to convince her that all he wants is to see his grandson, and since she admitted to helping with the escape, then she must also know where they are."

"Where is it that you lived?" Elizabeth's voice had an underlying shrewdness to it.

"You did not know?"

Elizabeth smiled. Teresa knew, then, that Elizabeth did know.

"Brantford."

"And the woman's name?"

Teresa felt that she was tumbling deeper into Elizabeth's trap. "Virginia." She swallowed hard.

"A last name?"

"She never told us."

"The child's name?" Elizabeth asked, a diabolical sneer on her lips.

"Santan."

"So … do you think Virginia is still in Brantford?"

"I don't think so. She would be a fool if she did not leave there, wouldn't she? Virginia was no fool. She managed to stay alive, and escape Basarab's clutches." Teresa returned to the front of the couch and sat down. "No, I am positive that Virginia would have left Brantford. She knows the count will return one day for his son."

"How is she surviving? Everybody needs money."

"Virginia is resourceful. I am sure she would have found a way to survive."

"She left Basarab's house with nothing but the clothes on her back. Is that not correct?"

"Yes."

"And she has a child, which means it will be difficult for her to work, and for more reasons than one. Her child is special—the son of a vampire. Who would she be able to get to watch him while she earned a living?" Elizabeth smirked.

"Possibly, Emelia gave her some start-up funds..."

"But how long would such funds last? Surely, by now they would be long exhausted, which means Emelia is still in contact with Virginia. Perhaps, she has a human liaison forwarding the money." Elizabeth rose to her feet. "I do hope you will have more information for me tonight. Are you meeting with Max?"

Teresa nodded, knowing better than to lie.

"Good. I am going to rest now. I will speak to you tomorrow." Elizabeth headed to the door.

"You do not sleep here?"

"No."

"Where then?"

Elizabeth sneered. The words slithered through her lips. "Where no one knows. Not Radu—not Jackie Boy—no one that I do not trust!" The door slammed shut as she left.

Teresa began to pace. Her plan was not going well. Elizabeth didn't even trust Radu; how could Teresa expect the woman to trust her, the wife of Basarab. She realized that she was in deeper than she and Basarab had expected she would have to go. Teresa felt heavy waves of deceit drowning her. She had done her own share of deceiving over the years, but nothing she had done could compare to what Elizabeth Bathory, the Mistress Deceiver, was capable of!

~

Teresa needed to make sure that Max had gotten Emelia safely away. She knew if she didn't come up with something, Elizabeth would get to Emelia, somehow. If that happened, Teresa was sure that Emelia would be no match for the wrath Elizabeth would mete out to extract what she wanted. Teresa sensed that Elizabeth's ultimate goal was to betray Radu and take the throne of power for herself. She didn't think that any man would be sitting by Elizabeth's side. When it was all over, Radu would be disposed of.

Teresa took a cape from the closet and threw it around her shoulders. She pulled the hood up, shadowing her face. She noticed a pair of sunglasses sitting on the dining table and slipped them on. Fully covered, she walked out the door, a plan already formulating in her mind. Teresa hoped that Elizabeth would not be lurking nearby, waiting for her to make a move—and stumble.

As she headed to the hotel, Teresa was hoping that her father had been successful. She felt that he would have been; she just needed to be sure. When she arrived at the hotel, Teresa went around to the employee entrance at the back of the building. A hefty man, in a cook's uniform, was entering the building; she slipped in behind him. He stared at her, a concerned look in his eyes.

"I noticed my husband waiting for me in the hotel lobby," she said, trying to look guilty. "I was out all night," she continued, and then laughed nervously. "Not something that one should do, if married to a jealous man."

The cook shrugged his shoulders. "Not my problem." His eyes raked over her before he headed off to the kitchen.

Teresa located the exit door, and opened it to a set of stairs. She headed up them, two at a time, deciding to seek out her father first. When she found his room empty, Teresa continued on to Emelia's room, which was on the eleventh floor.

Her eyes searched diligently up and down the hall. There was no one in sight. There wouldn't be—it was daytime—everyone would still be sleeping. Teresa crept down the hallway, making her way to Emelia's door. She knocked softly, with the hope that Emelia would not be there. She was just about to turn around and leave when the door opened.

"Teresa! What are you doing here?" There was a puzzled look on Emelia's face.

Teresa didn't have time to ponder on why her father hadn't gotten Emelia out of the hotel, but she was happy that she had thought to double-check. She would find out later; now she had to get Emelia away. She pushed her way into the room. "I need to talk to you. Our plan is not working out as we had hoped." She paused. "You are alone?"

Emelia nodded. "What plan is not working out?"

Of course, she would not know of the plan. Teresa quickly filled Emelia in on how she and Basarab had planned for her to get close to Elizabeth Bathory.

"Am I to believe this?"

"You need to."

Emelia turned her back on Teresa.

"Have any strangers contacted you recently?" Teresa questioned.

"No."

"Good … how long will it take you to pack, and get a flight out of Brasov?"

Emelia turned back to Teresa. "Why would I want to leave?"

Teresa plunged in further. "Elizabeth knows about Santan and Virginia; she demanded that I tell her where they are. She quickly figured out that you, the one who helped Virginia escape, would know where the child is—where Basarab's son is. For me to prove my loyalty to her, I need to obtain that information from you."

"And how did Elizabeth figure out that I helped Virginia?" Emelia asked.

Teresa could not look at her aunt as she replied. "I told her … but I was trapped, after I had said Virginia had had help, Elizabeth forced your name from me."

"So, why you are really here, Teresa?" Coldness filtered through Emelia's voice. "Is the story you told me just that—a story?—have you betrayed our family…"

Teresa cut Emelia off. Anger crept over the momentary embarrassment she had felt when having to admit that she had divulged Emelia's name. "No! I have not betrayed the family, not like you did, dear Emelia. But, unlike you, I am trying to head off the disaster I have possibly created through a slip of my tongue. You created a *situation* when you helped Virginia escape with the child. I am not a fool—I know that you know Virginia's whereabouts. And if I know, be assured that Basarab will assume the same. Only Atilla keeps him from obtaining that information, and from returning to Brantford for his son. I am here to make sure Elizabeth does not find you and force you to tell her where Santan is. You owe Basarab to get his son to safety. Virginia will never be able to protect him from Elizabeth!

"Now that the niceties are out of the way, I need you to pack and leave as quickly as possible. You must go to wherever the child is, and protect him. I do not want to know where. I told Elizabeth that Virginia would most likely never have stayed in the same city where she had been kept prisoner. Elizabeth will not leave anything to chance. Having me try to get the information from you first is probably just a ploy on her part to test me. I am sure that with whatever I come up with to tell her, she will still pay you a visit, either herself, or send one of her followers—maybe even Jack."

Emelia nodded. "How do I know for sure that you are telling me the truth? You never had any love for Virginia, or the child, for that matter."

"But I love Basarab—that you know. And he loves the child. I will not cause harm to what my husband loves. As for Virginia, I care not for her. I would cast her to a pack of wolves if I had the opportunity to."

"What are you going to do now, though? If I disappear, Elizabeth will surely discover your deceit and seek you out." Emelia sounded concerned.

"Let me worry about that. I am going to go to Basarab, once you are safely gone, and tell him our plan has failed and that I must hasten to the caves. Elizabeth is wilier than we thought— than Radu thinks. She even keeps her resting place a secret! She has gone there now, which gives us a small window of time to get you out of here."

Teresa noticed the continued misgiving on Emelia's face and realized that her aunt was still not convinced. She strode over to her, took hold of her hands, and looked into her eyes. "Emelia, I swear to you, I am telling the truth. If Elizabeth gets her hands on Santan, that could be the end for us. Basarab would go crazy! I have never seen him happier than he was the night his son was born—never! I won't take that from him—from the man who has given me everything."

"But he took everything from you, as well." Emelia still faltered. She was thinking about the fact that Basarab had more than one child that could be used as a pawn in this war. "Your mother—your humaneness..."

"He gave me a life with him, which is all that matters to me. There is no more time to waste, so if you refuse to listen to me, I will just leave. But I warn you, whoever walks through your door next will not be so concerned for your welfare." She started to walk to the door, with the pretence of leaving.

Emelia grasped hold of Teresa's arm. "Give me a few minutes to pack." She paused. "And, I will leave a note under Max's door, asking him to inform Atilla that I have had to leave. It is better that Atilla break the news to Basarab, under the circumstances of our current relationship."

On her return to the living room, she was carrying a small satchel and wearing clothing similar to Teresa's. She smiled as she put on her sunglasses. "Lucky for you that I have such attire."

"Lucky for you," Teresa retorted. "Shall we?" She opened the door and stepped out into the hallway, looking both ways to ensure they were still alone. Emelia headed toward the elevator. "No," Teresa stopped her. "We must use the stairs. We cannot chance being seen. After we deliver the note to Max's room we will head outside. Once outside, we will walk a few blocks and then hail a cab to the airport. When you purchase your ticket, I do not want to know where you are going. That way, if Elizabeth interrogates me, I will not have to lie—well, lie too much. I will tell her that I have not seen you; I will figure something out that will satisfy her. She is quite intuitive."

"Is it safe for you to return to her?" Emelia still sounded concerned.

"As I mentioned, I am going to speak to Basarab first, after I see you safely away."

They did not have any trouble getting a taxi. Teresa noticed how curious the driver was about them, more specifically, their clothes. He kept glancing at them from his rearview mirror. When he spoke, she knew she had been correct in her conjecture. "You ladies have a problem with the sun?" he asked.

"Something like that," Teresa returned. She was thinking that it was good he could not see the *hunger* in her eyes.

The driver reached for something on the front passenger seat. He must have scraped his hand because Teresa smelled the blood instantly. She watched as he raised his hand to his mouth, as he sucked the wound. She licked her lips. Emelia placed her hand on Teresa's leg. Teresa did not look at the driver for the balance of the trip.

When they arrived at the airport, Teresa directed Emelia straight to the ticket counter. "I'll leave you now," she said. "Will you be okay?" She had no idea why she was feeling so concerned; possibly it was the creeping feeling that something was going to go wrong—she couldn't shake it.

"I will be fine. I have travelled many times." Emelia chuckled, trying to break the iciness that existed between them.

"I guess you have." Teresa laughed, halfheartedly. Then she leaned over, embraced Emelia, and whispered into her ear: "Be safe, my dear aunt. I am sorry to have put you in this danger, and I will do whatever possible to remedy the situation. Keep the child safe. Take him wherever you need to, wherever it will be impossible for her to find him. Basarab's son must not be harmed." She kissed both of Emelia's cheeks, then left.

Teresa watched from outside the terminal as Emelia purchased her ticket. Emelia noticed Teresa, whom she still did not fully trust, watching her. She suspected that Teresa might try to see which plane she was going to board, so she turned and waved, then waited for her niece to leave.

Emelia procured a ticket for Montreal, but had no intention of going there. She assumed that Elizabeth would have someone check her destination, and was also aware that Elizabeth knew the child was somewhere in Canada. Emelia proceeded through security, and headed into the washroom. She had decided to take refuge there for the night. She knew her plane would leave without her and that her trip would be delayed, however, Emelia figured it was a worthwhile precaution. If Teresa doubled back, or if Elizabeth's minions were lingering in the airport, Emelia was confident that this move would throw them off her trail.

~

As Emelia exited from the washroom, it was daylight. It had been a long night, and her body was cramped from having been curled up on the cement floor of one of the toilet stalls. She had not slept, either, as people were coming and going the entire night. A couple of times someone had pounded on her stall door, not thinking that a locked door meant that it was occupied. Emelia felt lightheaded from not having had any nourishment for some time. She had not thought to pack any supplies. She needed to get to Adelaide's as soon as possible. Once again, she was compelled to depend on her old friend.

Emelia made her way out of the airport and headed to the train station, walking in the shadows as much as possible. She was just in time to catch the train to Kenora. Quickly, she bought her ticket, paying extra to secure a private compartment. Before boarding the train, she sent a telegram to Adelaide.

~

"Emelia!" Adelaide drew her into the apartment. "What is so pressing that you have come to me so? Your telegram sounded desperate."

"My dear friend, you have no idea what has transpired. Nothing good, that much I will tell you. But at the moment, I need some nourishment; were you able to get...?"

"Alfred should be returning any minute now with something for you," Adelaide assured her. She went around to all her windows and drew the shades down, and then motioned for Emelia to sit.

Emelia chose a large chair. She removed her headdress, and closed her eyes. "Just for a moment, my friend," she whispered. If Adelaide answered, Emelia did not hear her.

Adelaide gently shook Emelia's shoulder. Emelia was still groggy as she took the glass of liquid that Adelaide handed to her. She downed the contents in a few seconds. Adelaide refilled it. The second helping went down a little slower, but not too much. After the third refill, Emelia felt renewed. She set the empty glass on the table beside her and looked up at her friend.

"Elizabeth knows about Santan."

Adelaide gasped.

"She will probably throw a celebration feast if she finds out there are two children," Emelia added.

"How did this happen?" Adelaide wrung her hands worriedly.

Emelia filled Adelaide in on the events of her past few days—about the scheme Teresa and Basarab had concocted, about how everything started to backfire when Teresa had innocently let it slip that Basarab had a child. That had led to the disclosure that she had been part of the escape, and that most likely she also knew where the child was. Teresa had just done what she had thought was best, Emelia told Adelaide.

"However, if Teresa was being on the level with me, she is most likely in danger. I purchased a plane ticket to Montreal, and then spent the night hiding in the restroom. I am sure that Elizabeth will have someone check my destination, and that she will not be far behind me. It was the best way I could think of to throw her off my trail."

"But Montreal is still in Canada," Adelaide pointed out.

"Yes ... but I am hoping, when Elizabeth discovers the child is not there, we will have had time to move Virginia and the children to somewhere safe. I do not know how long Teresa will be able to keep up her ruse—if Elizabeth has not already figured her out." Emelia paused. "How long will it take you to prepare to leave with me?"

"I can be ready to leave tonight." Adelaide stood. "Should we notify Virginia of our coming?"

"No, I think it might be better if you just sent a message to Carla, letting her know we have a *situation* that we will explain when we arrive. You might ask Carla to check in on Virginia and the children, though, if she has time. I do not want Virginia to panic and take off because she will never be safe from Elizabeth if she does not have *family* protection."

"Are you strong enough to protect her from Elizabeth Bathory?" Adelaide flushed. She was apprehensive to even ask such a question.

"I will do what it takes," she sighed heavily.

"Perhaps Alfred should come with us?"

Emelia shook her head.

"I think you are wrong not to bring in whatever reinforcements you can. The children are familiar with both of us, and with Carla. Carla might even know of a good place where we can hide the children. Samara is a difficult child, but she will go where Santan goes. She loves Carla, too. Other than Santan, Carla seems to be the only one able to control Samara. Don't forget, Alfred and I do not have the scent of a vampire. Hopefully, the children's scent will not be strong enough, yet, to lead Elizabeth to them. This way, you will just have Virginia to worry about. Two women would be able to get about much quicker without having to care for children, especially children such as Santan and Samara. My guess is that they will follow Virginia's trail first, reasoning that she would not separate from her offspring. We will not tell Virginia where we are going, so if by chance she is confronted by Elizabeth, she will not be able to reveal our destination."

"That will put Virginia in a very precarious position," Emelia commented, a deep sadness creeping into her already troubled eyes. "Maybe even her death if I cannot stop Elizabeth."

Adelaide laid her hand gently on Emelia's shoulder. "That is a chance you must take, Emelia ... for the sake of the children ... for Basarab. This is your opportunity to do a good turn for him; and, if I might be so bold to add, I am sure Virginia would sacrifice her own life if it meant that her children would be safe. What mother wouldn't?"

"I am sure you are right ... I am not thinking straight ... too much going on."

"So ... about Alfred coming with us?" Adelaide reminded.

"I guess ... if you think it best." Emelia finally relented to having Alfred come along. "But ... I will decide once we get there what we do. I do not think, at the moment, that I want to let the children out of my sight."

Later that night Emelia, Adelaide, and Alfred boarded a plane bound for Toronto, Ontario. Emelia had donned her special clothes again, but this time, to detract from her dress, she walked hunched over and with a cane—an old woman—so old the ticket-takers would never believe if they were told the truth. Carla would be waiting for them at the airport and would take them directly to Virginia's.

Emelia figured that she had the entire trip to think about what she was going to do, but she ended sleeping for most of the flight. And she, who usually never dreamed, dreamed...

Teresa was standing on the upper landing in the house where she and Basarab had lived in Brantford. Emelia noticed a horror-struck look on Teresa's face, and that she was staring intently at something. Emelia moved up the stairway, walking cautiously toward Teresa, who was still as a statue, except for the slight flinching of her facial muscles. As Emelia approached the top step, Teresa turned to her.

He beds her again, even though he has what he wants from her. He told me that it would end there, but once again, he lies! What sort of a sorceress is she that he returns to her every night?

Tears were crowding the corners of Teresa's eyes. One slipped down her cheek. She wiped it off with the back of her hand. She pointed to the locked door. *He is with her now.*

You know these kinds of liaisons never last long with our men. Emelia hoped to ease Teresa's pain.

Teresa collapsed to the floor. *Vacaresti has never been unfaithful to you. You were fortunate enough to have your children before you crossed over and became a member of the family. I was not. If I am to be truthful, there are too many times when I gaze upon Santan that I wish the child had not lived. But here he is—strong and handsome—thriving on the blood-milk that flows from 'her' breasts! I cannot help some of the thoughts that flit through my head...*

Like what, my dear? Emelia felt a serpentine fear within the pit of her stomach—fear for the child of her beloved nephew—fear that Teresa, out of desperation, would do something drastic.

There was blank emotion on Teresa's face, and in her eyes, as she simply said: *I want the child dead, and I care not whose hand strikes the blow! Preferably mine...*

Emelia laid a hand on Teresa's shoulder, trying to calm her. She felt Teresa's muscles tense under her fingers, and then Teresa shrugged away from her. Slowly, she stood up. She pushed Emelia aside and began to descend the stairs. Emelia fell against the banister, gripping it just in time to prevent a tumble down the stairway.

He shall be sorry for this ... this time, I am going to make him pay ... no matter how long it takes ... I shall make him pay! Teresa was already halfway down the stairs, but her angry words easily reached Emelia's ears.

Emelia was still standing outside Virginia's room when Basarab emerged. She noticed a peaceful look on his face, not the usual stone-hard features he was so well-known for. She glanced into the room, just before the door closed. Virginia lay curled on the bed, half-buried under the covers. Her eyes were closed, but Emelia noticed the contentment on Virginia's face.

Basarab put his arm around Emelia's shoulders. *Ah, my dear Aunt Emelia; what brings you up here? Have you come to tell Virginia another story? I am afraid I have tired her out—she is sleeping soundly. Perhaps you could return later.* He laughed softly. *I thought I heard another voice out here—my wife's. Although I could not make out what she was saying, she sounded angry. Is there something I should be aware of, auntie?*

Emelia blushed. She had always had a difficult time withholding her emotions, and this moment was particularly difficult for her. She did not want to expose Teresa, because she hoped that whatever suppressed feelings Basarab's wife had been prone to when she had spieled off a few minutes ago, would pass. Teresa was not behaving like the young woman whom Emelia had come to know and love. On the other hand, what Teresa had suggested could bring danger to the child—to Basarab's child—even death. Emelia did not think she would be able to live with herself if Teresa followed through with her threat!

Basarab placed his hands on Emelia's shoulders and turned her to face him. *What is wrong, Emelia; why do you hesitate to speak to me? Is Teresa angry with me? Is she upset because I have paid another visit to our guest? Why can she not understand that I just toy with Virginia? Teresa is my queen. Does she not comprehend that I have done what is necessary to give her a child? She led me to believe that was what she desired...*

She is angry with you, Basarab—more hurt than angry. Emelia was trying to choose her words carefully. *She thought you would have nothing more to do with Virginia after the child was born.*

Ah ... so she is jealous.

Yes, and you should know, nephew, a jealous woman does not make a happy marriage. Your Teresa is beautiful, Basarab, so why do you find it necessary to flaunt your indiscretions in her face? All these years, she has stood by you— even saved your life! I understand that your original intention was to ensure a child for you and Teresa, and that she had given you leave to do whatever it took to accomplish that end. However, she feels you have carried on far beyond what has been necessary to achieve that end. You continued your liaisons with Virginia during her pregnancy, not stopping, even after the child's birth! It is not right, Basarab.

Did she threaten me with anything?

Emelia hesitated.

Your hesitation tells me that she did.

She is upset, Basarab. Go to her, nephew—calm her down. Promise her that you are finished with Virginia and...

I cannot promise such a thing, dear aunt, not under the umbrella of such a threat. Basarab's fingers released Emelia's shoulders. He turned and headed down the stairway. *If Teresa causes any harm to my son, I will not hesitate to end her life!*

Emelia sank to the floor and wrapped her arms around the wooden pillar. She could not stop shaking. Teresa and Basarab's words raced through her head ... *He shall be sorry for this ... this time, I am going to make him pay ... no matter how long it takes! ... If Teresa causes any harm to my son, I will not hesitate to end her life!*

~

Emelia awoke with a start.

"We will be experiencing some turbulence within the next few minutes. Everyone, please remain in your seats until further notice." The Captain's voice crackled through the intercom. The seatbelt sign flashed on.

Emelia glanced over at Adelaide and Alfred. They were sitting across the isle, as they had not been able to get three seats together. It appeared they too had been sleeping. Adelaide rubbed her eyes and yawned, and then straightened up in her seat. As she fastened her seatbelt, she smiled at Emelia, who nodded in return.

Half an hour later, a flight attendant announced that they would be landing at the Toronto airport in approximately twenty minutes. Emelia still had not decided what she was going to do. The dream had unsettled her. She was finding it difficult to think straight. In fact, her mind seemed to have gone blank. She began to think that she should just go with Adelaide's idea—leave the children with her, Alfred, and Carla, and then get Virginia away, somewhere where Elizabeth would never think to look. But to where? What could she really do, alone, if Elizabeth Bathory decided to come for her—for the children? Maybe she would be better off taking them all to Brasov, to Basarab. At least there, they would be protected.

~

On the way to Brantford, Adelaide and Alfred sat quietly in the backseat of the car while Emelia relayed to Carla the state of affairs they were in.

"Have you decided what to do yet?" Carla asked. "It sounds as if there is not much time to consider alternatives."

"I have no plans other than the one Adelaide suggested." Emelia paused briefly. "Do you think it will work?"

"It could. I purchased a property in the country, not far from Hamilton—Port Dover area, to be precise. It is relatively isolated. A long laneway ... small cottage on a cliff ... surrounded by trees ... a five-minute walk down to the lake. It has its own fenced, private beach, which can only be reached by water or the set of stairs the previous owner built on the hill. Adelaide and Alfred could stay there with the children. I have a friend in the computer business; he can install a security system and get us some secure cell phones so that we can keep in touch." Carla tapped her fingers on the steering wheel. "Yes, Emelia, I think that might work. The cottage has enough supplies to last for a few days; I can pick up more supplies at the local grocery store in Dover."

Emelia gazed out the window, noticing that a light snow had begun to fall. She was glad they had not run into a snowstorm that would have delayed their arrival. "Is the cottage fairly accessible?" she questioned.

"Yes. A local fellow ploughs the laneway if it snows, whether I am there or not. He just mails me the bill."

"And your computer guy—he is trustworthy?" Emelia was aware that she might be being paranoid, but there were a lot of lives at stake here, especially if there were too many loose ends left untied.

"Very."

"Okay ... I guess it is settled then. The children will go with you, tonight, if possible."

"What of Virginia?" Carla enquired.

"I shall stay with her, and by morning I hope to have thought of something concrete."

"I'll give you the key to my office in Hamilton, so you and Virginia can stay there for at least tonight, if that will help," Carla suggested.

"A possibility," was all Emelia said as she turned and looked out the passenger window.

The wipers swished the light dusting of snow off the windshield. The atmosphere in the car was one of quiet; the occupants each in their own world of thoughts. Emelia's stomach was in knots—maybe butterflies—either way, she felt edgy—more so than she had been for a long time. Despite the burning in her throat, she whispered a prayer to the God she had worshiped when she was a child—centuries ago.

Suddenly, the traffic started slowing down. Emelia looked ahead and saw the red taillights of rows of cars coming to a halt. Carla hit the brake. They were stuck behind a large transport truck. She turned on the car radio, tuning it to the local Hamilton station.

"Damn it!" Carla slammed her hand on the steering wheel. An ambulance sped past in the emergency lane, just as the radio announced there was a nine-car pileup on the 403 at Hamilton's Main Street cut-off.

~

They had travelled far. It was difficult for Emelia to believe that it all may end so horribly. Indications were pointing in that direction. A stranger's ill fate could cause a world catastrophe, like no war had ever done. *I was so close to saving your son, Basarab; now, I feel so helpless, stuck in this sea of cars.* The snow started coming down heavier, thick and wet, which made the road even more slick and hazardous. Two more ambulances sped up the fast lane, adding to Emelia's anxiety.

Adelaide and Alfred were sitting quietly in the backseat. Emelia glanced back at them and saw the distress on their faces. Carla was tapping impatiently on the steering wheel. She was a young woman who loved to be in control, and when something got out of her control, she was at a loss.

Emelia watched the cars on the other side of the highway, as they slowed down to take a look at the disaster, and then sped up again. There was one car, in particular, to which her eyes were drawn—a taxi with a roof sign that read "Brant Taxi." She felt her heart skip a couple of beats. The vehicle was in the outside lane, and it had slowed, like the other cars, to observe the accident scene. Emelia squinted, trying to see into the back of the car. There was only one passenger, and it appeared to be the silhouette of a man. Her breath caught in her throat—*Vacaresti?* Quickly, she turned her head and looked in the other direction. *What is he doing here, in Canada ... in Brantford?* She assumed that was where he was coming from, because of the name on the taxi. Where was he headed? From the corner of her eye, Emelia noticed Carla staring at her.

"Emelia, are you okay?"

"Yes. I am fine. I am just impatient about this hold-up. I cannot help thinking that we are going to be too late, that someone else has already gotten to Virginia and the children."

"Don't be silly, Emelia," Adelaide's voice came from the backseat of the car. "No one knows where she is."

"We don't know that for sure. Everyone has spies everywhere. Don't think, for a minute, any of us are safe. I should never have given Virginia the child. I should have just let her go. She would have left Brantford..."

"But she would still have Samara." Adelaide reached her hand over the back of the car seat and touched Emelia's shoulder. "Virginia would never have been able to handle that child on her own. Samara is more her father's child than her brother is. I know that, and so do you. Do not fault yourself for having done a noble deed."

Emelia reached her hand up and laid it over her friend's. She could feel her warmth. She closed her eyes and thought of the time when her own hands had been as warm. She thought of the man who had just passed by on the other side of the highway, and wondered if she had it all to do again, would she have crossed over? Would she have fallen in love with Vacaresti and married him, had she been privy to what he truly was, beforehand? It had been such a long, tiring road; one she had thought of getting off of, several times.

Her mind wandered back to the last time those thoughts had gone through her mind. It had been during the last great scourge by the vampire hunters. She and Vacaresti had split from the rest of the family. They had run through the streets, dodging into doorways and down alleys whenever they heard footsteps approaching. Somehow they had gotten separated. Emelia had not dared to call out for Vacaresti, for fear of bringing the hunters upon them. For hours, she had wandered, searching for her husband, but finally, as the sun had begun to rise in the east, she had given up. With a heavy heart, she had sought refuge inside a large, abandoned cardboard box. She had curled up and gone to sleep, thinking if she was found, so be it.

But she had not been discovered. When the stars spotted the sky, she left the box and took to the streets again. Emelia searched for another few hours and then finally gave up.

Vacaresti was nowhere to be found. There was only one safe place for her to go—Adelaide's.

She turned and glanced at Adelaide, patted her hand, and then returned her attention back to the slow moving cars.

Carla's voice permeated the silence. "It looks like the cars are beginning to move."

Emelia noticed brake lights going off and on as cars began crawling forward. She sat back in the seat and tried to relax, but knew that she would not be able to until she had Virginia and the children safely stashed away. She would do whatever she had to, to protect them.

It was another hour before they reached the part of the highway where the accident had taken place. The vehicles that hadn't been towed yet had been moved over to the inside lane, freeing up the rest of the road. Carla pressed her foot to the gas pedal and the car sped along the 403, heading toward Brantford. Emelia's heart pounded furiously as they turned off on the Wayne Gretzky cut-off. Carla turned left on the freeway, and then right onto Henry Street. They would be at their destination within a couple of minutes. Emelia started to shake. She gripped her hands together so that Carla would not notice how nervous she was. She saw the railway abutment. The laneway was just beyond that. Carla flicked on the turn signal.

As they turned into the laneway, Carla pointed out the recent tire tracks, even though they had started filling with the fresh snow. Emelia mentioned that it looked as though there were at least two different types of tires, both coming and going from the laneway—some, fresher than the others.

Carla nodded in agreement. "Look's like there has been some recent goings-on here," she stated.

Emelia nodded. She had lost the ability to speak.

Carla pushed the gas pedal to the floor, and the car spun up the snow-rutted laneway. Emelia could tell from the set of Carla's jaw that she feared they were too late, as well. She skidded to a stop at the back of the house. There were two vehicles parked there—Virginia's van and Randy's Volkswagen. Steam was coming from the hood of Randy's car.

"Well, I guess we know that one of the car tracks was Randy's," Carla stated. "I wonder who the other one belongs to?"

Emelia shook her head. She thought she might know, but how would Vacaresti have known where Virginia and the children were? She had always been exceedingly careful to cover her tracks when travelling to places she had not wanted him or the others to know of. Had he had her followed? Was he aware of what she thought was secret in her life—of Adelaide?

They all got out of the car and hurried toward the backdoor of the house. To their surprise, it was ajar. Carla stepped in front of Emelia. "Let me go in first." Her voice was gentle, yet commanding.

"No." Emelia's voice was just as firm as Carla's had been. "If there are vampires inside, I should be the one who enters first." She pushed the younger woman aside and stepped over the threshold, into the kitchen.

There was a sobbing sound coming from the living room. Emelia pushed forward, hope giving her strength. Perhaps they weren't too late, after all. Carla, Adelaide, and Alfred followed. The sight that greeted Emelia was not the one she had been hoping for. Randy was sitting on the couch. His head was buried in a pillow, and his shoulders were shaking uncontrollably as sobs wrenched out of him. Emelia went directly to him and sat down. She put her hand on his shoulder.

He looked up, startled. For a few seconds Randy just stared, speechless. Finally, he found his voice. "Emelia! They have her ... we had a fight ... sort of ... not an actual fight ... just a difference of opinion ... I left ... I was angry ... if only I hadn't left ... I could have saved her ... but now, they have her ... and Santan ... and Samara..." his words were staggering out of his mouth in piecemeal.

"Who has them, Randy? Did you see who they were? How many? Male? Female?" Emelia needed to know how many she might be dealing with.

Randy leaned back on the couch, still hugging the pillow to him. Emelia noticed the redness of his eyes, which told her that he had been weeping for some time. "I didn't see them clearly. They were coming out of the laneway, just as I was returning to apologize to Virginia. It looked like two people in the front seat, but it was so dark I could not tell if they were male or female. From the corner of my eye, I thought I saw someone in the backseat, pounding on one of the windows. When I realized that it was Virginia, it was too late. The laneway is so narrow; and, as small as my car is, I couldn't get it turned around. I didn't think to just back up! I drove all the way up to the house and when I got back to the street there was no sign of the car. I drove around for over an hour, trying to find it, but I didn't even know what model of vehicle to look for. I hadn't gotten that close a look, it all happened so fast." Randy swallowed hard, as though he was trying not to burst into tears again. "I have been out today, as well, and just returned about an hour ago."

"When did this happen?" Emelia asked, needing to know how much of a head start the kidnappers had.

"Last night." Randy's body shuddered. "Who would take Virginia and the children? Why? Can you tell me what is going on here?"

Emelia patted Randy's knee. "It is not your fault, Randy." She paused. "Did you call the police?" She was hoping that he hadn't.

"No ... oh no ... I am sorry ... I should have ... I was so confused..." Randy stuttered.

"It's okay, Randy; it's probably for the best that you didn't. If it is who I think it might have been, then not only would you have been no match for them, neither would the police have been."

Randy drew in a deep breath and glared at her. "What do you mean, Emelia? I would have done whatever it took to protect Virginia and the children!"

Emelia noticed the earnestness in his eyes.

"I think that you should tell him," Adelaide said.

"Tell me what?" Randy looked from Emelia to Adelaide.

Emelia stood up and walked to the back of the couch so that she would not have to look Randy in the eyes, and so she could still see Adelaide. What was her friend trying to suggest? There was no way they should be telling Randy what had really happened here! That would put him into more danger than he could ever bargain for. "Can't do that," She stated, throwing Adelaide a stern look.

"You have to, my friend. There is no other way. He is already involved."

Randy jumped up from the couch and spun around to face Emelia. "What is going on here? Tell me Emelia! What am I involved in? I have the right to know!"

Alfred spoke up for the first time. "The boy is right, Emelia, and so is my sister. He has been drawn into your world just by his association with Virginia and the children. He should be told so that he can either leave to protect himself, or he can stay and help us find the woman that he has fallen in love with. There is nothing stronger in this world than true love, Emelia. Give it a chance."

Emelia studied the people standing around her—Adelaide, Alfred, Carla, and Randy. From the looks on all of their faces, she knew she was defeated. She walked back to the front of the couch. "Sit down, Randy. It is time to tell you what you need to know. When I am finished, you can decide for yourself which path you want to take. But remember this, if you chose to stand with us after hearing what I have to say, it will be the roughest road you will ever travel."

Adelaide, Alfred, and Carla exited the room. Randy sat down on the couch and Emelia took the chair opposite him. She still hesitated, unsure exactly how to proceed, or where to start. Finally, she guessed the beginning would be best...

"Virginia was never married to the father of her children," Emelia began.

"Excuse me? I was informed that her husband died, that she was a widow." Anger crept into Randy's eyes. "Now, you are telling me that she was never married!"

Emelia sighed, knowing that what she was about to say to Randy could shatter his world. "The father of her children is a man called Count Basarab Musat. He is a Transylvanian vampire..."

Randy jumped up from the couch. He paced back and forth in front of Emelia. "First you tell me that Virginia is not a widow, and now you are telling me the father to those two precious little children is a vampire! Unbelievable!"

"Actually, he is the king of our kind." Emelia paused a moment, to note further reaction on Randy's face. The anger was still there, hooded by shock. "Please, Randy, sit down."

Randy stared at her for a moment, then obliged. He sat on the edge of the cushion and leaned forward.

Emelia continued. "Virginia found herself trapped in the count's house, because of her curiosity, so I was told. For a long time, the count had searched for a human woman to bear him a son. As you have obviously noticed, Virginia is a beautiful woman; she was very much to the count's taste.

"Max told me that at first she wanted nothing to do with the count and she begged to be allowed to leave, but it was too late for that. Basarab could not take the chance of releasing her; plus, once he saw her, he decided that she would be the one to bear his child. She did attempt several escapes, which ended badly for her, except for her final try."

"That would be when she came to me, then?"

"Yes."

"How did she manage to get out that time?" Randy's voice still had an angry edge to it.

"Everyone was sleeping … and … I helped her." Emelia lowered her eyes to the floor. "She chose to make a run for it after Santan's naming ceremony. I knew she would make one more try. I saw what transpired that night, afterward—when my nephew went to her room and did what he did, and then left her on the floor in a broken heap, while he and Teresa mocked her. I was hiding in the shadows when they walked away, arm in arm. I decided that if Virginia did what I felt she would do, I would help her, and I would give her Santan to take with her."

"I see."

"Max did tell me that Virginia tried to play a highly dangerous game with the count. She got the foolish idea that she could win his heart…"

"Are you telling me that she actually loved such a monster?"

"I don't know if she did or not; his charms have always been difficult to resist."

The fury in Randy's next statement shocked Emelia. "So she gave herself to him, like a common whore?"

"Oh, Randy." Emelia reached over and laid her hand on Randy's knee. "Your Virginia is not like that; you of all people should know that. A vampire is someone you do not have a chance resisting, if it is you that they want."

"How would you know? You are one of them, aren't you?" Randy snapped.

"It was not always so." Emelia looked away. "I was human once," she whispered. "I fell under the spell of my own count." She turned back to Randy. "Virginia thought she was controlling the game, but in reality, from the beginning, she never stood a chance against him. She thought she held the trump card––his child in her belly—something his wife could not give him.

Max tried to convince her otherwise, constantly reminding her that the count had no heart. Even Teresa tried to warn her. But, Virginia would not listen. She pushed forward, seducing him, with everything she had—body and mind. Max said that they would spend hours in the library, debating all manner of issues; and then afterward, Basarab would take Virginia upstairs to her room and make love to her.

"She thought she was winning. The count's wife became viciously jealous; Virginia was getting under her skin. But what she kept forgetting, despite the warnings, was that Basarab really had no heart. My nephew can perform with the best, in order to get his way." Emelia hesitated a moment when she noticed the look that had crept into Randy's eyes.

"So, I guess what you are saying here is that Virginia has been deceiving me all this time—using me as a shield. She has been playing me, as she tried to play this count—only in my case, I have a heart—something she did not think about when she started her game with me!" Randy's eyes flamed with indignation; his body was tense. He ran his hand through his hair, stood, and began pacing again. "I can't believe she would do something like that!"

Emelia felt a pang of sympathy for the young man. He had landed himself into the vampire world, in much the same manner as Virginia had—by chance. Only he had genuinely fallen in love, and not just with her, but with the children. Emelia knew that he had been willing to give up everything for them. "I understand what you are saying, Randy," she began, "but put yourself in her position ... she was fighting for her life. And then, when she found out she was pregnant, for the life of her child. Anyone can act out of character if they have to fight for their survival. Would you not do the same?"

Randy stopped and glared at Emelia, still in the throws of his anger. "I don't think I would go far enough to sell my soul! I rented Virginia this apartment without asking all the questions

that were running through my mind. What a fool I have been!"
Randy was on a roll, and Emelia decided not to interrupt, just to
let him spiel off. "I am assuming this is the reason her children
are so far advanced, too?" He shook his head, and she noticed
tears creeping into his eyes. He turned away from her.

"I asked Virginia to be with me, her and the children.
When she told me that it wouldn't work, I got angry. We fought;
I said awful things to her. I told her that I knew she was hiding
something in that head of hers ... too many things weren't adding
up. She asked me to leave. Eventually, we talked ... I apologized
... we started over. I never brought the subject up again, until a
couple of nights ago. After the children were in bed, I approached
her again, telling her that it was time to move on, that I still
wanted to be with her and the children, I hadn't changed my
mind. I tried to kiss her, but she pushed me away, telling me that
it wasn't me; it was just that she wasn't ready yet. That is when I
left. I was angry ... I felt she was using me ... how could I have
known..." his shoulders began to shake as the volcano of his grief
released once more. "I love her, Emelia ... I love her. At least, I
thought I did."

Emelia went to him, turned him gently around, and put
her arms around his trembling body. "You couldn't have known,
Randy; none of this is your fault. I know that you love her, and I
guess what I am about to ask you might be selfish on my part, but
we need your help. I am not sure exactly who has her and the
children at the moment, but I have a feeling that I might know. If
it is this person, if they are alone, then Virginia and the children
will be safe. But somehow I doubt the count would have sent
only one, especially with the way affairs are in Transylvania."

"What do you mean?" Randy interrupted, catching his
sobs in his throat, and pulling out of her embrace.

"That is another story, for another time. Humans are not
the only ones who have difficulties between families. There is
much trouble brewing in our home country, which is the main

reason Basarab had to return there. If it were not for that, he would never have left his son."

"So what is all this trouble in Transylvania, and what does Virginia and the children have to do with what is going on over there?" Randy had begun to recompose himself.

Emelia took a deep breath and pointed to the couch. "Sit down, Randy." He did. She returned to her chair and leaned forward. "Dracula's brother, Radu..."

Randy started to laugh. "Oh, this just keeps getting better and better! Now you are telling me that Dracula is still alive—and his brother?"

"Yes ... they are still alive. All with the blood of the Dracul family flowing through their veins still live, unless they were murdered by the vampire hunters..."

"Vampire hunters, too? Wow!"

"Randy, please ... you must take this seriously."

"I am trying ... I mean, well, the whole vampire craze is kinda fun, but this is too much! I always thought they were just great stories; I never thought that they were actually true."

"Well, now you know that they are true. However," a warning look appeared in Emelia's eyes, "this is something that we have tried to be cautious about, and now you must be too. As I was starting to say, Radu has decided that he wants the vampire throne, and he has amassed an army of rogues to try to take it. If this happens, not just vampires, but humans will be in jeopardy. Radu will not rule with the same reason as Basarab has."

"Why is this Basarab fellow the leader? I would have thought that Dracula would have been the obvious choice."

"The Gypsy who cast the curse on the family decreed it so. I believe she thought it would be a cruel joke on Dracula. To take away the supreme power and give it to the unborn child of his young cousin, Atilla—what trickery!" Emelia paused. "Now, to return to the importance of what we are dealing with here. Elizabeth Bathory, who is in league with Radu, has found out about Basarab's child. Of course, we can assume that Radu knows now, as well. Basarab's wife came up with a plan. She would infiltrate Elizabeth's organization in order to gain information for the family, but the plan backfired. Teresa disclosed more than she had intended. She was the one who told Elizabeth about Santan.

"Teresa helped me leave the country so I could get the child to safety, which most likely jeopardized her own life. I will not bore you with all the details; my priority, now, is to find Virginia and the children. I had no idea the count might send someone after me, and his son, as well. Unfortunately, on the way here, a huge car accident delayed us for several hours. I get the sense, though, that it was not Elizabeth who was here last night." Emelia stood up. "Wait here a moment; there is something I need to check out." She left the room and headed to the kitchen.

"Is everything okay?" Carla asked.

Emelia nodded, and then went outside to the place where she had noticed several footprints in the snow. She knelt down and lowered her face to the spot, sniffing the area. She stood. *Just as I thought. Vacaresti and Ildiko.* She returned to the house.

"It was not Elizabeth," she told everyone.

"Then who?" Adelaide enquired.

"My husband, and Ildiko."

"Basarab must know then?" Alfred surmised.

"Yes," was all Emelia said, before returning to Randy.

He stood as she entered the room. "What did you find out?"

"Randy, I need to know where you looked."

"Everywhere; I drove all over the city."

"Did you drive by *The House*?"

"Are you talking about the one I think you are?"

"Yes."

"I did. It was in total darkness."

"Did you notice tire tracks?"

"I never thought to look; there were no cars in the parking lot." Randy had a hopeful look in his eyes as he asked his next question: "Do you think whoever took Virginia and the children would have taken them there?"

"Maybe ... but I also think that they might not stay there for long. Especially, if the one that I think has left, is not there. The other one might make a move."

"Who are you talking about?"

"The one is my husband, the other, Ildiko, Basarab's cousin. I have the feeling that Vacaresti is headed to Montreal to find me. Ildiko is sharp; if she senses danger, she will be out of there in a flash, and she will take Virginia and the children with her—maybe even back to Transylvania. I think we need to take a drive to *The House*; I want to check and make sure that they are not there. I can think of no other place Vacaresti would be able to take them on such short notice. Will you drive me there? I think the others should stay here, though."

"I don't think we should separate, Emelia." Alfred walked into the room. "If they are there, you will need all the help you can get to either free them, or to convince Vacaresti and Ildiko, if they are the kidnappers, to release Virginia and the children into our custody."

"Alfred is right, my friend," Adelaide joined her brother. "We cannot separate."

"But then they will know about you, Adelaide."

"So be it. Better they know of me, than have you hurt, or killed. It is my guess that they already know—at least Vacaresti does."

"I think that we should wait till dusk, before leaving." Carla came into the room and stood beside Alfred and Adelaide. "If we do find Virginia and the children at the house, it will be much easier to escape under the cover of night. The children cannot tolerate sunlight."

Emelia felt defeated, again. She looked at her friends. "Okay, we will do it your way. We will have to take both cars." She turned to Randy. "Does it look as if there had been time to take any of their personal belongings with them?"

"I don't think so," he replied. "There didn't even appear to be a sign of struggle."

"We should pack some of their clothing, then, just in case we can get them out of there and to a safe place," Emelia suggested.

"Good idea." Carla headed into the children's room.

Emelia gazed into Randy's eyes. "It is not too late for you to back out, Randy. Be assured, we will not think less of you. I also want you to understand that by stepping further into this world, you will be putting yourself in imminent danger—and not just from the evil forces that are trying to seize power, but from Basarab himself. He will not be happy about the special relationship that you have forged with his son, or about your love for Virginia."

Randy returned the gaze just as intensely. "I would not have it any other way," he stated emphatically.

~

It was decided, after packing the cars with the children's basic needs, that everyone would grab a couple of hours rest before the sun went down. Emelia could not sleep, though, so she sat and kept watch, anxious for the moon to begin its ascent in the sky. Finally, night pushed the day aside. They piled into the cars and headed toward the place that Emelia knew Virginia had never wanted to see again.

Other books in the

NIGHT'S VAMPIRE SERIES

Night's Gift – Book One
Night's Return – Book Three

Author Page

Mary M. Cushnie-Mansour was born on November 15, 1953, in Stoney Creek, Ontario, Canada. She is a freelance creative writer who now resides in Brantford, Ontario, with her husband, Ed, and her cat, Princess.

In March 2006, Mary completed a freelance journalism course at the University of Waterloo, Ontario, after which she wrote freelance articles and a fictional short story column for *The Brantford Expositor*. During this time, Mary also published four poetry anthologies, a collection of short stories, and two biographies. From 2010 to 2013, Mary wrote the *Night's Vampire Trilogy*, releasing the first book in the trilogy, *Night's Gift* in 2011, the second book, *Night's Children* in 2012, and the third book, *Night's Return* in 2013. She also writes a blog, *Writer on the Run.*

In 2014, Mary will be working on a mystery series—murder, mayhem, and an oversized cat called Toby who loves to solve crimes. Watch for the first in the series, *Are You Listening to Me,* coming your way soon.

To check out Mary's books and blog, social media links, and to sign up for her newsletter, please take a moment and visit her website at www.marymcushniemansour.ca